MOLLY GREEN has travelled the world, unpacking her suitcase in a score of countries. On returning to England, Molly decided to pursue her life-long passion for writing. She now lives and writes in Tunbridge Wells. *An Orphan in the Snow* is the first of a series set in Liverpool during the Second World War.

An Orphan
in the Snow

MOLLY
GREEN

avon.

Published by AVON
A Division of HarperCollins*Publishers* Ltd
1 London Bridge Street
London SE1 9GF

www.harpercollins.co.uk

A Paperback Original 2017

First published in Great Britain by HarperCollins*Publishers* 2017

6

Copyright © HarperCollins 2017

Molly Green asserts the moral right to
be identified as the author of this work

A catalogue record for this book is
available from the British Library

ISBN 978-0-00-823894-0

Set in Minion 11/14 pt by Palimpsest Book Production Limited,
Falkirk, Stirlingshire

Printed and bound in Great Britain by
CPI Group, (UK) Ltd, Croydon, CR0 4YY

MIX
Paper from
responsible sources
FSC
www.fsc.org
FSC™ C007454

This book is produced from independently certified FSC™ paper
to ensure responsible forest management.

For more information visit: www.harpercollins.co.uk/green

To my dear friend June who was an evacuee in the Second World War, although nothing she experienced has found its way into this novel.

To all Dr Barnardo's orphans during the Second World War who were the inspiration for this series.

Before . . .

Cambridgeshire, 1936

June raced home from the last class of the day, wanting to make sure the bedroom she shared with her younger sister Clara was free so she could do her homework in peace. Good, she thought as she opened the front door. She could hear Clara downstairs talking to their mother.

'Mum, I'm home,' June called as she pulled off her coat and hat and hung them on a hook in the narrow hallway. She put her head in the kitchen door.

'Would you like a cup of tea, June, and a piece of sponge?' Her mother began to cut a slice from the cake. 'I've just taken it out of the oven.'

'I'll come down in a bit. I've got two lots of homework, and we've got an English test tomorrow.' She hesitated, then asked, 'Where's Dad?'

A shadow crossed her mother's face. 'He won't be here yet. He's up at the stadium.'

June blew out her cheeks in relief as she ran up the stairs, two at a time, to her room. She settled at the small table under the window, and had finally worked out how to solve the mathematics problem when she heard her sister flying up the stairs and footsteps thundering behind – her father's.

1

June's heart pounded as she threw down her pencil and rushed to the door.

'Don't, Daddy! Don't hit me!' Clara screamed as she tried to kick out to escape their father's powerful arms. 'I didn't do anything.'

'Leave her alone!' June used every ounce of her strength to wrench her sister away from her father's grasp. What little thing had Clara done *this* time to make her father so angry?

'Stop interfering, you!'

For a split second June was caught by his maddened eyes. She smelled the beer on his breath as he made to snatch Clara back. He cursed as Clara's foot caught him on the shin. June rushed towards her father, her hand up ready to hit him. Clara ducked out of his way and turned to run but she slipped on the rug, losing her balance. June tried to grab her but her hand clutched air. She could only stand frozen in horror as Clara slowly fell backwards down the stairs.

She didn't know if it was she or her younger sister who screamed.

Chapter One

Liverpool, December 1941

The train to Liverpool was nine hours late pulling out of Euston Station. When it finally departed, at five minutes to ten at night, it was to a cacophony of clanking and shouting, belching steam, and conductors constantly blowing their whistles. June stuck her head out of the nearest grimy window to catch the last glimpse of her aunt running along the platform. She kept up for a few seconds, her handkerchief a small white flag, but as the train gathered speed she fell back and her outline faded into the mist. Dearest Aunt Ada. June was going to miss her.

June drew back her head and took in a deep breath. She'd done it. Even though the train had been delayed for such an interminable time, causing her to spend hours sitting on the stone floor of Euston Station because there were no available seats, June could not suppress her joy. She'd been pressed up like a bookend against one of a small group of WAAFs who chatted nonstop whilst she waited, though thankfully a soldier had given up his seat for her aunt. And now she was on her way up north. Against all odds.

She only hoped that Liverpool was far enough away from

London that her father wouldn't come after her. She'd been brave enough not to give him the address; she hadn't even told him the village. 'Somewhere near Liverpool,' she'd said vaguely. 'I'll let you know when I'm there.'

Her heart beat a little faster as her father's words rang in her ears: 'All of you have left me now. First Stella, then Clara . . .' He'd bowed his head as he uttered Clara's name and for a second or two she thought there might be some sign of remorse reflected in his eyes. 'Then your mother,' he'd carried on, 'and now *you*.' He'd looked up slyly and she saw then that his eyes were as cold and grey as concrete.

Clara. June bit her lip. No, she mustn't think of her sister for the moment. She had to concentrate on what lay ahead. Think about her new job at Dr Barnardo's. But first she needed to find her compartment.

She struggled to manoeuvre her suitcase through a line of soldiers standing in the corridor, most of them puffing on cigarettes, and caught snatches of their talk as she tried to squeeze past.

'Where are you stationed?'

'The Isle of Tiree.'

'Oh, bad luck, old chap. That's the Met station, isn't it? Pretty desolate, I'm told.'

'Not the best posting but at least I probably won't get shot at. I've got a couple of days' leave before I go so I'm nipping in to see the parents – they're near Liverpool and—'

'Excuse me,' June said, now completely blocked by a tall, broad-shouldered man in an RAF greatcoat – an officer by the two bars on his shoulders – who appeared to be deep in conversation, his back to her.

'I'm sorry,' the man said. He turned round and even though the peak of his cap partly shaded his face, June found herself looking into eyes the colour of a summer sky. An appreciative smile spread across his even features. 'I'll be glad to help with that case.'

'No, I'm all right, thank you. I just need to get by,' June said, a little unnerved by his directness.

'Are you sure? That case looks heavy to me,' he said, briefly glancing down, then catching her eye again.

'I'm absolutely sure.'

The man held her gaze for a few more seconds, then shrugged and stepped aside, leaving a few extra inches of space. June nodded her thanks, conscious that she was forced to brush hard against him as she shouldered her way through.

Out of the corner of her eye she caught a mocking smile. *He was doing this deliberately!* She was glad he couldn't see her face grow pink.

Drawing admiring glances and a few whistles, she pushed her way through the heaving mass of soldiers along the corridor, the smoke from their cigarettes catching in the back of her throat. She was thankful to finally spot her compartment. She slid open the door to find it was already occupied by four uniformed women, chattering away, and a harassed-looking mother, her arms around a sobbing child sitting on her lap, trying to soothe her. A second child, a boy, was tapping his mother's arm, whining for something to drink.

Instinctively June smiled at the mother, who sent back an apologetic look and mouthed that she was sorry.

'Don't worry,' June said, heaving her case onto the rack. 'I'm used to children. My sister's got three boys who are little monkeys. I've been looking after them lately.' She sat down beside the mother, who was trying to hush the little girl's sobs. 'They must be tired at this late hour. How old are they?'

'Joe's six and Millie's five,' the woman explained. 'I'm Doreen, by the way.'

5

'And I'm June.' She opened her bag. 'I have some boiled sweets in here somewhere. Perhaps I could give them one and tell them a story?'

'*Would* you?' Doreen's face softened with relief.

'If you've got a cardigan or a shawl or something, we can tuck it around Millie so she's ready to go to sleep for a few hours. She'll feel better in the morning.'

The little girl stopped crying and looked at June with wide tear-filled eyes.

'The nice lady has a sweet for you, love, and she's going to read you a story.'

It worked like magic.

If only Stella's boys had been that easy, June thought wryly, a twinge of apprehension rolling down her spine. Instead of Stella's three boys, she'd be faced with ten times that many at the orphanage.

It was early the following morning when June alighted at Kirkdale railway station. The muscles in her legs and shoulders were stiff from being in the same position for so long. Rubbing the back of her neck and ignoring her rumbling stomach for the time being she opened the piece of paper with the written instructions she'd had from the matron of the Dr Barnardo's home – and *her* new home.

Catch the no 6 bus outside Kirkdale station. Ask the driver to put you off at the Ferndale stop. Turn left and after about five hundred yards turn left again down a lane. Walk for a few minutes and you'll come to a private drive on the left. It's uphill. Follow it all the way and you'll see a large red-brick house in front of you. That's Bingham Hall.

June was desperate for a cup of tea and something to eat before she could attempt one more minute of travelling or she was sure she'd faint. Maybe the station would have a café. She folded the piece of paper and tucked it in her coat pocket, then doubled back onto the platform.

She looked at her watch. Not even six o'clock. Everywhere was quiet except for the last stragglers coming off the train she'd been on. They too looked bleary-eyed, as though they hadn't slept much. She hadn't either, squashed between the mother with her two children, the other four women, and a tall uniformed man who'd rushed into the compartment at the last minute. For a moment, she'd thought he was the man in the greatcoat that she'd brushed against earlier; she'd felt an unexpected flicker of disappointment when she saw this man was a lot older. He'd given her an apologetic smile and settled in immediately, closing his eyes and only letting out a grunt and a snore now and then, much to the little boy's delight when he awoke.

The man with the blue eyes flashed through her mind again. She wondered where he was stationed; she hadn't noticed him get off at Kirkdale. There was no way of telling the colour of his hair under the peaked cap . . . but those eyes. They were such a bright blue they looked as though they'd been painted in by an over-enthusiastic child. She'd been rather abrupt when he'd only offered to help her. She ought to have been better mannered. Her mother would have reprimanded her. Then she remembered the way he'd enjoyed her discomfort and with a flicker of annoyance she marched into the station café. She sat down, ordered some tea and scrambled egg on toast, and opened her book, the one Aunt Ada had slipped into her bag for the journey. June grinned as she turned the page to her bookmark. *Mary Poppins* couldn't be more appropriate.

'Sorry it's powdered,' the waitress said as she put the plate down in front of her. 'We haven't had our usual order of eggs delivered this week.'

7

'I'm one of those strange people who quite like powdered egg,' June said with a smile.

'Most of the customers understand, but we've got one who grumbles every time. I always remind him there *is* a war on, and he gives me such an old-fashioned look. He don't know if I'm being saucy or not.' The woman chuckled, showing a wide gap in her teeth.

'I'm glad you remind him,' June said, her smile broadening.

'Where are you off to, if you don't mind me asking?' the waitress asked.

'I'm going to be working at Bingham Hall.'

'What used to be Lord and Lady Bingham's big house.' The waitress put both hands on her hips, her expression one of genuine interest. 'It's now the orphanage, isn't it?'

'Yes. Dr Barnardo's. Do you know how far it is?'

The waitress frowned and pulled one of her earlobes as though it might help her to think.

'It's quite a way from here. Are you going on the bus?' June nodded. 'It's about eight miles but the bus will stop at every stop so it'll feel three times as long. Anyway, you enjoy your breakfast and I'll go and bring you a pot of tea.'

June shivered as she rubbed her hands together through her gloves. The queue at the bus stop was long, the women chatting in such a strong accent she couldn't catch all they were saying. Stamping her feet, which were turning numb, she was thankful to see a number 6 bus approaching.

A large lady squeezed in by the side of her, pinning her against the window. June tried to read her book but the constant jolting made her feel nauseous and she was forced to give up. She turned her head to look out of the window, which was crying out for a good clean, and glimpsed hills and valleys and trees and the occasional small village. But her mind was busy with the thought of Bingham Hall. What would it be like? Could she make a real difference to the children's lives? June's thoughts rushed back to Clara. Even though the accident had happened more than five years ago it was still difficult to believe she would never see her sister again. Tears stung the back of her eyes. Somehow she had to make up for Clara's tragic end.

I want to do my bit in the war as well as everyone, she thought, as the bus rumbled along. She recalled that on the very day she'd received the offer from Dr Barnardo's she'd had a letter from the Auxiliary Territorial Service telling her she was to report for duty. She'd almost forgotten she'd applied in her excitement at Aunt Ada knowing someone at Dr Barnardo's and putting in a word. Thank goodness the ATS agreed that her position in an orphanage was important, and even essential, and they'd immediately released her. It had been such a relief to make her own decision about her future. Working with children, especially those who had very little, was her hope, her dream. An orphanage such as Dr Barnardo's just felt right.

The large woman beside her spread out even further and gave a long grunt of a snore. She smelled as though it had been some time since she'd had a bath. June sighed. She mustn't judge her. Who knew what her circumstances were? Just get this journey over and you'll be fine, she told herself.

But the time dragged. Once the bus turned round in a complete circle.

'We can't get through,' called out the conductor. 'There was a raid last night and our road is completely blocked. We'll have to do a detour. Probably add another half-hour on to the journey.'

The half-hour turned into an hour. Every time the driver

tried to take a detour, the detour road would come to a full stop and he'd have to turn back and try another route, negotiating his way past recently bombed buildings. Somehow she hadn't thought she'd see such depressing scenes so far from London, as Pathé News at the cinema always seemed to draw attention to London devastation. She prayed her aunt would keep safe. Dear Aunt Ada. When she'd been undecided about whether she should choose the ATS or the orphanage, her aunt had encouraged her to take up the position with Dr Barnardo's.

'You're a natural with children,' she'd said to June. 'And you don't want to waste your nursery nurse training. But don't forget to have a bit of fun sometimes. There'll be plenty of time for sadness if this war carries on much longer.' She'd looked June up and down, her eyes full of affection. 'You're very young still, and pretty as a picture, so don't tie yourself down to one man . . . and that includes Howard Blessing.'

Howard Blessing. June had had a crush on him when they'd first begun dating, but the attraction had quickly petered out – on her side, at least.

'Don't forget, you were the one who introduced me to him,' June said with a laugh.

'That's as maybe. But he was supposed to take you to the pictures and dancing, not ask you to *marry* him – at your age.'

'He was only kidding,' June said. 'Anyway, I don't love him and never did, so there's nothing to worry about. I just want to concentrate on my new job, but *if* I ever settle down it will be for love . . . though I shan't hold my breath.'

'You're also too young to be cynical,' her aunt had said with feeling. 'You'll fall in love, no doubt about it, and when it happens it's the best thing on earth.'

The conductor broke into her thoughts as he called out,

10

'Next stop, Ferndale. That's yours, hen,' he said, walking towards her, smiling.

Hen? Was he referring to her? What a strange expression. She was sure she had a lot to learn coming all this way from London.

'Oh, thank you.' June scrambled to her feet, which was difficult in the confined space. The large lady struggled up to let her out and June moved towards the front of the bus. Someone had shoved her case into the luggage space, and as she tried to lift it out the bus jolted to a stop, pitching her forward.

'Steady,' the conductor said, holding her arm. He glanced at her curiously. 'Where're you off to, hen?'

'Dr Barnardo's home. Do you know it?'

'Aye. It used to be Lord Bingham's house. That's where it got its name: Bingham Hall. It's up the lane on the left, then left again. A good twenty minutes' walk, I'd say, as it's quite a climb.' He threw her a cheeky grin. 'But you're young . . . you'll probably do it in less than that.' His eyes swept approvingly over her ankles before he asked, 'Are you a teacher . . . or visiting one of the young'uns?'

'I'm working there – matron's assistant.'

'You'll be working for Mrs Pherson, then.'

June nodded, pleased that someone knew her new employer.

'Well, good luck, hen, is all I've got to say. I think you'll be needing it – and not just with the young'uns.'

She wondered what he meant by this, but there was no time to think. The conductor had already kindly set her case down outside and waved her goodbye.

June's eyes stung in the bitter morning air as she watched the back of the bus disappear. She was the only passenger who had alighted. It was foggy now they were out of

11

Liverpool and she wondered how far away the orphanage was from the nearest village. Wherever it was, and however far, there was no going back. It had started to drizzle and grey clouds had begun to pile up. Pulling her scarf more snugly around her neck, and pushing back strands of the honey-coloured hair that whipped from under her hat, she clutched the handle of her mother's suitcase, somehow feeling close to her, and began the long trudge up the lane.

The house came into view almost brick by brick. The first things that struck her were the tall chimneys poking up into the heavy sky, smoke curling out of them. As she got nearer, the house looked even more impressive with its crenellated front, giving the air of a castle. Was this mansion really going to be her home? She thought of the little terraced cottage where she'd grown up – the small back yard – and pulled herself up sharply. She was being disloyal.

June wondered what had happened to Lord and Lady Bingham. Had the family fled when war was declared? How did the house come to be a children's home? Had he lent it to them just for the duration of the war? But what did it matter how the house came to be a Dr Barnardo's? Whatever had happened in the past, the house was providing orphaned children with a home. As she walked up the long drive the house took on such magnitude that she felt quite overwhelmed. Whatever must a child think, seeing a house like this for the first time?

At this moment she didn't feel much more confident than a child, but she allowed herself a rueful smile as she craned her neck to look up at the dozens of windows peering down at her, imagining them slyly weighing her up as to whether she was welcome or not. There didn't seem to be any sign of life.

She pulled the bell cord beside the massive oak door and

waited. No sound at all. No scuffling of shoes. No running footsteps. Nothing. She pulled again, harder and longer. This time she heard a man's voice shout something but she couldn't make out the words.

The door swung back, groaning on its hinges, and a short figure of a man appeared, dressed in black from head to toe, back bent as though he'd worked in the fields all his life, grumbling and swearing under his breath.

'I heard you the first time.' His tone was irritable. 'I'm not deaf, you know.'

'I'm sorry,' June said. What a rude man. She hoped she wouldn't have much to do with him.

'Are you the new assistant?' He looked at her through dazed watery eyes.

'Yes. I'm June Lavender.'

Was he ever going to ask her in?

He continued to stare at her. Did she have a smut on her nose or something? Her feet were beginning to freeze. She stepped forward into the doorway, forcing the little man back. 'May I please come in?'

He gave a grunt. 'You'd better come this way.'

June found herself in a magnificent hall. Her eye was immediately drawn towards the biggest fireplace she'd ever seen. It was built of stone, and rose twice as high as a man. A fire flared and snapped but from where she stood she couldn't feel any heat; most of it was probably going straight up the chimney. Unlit candles in sconces were set in niches near the fireplace, and several chandeliers shaped like individual flares hung from the ceiling, which was painted with what appeared to be hundreds of coats of arms. In the middle of the flagstone floor was a huge oriental rug, rucked up at the side.

It was just as she imagined the great hall of a castle would look. This was a grand house indeed. She took a deep breath to still the nervous fluttering of her heart.

'Is that Miss Lavender, Gilbert?' A strident voice came from above and a woman poked her head over the curving oak staircase.

'Yes, ma'am. She's arrived.'

The figure made her way slowly down the stairs, holding on to the banister. She was an exceptionally tall, large-framed woman, her grey hair scraped into a tight bun on top of her head. She stopped short, and from behind a pair of rimless spectacles her piercing steel-grey eyes regarded June from top to toe.

'You're not very big.'

'I'm five foot four.' June drew herself up to her full height. 'And I'm not a weakling.'

'Mmm.' The woman pursed her lips, her head cocked to one side. 'We've nearly all boys here. They can be a rough lot.' She glared at June. 'You sounded much older in your letter but you don't look more than sixteen.'

'I'm twenty-one next summer,' June said firmly. 'And I'm used to unruly children. As I said in my letter, I've been looking after my sister's three boys for the last two years and they're quite a handful.'

'Not such a handful as *thirty*-three little devils, not counting seven girls who never stop crying.' June was about to answer when the woman said, 'I'm Mrs Pherson, the matron. And that's what you call me – Matron,' she repeated, as though she had no doubt that she was dealing with a simpleton.

June offered her hand but the matron barely touched it with her fleshy fingers. 'Take Miss Lavender's case upstairs, Gilbert.' Her eyes swept back to June. 'There'll be a cup of tea for you in the kitchen.' She pointed to a corridor at the

14

far end. 'First right along the passage. I will meet you back here in' – she pulled the chain of her watch towards her and glanced at the hands – 'twenty minutes exactly. Please don't keep me waiting.'

She certainly runs a tight ship, June thought tiredly, remembering the conductor's words, which now made a lot more sense. For the moment, all she wanted to do was get to her room, drop her suitcase and find the kitchen. Her mouth was dry from the little she'd had to drink during the long journey from London, and the thought of a cup of tea was bliss.

'Tea would be very welcome, thank you.' June glanced at Gilbert who was standing nearby, a sullen expression spread across his small mean features. 'I can carry my own case upstairs if you'll just show me where to go.'

'Suit yourself.'

Gilbert stomped up the stairs in his scuffed black boots with June following, heaving her case. Then another flight, and another. When they reached the fourth floor she thought she would drop with tiredness. Gilbert waved her towards a door and nodded.

'That's it, yon,' he said, and, muttering to himself about having more work to do with extra staff, he vanished.

It wasn't a good start, June thought. The first two people she'd met weren't in the least welcoming, but then she was used to difficult people. She'd had plenty of training with her father and, although she'd loved her mother, she'd not been easy to look after when she'd been drinking. And her sister Stella was always known for her quick temper. June breathed out a long sigh. She would just have to do her best to get into Matron's good books by showing her she could cope with thirty-three boys and seven girls. They couldn't be that bad.

She opened the door and a smell of damp filled her nostrils. By the look of it, the bedroom hadn't been occupied in months. Gingerly she stepped inside and shivered even though she still had her coat on. The room was big enough to warrant a fireplace, though there were no ashes, nor logs nearby for the next fire to be lit. An ugly brown wardrobe and mismatched chest of drawers had been pushed against one wall in a lopsided manner, and when June went to inspect a table under the window she pulled back in disgust. Unrecognisable flowers were festering in a glass vase with an inch of slimy green water. June wrinkled her nose as she unfastened the window, letting in a blast of air. It was freezing, but it couldn't be helped, she thought. The room needed fresh air. She couldn't see much of a view as it was still foggy so she'd have to be patient until it lifted.

How was she ever going to sleep in such an atmosphere? Or was she being too fussy after Aunt Ada's neat-as-a-pin flat? Her own mother had done her best to be tidy and clean before she became sick but her father had never taken any notice, tramping in from the garden in his boots no matter how many times her mother asked him to remove them, and leaving his dirty clothes on the floor for her to pick up and wash.

June pushed the image of her father away. She'd give the room a good clean the first chance she had, but first, even before her tea, she decided to unpack.

She hung her few clothes in the wardrobe, which smelled of mothballs, set out her brush and comb and placed her bag on a cane-seated chair, though most of the cane poked underneath like a long fringe. There was no mirror to check if she looked tidy but she mustn't complain. Plenty of people were much worse off. At least the house was quite a few miles from Liverpool, she reasoned, and the drive itself must

16

be a half a mile long, so the children should be safe from any bombs.

Although June was getting more tired by the minute, her mouth curved into a delighted smile. There'd be wonderful gardens to walk in and where she would play games with the children. She'd soon make her room homely. It was just a matter of getting used to everything.

Chapter Two

Five minutes later a maid directed her to the kitchen where a pot of tea and some cups and saucers were grouped on a scrubbed pine table. Two young girls were scurrying round a plump woman in a wraparound apron and white cap who stood over an enamel bowl as big as a baby's bath, hands flying up and down as she crumbled in fat and flour for her pastry. She looked up as June entered.

'Are you the girl come to help with the children?' she demanded, though her tone was friendly.

'Yes. I'm June Lavender – just arrived from London.'

'Och, you talk funny.' The woman wiped her hands on her apron and stuck out a floury hand. 'Name's Marge Bertram. Call me Bertie. Everyone does. I'm from Scotland. Buried the second husband and decided to have a change and cross the border.' She laughed. 'It's a couple of degrees warmer here, I'll give it that. Little did I realise how close Jerry would be, trying to smash the docks to smithereens.' She looked at June, who was waiting to be told to take a seat. 'Still, you don't want to hear all that right now. You must be worn out. Tea's on the table. Help yourself, hen. You'll have to excuse me getting on as I'm in the middle of cooking dinner.'

'What time will that be?' June asked, a little embarrassed but hearing her stomach rumble again. One piece of toast and a spoonful of scrambled egg at six this morning hadn't gone very far to stave off her hunger.

Bertie looked up at the wall clock, which showed five minutes past eleven. 'Not until one o'clock.' Her eyes pierced June's. 'Here, I'll cut you a slice of cake. Don't tell anyone, mind. It's supposed to be for the children's teatime.'

'I haven't heard any sound from them,' June ventured, pouring herself a cup of tea. 'Are they out somewhere?'

Bertie snorted. 'No, dear, not at this time of the morning. They're all in class. These walls are solid. The Victorians really knew how to build. You'll not hear a peep unless they're in the next room or right on top of you. Except the wee bairn in the corner.' She jerked her head to where a child sat silently watching on a three-legged stool in the unlit corner of the room.

June glanced where Bertie had gestured and saw a little girl with pale blonde hair tied up in plaits, and a face like an angel, sucking her fingers. How could she have not noticed her? And there was something familiar about the child. June looked closer and her heart suddenly gave a great lurch. She gasped. The little girl looked the spitting image of her sister Clara when she was that age.

'Say hello to the nice new lady who's come to look after you and the other children,' Bertie said to the child, then turned her head to June and lowered her voice. 'Poor wee lass doesn't talk. She's not said a word since she came here ... that'd be a coupla months now. We all thought she was dumb at first. Now we know it's a mental thing.'

Poor little girl. Whatever could have happened?

June half rose from her chair, but Bertie put a warning hand out. 'Maybe not come too close at first ... don't want to frighten her any more than she is already.'

'How old is she?' June whispered.

19

'Three and a half.'

Her eyes filling with tears at such a likeness to her sister, June managed to smile across at the child. 'Hello, little one. Can you tell me your name?'

'She won't answer,' Bertie cut in. 'Her name's Lizzie. But it doesn't seem to mean anything to her. No reaction or nothing. I'll explain later – when she's taking a nap – how she ended up here.'

'Hello, Lizzie,' June said, still smiling. The child stared. Even from several feet away she could see that Lizzie's eyes were dark, unlike Clara's, which had been a grassy-green just like June's own, but the child's other features, the shape of her face – it brought back all the pain again. She felt herself tremble, her nerves on edge. Trying to calm herself she sipped her tea, her heartbeat slowing. She'd be all right. She'd be safe here. Mustn't go to pieces or she'd be no help to the children. Bertie was right. It was best to keep a distance until Lizzie began to trust her. Something terrible must have happened that had shocked the child.

She finished her tea just as a nurse, a halo of dark curls escaping from her cap, put her head around the door.

'Oh, there you are. The Fierce One told me you'd arrived.' She grinned and came into the room.

'The Fierce One?' June questioned.

'Matron.' The nurse laughed and Bertie joined in. 'That's what we all call her – Pherson, the Fierce One.' She looked June up and down and stuck out her hand. 'I'm Iris Marchant. And you are . . .?'

'June Lavender.' June took Iris's warm hand in her own cold one.

'Well, we should get on a treat,' Nurse Marchant said, shrieking with laughter, 'what with us being a couple of flowers.'

June laughed too. How wonderful that there was a young woman, not much older than herself, working at Dr Barnardo's. She was sure they'd be friends. Iris poured herself a cup of tea and gulped it down in a few mouthfuls.

'And months,' June added, grinning. Nurse Marchant looked puzzled. 'June and March . . . ant. And I was born in June – hence my name.'

'Oh, I get it.' The nurse chuckled. 'By the way, I'm Iris when we're off-duty – and you'll be June. But definitely not in front of the Fierce One, whether we're working or not.'

'I wouldn't dream of it,' June said, glancing at the clock. 'She sounds a stickler.'

'She is.' Iris nodded. 'You need to keep on the right side of her, which is difficult, as it's nigh impossible to tell what her right side is.' She chuckled again.

'You don't sound like a northerner,' June said.

'Me?' Iris pointed to herself. 'Definitely not. I couldn't live up here for good if you paid me. I'm from Kent. Not a good place to be in this bloody war.' June flinched at the swear word. 'Though it was quite thrilling seeing the Battle of Britain going on right above my head. My two young brothers went mad with excitement. Daft little buggers. They can't wait to be old enough to join up.'

June took a piece of Bertie's delicious fruit cake, barely taking in all Iris was telling her. 'I've been sent here and here I'll stay,' Iris rattled on, 'but not a moment longer after the war's over . . . whenever that will be. Luckily, the children keep me on my toes with their various shenanigans. And there's plenty of food. That's a draw in itself.' She grinned.

'Isn't the food rationed?'

'Some things,' Iris said. 'But the government looks after

21

institutions, particularly when there are children. And we grow our own vegetables and have a few chickens so we do all right here.'

June put her cup down. The twenty minutes must be up by now.

'I'm to meet Matron after I've finished my cup of tea,' she said.

Iris pulled a face. 'She's such a tartar. Barely gives you time to unpack before she has you working. You'd better get going then. Don't want to get in her bad books on your first morning.'

With more than a flicker of apprehension June went in search of Matron, who was already waiting outside her office, tapping her large foot impatiently.

'Right, there you are at last,' Matron said abruptly. 'We'll do the classrooms first.'

With that, she strode down the corridor, June following closely. She opened a door without knocking, then marched into a classroom of about fifteen children. Immediately the children scrambled to their feet, even two small boys not more than five or six years old, looking wide-eyed at the new lady in their midst. The older children, maybe ten or eleven years old, shuffled as they stood, and June saw a yellow-haired boy dig a dark-skinned child in the ribs. The child gave a yelp. All of them stared at her.

'Miss Graham?' Matron said, almost as a demand.

A woman of about June's own height and figure, her strawberry-blonde hair pulled back in a soft, shining Victory Roll, finished wiping the blackboard and put the rubber neatly back on the ledge. June couldn't help being conscious of her own hair, so thick it refused to be properly styled and would simply fall to her shoulders in unruly waves if she didn't keep it tied back. The young woman, Miss Graham, came towards them with quick determined steps, her heels clicking on the wooden floor.

'Miss Graham, this is Miss Lavender,' Matron said. 'She's my new assistant – come to help me with the load.'

'Nice to meet you.' Miss Graham had a clipped accent. Her hazel eyes held no gleam of enthusiasm as she extended her hand to June. 'I'm Athena Graham.' June sent her a questioning look. 'Yes, ghastly, isn't it? Blame it on my mother, who was a Greek nut. I teach English and mathematics, by the way – to all ages, as you can see.' She dropped her hand. 'I hope you'll be happy with us.'

Athena Graham didn't sound a particularly happy person herself. Maybe the boys played her up, yet somehow June couldn't see her allowing them to get the better of her.

'I'm sure I will be.' June smiled. 'I'm looking forward to it.'

Miss Graham turned towards the class. 'You may sit.'

There was a scuffling of chairs as they sat down with expressions of undisguised curiosity. June looked over at the sea of faces. All boys. They began muttering and one of them gave a low appreciative whistle when June sent them a shaky smile.

'Enough of that, Jackson,' Matron admonished. 'Where are your manners?'

'Left them in the dorm this morning, Matron.'

The other boys sniggered.

'What did you say your name was, Miss?' another boy asked cheekily. He had a too-thin face and dark, greasy hair which flopped into his eyes.

'I didn't say,' June began, 'but I'm Miss Lavender.'

The boy flicked his head back and the swathes settled into place for a few moments. 'How *do* you do, Miss Lavender?' he said in what he obviously thought was an upper-class accent. The boys giggled again.

'Hello to all of you.' June smiled. 'I hope to get to know your names very soon. It'll take me longer than you because there's only one of me, but I'm sure—'

'That'll be all, Miss Lavender,' Matron said, taking hold of June's arm. 'We must continue our tour. No doubt we'll see you at dinner, Miss Graham.' And with a nod she firmly escorted June out of the door.

'Now the art studio,' Matron said. She opened the door and June inhaled the familiar smell of paint and turpentine. It took her straight back to her home in March, where she would help Clara to make a painting for their mother. June noticed the atmosphere in the studio was far more relaxed than Miss Graham's class, as this teacher was walking around, looking over the children's shoulders and smiling encouragement at their work.

'That's coming along really well,' she was saying to one of the girls.

'Mrs Steen – needlework and art,' Matron snapped out as though she was contemptuous of Mrs Steen's particular subjects.

'Barbara,' the teacher said in an undertone so the pupils wouldn't hear. She grinned as Matron flashed her a warning look, and her friendly grey eyes lit up her plain features. She took June's hand firmly in her own plump one, and June warmed to her instantly.

'And the third teacher we have is Miss Ayles,' Matron said, as they left the art studio and she strode ahead into the next classroom. 'She's the senior teacher and has the older children. She teaches religious instruction, history and geography with particular emphasis on our glorious Empire.'

From Matron's tone, history and geography were far more acceptable.

Miss Ayles was thin as a stick, with spectacles halfway

down her nose, and an abundance of liver spots on her face and hands. Her grey hair was drawn back into a severe bun, every hair held in place at the sides by two black combs.

'Miss Lavender is my new assistant,' Matron said, edging June forward.

June smiled and put out her hand. Miss Ayles's lips lifted a fraction at the corners in acknowledgement, but her dry handshake was brief and gave nothing away.

It was plain that some of the staff didn't seem best pleased to have her there. June pressed her lips stubbornly together. She'd show them she was a hard worker who would put her heart and soul into whatever was in store for her. Her thoughts flew again to Lizzie. She was just about to summon the courage to ask if they could go up to the nursery, when Matron said:

'We'll put our heads in the door of the sick ward. Don't want to go in and catch anything. Nurse Manners will be there. She's got two of the girls in, both with tonsillitis. They're twins – Daisy and Doris Smith – and when one gets something, so does the other. They've been ill for a week now.' Matron sniffed and spread her fingers wide down her navy-blue dress as though smoothing out a crease, and June couldn't decide if she was annoyed with the twins catching everything at the same time or didn't have much confidence in Nurse Manners' nursing abilities.

'I've met the other nurse – Nurse Marchant. She seems very nice.'

Matron's lip curled. 'She's nice enough though she's an argumentative little madam and I won't tolerate it. She wouldn't get away with such behaviour if nurses weren't so thin on the ground because of the war – which the British shouldn't have been involved with in the first place.'

June managed to hide her astonishment at Matron's

outburst. She'd hardly been in the orphanage more than an hour or two. It made her feel uncomfortable that Matron should say such things about Iris, whom she'd taken to immediately. What a dragon. She wondered how many years Matron had been at the home and how the staff got on with her, having such threats hanging over them.

They walked down some steps at the far end of the house. Matron hesitated, then knocked and opened the door. June hovered outside, not wanting to disturb the two sick little girls.

'It's better to wait for me to tell you it's all right to come in,' a voice said in a firm tone, and a short, stocky young woman appeared, her face flushed and frowning, her arm thrust out as a barrier.

'I'm the matron. I can come in whenever I choose.' Matron tried to brush the nurse's arm aside, but the younger girl's arm was strong.

'No, I'm sorry, you can't. The girls are sleeping and I won't have them disturbed. You know I'll call you if they take a turn for the worse.' The nurse gave June an apologetic smile. 'I'm Kathleen Manners.' She turned to Matron. 'I'll come over later with a full report on the girls when Iris takes over this evening.'

'See that you do.' Matron's face was red with annoyance as she turned. The door clicked behind them.

Someone else who wasn't going to take orders from Matron. June was pleased that Kathleen hadn't succumbed. But she made a mental note that Matron was displeased if anyone didn't agree with her.

'Saucy slip of a girl,' Matron was saying. 'I'll be putting in my own report.' Her chest was heaving with frustration and her breathing was loud enough to reach June's ears.

'I was hoping I might see Lizzie,' June ventured, wanting to change the subject. 'Poor little mite. What happened to her that she can't speak?'

'*Refuses* to speak,' Matron said with such vehemence June took a step back in shock.

'Oh, surely not.'

'Surely so. It's obvious. The child's seeking attention. She's got another think coming if she reckons she's going to get it. That's why I've kept her separate. The other children think she's peculiar and then they start acting up, pretending not to hear or speak, the way *she* does.'

'May we go and see her?' June asked.

'No. My legs won't carry me up the all those flights more than once a day. The nursery's on the top floor. Where you and the maids are. But you'll meet Hilda, the nursery assistant who looks after her, soon enough. The girl eats like a horse. She'll be first down to supper, mark my words.'

'So Lizzie sees the other children at mealtimes?'

Matron threw her a sharp look. 'No. I've just told you the child has to be kept separate. She has her meals in the nursery. Hilda's a fast eater. She bolts hers down and then brings Lizzie hers.'

'Do you mean Lizzie is alone while Hilda goes to have hers?' June asked. She didn't like to think of the scared little girl locked in a room on her own. 'Isn't there someone who could keep an eye on her for a short time – in case something happened?'

'No,' Matron said. 'We're short-staffed and I'm on a tight budget.' She drew her eyebrows together. 'The child is hardly "alone", as you call it, not with everyone here.' She gave June a sharp look. 'You ask rather too many questions on your first day, my girl, and you'll do everyone a favour to keep those opinions of yours to yourself.' With that she stomped down the stairs leaving June trailing after her, her heart beating a little faster than it should.

'I must get on,' Matron said over her shoulder. 'I've got paperwork to do so perhaps you can get one of the others to finish showing you around.'

June chewed her lip as she gazed after the unbending figure. She had a horrible feeling Matron wasn't going to take any notice of her experience as a nursery nurse. She was the kind of woman who knew best, that was plain to see, and wasn't interested in anyone else's suggestions.

She felt bad thinking such things when she'd only just arrived but Matron certainly didn't put herself out to make people feel at ease. June was determined she wasn't going to make an enemy of her. That would be fatal. She squared her shoulders and began her tentative exploration of this mansion she must now call home.

Chapter Three

No one took the slightest bit of notice of June as she opened all the doors on the ground floor, taking note of the common room, the dining room, the cloakrooms, and a few steps down to the laundry room, where she could just make out two figures who were plunging what looked like poles into two enormous copper boilers and giggling through the steam. One of them looked up, sweat pouring off her forehead, and waved. There was also a playroom and a grand library. She had a few minutes' quiet browse around the shelves, looking over her shoulder every so often in case she was spotted and reprimanded. What a luxury if she was allowed to borrow a book now and again, although most of these seemed very highbrow. She couldn't see any novels, for one thing. At home she'd built up a small collection of books but she'd had to leave them behind when she went to London, and her room here felt bare without them. They'd been her friends when she'd had no one else. She shook herself. Mustn't think . . . .

She climbed the main staircase and looked into the bedrooms. There were five large rooms, laid out like dormitories, containing eight identical narrow beds with a small locker next to each one. And near the door there was a larger single bed, she guessed for one of the adults to keep an eye on the children. Everywhere was clean and neat. Nothing out of place. It didn't look as though any children lived here.

She thought of the state of her childhood home. Before she'd left at 16 to train as a nursery nurse, it had been chaos. Stella had already left home three years before to get married and move to Wisbech, leaving June with their violent father and a drunken mother. A mother who when Clara died had only found solace in drink, and as a consequence had neglected the home. June had done her best to keep everything going but it was almost a relief when her mother drifted into a coma one sunny morning in her bed. A once attractive woman lay on the pillow, her mouth open, her eyes wild, looking haggard and beaten before she gasped her last breath. June swallowed hard as the memories reached out to pull her back in – forcing her to relive it as she had already done, over and over, hundreds, maybe thousands of times, since it had happened. She'd been left with her father, an unkempt bully of a man, with a temper which erupted at any moment. He'd had not a shred of decency or compassion for comforting his grieving wife after Clara's death.

The only time June had seen any sign of distress in him was after her mother's funeral when June told him she was leaving home and going to live with Aunt Ada. He'd realised with a jolt of fear there was no one left to look after him. June's lip curled in disgust, willing the old images to stop replaying. But they were too strong.

June had flown down the stairs to where Clara lay crumpled at the bottom. She cradled her sister's head in her arms. Clara's eyes were wide with terror. Thank God she was still alive.

'Clara, darling, I'm here. You're going to be all right.'

Clara smiled – an angel's smile. Her eyes held a wise

expression and June felt her heart sing with joy that her sister would indeed recover. She smiled back at her.

And then June heard a long sigh escape Clara's lips as her head lolled to one side.

Clara had just had her eighth birthday.

As long as June lived she would never, ever forgive her father. And one day she would see that justice was done.

Tears fell from June's eyes as she pulled the dormitory door shut. Would she ever stop reliving that nightmare? She brushed the tears away with the back of her hand, hoping against hope that no one would spot her and ask what was the matter. She could never tell anyone.

A bell sounded.

She heard footsteps behind her and spun round to see Iris.

'I came to see how you were getting on. If I could answer any questions.' Iris looked at her sharply. 'You've been crying. Are you all right?'

'Yes. I'm all right.'

Iris didn't look convinced. 'By the way, that was the bell for dinner. Are you hungry?'

'Starving,' June said, thankful the subject of her crying was closed. She followed Iris back into the hall. A noise like thunder crashed over her head and seconds later a stream of children came flying down the stairs, pushing and shoving and calling out.

'Where on earth's Matron?' Iris sounded irritated as she glanced about her.

'I'm here.' Matron appeared from one of the oak doorways. 'Right, children.' She clapped her hands loudly and they immediately stopped their noise. 'Before you go in, I want you all to know Miss Lavender is going to help keep you lot in line.'

'Hello, Miss. You came in our class,' a boy of about ten with a cheeky grin shouted over the banister. 'Have you got any sweets for us?'

'You're not allowed sweets,' Matron told him. 'Now come on down, all of you, and line up, so Miss Lavender can take a look at you all . . . and keep your traps shut for once.'

June flinched. This was not the sort of language she ever used to keep children in order, but she knew she mustn't make a comment – not yet. The children lined up, still shuffling and muttering, but they were obviously in awe of Matron as they'd quietened right down.

'Can you all tell me your names and how old you are?' June said, smiling at the first child and letting it travel along the row until it fell on the last. 'I shan't remember them all right away but I'll do my best, and I'm sure you'll remind me.'

'You can do that after we've had dinner,' Matron interrupted, clapping her hands again. 'It'll be cold at this rate. File in, all of you.'

'I'm worried about the little girl, Lizzie,' June whispered to Iris. 'Matron said she has her meals in the nursery.'

'I don't agree with it at all,' Iris said under her breath, 'but Matron says she's a disruptive influence over the other children.'

'What did she do that's disruptive?'

'When she first came they put her in the dining room with all the other kids,' Iris explained, 'but if one of the teachers told her she had to eat what was on her plate and she didn't like it, she'd throw the plate on the floor.' Iris smiled ruefully. 'We lost a lot of plates that week. Matron got angry and said Lizzie had to have her meals in the nursery from now on.'

'But she'll never learn to behave if she's taken out of a normal situation like eating with the others,' June protested.

'I said as much to Matron but she ignored me. Matron is always right. You'll soon find that out – if you can put up with it.'

June knew that Iris was warning her that she might not be able to put up with it; that Iris wouldn't be at all surprised if she left. June pressed her mouth tight, resolving that it would take a lot more than that for her to give in her notice. In her experience Lizzie needed to know she was part of the home, whether she was naughty or good, and mix with the other children. June was sure it was the only way to encourage her to speak.

'You'll have to help serve at that table over there,' Iris said, pointing, 'and I'll take this one. Don't know where Kathleen's got to – she's the other nurse.'

'Oh, yes, I met her in the sick bay.'

'Of course. She takes the third table . . . oh, here she is.'

Kathleen shot in and gave Iris a wave, smiled at June, then rushed to her place, and the dining room became a crescendo of noise again until Matron appeared and banged on the table.

'Fold your hands together for Grace,' she said, raising her chin, her eyes rolling back in their sockets, her hands clasped, as though she were in direct contact with God. 'For what we are about to receive, may the Lord make us truly thankful. Amen.'

'Amen,' repeated the children.

There was a clatter of plates and cutlery as two kitchen maids brought in the steaming bowls of stew and potatoes. When June had served all sixteen boys at her table, there was another kind of noise – slurping, gulping, hiccupping – but at least they were clearing their plates. She took a few bites but the excitement of the day seemed to have rid her of her appetite.

But now she had a purpose. She was going to look after the children who lived in this huge old house. Try to make it up to Clara. Make sure she would never forget her dearest sister.

After the children had all taken turns to tell June their names and ages, she looked round for Matron, but the woman was nowhere to be seen. Not knowing what to do next, she went to Matron's office and tapped gently on her door but there was no sound from within.

'Are you looking for Matron, Miss Lavender?'

June turned to see Miss Ayles, the history and geography teacher, regarding her from behind her spectacles.

'Yes. I was wondering what she'd like me to do. And if sometime this afternoon I could clean my room. It smells of damp and I don't think it's good to sleep in such an atmosphere.'

'I'm not surprised. It's been empty for quite a while. We've not had an assistant to Matron since the war started but now we've got ten more children – evacuees – it's not been easy with the shortage of books and pencils.' Miss Ayles peered at June. 'So I should go and get your room done, Miss Lavender, while Matron takes her hour-and-a-half nap.' She wrinkled her thin nose. 'Some nap,' she added under her breath. 'This might be your only opportunity before bedtime.'

'Does everyone live in?'

'The teachers and nurses are up on the third floor, the maids on the fourth. I have my own cottage as do Cook and Matron.' There was a note of triumph in her voice and June hid a smile. 'Is there anything else I can answer?'

'No, you've been most helpful,' June said. 'I think I'll go to the kitchen and ask Mrs Bertram where I can find some cleaning things.'

Cleaning took longer than she'd thought. She went downstairs more than once to check Matron wasn't looking for her but all was silent. The children were in class, or if they were in the younger group they were having a nap themselves. But, two hours later, June ran her eye over the room. She'd managed to straighten the wardrobe, get rid of the dead flowers and clean out the vase, and she'd washed everything down, including the windows and frames and wainscot, with soap and vinegar and bleach. It was a remarkable improvement though the room still looked sadly stripped of homely items. Somewhere she had a photograph of herself and her sisters with their mother. She delved into her travel bag, unwrapped it from its newspaper and smiled as she set it on the shelf above the fireplace. She stood back to admire it. One photograph, but it made all the difference.

A few paintings – prints of course – would brighten the room but she had no money to buy anything extra. Maybe she'd find something in a second-hand shop when she'd settled in properly and saved a bit of cash. Until then, she was satisfied the room looked infinitely cleaner and smelled infinitely fresher. After the long journey she'd surely sleep tonight.

Chapter Four

June opened her eyes and for a few moments wondered where she was. Then she smiled. She now lived in a grand country house all the way up north in Liverpool. If her mother could see her she'd be amazed. But grand house or not, the room still felt deadly cold. She sat up, wrapping the extra blanket she'd found in the wardrobe last night around her shoulders, and let her mind drift over the last twenty-four hours. Bingham Hall was certainly a different world from her last two years living with Stella and her three boys in Wisbech. She pictured them all and suddenly felt a stab of homesickness. They were the only family she cared about now, besides Aunt Ada. A tear trickled down June's cheek and she quickly brushed it away. She had a new life now, and she was determined to make a difference to these children's lives.

Well, she wasn't going to make a difference in anyone's life by sitting here thinking. She scrambled out of bed and pulled back the short velvet curtains, which were spotted with age. She peered through the glass panes, pleased she'd cleaned them yesterday, though she could still smell the traces of the vinegar she'd used. The fog had cleared and everywhere was white. Snow, like giant bales of cotton wool, lay over the fields and trees as far as her eyes could travel. Thick and white and silent.

She couldn't see another house in sight. She'd never lived anywhere this remote in her life. But standing there looking out of the misted-up window at a fairyland view, she felt a sense of calm seep through her bones. Her mother, bless her, was finally at peace. June had been grateful Stella had given her a home, but it hadn't been easy looking after the three boys while her sister's husband had been away fighting. Stella had had little control over her sons, leaving them to June. 'I'm better to go out to work,' Stella told her sister, as she left each morning to work in the munitions factory. 'And I need the company,' she'd added, never thinking her sister might occasionally like to be with people her own age too, June had thought at the time. After her husband was killed Stella had gone out dancing or to the pictures most nights, and six months later she'd found herself a new boyfriend. She'd been astounded when June told her she'd been offered a job up north.

'What will I do without you?' she'd said. 'The boys need some stability and you know how fond they are of you.' Her eyes pleaded with June.

June wasn't at all sure that was true – it was much more likely that Stella wouldn't have the freedom she'd enjoyed lately – but it didn't stop her feeling guilty that she was leaving her sister in the lurch.

It had been a shock to June when she'd moved from sleepy Wisbech and stayed with her aunt in London those last three days. When she'd lived there while training to be a nursery nurse there'd only been rumours of a war. This time she'd seen whole streets reduced to a pile of rubble, and the bombs at night had left her tired and jumpy. She had no desire to live in London again. How had the Londoners gone through bombing, night after night, day after day, with such bravery? Was she being a coward to escape it all? But surely vulnerable orphans and evacuees at Dr Barnardo's needed help just as much as wounded soldiers and citizens.

Now June gave a sigh but it was more of contentment. Whatever lay in store for her, for once she hadn't been manipulated or made to feel guilty. This new life was of her own making. She'd take the consequences whatever they were.

Feeling more sure of herself she washed and dressed and half ran down the four flights of steps. Iris was the first person she spotted.

'Bet you haven't seen snow like this in London.'

'I must admit I've never seen it as thick.'

Iris glanced at June's shoes that Aunt Ada had bought her. 'You need boots for our northern winters,' she said. 'Those shoes won't do at all.'

'I didn't bring any.' And had no money to buy them, June wanted to add.

Iris considered for a few moments. 'We need to fix you up with some proper footwear right away so I'll have a word with Matron. What say we go into town this morning? I have a few hours to spare as I'm on evening shift this week. But you'll have to brace yourself. We had a very bad raid in May and parts of Liverpool are in a terrible state. They usually aim for the docks but I think they enjoy giving the civilians a good fright as often as they can as well.'

'Don't worry about me – I'm used to London, which you wouldn't believe the terrible hammering it's taken . . .' She stopped, realising she sounded as though she was making light of Liverpool's hardship. 'Though I read Liverpool is a close second,' she added quickly. 'I suppose it's because it's a port.'

'A major one,' Iris said. 'The docks have taken the brunt of Hitler's planes because its position is convenient for

American ships to bring us crucial supplies. Not just American but Canadian and Australian ships deliver here as well. If the Germans have their way and smash the docks to pieces we'll have had it. Nothing will get through – food, fuel, arms – everything we depend on. It'd be a disaster.'

June shivered. She could tell by Iris's upset expression that her friend was not exaggerating.

'Anyway, enough of that,' Iris said smiling. 'Are we on? Our jaunt into town?'

'But what about the twins in the sick bay?' June asked. 'Don't you need to see to them?'

'Kathleen's here to look after them.'

'I don't know . . .' June hesitated. It might not look right if she wasn't there to learn the ropes on her first full day and she felt guilty that Matron still hadn't appeared after she'd finished cleaning her bedroom yesterday. She'd spent the rest of the time until supper in the library. 'Matron hasn't told me yet exactly what she wants me to do. I thought she'd have given me a list of jobs by now.'

'She's not the most efficient,' Iris said. 'But I'm sure she'll let you know soon enough. But as far as going into town, leave it to me. We might be able to get a lift with Harold – he's the only one here with a car and more or less acts as a chauffeur. We have to take advantage when he goes in, which is usually only once a week as fuel's rationed, of course. Anyway, I'll have a word with the Fierce One.' With a chuckle Iris vanished.

June had told Iris not to worry – that she was prepared for a city that had borne the brunt of constant bombing attacks – but she hadn't expected the sights that met her. Whole streets were razed to the ground, and when they turned a corner they saw flames burning in what had obviously been

39

a sizeable commercial building. They watched a group of firemen trying to bring it under control.

'Jerry were busy last night,' said one of the firemen, nodding in their direction.

'Lewis's department store,' Iris said with dismay. 'It's my favourite shop – or was. But that's nothing compared with so many of the wonderful old buildings – our landmarks – vanished or standing like empty shells. Most of it happened in May when they blitzed us. They even managed to hit the cathedral but it wasn't damaged too badly so if it comes through the war, they'll repair it. It's so ghastly.' She turned her face to June, her eyes moist. 'Let's go, June. It makes me feel sick looking at it. Oh, I'm so fed up with this bloody war.'

The scene was so terrible that this time June didn't even cringe at Iris's swear word. And it *was* bloody. Men and women were dying in England, in France, and of course in Germany, and though she couldn't feel quite so sympathetic about the enemy, it was still a tragic waste of lives. A shiver of horror ran down her spine as she saw an old man lying on his back by the side of the road, still and pale, his eyes open. A woman came out of one of the shops and put a blanket over the figure, pulling it right over his head.

'Don't look,' Iris said. 'He's dead. Probably had a heart attack. It's happening quite a bit to the elderly. I had to give some first aid to an old lady the last time I was in town. Thank goodness she came round but there's nothing we can do here. Someone will see to what needs to be done.' She took June's arm and moved her away.

'So many people have lost their homes,' June said, her eyes pricking with tears. 'Look over there – those poor people picking through all those bricks for their belongings.'

Her stomach sickened at the sight of houses where their

owners' once precious belongings had been proudly on show to their visitors, and now spilled out of blown-out walls and down smashed-up staircases – beds, mattresses, tables, washstands, stoves, pictures, clothes – all looking as though they were ready for the rag-and-bone man.

'We're not going to be sad,' Iris said firmly. 'We're going to get you the best boots you've ever had. And then we'll go and have tea in one of the cafés.'

Iris led her down one street and then another, June's feet becoming colder by the minute. She wished she had a street map to see where she was going. Maybe she could pick one up in a stationer's or a bookshop.

'Here we are,' Iris said. 'One of my favourite shoe shops – they don't have quite the choice these days but they're bound to have something suitable.'

'They're too expensive,' June said, peering in the window at the price tags.

Iris laughed and practically pushed her inside.

'Try these.' Iris held up a pair of sturdy leather boots with a fur lining. June could tell at a glance they'd be dear.

'They're too big.' June shook her head but Iris ignored her and asked a smartly dressed lady if she would measure her friend's foot.

'You have very small feet, Miss,' the saleswoman said, scrutinising the measurement. 'Only a three-and-a-half. I'll see if I have them in your size.' She unbent with a wince and threw back her shoulders. 'Back in a jiffy.'

True to her word she was back with another box and a shoehorn. When she was satisfied June's foot was in the correct position she said, 'Now try walking in them.'

They felt as though they'd been made for her.

'How do they feel, June?' Iris looked down and gave a satisfied nod.

'They're lovely and comfortable, but—'

'But you can't afford them,' Iris finished. June reddened. 'I'll lend you the money. Pay me back when you can. You just need six coupons. Have you got your ration book with you?'

'Yes, but—' She didn't want to admit she'd used up most of her yearly allowance of sixty coupons already when she'd been offered the job. Aunt Ada had insisted she buy a desperately needed coat, and the shoes that she'd just taken off, as well as a skirt and blouse, camiknickers and stockings. June bit her lip, mentally adding them up. Six more for the boots. That would only leave eight to last until the end of May.

'We'll take the boots, thank you.' Iris walked over to the lady at the till and fished out her purse.

'But—'

Iris put her hand up. 'Stop! Those shoes you're wearing will let in all the wet. In fact' – she turned back to the lady at the till – 'my friend will wear the boots straightaway.'

There was nothing June could do. She could tell Iris was determined and used to taking charge. She had to admit the boots were warm and the soles thick enough to practically skim over the snow.

'Thank you, Iris. I'll pay you back soon, I promise.'

'See that you do,' Iris said with mock firmness. She looked at June and grinned. 'You've got some colour in those pale cheeks now. You're pretty, but I expect you know that. Bet you've got all the boys after you.'

'I haven't got a boyfriend at the moment,' June said, a sudden image of the tall, broad-shouldered man in the greatcoat with the mocking smile making her go pink.

'You will soon, what with the RAF station nearby.'

'What do you mean?'

'Speke. The RAF station. It's only a few miles away. The

boys there go to dances. And *we* go to dances. There's never enough girls so we're never short of partners. You're coming with me to the next one.'

'I've never been to a dance.'

'Well, now's the time.' Iris slipped her hand through June's arm as they left the shop. It felt nice. It had been a long time since she'd had a real friend. 'Are you ready for a cup of tea, Junie, or what would you like to do?'

Junie. The only person who had called her that was Clara. June swallowed.

'Do you mind me calling you Junie?' Iris asked as though she'd read June's thoughts.

'N-no, not at all,' June stuttered. The pain was always close enough to burst out at any moment. She blinked back the tears. 'I was wondering if there was a second-hand book-shop anywhere.' She looked around vaguely as though one might spring out at her. 'I could do with a map of Liverpool and I'd love a new book to read.'

'I'd have thought there would be plenty of books in the library at the home,' Iris said.

'I had a look yesterday but they're mostly what I'd call scholarly. I just want something light to read in bed before I switch my light out.'

'Lucky you to be able to see to read,' Iris said grimly. 'My light's awful. Maybe I'll see if I can find a stronger bulb . . . buy it myself 'cos Matron will never give me one.' She stopped, her forehead puckering. 'Let's see . . . there are two second-hand bookshops near here . . . more or less the same, except one has a bad-tempered owner and the other one is just the opposite – polite and helpful.'

'Could we go to the polite and helpful one?' June smiled. 'I don't think I'm in the mood for bad temper today.'

'They're both up in the High Street, on the right-hand

side as you go down. Only a couple of shops in between so I'll leave you to it. I won't tell you which one's which,' she added with a wicked grin. 'I need to pick up some things from the chemist and I'd like to have a wander, even if there's nothing much in the windows. Shall we meet over there at the fountain' – she looked at her watch – 'say, half-past eleven? Will that give you enough time to poke around some dusty old bookshop?'

'That would be perfect,' June said, delighted. It would be fun to go to both bookshops and have a browse. She wondered if she would be able to tell which owner was which.

The snow was already beginning to melt and June wished she wasn't wearing her beautiful new boots. They'd be ruined through all this slush. Then she smiled. They were made for that exact purpose. She'd give them a good clean and drying-out when she got home.

Home. Dr Barnado's. Who would have thought it?

She crossed the road, narrowly avoiding a car coming at a pace along the slushy high street. Further along, the damage the Luftwaffe had done on their air raids made her sick to her stomach again. A whole row of terraced houses had been turned into a mountain of rubble – except for the end one, which didn't look as though it had acquired even a bruise. Horses towing carts carrying the remnants of people's homes patiently picked their way through the debris. Several shops had their windows boarded up but most of them had a notice on the door saying: 'Open for business as usual'.

'Usual'. June grimaced as she slowly walked along the pavement wondering how people could manage to run a business in such chaos.

The first bookshop she came to was simply called Brown's Books. She opened the door and from somewhere within a bell clanged.

An RAF officer, his back towards her, was talking to an older man behind the counter.

'We don't keep maps any more since the war started,' the bookseller was saying. 'You ought to know more than most they could end up in the wrong hands.' June saw him glare at the man in the blue coat, who turned at June's approach. She gave a start.

The officer smiled and removed his peaked cap, then his blue eyes sparked with recognition. He beamed at her, showing strong, creamy-white teeth. She hadn't been able to see his hair before. It was tawny-coloured.

'Well, if it isn't the independent miss who wouldn't let me give her a hand with her luggage,' he said, smiling.

June flushed. 'I really didn't mean to be rude but I was trying to . . .' she trailed off, wishing her heart would stop pumping in her ears.

He chuckled. 'It's all right. I forgave you straightaway when I looked into those green eyes of yours.' June felt her face go even redder.

'Looking for anything in particular, Miss?' The man behind the counter tipped his glasses back to the bridge of his nose.

'Not really,' June said. 'Do you mind if I just have a browse and maybe I'll see something?'

'You go right ahead, Miss.'

'What sort of books do you read?' The officer made the question sound as though her answer was important to him.

His eyes were even more blue than she remembered.

'Oh, whatever I can get hold of,' June said, a little disconcerted. What a stupid answer. He would think she had no taste. 'I enjoyed Monica Dickens' book *Mariana,* and I tried to get her previous one from the library but they didn't have it.' It sounded just as feeble.

'That'd be *One Pair of Hands*,' the bookseller put in. 'I should have a copy somewhere. One of my regulars brought it in a few weeks ago. Let me have a look.'

He tottered from behind the counter. 'I think I'll need those steps.'

'Allow me, Mr Brown.' The officer set them beneath the overladen shelves.

Mr Brown was up the ladder in a flash. 'Ah.' He triumphantly pulled out a book and clutched it with one hand as he backed down the steps. 'You can have this for one-and-six, seeing's how the jacket's torn a bit.'

He made to hand it to her but the younger man was too quick for him. Forehead creased as though he was inspecting a valuable document, the officer flicked through the book, bending back some of the corners on the pages that had been turned down. 'What about a shilling from the young lady?' he asked Mr Brown, then looked up and sent June a wink and a smile.

Put out somewhat by his flirtatious manner, she frowned, which caused his smile to widen even further.

'Seems fair to me when several pages are quite grubby and creased,' he added, then handed the book to June, who removed her gloves and leafed through a few pages. The book was actually in a very respectable condition, she thought.

'I'll take it if a shilling is acceptable,' June said, wanting to escape as quickly as she could.

Mr Brown frowned. He looked at the officer, then nodded. 'All right, then. This young man here has twisted my arm. It's yours. Shall I wrap it?'

'No, don't bother. It doesn't look like rain.'

'More snow, more like,' Mr Brown said with a grimace.

The officer reached in his pocket and brought out a

ten-shilling note. 'As we've already met, I'd like to buy it for you, if I may – as a small gift.'

This was a pick-up, no doubt about it. June shook her head. 'Thank you, but I would prefer to pay for the book myself.' Her voice was sharper than she'd intended.

Disappointment spread over the officer's face.

'I'm sorry – that sounded awfully rude,' June said, conscious of Mr Brown gazing curiously at the two of them. 'It's very kind of you but really I don't—'

'You don't know my name,' he finished. 'Then let me introduce myself. Flight Lieutenant Murray Andrews. RAF Speke.' He gave a mock bow. 'At your service.'

Of course. A pilot. And cheeky with it. Not that she knew any but she'd been told often enough. Apparently they all had that charm. And he was at the station Iris had mentioned.

She offered her hand. 'June Lavender. It's been very nice to meet you again, Flight Lieutenant Andrews. And thank you for helping me to decide on the book.'

He took her hand. She hadn't put her gloves back on and it was as though the warmth of his skin flowed between them. 'I wouldn't mind reading it after you.' He finally allowed her hand to drop but kept his gaze on her.

A little shaken, she gabbled, 'I don't think it's a man's kind of book if the other one's anything to go by.'

'It's a true story, isn't it?'

June turned the book over. Monica Dickens smiled from the jacket cover. 'Yes, it's her autobiography.'

'Then try me.'

By the look of his grin he was flirting with her. Willing her cheeks not to burn and trying her best to ignore the nearness of him, June handed over a shilling and said goodbye, but Murray Andrews reached the door before her.

'Can I at least take you for a cup of tea, Miss Lavender? That wouldn't be too forward of me, would it?'

His hand on the door frame. A strong, capable hand. Only moments ago her own hand had been lost in it. An image of him in his flying suit in the cockpit, blue eyes fixed firmly ahead . . . that same hand on the controls . . . *Look away.* Her eyes roved to a clock on the wall above Mr Brown. Oh, no. It was already five minutes over the time Iris had given her.

'I'm really sorry but I'm late meeting someone.' And with that June rushed out.

'I'm ready for that cuppa,' Iris said, holding the café door for June, who thumped her new boots up and down to kick off the snow.

The café was heaving. Iris pulled a face. 'Ugh, I hate the horrible smell of dandelion they're all using now instead of coffee. Camp. Who thought of a name like that? And who do they think they're fooling?'

'I suppose they can't help it with the rationing.' June looked about her and spotted a table. 'Oh, that couple by the window are just leaving. And it doesn't look quite so smoky.'

'Did you go to both bookshops?' Iris asked, when they'd settled in the still warm seats.

'No, only Brown's. He was very helpful so he must be the nice one.'

Iris smiled. 'I'm glad you got on well with him.'

'He found me exactly what I wanted. Maybe because I bought a book it cheered him up . . . even though a customer knocked him down from one-and-six to a shilling – on my behalf.'

'Oh? Who was that then?' Iris gazed at her, curiosity sparking in her sapphire-blue eyes.

48

'Just some man.' Blast. She hadn't wanted to mention Murray Andrews.

Iris immediately pounced. 'What man? Another old boy?'

'No. He was an officer – a pilot at that RAF station you mentioned.' June hesitated. Might as well give the full account now. 'Actually, I first saw him on the Liverpool train. He offered to help with my case but I wouldn't let him.'

'Gosh, it doesn't take *you* long to get yourself a boyfriend.' Iris laughed.

'Don't be daft. I doubt very much I'll ever see him again. Anyway, he was nothing special.'

'Then why have you gone pink?'

June put her hand to her cheek. 'Because it's so hot in here. I'm going to take my coat off.' She was relieved to see a waitress hurrying over.

'Tea for two, please, and two scones and jam,' Iris said. She leaned across the table and gazed at June, her eyes full of mischief. 'Don't think you can change the subject. I want to hear all about your pilot. Every detail.'

'He's not my pilot and there's nothing to tell,' June said, annoyed with herself for starting all this. 'He was after a map but Mr Brown told him in no uncertain terms there was a war on and a map could end up in the wrong hands. So of course I couldn't tell him I was also after a map.'

Iris chuckled. 'Well, you're bound to bump into him again at one of the dances. Maybe he has a nice friend.' She patted June's arm. 'It'll be fun going with you. Sometimes a couple of the maids come and we catch a bus together but they giggle over nothing and have no conversation except boys and moaning about Cook. Course, they're still wet behind the ears.'

The waitress set a tray of tea and the scones on the table.

'No butter.' Iris wrinkled her nose at the margarine. 'But at least we've got a teaspoon of jam.'

June was relieved the conversation had taken a turn away from Murray Andrews. Iris chattered on about her family, then said, 'Do you have brothers and sisters?'

It was the question June was dreading.

She swallowed. 'I had two sisters, but one – Clara – died when she was only eight.'

Iris covered June's hand with her own. 'I'm so sorry, Junie. That's awful. How long ago?'

'More than five years but it still seems like yesterday. That's why I'm here – to help children who need me.'

'What about your parents?'

'Mum died two years after Clara's accident, when I was sixteen. She was broken-hearted and became . . . ill.'

'Oh, poor you. And your father?'

'I . . . he . . .'

'Don't tell me if it's painful.' Iris looked over at the wall clock opposite and shot to her feet. 'C'mon, kid, we've got to get back. Harold won't be able to take us home as he's got to take the car in for repair. But we can get the bus if we hurry.'

'This is my treat.' June got out her purse and left the coins on the table. She dipped in again and drew out a thruppenny bit, hoping it was enough for a tip, and buttoned her coat. She picked up her bag and the shoebox with her old shoes and hurried after Iris.

An hour later they were back at the home. Just as Iris put her hand out to pull the bell cord the heavy oak door swung wide. Matron stood there, her face red and perspiring, eyes wide as though she were about to burst.

'Have you heard the news?' Matron threw her hands in the air.

June and Iris glanced at each other, puzzled

'No, we've been—' Iris began.

'The Japs have bombed one of the American naval bases in Hawaii!' Matron's voice rose a decibel. 'That means the Americans will be over here in droves, you'll see! With all their money and fancy goods.' She gave a contemptuous twist of her lip and shook her head with such force her cap hung at a precarious angle.

Iris shouted in delight. 'But that's wonderful news, Matron. They'll be here to help us win the war – and not before time.' She grabbed hold of June, who was trying to take it all in. 'Isn't it exciting, Junie?' Iris whirled her so hard June's head swam. 'Junie, say something.'

'I bet Mr Churchill's relieved,' June gasped, laughing as she nearly lost her balance when Iris suddenly let her go. Out of the corner of her eye she saw Matron's grimace before she disappeared inside. June suddenly thought of all the boys and men and women who had already died. How many more would have to die before the world came to its senses? But at least it looked as though Mr Churchill would finally have help.

'He'll be dancing for joy like us,' Iris said, this time pulling June into another spin. 'The Yanks are coming – they're really coming,' she sang out. 'Oh, thank God! We're going to win this bloody war, you'll see. This time next year it'll all be over.'

Even the welcome news about the Japs invading Pearl Harbor wasn't enough to stop Murray Andrews thinking about the girl in the bookshop. Fair enough, she was pretty, but he'd known loads of pretty girls. So what was so special about June Lavender? Was it her quiet determined manner? Or the hint of mischief behind those grassy-green eyes? Was it because she shared a love of books? Was it simply because she hadn't shown the slightest interest in him when she'd tried to get past him in the corridor of the train? Her polite but firm reply when he'd offered to pay for her book? He was so used to women being impressed with his being a fighter pilot that it was odd not having to fend off yet another pretty girl.

He grinned. If he wasn't careful he'd get the reputation of being a cocky sod. And that was best left to the likes of the handsome, full-of-himself Yank, Captain Charles ('Call me Chas') Lockstone, who'd breezed in six weeks ago along with a handful of other American volunteer pilots by going over the border and joining the Royal Canadian Air Force. It was inevitable that today's news would bring the Yanks into the war and a lot more of them would soon be over here. No question we need them, Murray thought, lighting a cigarette, even though he couldn't work up a lot of enthusiasm. He'd heard too many stories about them – many of them not very favourable – to look forward to their arrival. But Churchill would be ecstatic as he'd tried so hard and for so long to convince Roosevelt to enter fully into the war, so surely now the tide would turn in the Allies' favour.

Murray tried to concentrate on his newspaper but it was impossible. Everything was bound to change now.

Chapter Five

The news about the Americans coming into the war was the only topic in the dining room at dinnertime. Even Matron couldn't stop the children cheering and shouting 'hurray' when they heard the grown-ups talking and laughing that Jerry wouldn't know what hit them now the Americans were about to swell the numbers in the military. Everyone joining in except Lizzie, June thought sadly. It didn't matter that Lizzie and most of the children were too young to understand how much it meant that finally Churchill had got his wish. It was enough that they were following the older children, who were clearly excited. But not Lizzie. The little girl would be upstairs in the nursery having her dinner, but there'd be no childish laughter escaping the room as there were no other children to share it with. June was certain that if only she knew the full story she'd be able to help Lizzie, whom she hadn't seen since those few minutes yesterday. She'd settle in for a few days and have a word with Iris and Kathleen – ask them their opinion – but until then she'd make sure to go to the kitchen every morning, where she knew Lizzie regularly curled up under the watchful eye of Bertie, and speak to her even if the little girl never answered. Momentarily, June closed her eyes. Lizzie reminded her so much of Clara.

'Let us hope you've enjoyed your morning off,' Matron

said, a touch of sarcasm dripping through the words. 'There's plenty to learn and I want you to start right away, so please come to my office as soon as you've finished.'

June helped serve the dinner, which was stew and bread, with rice pudding to follow, all the while thinking of Lizzie alone in the nursery, though it was hard to think straight with all the noise. The children were not allowed to talk but that didn't stop them scraping their chairs, coughing, slurping, sniffing, whispering. One child was making a racket with two spoons and June was surprised Matron hadn't reprimanded him. Then she realised. Matron would be watching to see whether she could control the children on what was only her second day.

'Will you please stop banging those spoons,' June said in a firm voice. The child took no notice, just grinned and carried on doing it. The child opposite with ginger hair and freckles began to giggle. She had to say something or else they'd get the better of her, though it was difficult as they were several seats away.

'The boy who would love to play drums and is practising with two spoons – what is your name?'

There was a silence. The children's heads swivelled to look at the offending boy. The boy banging the spoons gave another loud clash.

'Could someone tell me his name if he can't answer for himself?' June persisted.

'It's Thomas, Miss. He's always mucking about,' said the ginger-haired boy.

'No, I'm not,' Thomas shouted.

'No talking!' Matron glared across from the neighbouring table. 'That goes for you, too, Miss Lavender, unless there is an emergency.'

Several children giggled. June went red with annoyance.

54

If Matron was going to pull her up in front of the children, she didn't stand a chance. The children would think they could get the better of her every time.

'This *is* an emergency, Matron,' June spoke in such a low voice she wondered if Matron would hear. 'If I hear any more from you, Thomas, I will . . . I'll . . .'

'What, Miss? What will you do?' His eyes were like two shining pieces of coal, challenging her.

'You will be promoted to monitor of the games room. And you will clean it up after the children every day for a fortnight whether you've played in there or not. They won't have to do it – *you* will.'

'That'd be right good, Miss,' Peter said, grinning at the scowling Thomas.

'Now no more talking. That goes for all of you.'

'Even you, Miss,' Thomas muttered under his breath.

The rest of the meal passed in silence allowing June's thoughts to stray to Lizzie again. She couldn't get the little girl out of her head. A child who had suffered such a terrible shock it had made her dumb. It was wrong that Matron would not allow her to join in with the other children who might even be able to encourage her to speak. And she still didn't like the idea that Lizzie was left alone while someone came downstairs to eat a meal, no matter how quickly, and then go back upstairs. Anything could happen in between. Hilda was not acting at all responsibly but Matron had clearly sent a warning not to interfere. Well, she was afraid she might not be able to heed that warning. Where was Hilda anyway?

Completely forgetting Matron's order to report to her office, June jumped to her feet and stacked the plates nearest to her.

'Can you finish this?' she mouthed to Iris, who nodded. June dumped the dishes in the kitchen and practically ran up the flights of stairs, her heart hammering as though she were a naughty schoolgirl about to get found out. Past her own room and the maids' to the end. A door in front of her was conveniently marked 'Nursery' and she tried it. It was locked.

'Lizzie, are you in there?' June shook the handle. There was no sound. Of course – the child couldn't make herself heard. She thought she heard a scuffle of shoes. 'Lizzie,' she called again. 'It's Miss Lavender, the new lady who has come to help look after you and the other children. Is there a key in the door? If there is you could turn it. Open the door. And I could say "hello" to you.'

She stood quietly, straining her ears to pick up any noise of a child. Nothing. She must have imagined the other noise. Bending down she put her eye to the keyhole but her view was restricted. She could just make out what looked like the end of a cot.

'Can I help you, Miss?'

June jumped to her feet at the sound of Gilbert. She hadn't heard his approach and it unnerved her.

'There's a child in there. I was worried that she's alone and frightened.'

'Why do you say that?'

She shouldn't have passed any remark to Gilbert. He'd made it clear that he disliked her on sight and she couldn't say in all honesty she felt any better towards him. But it was too late. He was asking her questions.

'Matron said Hilda leaves her while she has her meal.'

'Aye. That's right.'

'But if the child should have an accident . . .'

'I'm here if anything like that happens.'

'But you can't be everywhere,' June said, knowing it was the wrong thing to say, but not able to help herself.

'What right have you got coming here, poking your nose in things which don't concern you? You've been here five minutes and want to change everything.'

'No, you have it wrong, Mr Gilbert. I just want the children's safety.'

'You want to leave well alone, Miss,' he said. 'That's my advice.'

What was going on here that two people were warning her to mind her own business? Why wasn't a child's safety and well-being of paramount importance? June sighed. Why was nothing straightforward? All she wanted to do was help. That's what she was here for, wasn't it?

Suddenly remembering Matron, she simply nodded at Gilbert and rushed down the stairs.

'Where have you been?' Matron demanded as June entered the office. 'I said for you to come straightaway . . . wasting my time.' She removed her spectacles and glared at June.

'I'm sorry, Matron. I needed something from my room.'

'Well, we'd better get on with it.' Matron pursed her lips as she handed June a sheet of paper. 'Perhaps you'll read that and ask me any questions.'

June quickly scanned the paper. Everything was timed from the moment she rose from her bed. She was to help the children get washed and dressed, take them downstairs for breakfast, and make sure they cleaned their teeth. From that point the teachers took over until dinnertime at one o'clock, where she would help the teachers to supervise them. While the children were in class she was to make the beds of the very young children, help Hilda clean the dormitories, sort out their dirty washing for the laundry room and help there when needed, mend their clothes, darn their socks, and help Hilda with the ironing. Then help the teachers to supervise the children's supper at six o'clock. She would have an hour off every afternoon.

With that list of chores for forty children she wondered how she'd fit in that hour for herself.

'Any questions?'

'Yes, Matron. I wasn't told I'd have to help in the laundry or do the ironing. I thought that was Rose and Mabel's job.'

'Several of the orphans frequently wet the bed. It's too much for the two girls without help.'

'Couldn't Hilda help out?' June's heart was beating nervously, hoping she wasn't speaking out of turn.

Matron frowned. 'She's kept busy all the time. As I've told you before, we're short-staffed as it is. There's a war on, you know.'

'Yes, I do know.' June nearly added, 'and my sister's husband was killed in it,' but managed to stop herself. 'I'm not afraid of hard work, but—'

'But nothing.' Matron's eyes flashed. 'These orphans are obviously more of a challenge than your sister's three boys. So if you don't feel you're up to the job, perhaps you should be looking elsewhere.'

'No, of course I'll do my very best.' June folded the sheet of paper and put it in her overall pocket.

'Then that'll be all, Miss Lavender.'

'I wondered where you'd got to,' Iris said under her breath as June slipped into the common room.

'I was worried about Lizzie and went up to the nursery but the door was locked so I couldn't get in. Then Gilbert sneaked up behind me, making me jump, and asked what I was doing. He was quite rude.'

Iris's face was serious. 'Don't take any notice of him. And no, I don't approve at all of her being left alone, and neither does Kathleen. But you can't tell Matron, and I'm afraid Hilda hasn't got much between the ears.'

'I've just had a bad run-in with Matron.'

'Haven't we all.' Iris grinned. 'What happened?'

June told her briefly what had taken place, and showed her the long list of duties.

'She's having a laugh,' Iris said. 'You're a trained nursery nurse. You shouldn't have anything to do with the laundry. You're Matron's assistant.'

'But I have no idea what Matron does.'

'As little as she can get away with,' Iris said. 'She disappears several times a day. We've all seen her sneak off to her cottage. Probably has a quick one. You can always smell it.' She wrinkled her nose.

'Do you mean a cigarette?'

'That, too, I expect,' Iris said. 'But mainly a drink, and I don't mean a bottle of lemonade either.'

June's heart plummeted. Knowing how her mother had taken to drink after Clara died, June knew Matron was not going to be easy. But she wasn't here to make such observations. Her duties lay with the children.

'You said you'd tell me what happened to Lizzie.'

Iris looked from side to side out of the corner of her eyes. 'Let's go to my room and I'll tell you what I know.'

Although Iris's room was bigger than June's it was so untidy it only looked half the size. Her nurse's uniform was half dangling over a chair, the cap fallen to the floor, and to June's embarrassment there was a brassière and a pair of knickers underneath. And a distinct smell of tobacco.

Iris laughed. 'You're obviously the neat type, Junie,' she said. 'I can't keep anything in order in my own room but I'm completely the opposite when I'm working. Fussy as a housewife with her front doorstep, that's me. And I never

59

want to be one of those – housewives, I mean.' She laughed again. 'Here. Sit on the end of the bed. It's more comfortable than the chair.' She hauled a pile of papers and a pair of slippers off the only chair and dropped into it.

'Don't you want to get married one day?' June ventured a little tentatively. She wasn't used to asking personal questions of people she hardly knew, but Iris was different.

'What? Tied down to some man who expects you to wait on him hand and foot. Then a load of snivelling kids to bring up single-handed because he's gone all day.' She glanced at June's disbelieving face. 'I'm put off having my own when I see my friends' brats. No, thanks. Definitely not for me.'

'But you're here working with children.'

'True. But these kids are different. They're a challenge. They don't have a normal home. This is all they know, poor little blighters. I don't mind *them*.'

'So tell me about Lizzie,' June said, relieved that Iris was just as nice as she'd first thought.

'It happened a couple of months ago. Lizzie was at her grandmother's house for a few days and while she was away her house was hit in a bombing raid and caught fire. It was terrible.' Iris's voice began to quiver. 'The fire engine got there too late. They all died. Her brother, who was only seven, and both parents.'

A shiver ran down June's back making her gasp. She could feel tears pricking at the back of her eyes, imagining Lizzie, not even four, trying to understand where her mummy and daddy and brother had gone.

'Since she came here the poor little kid hasn't spoken a word.' Iris searched in her bag for her packet of cigarettes, took one out and offered it to June, who shook her head. Iris put it between her own lips and flipped a silver lighter until it flared, then inhaled deeply before she let it out in a stream.

June felt the smoke catch the back of her throat and she tried not to cough.

'What about the grandmother?' she asked.

'She used to come and see her once a week,' Iris said. 'But she's getting old. Said she couldn't bring up the child on her own. It was too much responsibility. And it was her son who died in the fire, and her grandson. She's beside herself with grief. It was just too much for her. You can't blame her.'

'And Lizzie doesn't even talk to her grandmother?'

'Not a word. She stares at her as though she doesn't even recognise her. It breaks Mrs Dixon's heart. She hasn't been to see her lately. I don't think she can bear it, poor thing.'

'Can we go and see Lizzie?'

'I don't see why not. C'mon, let's go now while the kids are having their nap.'

The two girls ran up the flights of stairs and Iris took out a bunch of keys from her pocket, unlocked the door and pushed it open. Apprehensive of what she might see, June noticed Lizzie curled up in a corner like a frightened animal, clutching a ball of wool.

'Hello, Lizzie, it's Nurse Iris come to see you. I've brought Miss Lavender.' Iris caught June's arm and gently propelled her forward.

Lizzie curled up even smaller if that was possible, her eyes staring, her expression blank. She had three fingers in her mouth.

'Take those fingers out, lovey, and say hello to Miss Lavender.'

'Hello, Lizzie.' June stepped a few inches closer. Lizzie tightened up, letting the wool fall on to the floor, her hands covering her eyes. 'Lizzie, do you remember I came into the

61

kitchen yesterday and said hello to you? Can you take your hands away so I can see your pretty face?'

The little girl moved her hands a fraction so June could just see part of her eyes.

'Maybe tomorrow you'll let me see you properly,' June said.

'Here – what's going on?'

June turned at the harsh voice from the door. A girl of about 16, built like an ox, stormed in. Lizzie began to cry.

'Hilda, this is Matron's assistant, Miss Lavender,' Iris explained. 'I'm introducing her to Lizzie.'

'You can see you've frightened her,' Hilda squealed. 'If you don't leave this minute I'll report you to Matron – both of you.'

Lizzie cried even louder.

'You need to watch yourself, Hilda,' Iris said, irritation with the girl colouring the words. 'I may be putting in my own report – and it won't be to Matron, either.'

'She's not the right person to be in charge of Lizzie,' June said, when they were downstairs again. 'Lizzie needs someone gentle and understanding and encouraging. I don't think she'll ever get that from Hilda.'

'You're right. She was only here a few weeks before Lizzie arrived so I don't know her that well, but I'm not keen, I must say.' Iris turned to look at June directly. 'What do you think, June? Do you still think we should force Lizzie to play with the others? Have her meals with them?'

'Maybe not right away, and I don't think we should force her to do anything, but little by little I think we should include her in some games, and if all goes well, let her sit with us at mealtimes.'

'I agree. She's such a dear little poppet . . . must be lonely as hell. Pretty little thing too.'

'It doesn't really matter if she's pretty or not,' June said, her eye on Matron's door. 'She should be treated kindly and lovingly. She's just lost both her parents and her brother. She hasn't anything more to lose – except her voice,' she added soberly. 'That's what's so terrible. She can't communicate with anyone.'

'Any suggestions?'

'Not yet, but I'm going to make it my mission to help her.'

Chapter Six

The next two days slipped by quickly as June tried to take everything in and work through Matron's list. Daisy and Doris came out of the sick ward but they didn't join in with the younger children's favourite game of hide-and-seek or practise with the skipping rope, and June noticed they left half their food. She wondered how long they'd been at Dr Barnardo's, and the reason why they'd come. She'd ask Matron. She'd also ask Matron if she could see a list of every child's name and date of birth, and who their parents were, if known, and how the child had come to be at Dr Barnardo's. It was important to know everything possible about each child and Matron was bound to keep a book with those sorts of details.

She decided to waylay Matron immediately after the children went to their first class of the morning.

'Matron, it would help me a lot if I knew the different backgrounds of the children and I wondered if I could have a look at the records—' She broke off when she saw Matron's frown. 'Just to acquaint myself,' she added hurriedly.

'I don't see that's necessary at all, Miss Lavender. They're confidential.'

'Yes, I understand, but surely not to the people who work with the children. It's difficult to know how to handle them when I know nothing about them. They're all individuals with different stories and I feel I'd be able to help them far more if I knew them better.'

'You will know them better when you've been here longer, I'm sure.' Matron's voice and body were stiff with annoyance that she was being challenged.

'No, they don't say much about the reasons why they're here. Not the orphans anyway. The evacuees sometimes tell me about their mums and dads. They have their own problems of homesickness, but the orphans are the ones who I believe need more attention. And sometimes the evacuees taunt the others. Only the other day I heard Arthur say to Jack, "*I've* got a mummy and daddy and you haven't. I'll go home soon and you've got to stay here forever."'

'Bates is always playing up.' Matron pursed her lips. 'He's a troublemaker.'

'Yes, he can be difficult.' June sighed inwardly. She didn't feel she was getting through to Matron at all. 'But I don't think he's deliberately being horrible. I'm trying to show him his remarks are hurtful, but I have to tread carefully not to make him worse. If I knew more about him—'

'Yes, yes, you've already told me,' interrupted Matron pulling the chain of her watch out and looking at the time in a pointed manner. 'Well, Miss Lavender, I've enjoyed our little chat, but I must get on. I believe you are down to darn their socks this afternoon, am I not correct?'

'Yes, but—'

June's words were lost as Matron turned on her heel and marched off, her shoes clacking on the wooden floor.

How was she going to find out about the children? A few of them had told her snatches, all of them sad stories, but several of them refused to discuss it. The boys were more secretive than the girls, and bit back their tears. She longed to take them in her arms and comfort them the way a mother would, but she daren't. Matron had said only yesterday that displays of affection didn't sit well at any Dr Barnardo's home. Made the children weak, she'd said. They'd have to go out in the world as soon as they were old enough and needed to be independent. They'd thank her one day.

'Are you coming to the dance, Junie?' Iris asked, when the two girls were in the common room that evening after supper and the younger children were tucked up in bed. June had read them a story and was pleased to see they were all listening to her intently. When she asked who usually read them one, the answer took her by surprise.

'No one, Miss.'

'No one *ever* reads to you?'

'No, Miss.'

'Did you enjoy the story?'

'Oh, yes. We'd like a story every night. Can we?'

'Can we?' Two children jumped up and down on their beds.

The others followed, all calling out, 'Can we, can we?'

'You're not too old?'

'No,' they all chorused.

'Well, all right, so long as you behave,' June said, smiling. The children had settled down instantly. 'And if I'm not ill or too busy, I'll read you a story every night.'

'Will you really, Miss?' Peter's eyes had shone with delight. 'That'd be grand.'

Now Iris broke into her thoughts with talk of the dance.

'I'm working,' June told her, annoyed with herself for wondering not for the first time if Flight Lieutenant Andrews would be there, and trying to pretend her heart didn't give a tiny leap each time. 'And I don't want to ask Matron any favours when I've only been here such a short time.' June leaned towards the nurse. 'Iris, can I ask you something?'

'Sure.'

'How long have you been at Dr Barnardo's?'

'Oh, dear, I thought you were going to ask me a really tricky question.' Iris leaned back in her chair and laughed. 'Let's see. It must be coming up two years.'

'Do you like it here?'

'It's as good as anywhere,' Iris said. 'Better if we had a nicer matron – a proper one who actually works. The Fierce One's a harridan and lazy with it. That's why she's got you here. She can push all the jobs she doesn't like on to you. She's been here forever and thinks she owns the place. And she's got no kids of her own – not that I have' – Iris threw June a grin – 'but she doesn't have the first clue that the kids need affection and individual attention, and it's just as important as their food and a roof.' She pulled a packet of cigarettes from her handbag and plucked one out. 'You're changing the subject, Junie, and I'm not taking no for an answer. *I'm* going to have some fun. And you're coming with me.'

'Message from Matron,' Kathleen said, flopping down in the chair next to June. 'She wants to see you in her office – NOW!' she barked in Matron's strident voice. Barbara, who was crocheting a bedspread, chortled.

June's heart dropped. Iris had warned her that Matron didn't usually call you into her office unless it was something serious. Her usual habit was to waylay you in front of as many people as possible to criticise you – her way of feeling superior, she supposed. But if she wanted to give you a real dressing-down, that's when she sent for you.

June went straight to Matron's office and knocked.

'Enter.'

June turned the handle and opened the door to Matron's

office. The room was so full of smoke she could hardly make out the figure sitting behind the desk. Matron had an accounts book open and was reading the figures, but June had the distinct feeling the woman didn't understand them from the way she was flicking the pages back and forth. June cleared her throat in a pointed way. Matron looked up.

'Oh, there you are, Miss Lavender. You can be seated.'

June sat with her hands quietly folded in her lap, determined not to be intimidated by the woman. She drew in a deep breath, wondering what was coming.

'Hilda Jackson has put in a complaint about you which I take very seriously indeed.'

Lizzie.

'You interfered with one of her special charges, Lizzie Rae Dixon.'

June opened her mouth.

'No, Miss Lavender. I would prefer not to hear any excuses. Hilda has explained exactly what happened. The child needs special attention and Hilda has been assigned to give it to her. She did not take kindly to your interference and I will not tolerate such behaviour. You are *not* to go up to the nursery again, do you hear me?'

'Matron, I didn't interfere, as you call it. I just—'

'Silence!' Matron slapped her hand hard on her desk. 'I will also not tolerate such rudeness. I shall be keeping a close eye on you, so watch your step in future, Miss.' She snapped the accounts book closed. 'You are dismissed.'

June bit her lip in fury to stop herself making a retort. How dare Matron speak to her as though she were a naughty child. If she'd only let her tell *her* side of the story. How Hilda did the complete opposite of giving the little girl attention and love which the child was crying out for. Leaving her completely on her own while she went down to the dining room and ate her own dinner, and then bringing a plate back for Lizzie. The child could get up to anything in those twenty minutes. No, Hilda was *not* the right person to be put in charge of her. But how on earth was she ever going to convince Matron? But whatever Matron threatened, June was determined she was going to try to talk to Lizzie again. To break through that wall of silence.

The only place Lizzie would go outside the nursery was into the kitchen with Cook. That was the best place to talk to her, June thought, because at least Bertie had shown the child kindness. But she couldn't risk Matron's temper if she went to see Lizzie in work time. No, she'd leave it until her next day off. Then she could do what she liked. Go into the kitchen and have a cup of tea with Bertie if the cook wasn't too busy and maybe Lizzie would be there. Even so, it wouldn't be easy. The child was suspicious of everyone, it seemed, with the possible exception of Cook.

June fell into bed, exhausted by the children. It was as though they sapped all feeling, all strength, until her head spun. But at least she now knew their names. The worst of it was she already had favourites. She'd been determined not to. It wasn't fair on the others. But who could resist little Betsy with her skin the colour of treacle and her dark-brown eyes which she used in a comic fashion when she wanted to make you laugh? June couldn't help smiling at the vision. And Harvey with his mocking grin and legs that showed recent scars, which could only have come from someone beating him. He bragged he could play any tune you asked for on the mouth organ, and so far he'd never wavered. Then there was quiet little Janet, a shy plump child with an extraordinary vocabulary for an eight-year-old. She'd sit for hours making tiny books and writing and drawing in them.

The children took her mind off painful memories. But June always came back to Lizzie.

Once or twice June had been tempted to remind Iris about the dance, but decided her friend would immediately tease her that she was looking for a man. She momentarily closed her eyes. A certain face whose image refused to go away. A strong face with the bluest eyes that crinkled when he laughed. The cleft in his chin like Cary Grant's. The shiny hair, the colour of a tawny lion. You see, it's happening right this minute, she berated herself, trying to push his image away. She was being ridiculous. Their encounters would have meant nothing more to him than a brief exchange of pleasantries. Actually, that first time on the train was more of a battle. She couldn't help smiling at the memory, and Iris, who was collecting the dirty supper dishes, caught the smile and grinned back.

'Penny for them.'

June went pink.

'Ah, I thought so,' Iris said, nodding sagely. 'It's the RAF chap. Well, the only way you're going to see him again is if we go to the dance on Saturday. The girls in the kitchen aren't going as it's an officers' do and they don't feel comfortable with them, even though they admit they look gorgeous in their uniform. But they prefer the soldiers.' She gave June a sharp look. 'What's the matter? You're very quiet all of a sudden.'

'I'm not sure *I'll* feel comfortable with a load of posh officers.'

'Posh?' Iris threw back her head and roared. 'You should hear some of them. Granted, they might talk hoity-toity but believe me, we're just as good as them any day of the week.'

'All right, you've convinced me,' June said, grinning. 'And

70

maybe one of these days I'll surprise you and take you up on that offer of a cigarette. I've never tried one but everyone else seems to enjoy it. Maybe it's time I did something different.'

She didn't know what made her say this. Smoking was something that had never appealed, but in her new job at Bingham Hall she badly wanted to fit in.

Her eyes gleaming with mischief, Iris gave June a sly nudge. 'That's my girl. We'll give it a go this evening. I'll get Gilbert to light the fire early in the common room so we'll be nice and cosy and can have a girls' natter. There shouldn't be anyone in there tonight as they've nearly all signed up for Barbara's new evening art class.'

June changed her mind a dozen times as to whether she should go with Iris to the dance or not. She really didn't have anything to wear such as a party dress, as she hadn't envisaged needing one. And even if she had, she didn't have the coupons or the money to buy something that wasn't practical – something she'd hardly ever wear.

'You're coming, and that's all there is to it,' Iris said as they sat in the common room drinking a cup of tea.

They were on their own except for Athena, who had her head in a book and didn't seem to be taking any notice of their conversation.

'What will you wear?' June posed the question to Iris, half dreading her friend would come up with something really glamorous.

'I'm going to wear my navy spotted dress with white collar and cuffs. I bought it before the war so it's not new, if that's what you're thinking.' She turned her sapphire-coloured eyes to June. 'You don't need to worry about wearing sequins for the dance. The chaps are just grateful to see any woman,

71

whether she's in uniform or just come off the land smelling of manure with corn sticking out of her hair and a bag of turnips in her arms.'

June couldn't help laughing. 'Gosh, they must be desperate.'

'I think some of them are.' Iris's expression was suddenly serious. 'These boys really see life – and it's often extremely unpleasant with your friends getting injured and blown up at any time. So a dance means more to them than we'll ever know. They always seem optimistic that they just might meet the girl of their dreams. Even if it's only someone who'll write to them when they're abroad to stop them going mad. Can you imagine their lives – flying around trying to shoot down Germans and desperately trying not to get killed them- selves?'

'I can't.' June felt sick at the idea. Murray's face flitted across her mind. She'd been curt with him when he hadn't deserved it and it made her feel thoroughly mean. He'd only been trying to be nice and she'd cut him off – more than once. Was it because she liked him and didn't want to let herself become interested in anyone who might be killed at any moment? A shudder ran across her shoulders.

'. . . and I don't suppose your Murray is any different.'

June gave a start as she heard Iris say his name.

'Junie, have you heard a word I've been saying?'

'I'm sorry, Iris. I was miles away.'

'Thinking of Murray Andrews, were we?' Iris's eyes twinkled mischievously. 'I daresay he'll be at the dance.'

June's heart skipped the next beat.

''Course I wasn't,' she answered crossly. 'I was thinking of what you said about all of them. It must be awful.'

'Well, they'll soon have a load of Yanks to see to,' Iris said. 'It will give them something to grumble about. I've heard

72

their uniforms are much more attractive than our boys', and they've got more money too. *And* they're very generous with their gifts, so I'm told – nylons and chocolate and all sorts of luxuries we can't get.'

Athena looked up from her book. 'Can't you two talk about something else besides men?' she said. 'It's getting on my nerves.'

'Can't think of anything more fun,' Iris retorted. 'You're always so quiet, Athena. Have you got a boyfriend?'

'None of your business if I have or not.' Athena snapped her book shut. 'I'll leave you two alone. You've obviously got private stuff to talk about.' She rose up.

'Don't know what's got into her.' Iris frowned at the disappearing figure.

'How long has she been here?'

'Not that long. There's a rumour her fiancé jilted her at the altar and that's why she's so touchy.'

'Oh, how dreadful,' June said, full of concern for the young woman. 'But if he can do that, she's well rid of him, I should think.'

'Yes, but there's no need for her to be so bitter and twisted. There's plenty of women who've had worse – their men killed or injured in this bloody war. You just have to get on with it.' Iris wrapped one of her dark curls around her finger and let it spring back.

'We could ask her if she'd like to come with us,' June ventured.

'I've asked her two or three times. She always declines.'

'Maybe I'll have a go. If she's unhappy it might do her the world of good.' June looked across at Iris. 'I know how I would've felt if it hadn't been for you and Bertie. Perhaps she just needs a friend to talk to.'

73

Chapter Seven

June glanced out of her bedroom window as she cleaned her teeth after the usual breakfast rush. It had snowed through the night and icicles had formed on the window panes, making the room feel even colder than usual. She shivered as she put her toothbrush in the glass over the washbasin, her breath appearing in short puffs, clouding the mottled mirror that she'd found in an empty room and installed in her own. At the same moment she heard screams coming from the floor above. She dashed up the flight of stairs and, without knocking on the nursery door, rushed straight in. Hilda was shouting and screaming with rage and gripping one hand with the other.

'Oh, goodness, what—?'

'That little tyke bit me.'

'Let me see.'

Hilda thrust out her arm and June looked closely. There was a bite mark, no doubt about that, but it was minute and had only brought up red marks – there was no blood. Not exactly warranting such a fuss, June thought. But this was her opportunity.

Her eyes flew to Lizzie who was cowering in the corner. She was pulling on her thumb, her eyes wild with fear.

'Look at her – she's not even sorry.'

74

Keep calm, June said to herself. Don't rise to her. She walked over to where Lizzie was curled up.

'Lizzie,' she said quietly so as not to alarm her even more, and sat on the floor beside her. She touched Lizzie's arm but the child pulled away immediately. 'Please tell me what happened. I know you didn't mean it.'

'As if she'll speak,' Hilda broke in. '*I'll* tell you what happened. She meant it all right. All I did was tell her off because she crayoned over the walls. Look!' Hilda pointed to the bottom of the wall by a cupboard door. Lizzie had drawn a childish picture of a house with four figures, two grown-ups and a boy and a girl, all holding hands, and then she'd put a great big black cross through it.

Tears filled June's eyes as she realised immediately what the child was trying to say – that she once had a family – a mother and father and brother – and they all lived together in a house. The black cross had wiped them all away, which must have been how it seemed to Lizzie. Now she had no one. June's heart went out to the little orphan. It was hard to imagine how desperate Lizzie must be feeling, especially with all her words trapped inside her.

'I snatched the crayons away from her and that's when she bit me,' Hilda said, half turning away and giving the slight mark on her arm a little squeeze.

I'll pretend I didn't see that, June thought in disgust. 'That bite needs attention,' she said, awkwardly rising to her feet. 'Why don't you go and see the nurse and I'll wait here with her until you come back?'

'I'm not supposed to leave her,' Hilda said sullenly.

'You'll only be gone the same time as you leave her every day at dinner.' June deliberately made her voice reasonable so Hilda would have no reason not to leave the nursery. 'Just go and get it seen to.'

Hilda slammed out of the door and June breathed a sigh of relief. She'd need more than twenty minutes to tackle this intolerable situation but there *was* something she could do immediately.

'Lizzie.' June bent down again. 'Would you like to come for a walk with me in the garden and make a snowman?'

To her joy, Lizzie nodded.

'Have you got a coat?'

Lizzie shook her head. She must have, June thought. Every child had a coat.

'A warm jacket?'

Lizzie shook her head again and screwed up her face. Worrying that she couldn't take the little girl outside in the snow with no coat, June went over to one of the cupboards. She swished the hangers and pulled out a grey wool jacket. Luckily there was a pair of mittens pushed in the pockets, held together by a string.

'Try this, Lizzie. And you can borrow my scarf. I'll pick it up from my room on the way downstairs. Come on. Let's hurry.' She smiled at Lizzie. 'This is going to be fun and our little secret.'

June put her hand out and pulled Lizzie up. She put her finger to her lips and Lizzie put her own little finger to her rosebud mouth. This was progress indeed, June thought, smiling at the child. They sneaked out of the door and down the four flights of stairs, Lizzie clutching June's hand. It felt wonderful to feel Lizzie's hand in hers – to know the little girl trusted her enough to leave the safety of the nursery. Her ears pricked for any sound but no one was about. The children and teachers would already be in class and Bertie and the two kitchen maids would be busy making dinner. The only person June dreaded running into was Matron but her door was firmly shut as they stole by.

June heaved open the front door and the two of them were about to slip outside when a tobacco-riven voice behind her made her jump.

'Where might you be going with the dumb child?'

She turned. Blast! Gilbert. Why was he so interfering? June fought down a bubble of anger. Calling Lizzie a dumb child in that contemptuous tone of voice. She felt Lizzie cling even harder to her hand. Whatever Gilbert had to say, she would *not* be intimidated.

'*Lizzie*' – she emphasised the little girl's name – 'is cooped up in the nursery every day. We're going for a walk.'

'And who's given you permission to take her outdoors?' Gilbert might have been short, but his steely eyes under bushy brows were menacing.

Who did he think he was, questioning her decision on the child's well-being?

'I'm not sure your question requires an answer,' she heard herself replying, and, practically dragging Lizzie, she slipped out of the door.

'We'll go round the side,' June told Lizzie, 'so no one can see us. We're going to build a lovely snowman.' She looked down at Lizzie, who was gazing around her as though she'd never seen the garden before. 'Lizzie, have you ever built a snowman?'

Tears flooded Lizzie's eyes as she nodded.

Poor little soul. She'd probably built one with her brother when they'd last had snow. June scooped up a ball of snow and then another, and pressed it down firmly. Soon Lizzie began to bring her own small balls of snow to place on the body. June glanced over her shoulder at the little girl. Already she had a pink tinge to her cheeks and her eyes had lost their dull expression.

They made a head and stuck it on the top. 'I know he

doesn't look anything much at the moment, Lizzie,' June said, 'but I'll ask Cook for a carrot for his nose and get two pieces of coal from the bunker for his eyes. I'll have to think about his mouth. Then we need an old hat and scarf, and maybe some more bits of coal for his buttons down his coat.' She noticed with satisfaction that Lizzie was hanging on to her every word. 'Do you think you can help me collect all the things we need?'

Lizzie nodded.

'Maybe when the snowman has a face and is dressed you might be able to say hello to him. What do you think?'

Lizzie's little face immediately dropped.

'Don't worry, Lizzie. It doesn't matter. But I know he'd be awfully pleased if you could say something to him.'

Lizzie looked up at her and opened her mouth. In that instant June was certain Lizzie was about to speak. Then she pressed her lips even more tightly together. But somehow June felt there had been a lot of progress made in only – she looked at her watch. Oh, no. They'd been gone for nearly three-quarters of an hour. Hilda would definitely have reported her to Matron, who would be furious.

'And where do you think you've been, Miss Lavender?' Matron, her voice enunciating every word, barricaded the door as June tried to look as though it was normal for her and Lizzie to be out in the snow together.

'I thought Lizzie should get some fresh air – she's so pale. And she's helped me build a snowman. I'm so encouraged that she's joined in with something all children love making . . . and she really enjoyed doing it.' June knew she was gabbling.

Matron drew herself up and threw back her shoulders. Her head and bosom trembled with fury.

78

'You will *not* take Lizzie out of the house ever again. She hasn't even got a coat on. If she catches her death it will be your fault, my girl.'

'Honestly, Matron, we've been working and moving around. She's not a bit cold with her jacket and—'

'Silence! In you go this minute. You, child, come with me. You're off upstairs – Hilda's waiting to take you back to the nursery.'

Lizzie broke into sobs and looked up at June who could cheerfully have throttled Matron. There wasn't a shred of kindness in the woman – she couldn't even bring herself to say Lizzie's name. Matron stretched out her hand for Lizzie, who sobbed even harder and hung on to June.

'She was so happy outside,' June told the angry woman. 'At least let me take her upstairs myself.'

'Certainly not. And if I have any more nonsense like this, I shall send you packing. One more time . . .' Matron swiftly ducked and grabbed Lizzie's arm, forcing her to let go of June. The little girl screamed and Kathleen rushed into the hall.

'What's going on?' The nurse looked from Matron to June, and down at Lizzie, who was crying uncontrollably. 'Lizzie seems very upset, Matron.'

'You can blame Miss Lavender for that, Nurse.'

June opened her mouth to say something in her defence but stopped as Kathleen shook her head in warning.

'Let me help by taking her jacket and washing her hands ready for dinner,' Kathleen said.

'Where's Hilda?' Matron's angry eyes swept round the empty hall.

'She's gone to lie down. The shock, I expect, from the bite. I've dabbed some TCP on it. She'll be fine.'

Matron hesitated and June was sure she was trying to

work out what to do to save face, not necessarily what was best for the child. She was obviously reluctant to let Lizzie out of her clutches but Kathleen ignored her and calmly held out her hand.

Lizzie snatched her hand away from Matron's and took Kathleen's, but not before she'd turned round to June and given her the smallest sweetest smile.

Throughout the rest of the day June fumed. Not for the first time did she think Matron was unsuitable for such a responsible job. It was clear Lizzie needed careful handling before she would start speaking again. If only Matron would have let her explain how happy Lizzie had been helping to make the snowman, and how disappointed she'd be if she wasn't allowed to go out tomorrow and finish him. June drew her lips tightly together. At least Kathleen had rescued poor Lizzie. And she had seen Lizzie smile for the first time in the week June had been at the home. That was surely a good omen.

Kathleen and Iris were already in the common room when June went in that evening after supper. She'd had no time to tell them what had happened as Matron had kept her busy all day long cleaning the narrow windows in the children's dormitories, mopping the floors, sweeping and dusting. Not that she minded doing these jobs but there were two competent cleaners who came every day from the village, and she was, after all, supposed to be Matron's assistant. She had a feeling Matron was deliberately not letting her near the children as a kind of punishment.

June shivered as the cold air greeted her even though there was a fire burning. Mr Gilbert never lit it until five o'clock so the room hadn't had a chance to warm up properly by the time the staff had finished supper and wanted to relax a little after a day's work. But the two young women's smiles of welcome more than made up for the chilly atmosphere.

'You were brave to take Lizzie out,' Kathleen said, when June had settled into one of the sagging armchairs and was sipping her cup of tea.

'It was my chance of getting some fresh air into her lungs. She's so pale. They're all treating her like an invalid and I believe she'd do so much better if she could be with the others – hear them laughing and talking. Children can accept something unusual like Lizzie not talking if they're left to it, but until they let her mix with them, Lizzie will take far longer to recover, I'm sure of it.'

'Did you see the bite mark?' Kathleen asked.

'Yes. It wasn't even a scratch but Hilda acted as though her hand was falling off. She's not fit to be put in charge of a child like Lizzie – or any child, for that matter.'

'What experience does she have with children – do we know?' Iris said.

'No telling, but from her actions I'd say none whatsoever,' Kathleen said, drawing up a stool and putting her feet up. She let out a deep sigh. 'Oh, that's better. I've been on my tootsies for ten solid hours.'

'We should ask Hilda. In an interested sort of way,' Iris said, 'not as though we're threatening her at all.'

'She'll still be suspicious.' June put her cup down on the small table beside her chair. 'She's on the lookout for a fight all the time.'

'We need to make a plan,' Iris said firmly. 'She's doing more harm than good, and June's right – at this rate Lizzie's going to take much longer before she improves.'

'If she ever does,' June cut in crossly. 'Between Hilda and Matron the poor little kid doesn't have a chance.'

'We'll think of something.' Iris drew her brows together. She looked at her watch. 'I'd better go down to the ward ready for the night shift.'

At least these two girls feel the same as I do, June thought, as Iris vanished. And dear Bertie was sympathetic too, the way she had Lizzie in the kitchen, keeping an eye on her in the mornings. She wasn't alone in trying to think of some way that Lizzie could be brought into the daily life, along with the others. The three of them – four, counting Bertie – would come up with something. Lizzie would begin to speak again, June was certain. That little secret smile they'd shared gave her hope.

Chapter Eight

'We should ask Kathleen if she's coming to the dance with us tonight,' Iris said when the children were filing out of the dining room after breakfast. 'She usually does, even though she's got a boyfriend.'

June raised her eyebrows in surprise. She didn't like to comment that if *she* had a boyfriend she didn't think she'd be interested in going to any dance.

'You look rather disapproving.' Iris got hold of a young lad who was trying to push in front of her. 'Just watch it, young Baker.' She turned to June. 'Kathleen says she wants to have a bit of fun as you never know when your last day might come. She says she's sure Dick is enjoying himself when he gets some time off.'

'I didn't mean to look disapproving,' June said quickly. 'I'm sure she doesn't mean any harm but with such a shortage of girls she might have her head turned . . . especially if all your stories about the Americans and the money they spend on their girlfriends are true.'

Iris laughed. 'Dick would soon put a stop to anything like that, though he's not near enough to keep a close eye. He's somewhere the other end of England and she hasn't seen him for six months or more. Anyway, I'll ask her, if it's all right with you.'

'Of course it is. I like her company.'

'And you're definitely coming? You're not going to back out at the last minute?'

'No, I'll come. Just don't expect me to appear in anything special. I've only got a black skirt and a green blouse – not at all suitable for a dance. But it will have to do.'

'We may have to make you a dress from the curtains in the common room.' Iris giggled. 'Like Scarlett O'Hara in *Gone With The Wind*.'

June grinned. 'That was wonderful, wasn't it? She certainly had Rhett Butler fooled – for a while anyway.'

Even though June worried that her outfit wouldn't be good enough and she'd be embarrassed, she couldn't help feeling a little buzz of excitement. She hadn't been out for the evening since her arrival and it was less than a fortnight until Christmas. In fact, this was the RAF's Christmas 'do'. It would be nice to be out of the home, magnificent as it was, for a change. She wouldn't allow herself to think beyond that.

Kathleen didn't go with them after all. She'd finally had a letter from her boyfriend and told June and Iris she was going to stay in her room and reread his words to her heart's content.

'I've got to stay faithful for once in my life,' she said, a wicked gleam in her eyes.

'Next time, maybe,' Iris said. 'Right, Junie, are you nearly ready?'

June had spent a miserable hour trying to make herself look more feminine than she'd felt lately. She'd powdered her nose, and dabbed on some lipstick. Even though she'd eked it out, the stick was going down at an alarming rate. But tonight she wanted to look her best, especially when she didn't have a nice dress to wear.

It was her hair that was giving her the most trouble. It was so thick it refused to stay in place no matter how many times she practised the Victory Roll. Athena Graham always had a perfect one. So why couldn't *she* do one? In the end she pulled up a hank of hair at each side and stuck two tortoiseshell combs in. Her only real touch of glamour, she decided, would be the pearl necklace her mother had given her before she died. It had been her grandmother's before that, and now it was June's. She bent her neck and set the string of pearls just above her collarbone, fastening it at the back. It was beautiful. Nodding with not exactly satisfaction, but at least approval that she looked clean and tidy, she smiled at the image and the image smiled back at her. There was no more she could do. If they didn't think she looked right it was just too bad.

'It's still snowing,' Iris said, looking her up and down as was her way. 'You need your boots. You can take your shoes in a bag and change them once you get there. That's what I'm going to do.'

June sent her friend a grateful smile. She'd worried that she would look odd changing her shoes at the RAF station. She grabbed her coat and hat and they shot out of the door. The walk to the bus stop seemed shorter now she was used to it and soon they were in a warm bus on their way to Speke RAF station

As the bus jolted along and Iris chattered away, June began to look forward to the evening. She had a strong feeling Murray Andrews would be there and her cheeks warmed like the pearls nestling in the curve of her neck.

The dance was obviously a popular event with the officers, June thought, judging by the amount of noise coming from that direction as she and Iris sat on chairs by the open door, eased off their boots and put them neatly beneath their coats, now hanging on a rail. Her heart started to beat a little faster and she felt her new-found confidence ebbing away as she looked down at her attire, which could never pass for evening wear: her best flower-printed green blouse with short puff sleeves and a plain black skirt that had to go with everything. Well – nothing she could do about it now.

Drawing in a deep breath she put her arm through Iris's and the two of them stepped into the hall. Officers, all in uniform, dominated the dance hall, which was decorated with paper chains and balloons ready for Christmas. Clouds of smoke wafted towards the ceiling and the room was filled with chatter and Glenn Miller's music from a small group of musicians at the far end. Uniformed officers were throwing their heads back as they laughed with their friends, for all the world as though they didn't have a care. As Iris had promised, there were many more of them than there were women. Several of the latter were dressed to the nines, as her mother would have said.

'You mustn't ever be caught wearing bright-red lipstick, dear,' she'd told June once. 'Men don't like it and you don't want to be accused of being fast.'

June's stomach turned. Cold perspiration gathered on her forehead. She wasn't dressed properly for a dance at all. She turned away, ready to bolt out of the door and run for the next bus, when she felt Iris's hand give hers a reassuring squeeze.

'Not everyone's dressed to kill,' Iris whispered. 'Look, there are some girls over there in uniform.' She gave a casual wave then glanced at June. 'With your face and figure you'll be a match for any of 'em.'

As though to confirm Iris's remark an exceptionally tall

man with a GI crewcut strode up. You could only describe him as handsome, June thought, and he knew it.

'Hi, girls. Have y'all just arrived?' He looked and sounded like one of those American film stars Aunt Ada was so fond of. 'Name's Charles Lockstone. Well, I'm usually called Chas – or worse, Chuck – straight from Savannah, Georgia.' He grinned at both women but his eyes lingered on June. They were a light blue, flashing with merriment. 'So tell me your names, beautiful ladies.'

June gave a small smile just for good manners. She wasn't used to such a blatant introduction.

'I'm Iris, and this is my good friend June,' Iris said before June could answer for herself.

'And where have y'all sprung from?'

'We haven't exactly sprung from anywhere,' Iris answered. 'We've come from Bingham Hall – the grand house just outside Bingham village.'

'Have y'all been kept prisoners there?' Chas broke into a grin again. 'And did you tie a knotted sheet and climb out of your prison window and escape to give us poor guys a bit of feminine company?' He had an attractive drawl.

'Hardly,' Iris said. 'It's a Dr Barnardo's home.'

Chas looked puzzled.

'Have you never heard of them?' Iris asked, and Chas shook his head.

'It's a home for orphans,' Iris explained. 'And we work jolly hard there. I'm a nurse and June is Matron's assistant, even though she's trained to be a nursery nurse.'

June envied the easy way Iris had of talking to a strange man, and an American at that. He sounded just like Rhett Butler.

'Say, can I buy you girls a drink?'

'Thank you – that would be lovely,' Iris said quickly,

throwing Chas a wide smile. 'I'll have a gin and tonic, please.'

June rather wished Iris hadn't accepted a drink from the first person who'd set eyes on her. Deep down she hoped to see Murray Andrews. Thank him properly for getting her book at a reduction. Her eyes scanned the room but it was already so crowded it would be difficult to pick out anyone, especially someone she'd only briefly met.

She felt the American's eyes on her, waiting to be told what she would like.

'Nothing for me for the moment, thank you,' she said.

'You sure about that, ma'am?' His smile was wide and didn't leave her face.

'Quite sure, thank you.'

'I'll get ours then, Iris,' he said, and disappeared.

'You were awfully quiet, Junie, but it's quite obvious you've made a hit with him.'

'I don't want to make a hit with anyone,' June said sincerely. 'It's nice just to be here and maybe have a dance or two. But that's all. I want to concentrate on the children, not some man who thinks I'm only after a good time.' She managed to stop her eyes sweeping the room.

'You have to forgive them – the Americans, I mean. They're all like that. Much more open and friendly than the English – so I've been told, anyway.' Iris laughed. 'I wouldn't say no to a lovely American officer.'

'You can have him with my complete approval,' June said, smiling.

'I would if I could. But you can see he's only got eyes for you.'

'You're wrong, but even if it's true, I'm not interested. All I want is to try out my dance steps which Aunt Ada taught me.'

The music changed at that moment to a quicker rhythm

which June had never heard before. Chas came towards them, a glass in each hand. As he wove his way through the crowd, June realised he was head and shoulders taller than almost anyone else.

'I've found the only table,' he said, gesturing with a jerk of his shoulder. 'Had to give the barman a quid, I think you call it, to reserve it for us. Now which one of you lovely ladies wants me to teach her the jitterbug?'

June's annoyance grew. Thanks to Iris she wasn't going to be able to get out of this. But then she heard a voice behind her.

'Good evening, Miss Lavender.'

June turned and found herself looking up into a pair of sky-blue twinkling eyes. Flight Lieutenant Andrews in full uniform. She'd only ever seen him in his greatcoat. Her breath caught. He wasn't nearly so handsome as Chas but there was something about the way his tawny hair fell forward over darker eyebrows, his smiling mouth, the cleft in his chin . . . She grew hot under his gaze, feeling more uncomfortable as she sensed Iris watching her with open curiosity.

'Flight Lieutenant Andrews – how nice to see you again.' June fought to keep her voice steady as she held out her hand. He took it in both of his. The warmth of his skin . . . she felt a tremor . . . was it from his hand, or her own?

'Say, you already know Andrews?' Chas glanced at Murray and lingered on June.

'Oh, yes,' Murray put in quickly before June could think what to say. 'We've travelled together on the same train from London, we've chatted in a bookshop in Liverpool about Monica Dickens, we *nearly* had a cup of tea together' – he turned to June and winked – 'but unfortunately she had to rush away.'

'I'd hardly call it travelling together when I just asked to get by in the corridor,' June protested, which made Murray's smile even wider.

'Seeing as Junie's not going to introduce us, I'm Iris.' Iris stuck her hand out and Murray immediately shook hands with her.

'What will you have to drink?' Chas addressed Murray.

'Let me get them,' Murray said. He turned to June and Iris. 'What would you like?'

'I've got mine,' Iris said, holding up her glass.

'Miss Lavender?' The blue eyes turned to her.

'Just a lemonade for me, please,' June said quickly, unaccountably pleased that it would be Murray buying her a drink and not Chas.

'No dice, Andrews. I asked y'all first. Sit down at the table or I've wasted a quid. I'll get you a beer and a lemonade for June.'

'I'll come with you,' Iris said, giving June a huge wink which she pretended to ignore.

'Have you just arrived?' Murray asked when Chas and Iris disappeared.

June nodded. 'I wondered if you might be here.'

Oh, why did she say that? Her mother would have told her off for sounding too forward. She only hoped the dim light disguised her tingling cheeks.

'Did you? Did you really?' Murray's expression was eager.

'Yes. I wanted to apologise.'

'Whatever for?'

'For rushing away, as you just told them.'

'Well, you did, didn't you?'

'I was supposed to meet Iris at half-past eleven for coffee and was already late. That was all.'

'I thought you might have had an appointment with a boyfriend.'

90

'Flight Lieutenant Andrews, I haven't got time for that sort of thing. I'm working six days a week and long hours.'

'Murray, *please*.' Murray gave a theatrical sigh. 'So that's me out, is it?'

'Afraid so.' The retort was out before she could stop it. She wanted to retract it. Tell him she hadn't meant to sound so abrupt. She'd been like it in the bookshop as well and it wasn't in her nature to be rude. A stream of smoke wafted towards them and she felt it thick in her throat. She swallowed, trying to stop herself coughing.

The conversation was going nowhere, she thought, but she hadn't reckoned with Murray.

'Miss Lavender – June, if I may – I'm really happy you came tonight. Tell me – how are you getting on with *One Pair of Hands*? You know I really want to borrow it after you.'

'I'm surprised you remember it.'

'I remember our whole conversation,' Murray said. 'Would it be rude not to wait for the others and have this dance?'

Before she could answer, Murray had guided her on to the dance floor. The music had changed from a slow waltz to a quickstep.

He held her firmly. She was close enough to detect the faint musky cologne which seemed part of the masculine smell of his skin. His hand firmly holding hers was warm and strong and she allowed herself to be swept away by the music, her steps matching his as they flew across the dance floor. Suddenly he whirled her round and round until she clung on dizzily. He gripped her tighter. It was only when the music stopped that she saw his grinning face. He'd done it on purpose, just as he had in the corridor of the train when he'd stood in her way. She tried to ignore the spurt of irritation at his overfamiliarity.

'We're taking a fifteen-minute break,' one of the musicians announced. 'Don't go anywhere, folks. We've got more of the same, and more of even better.'

'Wondered where y'all had got to,' Chas said, standing up when June and Murray walked back to the table.

'Thought we might as well have a dance while we were waiting.' Murray pulled June's chair out.

'Don't blame you.' Chas downed nearly half a glass in what looked like one gulp. He screwed up his face. 'How do you guys drink warm beer? We always have it ice cold. Can't stand it if it's not chilled right.'

'We're the exact opposite.' Murray took a deep swallow. 'Thanks, Lockstone. Thirsty work.' He put his glass down, leaving a wet ring on the table, and winked at June. 'It's been a long time, Ginger. Glad you remembered everything I taught you.'

June couldn't help laughing as her irritation dropped away and she fell in with his mood. 'And don't forget, Fred, I wear high heels and have to do everything backwards, but you're the best partner I've ever had. No one can touch you on the dance floor . . . when you're really concentrating, that is.' She kept a straight face as she played the part of Ginger Rogers to his Fred Astaire.

Murray chuckled. 'Hard to concentrate with such a beautiful girl in my arms, Ginge.'

'Well, thank you, Fred. That's nice to hear.'

He was bantering. Of course he was. But he said I was beautiful. Her heart gave a tiny flip.

'Seriously,' Murray said, his eyes not leaving her face, 'I do like dancing since I had lessons. Did the whole gamut. Just try me. Anything.'

Their eyes held.

June took in a shaky breath and with an almost apologetic

smile turned to Iris, not wanting to leave her out, but Iris was taking no notice of them; she sat there mute, her eyes raking the dance floor, an unreadable expression on her face. Chas was frowning but he smiled when June glanced at him.

'May I have this one, June?' He stood up, his hand outstretched.

'I think I'll stay here a few minutes and catch my breath,' June said. Even in the dim light Iris's skin was flushed and her eyes unnaturally bright. A complete contrast to fifteen minutes ago.

'Iris, are you all right?'

Iris twizzled the stick in her glass and didn't raise her eyes. 'I'm going to the Ladies, June. Do you want to come?'

Her voice was so pleading June immediately jumped from her seat.

Two girls were at the basins rinsing their hands, and the familiar smell of Ivory soap wafted in the small space; one very blonde girl hogged the mirror re-applying her lipstick. Iris shook her head at June.

It seemed that every time the place cleared, more women and girls came in, chattering and laughing.

'We can't have any conversation in here,' Iris grumbled, 'and if we go outside to have a cigarette, which I could well do with, the men will wonder what on earth's happened to us.'

'You seem upset about something.'

'C'mon, Junie, let's go. I'll talk to you later.'

But the pleasure June had felt on seeing Murray Andrews again had dissipated with her concern for Iris, and she found herself pushing through the crowd as strongly as the tall dark-haired figure of her friend in front, wondering what could have made her change so abruptly.

Both men stood up as soon as they saw the girls approach their table.

'It's not the usual way,' Iris said, looking at Chas, 'me asking you, but could we have this dance?'

Chas hesitated no more than a second before he rose gracefully from the table. 'Sure we can. Be glad to.' He held his hand out and stepped with her on to the dance floor.

'You seem preoccupied, June,' Murray said as she sat down.

'I'm sorry.' Through the crowd of dancers June spotted Iris clinging to Chas, though even from a distance June could see her eyes darting this way and that over his shoulder. Her friend didn't seem to be behaving normally. June dragged her gaze from the dance floor and gave Murray a wry smile. He put his hand on her bare arm for a moment and her skin shivered into goosepimples.

'What is it? Can I do anything to help?'

'No, no, really. Thank you. It's just – well, Iris seems upset about something but we haven't had a chance to talk about it.'

'Is she ill?'

'I don't think so. But she's not acting herself.'

'Maybe she's tired. It can't be easy working at the orphanage with all those children.'

'It's not,' June admitted, 'but I love it. There's only one – no, two big problems.'

'Do you want to tell me about them?'

'Not in here,' June said. 'I can hardly hear myself speak above the band.'

'When is your next day off?'

'The day after tomorrow – Monday.'

'If I can get a couple of hours off, why don't we meet? A problem shared is a problem halved, they always say.' He smiled. She noticed one of his teeth at the bottom was crooked. She rather liked it. It made him look somehow vulnerable.

'That's kind of you.'

'Maybe we could meet in Liverpool at the same bookshop and go for that cup of tea we never had.' His blue eyes twinkled. 'Say three o'clock?'

'That would be lovely.'

'Good. I know a place where they do delicious cakes that seem to have escaped any rationing.'

They only stayed another half an hour. June was a little disappointed not to have another dance with Murray but she was conscious that Iris wasn't in the mood. Chas asked if she would like a dance and she said yes, but he had an awkward two-step style and kept apologising for stepping on her toes. It might have been because there was such a difference in their height and he had to hunch over her. Whatever it was, she couldn't relax or enjoy it the way she had with Murray. Besides, she felt Murray's eyes on her every time it seemed that Chas pulled her closer. At the end of the dance Chas excused himself and the next time she saw him he was with a pretty redhead.

Iris was still quiet on the bus back but again there was so much noise they couldn't really hear one another.

'Would you like to come to my room?' June said when they finally slipped inside the door. 'At least we'll get some peace. We shouldn't disturb anyone as I'm the only one on that floor as far as I can make out.'

'I'll bring us a cup of cocoa,' Iris said.

She kept to her word and ten minutes later the two girls were sipping cocoa and munching a Rich Tea. June waited patiently for her friend to speak. Iris was still looking a little flushed but her eyes didn't glitter quite so ferociously.

'I saw Paul dancing with another girl.' Her voice was flat.

'Who's Paul?'

'My boyfriend, of course.'

'I didn't know you had a boyfriend. You never said anything about him.'

'It's too new. But I thought it would develop into something more serious. I thought he liked me. And I really liked him. Until I saw him dancing with that awful woman this evening.'

June fell silent. What should she say? 'Would I have seen him?' she said eventually.

'You might – he's about my height, and very dark and very handsome. Though I doubt he's rich.' She tried to smile but June could tell she was upset.

'When did you spot him?'

'When I went with Chas to get your friend Murray a beer. Paul waltzed by without even noticing me. He only had eyes for *her*.'

'Then don't give him any more attention. He's not worth it,' June said firmly. 'Why don't you go for Chas? He's good-looking as well, *and* he's very tall. You know how you always grumble that men seem to be shrinking.'

'You can't switch off from one to the other like that,' Iris said, draining her cup. 'Ah, that was just what was needed.' She turned her attention back to June. 'Trouble is, I did try with Chas. I wanted to make Paul jealous by dancing close to Chas. *See how I've already got a new boyfriend, Paul?* Then he saw me. Raised his eyebrows and smiled – a stupid sort of apologetic smile. So it didn't work. And anyway, Chas talked about *you* all the time.'

'*Me?*' June put her cup down, splashing some of the brown liquid on the table. She jumped up to grab a cloth.

'Yes, he's quite taken with you and very disappointed you seem to be going with a British pilot.'

'I'm not going with anyone.'

'Well, he thinks you are. And by the look on your face when you were dancing with your pilot you seemed very happy.'

'It was just a dance,' June protested. 'And yes, I like him, but I don't want to get serious with anyone. I always seem to lose anyone I really love.' Her eyes misted as she thought of Clara. And her mother – her miserable life with a bully of a husband, who was the direct cause of Clara's death. If her baby sister hadn't been scared of him, if she hadn't run, then she wouldn't have tripped and fallen down the stairs and broken her neck . . . The tears gathered in her throat and she swallowed.

'June, are you okay?' Iris was by her side. 'What's the matter, Junie?' She put her arm around her friend's shoulders.

'I was thinking about my sister.'

'I thought you were. C'mon, kid. You've got a lot of children here who need your help badly.'

'I don't seem to be doing much at the moment. Every time I want to see Lizzie, Matron or Hilda are there barring my way.'

'It'll be Christmas week after next,' Iris said. 'Last year Matron went to her sister's over Christmas which allowed the kids to be normal children for once.'

'Maybe without her I can bring Lizzie down from the nursery. Let her help decorate the tree or something.'

'Good idea. We'll make a plan. And Junie' – Iris's old grin was back – 'for once in your life, you're right. I'm going to forget that rotter. I deserve better. And who needs a man anyway?'

June decided now was not the time to tell Iris that she was going to meet Murray on Monday afternoon.

Murray closed his eyes, remembering the feel of her in his arms as they'd danced the quickstep. She'd been a wonderful partner, light on her feet, following his every movement, her small hand – the lightest touch – on his shoulder, her other hand lost in his. His head had been in a whirl and it wasn't just the way he'd spun her round and round at the end of the dance.

Then the way she'd picked up on his joke about them being Fred Astaire and Ginger Rogers. She'd known immediately who he was talking about and had responded in exactly the same vein. He liked that in a girl. A sense of fun. It was what was needed even more urgently in this bloody war. If it wasn't for the cinema and the monthly dances at the station, there'd be no let-up from trying to beat Jerry. Not that he often went to the dances. He'd become cynical every time a busload of girls arrived, many of them so heavily made up it was difficult to see who the person might be underneath it, and it would get worse now a handful of Americans had already arrived. But he'd decided to go because there was a certain girl – a girl with fair hair like ripened corn, and green eyes – who might, just might be there too. And she had. And it was heaven. Just like the song Fred Astaire sang to Ginger Rogers in one of their films as they were dancing. Murray grinned. He was getting far too soppy.

Concentrate. Get June Lavender out of your head. For now, anyway.

He fell instantly asleep.

Chapter Nine

The thought of seeing Murray the next day gave June a tiny thrill of pleasure. She liked the way they'd bantered about the Fred Astaire and Ginger Rogers films. The way they both liked books. And now she could add dancing to the list. She smiled to herself. It was certainly different dancing with him than it had been with Aunt Ada.

She turned her thoughts to the day. Sunday was always quieter in the home. The children were getting ready to file into the turret room, which had been converted into a small chapel, complete with beautiful stained-glass windows. The vicar would be there promptly at eleven o'clock to take the service, and her job was to make sure all the children were in their Sunday best; no runny noses, no hair uncombed, no shoes unpolished, ready to hear Reverend Halliday tell them they were sinners. June was never sure why even innocent children should be called sinners, but at least Reverend Halliday showed them how to behave themselves and pray so that God would forgive them.

Today there were the usual grumbles and protests.

'Bobby, stop that snivelling.' Kathleen was nearby helping to get some of the children dressed. 'You'd think I was sending you to the dungeons to hear you.'

'Don't want to go and pray. What's the use? God let me Mam and Dad die. He doesn't care.'

'Of course he does. He needed your parents to help him. They're watching over you all the time, hoping you're growing up to be a good boy.'

'I don't believe it.' Bobby fought with the sleeves of his jumper as Kathleen tried to pull it over his head. 'Alan told me it was all a pack of lies about God and everything.'

'Then Alan should be ashamed of himself.'

June at that moment was having her own battle with the shameful Alan; aged twelve, he was three years older than Bobby, and becoming too cocky for words.

'Did you tell Bobby God was all a pack of lies, Alan?' she asked as she whipped away a penknife which was partly sticking out of his pocket. 'You won't be needing that in the chapel . . . or anywhere.'

'Don't take it, Miss.' Alan's eyes were black with rage. 'It's mine. I keep it with me all the time. It's useful for all sorts of things. I don't do nothing bad with it.'

'I'm sure you don't but I'm taking it anyway. You haven't answered my question. Did you tell Bobby that God was all a pack of lies?'

'Yes, and it's true.' Alan turned on her. 'And grown-ups know it's all lies, but it's a good way to send us to church and the like, to keep up us out of their hair.'

In spite of herself, June admitted there was a lot of truth in Alan's outburst. She remembered how she and her two sisters had had to go to church twice on Sundays, Stella hating every minute.

Before she could answer him there was a squeal from behind. She swung round to see Betsy, her eyes wide with fear, pointing to something on the stone slab floor. 'Miss! Miss! It's a hugest spider.'

'It won't hurt you.' June rushed over to the child, then took a step back. Betsy was right. It was the biggest, blackest spider she'd ever seen. Shaking, she rushed to the nearest classroom and grabbed the blackboard rubber.

'Not sure what you're going to do with that, hen.' Bertie laughed, coming out of her kitchen to see what all the commotion was about. 'Keep your eye on it. I'll get the spider-catching kit.'

'A spider-catching kit?' Alan's face was agog with curiosity, the confiscated penknife seemingly forgotten.

Cook was back in a twinkling and, bending down, she deftly got the spider in her Pyrex pudding basin and quickly put a plate over the top. 'Somebody open the front door, please,' she called.

'Kill it!' Betsy shouted.

'Kill it, kill it!' More shouts from the other children, who rushed over to see if the spider was really that big.

'This is one of God's creatures,' Bertie said to the children now crowding round and watching in awe as the spider struggled up the side of the basin and fell back. 'Why would you want to kill it?'

'Because it's horrible, Cook. It'll bite,' said Megan.

'Get away with you, child, it won't bite. Aye, he's been nice and cosy in the corner but I'm putting him outdoors. But don't be surprised if he finds his way back in again. They don't like the cold.'

The children stopped shouting and began to take a real interest in the trapped spider, which was desperately trying to escape. Three or four of the older ones followed Bertie and in a couple of minutes they were all back inside.

'I've let the poor thing out near one of the kitchen sheds,' she said, laughing. 'He'll get in there through one of the wee cracks. He must have wondered what on earth was happening.'

101

The doorbell interrupted any further discussion about the spider, and one of the maids hurried to open it.

'Do come in, Reverend Halliday,' she said. 'The children are all seated ready for you.'

The children left the chapel looking slightly dazed from the long service. June told them there was pop for them, and tea and biscuits for the grown-ups, laid out in the dining room. When she followed the children in, trying to keep order, she was surprised to find Hilda pouring out the drinks.

'I hope you're satisfied,' Hilda said between gritted teeth when June went to collect her own cup of tea.

June's first thought was to ignore the girl. But Hilda was plainly waiting for a response.

'What do you mean?'

'That bitch Iris reported me.'

June took a step backwards from the vehemence in the girl's tone.

'Don't call her that, Hilda. It's a horrible word.'

'It's too good for her, if you ask me.'

June drew in a sharp breath. 'What are you talking about, anyway?'

'You know perfectly well what about – Dumb Lizzie who pretends she can't speak.'

June's stomach turned. 'Has something happened to Lizzie?'

'No, but the way Iris went on, you'd think it had.' Hilda angrily poured tea into the next cup and it sloshed into the saucer.

'Who did she report to?'

'Matron, o'course. Who told me I didn't have to look after Lizzie no longer. I'm needed to help Cook. I *hate* kitchen

102

work.' Hilda practically spat the words out. 'I *like* looking after Lizzie.'

June swallowed her delight. This was marvellous news. If Matron was finally convinced Hilda was not capable of looking after a child who needed special attention, then she might be able to talk her round to putting little Lizzie in her own care. Mixing her in with the others.

'So who's looking after Lizzie right now?'

'Who d'ya think? Matron.'

June's heart plummeted. This was almost worse than Hilda. But at least if there was one thing Matron loved it was her days off. She couldn't be in sole charge of Lizzie every single day. She'd be forced to put Lizzie in someone else's care. June was determined it would be herself.

'Hilda told me she was no longer in charge of Lizzie,' June ventured when she was sitting down in Matron's office. She'd made an appointment to see Matron but her reception had been anything but welcoming. Matron had curtly told her to take a seat. As usual she had the accounts spread out on the desk in front of her, and once again June was sure she didn't really understand what the figures meant.

'Yes, that's right. Nurse Marchant reported her to me. I didn't realise Hilda was leaving the child on her own when she went to get her dinner.'

'But you were the one who told me—' June started, but Matron put her hand up.

'So *I* will now be in charge of her well-being.'

'What about when you have a day off?'

Matron glared over the top of her glasses. 'I rarely have a day off, but when I do I'll put her under Nurse Marchant's care. She's a nurse, after all.'

'But if she's busy in the sick room—' June tried again.

'Please don't argue with me. I know what I'm doing. I believe I have *slightly* more experience than you with the orphans.' She kept her eyes glued to June's. 'That will be all, Miss Lavender.'

'May I ask where Lizzie is at the moment?'

'Look around.'

And there in a dark corner of Matron's office was Lizzie, staring in front, her three fingers in her mouth. There was no sign of recognition in Lizzie's blank eyes. It was as though she'd never been outside to build a snowman and given a little smile to June to share their secret.

'Quite safe, you see. Now would you please leave? I'm very busy today getting the books in order for the accountant.'

June left the office fuming. What a horrible woman. But at least she'd come to her senses and stopped the twenty-minute time lapse when Lizzie had no one in the nursery with her. But what kind of a life was it stuck in a chair in Matron's smoke-ridden room? June was desperate to change things – but how? Maybe Murray would come up with a suggestion tomorrow. She hugged the thought to herself. Tomorrow she would see him.

Until then she'd go and find Iris. She couldn't wait to hear exactly what her friend had said to Matron.

Chapter Ten

Iris was in her usual chair in the common room when June finished getting the children to bed. They'd been more noisy than usual with Christmas looming.

'Only ten days and four and a quarter hours till Christmas, Miss,' Gordon had reminded her. He was a tall, thin boy with a frowning forehead, giving the impression he was older than his eight years. He could add any numbers in his head before the other children had even written them down, no matter how complicated they were, and loved impressing them with his practically infallible memory, though he wasn't a good mixer. He preferred to speak to the grown-ups.

'That's right, but best not to mention it too much to the younger children as they get over-excited about Father Christmas coming down the chimney with his sack of presents.'

'Good job it's a large chimney, isn't it, Miss?'

June couldn't tell whether he was simply making a comment or being sarcastic because he no longer believed in Father Christmas. If so, she hoped he wouldn't tell the other children and upset them the way Alan had.

'You're looking all sparkly-eyed, Junie,' Iris said as June slumped down on one of the nearby sofas. 'What's up?' She squinted at her. 'Oh, I bet it's Murray. Well, when are you going to see him again?'

'It's supposed to be tomorrow afternoon at the bookshop. I thought I could slip away as it's my day off and also Matron's. I never understand why she and I don't have different days off. After all, I'm supposed to be her assistant.'

'So she can keep her eagle eyes on you, of course,' Iris said. 'She doesn't want to risk you having a day without being under her control. You might do something she wouldn't approve of.'

'I might at that. It's so frustrating when I can see what a bad effect she has on the children – and on me.' June sighed.

'I agree.' Iris lit a cigarette. 'Sorry – forgot to ask you.'

June shook her head as usual, then laughed. 'I said I'd join you one of these days, didn't I?'

'You ducked out the other evening.' Iris lit one for her. 'What an awful woman Matron is,' she continued. 'She can't possibly keep Lizzie cooped up in her stinky office all day. Poor little kid. She's never going to speak at this rate.'

June inhaled. The smoke hit the back of her throat and she coughed so hard she felt she was choking. Iris jumped up and got her a glass of water.

'Thanks, Iris.' June took several gulps, her eyes stinging and tears pouring down her cheeks. 'I don't think cigarettes and I agree with each other.' She gave Iris a rueful smile. 'I hear you spoke to Matron.'

'Yes.' Iris flicked her ash into a nearby ashtray. 'I told her Hilda wasn't fit to look after children. And especially not to have sole charge of a child who needed special attention.'

'I've said the same thing so many times.' June felt a little peeved. 'She told me flatly Hilda had the job and that was that. So why did she listen to *you*?' She didn't mean it but it came out as an accusation.

'Because I'm a nurse, I expect.' Iris laughed, patting June's hand. 'I'm supposed to know these things. And if she doesn't make any changes I'm going to report her to Head Office. It's gone on long enough.' She took another puff of her cigarette. 'Anyway, about tomorrow. I can switch my day off with Kathleen and we can go to town together. Then separate and you can meet your pilot.'

'We're only going for a cup of tea,' June said, flushing. 'And he's not *my* pilot. I wanted to ask him some questions, that's all, and he thought it might be a good idea for us to meet there. And it would give me a chance of a few hours away from the home. Much as I love it, it can be rather oppressive sometimes.'

Murray kept popping into her mind all through the following morning. She visualised those incredible blue eyes. His capable shoulders. The strong jaw. Every time she pictured him her heart did a somersault. It was ridiculous. But she couldn't help smiling.

June barely tasted her dinner. She put it down to the grumbles of some of the younger children because it was liver and bacon. The twins were pushing it around their plates, and she spotted Betsy hiding the pieces of cut-up meat under her mashed potato. June wasn't that keen either but she knew they were lucky to get such good food when so many mothers had to queue for hours and still came home with barely enough to feed a family. She hoped the other children wouldn't start making a fuss as there was no alternative, though she had to admit that most of the older children didn't moan or complain too much. It had been drummed into their heads that there was a war on, but they were fortunate at Dr Barnardo's. There was always enough good basic food.

But that didn't stop Bertie from preparing special treats for Christmas.

107

'I've been saving up rationed ingredients for the cakes and puddings since September,' Bertie told June when she brought in a pile of dirty plates from dinner. 'A wee bit here and a wee bit there. It takes some juggling, I can tell you.' She pushed the large mixing bowl across the pine table to June. 'Here, hen, give a stir and make a wish.'

Immediately, June's eyes went to the small child crouched in the corner in her usual position.

'Lizzie, come and help me stir the puddings. You can make a wish.'

Lizzie slowly took her fingers out of her mouth, each one making a small sucking noise. Her eyes brightened with interest. Slowly she uncurled and trotted over on unsteady legs.

That's because she hardly ever uses them, June thought. This is ridiculous. Something has to be done.

Bertie brought a stool over and lifted the little girl up on it. 'Make a wish, Lizzie.' She handed the child the wooden spoon.

'Poor wee bairn,' Bertie said under her breath so only June heard, then spoke normally to Lizzie. 'Why don't you ask for Father Christmas to come down the chimney and bring you a pretty dolly to take care of.'

Lizzie put the spoon in the mixture and tried to stir it but it was too stiff. Before June could come to the rescue the child burst into tears of frustration and tried to climb off the stool.

'Oh, Lizzie, please don't cry, my angel.' June put out a steadying hand as Lizzie was about to lose her footing. She longed to take the little girl in her arms, comfort her, but she didn't dare. If she frightened her at this early stage she might not ever gain her trust. 'You'll make *me* cry next. Here, lick the spoon. No one will notice. That always used to be my favourite thing to do on baking days.'

108

To her relief, Lizzie sniffed back the tears and put her little pink tongue out and flicked it over the spoon. Just like a cat. June felt a ripple of pleasure that Lizzie was enjoying it. And then she turned to June and gave that small sweet smile again. And June had to steel herself from crushing Lizzie to her, feeling her warm, soft little body, and telling her how she loved her and would always keep her safe.

She felt Bertie watching her curiously.

'I'll have to say something,' she said. 'You're better than anyone with the child.'

'I'm glad when I know she's with you, Bertie, and not in Matron's smoky office. It can't be good for her. But I so want her to join in with the other children.'

'I've mentioned the same myself to Matron,' Bertie said, folding a tea towel and hanging it on a rail by the sink. 'But the woman never listens. She might now she's got you though.'

'I'm just a silly little girl, as far as Matron is concerned,' June told her.

'Give the Fierce One a bit more time to get to know you,' Bertie said. 'But don't let her get you down. She might even break into a smile, one of these days.'

That was all very well, June thought, but it didn't help Lizzie now, when she needed it most.

The mixture smelled wonderful even before the puddings had gone into the oven.

'Not as good as they should, hen,' Bertie said when June complimented her. 'I've usually got them all made by August. Earlier the better. But it takes longer these days to collect enough coupons to get all the ingredients. And even if you have coupons there's no guarantee they've got what you need.'

June glanced up at the kitchen clock. Quarter to two. She only had a few minutes to change and would be lucky to walk to the top of the lane and then catch a bus into town – all in an hour.

'Junie, are you ready?' Iris called. 'Harold is outside waiting to give us a lift in the motorcar. He's going into town.'

June didn't need any persuasion. The sooner she was in town the sooner she'd see Murray. She was out of the door in a flash, Iris laughing and running behind.

'Give Murray my very kind regards,' Iris said, as the motor came to a stop in the High Street and Harold went to open their door, 'if you can remember,' she added, tweaking June's hat so it sat straighter on the honey strands.

'You're making too much of it,' June protested. 'Really, it's nothing.'

'Tell me that after you've spent a few hours in his company.' Iris looked wistful. 'I'm going to leave you here and make my own way back. I need to buy some sewing needles and replenish the first-aid tin, then I'm back on shift in a couple of hours.'

She waved goodbye and was soon out of sight. June thought she'd feel pleased to be left alone, ready to meet Murray in private, and was surprised to find she half wanted to run after Iris – tell her not to go – tell her to join them for a cup of tea. All of a sudden she felt nervous. She closed her eyes for a second and took a deep, calming breath. She was a grown woman. All she was doing was having a cup of tea with a very nice man.

But she knew she was fooling herself.

She turned the corner and there he was, outside Brown's Books. As she approached him she could see a smile begin to tug at his mouth. For an instant she wished they were courting. Then she could run into his arms and be enclosed and safe. He would kiss her warmly – on her lips. Tell her how much he'd missed her. But they were just friends, and that was marvellous as well. She smiled, as much at her silly daydreams as at Murray himself.

'I didn't know if you'd really come,' Murray said, beaming, as he pecked her on the cheek.

'I told you I would. Something or someone would have to stop me from keeping my word.'

'I'm the same way.' Murray took her hand, his eyes seeking hers. 'Do you want to walk a bit or shall we go straight to my favourite teashop? If it's not too busy we can talk. You said you had two problems, and I'm a good listener. Have even been known to resolve a problem or two occasionally.' He gave her hand the gentlest squeeze.

That familiar tingling when he touched her, even though he was wearing his leather gloves. She felt her cheeks warm. Did he realise what an effect he was having? He still had hold of her hand and it felt right. She could hold his hand forever and not get tired.

'That sounds lovely.' Her voice came out a little shaky and he gave her a sharp look.

Murray took her to a different café from the one she'd gone to with Iris. This one was more modern and the tables were farther apart. And it wasn't so smoky, thank goodness. Murray helped her off with her jacket and settled her into a comfortable chair with a cushion.

'What would you like?'

'I'm dying for a cup of tea,' June said. 'It doesn't sound very sophisticated but that's what I would love.'

'Who cares about being sophisticated?' Murray laughed. It was a good sound. A strong, masculine sound. June felt a quiver run down her back.

'Something to eat? A sophisticated cake, perhaps?' he asked, giving her a cheeky wink as the waitress appeared.

June laughed. 'Oh, no. Tea's just fine.'

'Not enough for a slim little thing like you,' Murray said. He looked up at the waitress and smiled disarmingly. 'Can you bring your best cream cakes for the lady?'

'I'd honestly prefer something plainer,' June said. 'I told you I wasn't sophisticated.'

'Then two toasted and buttered teacakes, please. And be sure it's real butter.'

'We can't always guarantee it, sir,' the waitress told him, 'but I'll do my best.' She hurried away.

Murray turned to her and she thought she would drown in his blue eyes. 'What do you want to talk about, June?'

'It's hard to know where to start.' June twisted the corner of the tablecloth without even realising. 'Like I told you, there are two things. One is Matron, the other is Lizzie. And it's Lizzie I'm much more concerned about.'

'Is she a teacher or one of the children?'

'Oh, sorry, of course you don't know. She's one of the newer children.'

'Is she very naughty?'

'No.' June hesitated. 'Well, she is a little, but it's complicated. She's been through a lot. She only arrived a few weeks before me, but she's never mixed with the other children and has never spoken a word since. I would love to help her and I think I could if I was given the chance, but Matron won't allow me to have any contact with her. So that makes Matron the second problem.'

'Have you spoken about Lizzie to Matron?'

'Oh, yes, several times. I always seem to infuriate her. I have different ideas to her on how to handle a child who's still in deep shock. Both parents and her brother were killed in a fire. Lizzie was at her grandmother's house, else she would definitely have gone like the others,' June explained. Just saying the words made her bottom lip tremble.

'So we have to think of how to persuade Matron to let you try to help the child?'

'That's exactly it. But I keep coming up blank.'

'You're probably quite short-staffed with the war, aren't you?'

'Yes, very,' June said. She was finding it difficult to concentrate with those bright-blue eyes focused directly on her. 'Matron's finally realised that Hilda's not capable of looking after Lizzie – she's an untrained girl who I don't think is terribly bright – but there's no one else except me, which Matron won't even consider. So now poor Lizzie has to sit in Matron's office, which reeks of smoke, until Bertie the cook lets her stay in the kitchen for a change. It's an awful situation.'

'What happens when Matron has a day off?'

'That's what I asked her. She says she rarely has time off and if she does she'll ask Iris, who you met at the dance, to watch her. Iris is a nurse but she's too busy at the moment with all the coughs and colds and minor emergencies to spend a lot of time with one child. I'm in the best position because although I have to help with *all* the children, I wouldn't isolate Lizzie. She'd be part of the other children's lives, mixing with them and taking her chance – just like they do. And I think she'd finally open up and start speaking, but she'll remain dumb, I'm sure of it, if Matron carries on like this.'

June was suddenly struck with the thought that she'd rambled on too long and Murray would be bored.

'I'm sorry, I shouldn't involve you in all this.'

'No, don't apologise. I'm glad you're involving me.' Murray put his hand over June's and this time, instead of

113

his leather glove, she could feel the warmth of his skin. She felt a glow of gratitude that she could talk freely to him and he seemed genuinely interested.

'Let me think about it,' Murray finally said, as the waitress came towards them with a full tray. 'I'm sure we can come up with something.'

June liked the way he said 'we'. It made her feel she wasn't alone with her problems. Looking at his strong face and capable hands she felt he was bound to come up with a plan.

They talked of other things: books they'd read, their families, though June didn't give too much away on hers. There were so many sad stories connected with them and she didn't want to make their afternoon gloomy. In fact, she felt much more positive than she had since she'd started work at Bingham Hall. She'd find a way to help Lizzie – maybe with Murray's help – and Matron would see the sense of it, and even if she grudgingly handed over the responsibility of Lizzie to her entirely, June wouldn't mind at all. She only wanted the best for the child. The best for every child, but Lizzie was special. It shouldn't have any influence, but Lizzie so much reminded June of Clara. Yes, Lizzie was the one who needed the most help right now.

'The waitress managed to put real butter on the teacakes then,' Murray said approvingly as he took a large bite of his bun.

'They're delicious.' June bit off a rather more delicate piece. 'Perfect with the tea.'

To her surprise Murray leaned across the table. His head was so close she could smell the soap he must have used before coming to meet her. For a split second she thought he was going to kiss her. Instead, he reached for the napkin. 'You have a smear of butter on the top of your lip,' he teased. 'Let me get it.'

To June's acute embarrassment he gently wiped it off. It seemed such an intimate gesture and yet it was nothing – nothing at all. So why was her stomach turning upside down?

'There. All gone,' Murray said grinning, as though he were talking to a child. He looked at his watch. 'Oh, June, I'm so sorry, I have to go. They didn't give me much time today as they're really busy. But can I see you soon?' Before she could answer he said, 'You can't say no because I just might have a plan for Lizzie by then.'

'I wasn't going to say no anyway,' June said boldly. 'I've enjoyed having tea with you.'

'Next time I'll take you somewhere a bit more glamorous,' Murray promised. 'To the kind of place you should be seen.'

'Oh, no, I don't bother about that sort of thing at all,' June said quickly. 'I don't have to be impressed. I haven't got the right clothes anyway for anywhere glamorous. All I really want is this war to be over and everyone get back to normal. And keep my job at Dr Barnardo's.'

'Things will never be as they used to be before this damned war.' Murray stopped. 'Oh, I'm sorry. I shouldn't swear in front of a lady.'

'I don't mind. I feel like swearing myself sometimes,' June said, surprising herself by admitting it. 'Men are lucky. They can vent their anger. Ladies are supposed to be ladies at all times. And it's not always easy.'

'I don't suppose it is,' Murray said, reaching for his coat, which he'd slung on the back of his chair. 'But sometimes the boys get carried away and their language gets very colourful for my tender ears.' He winked, and she knew he was teasing her.

'It sounds as though you get on well with them.'

'I do. They're good chaps. But now the Americans are coming over it'll change us – and I'm not sure for the better.'

'I thought they already had – joined us in fighting the Germans, I mean,' June said, and Chas immediately popped into her head.

'No, they're not coming till the end of January.' Murray raised his eyes to the ceiling.

It struck her that Murray was not very happy with the idea.

'But Chas—'

'He came over early.' Murray shrugged. 'Volunteered, I believe, to get stuck in straightaway. He's okay, I suppose. Oozes the charm . . . obviously comes from a wealthy family. Bit of a womaniser, I'd say.'

Handsome, confident, relaxed Chas. A womaniser. She wasn't that surprised. She had to admit Chas would turn any girl's head. But in a crisis she knew whom she would rather be with.

Sitting on the bus back to Bingham Hall, June went over her conversation with Murray. She had every faith he would come up with an idea to resolve the problem that loomed larger and larger in her mind, but they hadn't been able to make a definite time to meet because he didn't know when he'd have a few spare hours. She'd been adamant that he shouldn't ring her at the home because of Matron. The woman would never let her hear the end of it.

'I'll think of a way,' he'd promised as he held her for the briefest moment and she felt his lips gently brush her mouth.

'Did you mind me kissing you?' Murray's eyes were anxious.

'N-no, of course I don't mind.'

How could she tell him that it had taken all her willpower not to fling her arms round his neck and beg him to kiss her again, only this time longer and deeper. Her cheeks

116

reddened at the thought of what on earth he would say – worse, what he would think of her if she had. He would think she was a brazen hussy. That's what Dad had called her that time when a boy in her class carried her satchel from school one day when she'd fainted in Assembly. She'd only been 13 and had had no idea what her father was talking about.

'I hope we can meet soon, Junie.' Murray looked into her eyes as though he was desperate to know what she was thinking. 'May I call you that? It seems to suit you somehow.'

Iris, and now Murray.

'Yes, you can call me Junie, if you like.'

June trudged down the lane and up the drive almost unaware of the cold drizzle which had started as soon as the bus had dropped her. It was already dark and she felt in her bag for her torch. She needed to get inside quickly before her shoes were ruined so she walked a little faster, the torch's thin light illuminating only a few steps ahead. She half covered it with her hand, feeling a bit of an idiot, as though an enemy aeroplane might spot such a pathetic beam and strafe her. At last the heavy door was in sight and moments later she was safely in the hall where a fire roared away. She blew out her cheeks. It had been quite a day.

Chapter Eleven

'June. Junie. Wake up! Please wake up. I—'

June came to with a start and bolted upright, her eyes wide.

'Iris! Whatever's the matter?' But immediately she saw the expression on her friend's face her heart began to beat wildly. Something was horribly wrong.

'Oh, Junie. Lizzie's not in her bed!'

Dear God, no.

'Maybe she went to the toilet.' June forced herself to say the words calmly.

'No, I've looked. In fact, I've been all over the house.'

June sprang out of bed and hurriedly pulled on her skirt and jumper, which she'd left over the arm of the chair the previous evening. 'How long do you think she's been gone?'

'I don't know. I'm on nights and the last time I checked must have been about two hours ago. She was sound asleep then. So was Hilda, for that matter.'

Hilda again.

'What time is it?'

'After midnight,' Iris said.

'She might have gone outside.' June looked at Iris, who was wearing her nurse's uniform. 'Let's get our coats and check there first. If we don't find her in the next half an hour we'll have to telephone the police.' June summoned up all her common sense, but inside she was sick with fear.

It was still snowing. No child would survive outside more than an hour without proper clothing.

'Not on her own, surely.' Iris sounded agitated. 'She'd be too frightened. And anyway, how would she have got out?'

'Maybe the back door from the kitchen was left open. Bertie forgot to lock it the other night.' She flung her coat on and hurried to the door, Iris on her heels.

'I've brought a blanket for Lizzie,' Iris said as she caught up with June in the kitchen. 'Oh, Junie, she could get pneumonia or frostbite or—'

'We'll find her,' June cut in, 'but let's hurry. You go towards the drive and I'll search round the back.'

Her words were whipped away by the wind as Iris flew off.

'What's going on, Miss?'

To June's surprise Alan, who Barbara had mentioned was the class trouble maker, appeared at her elbow, already dressed in coat and hat.

'You should be in bed, young man.'

'I couldn't sleep. I heard you and Nurse going up and down the stairs. I thought you were burglars.'

She was about to tell him to go back upstairs when she saw the concern in his eyes.

'Lizzie's not in her bed and we're worried. If she's out here she could catch pneumonia.' A thought struck her. 'Do you have a torch?'

'A bigger one than yours, I betcha.' Alan held out one of the hall lanterns. 'This'll find her. Good job we're in the country. One lantern isn't going to show the Germans where we are.'

What a sensible boy he was, June thought. 'Keep within calling distance,' she warned him. 'I don't want you to go wandering off and have to look for two children.' She caught

119

hold of his arm before he turned away. 'Do you promise, Alan?'

'Oh, all right, I promise.'

'Have you any idea where she might be?'

'No. Maybe she's run away.'

Fear clutched June's chest. If Lizzie *was* outside with no coat she'd freeze to death. They *had* to find her.

Her torch with its meagre light did little but she was thorough. She searched the sheds, all five of them, the Victorian greenhouses, all the outbuildings she could see. But there was no sign of a child. The children had been playing outside that morning and the snow was scuffed with their footprints. There'd been no new fall of snow so Lizzie's footprints might or might not be muddled in with the other children's.

June looked back at the house, but the blackout curtains had been drawn long ago. Alan's whistles and calls sounded further away. She swallowed, praying Lizzie wasn't out here. Wishing she'd changed into her warm boots she gave an involuntary shiver, and the hairs in her nostrils turned to icicles. It was an unpleasant feeling but she tried to ignore it and concentrate.

The top of her head felt icy cold. Why hadn't she stopped to put a hat on? She wondered if she should go back for it, but that would use up more than five precious minutes. She'd have to bear it for Lizzie's sake.

'Miss! Miss!' Alan's voice was faint but she picked up the sound.

'What is it, Alan?'

'Miss, come here. Come and look.'

He'd found her. She knew it. And Lizzie . . . oh, she daren't think any further.

'I'm over here, at the back of the clocktower. Come *on*.'

She stumbled in the direction of Alan's voice, thankful

for a sliver of moon which just caught the face of the clock to guide her.

'In this little barn,' Alan called. 'Where they keep the hens at night.'

Terrified of what she might see, June opened the barn door, which was already ajar. She'd never been in it before – didn't even know it was there. Alan swung round, his lantern aloft, and to her joy he was smiling.

'Here she is, Miss. Safe and sound.'

Lizzie was curled up in a corner amongst bales of straw sound asleep, three fingers in her mouth, her other arm clutching one of the hens.

'Alan, you're wonderful. What made you think of looking this far?' She tried to hug him but he wouldn't have it and backed away with embarrassment.

'I didn't. I heard the farm dogs barking from over here and thought I'd have a look inside. I think they were trying to tell me.'

June made her way stealthily over the barn floor.

'Lizzie. Lizzie.' She shook the child gently by the shoulder. Lizzie stirred. Gently she took the sleeping hen from Lizzie's arm. 'Lizzie, wake up. You need to come inside out of the cold.'

A pair of brown eyes suddenly opened, then went wide with terror as Lizzie realised she wasn't in her bed. She opened her mouth but nothing came out. June raised the little girl into a sitting position. Lizzie's silent sobs shuddered against her chest.

'You had us all very worried, Lizzie,' June said. 'We wondered where you were. Why did you leave the nice warm nursery?'

Lizzie opened her mouth again, but this time a determined expression crossed her little heart-shaped face.

'The snowman got losted – then Lizzie got losted.'

Chapter Twelve

June stretched out in the narrow bed, wondering why the mattress felt more lumpy than the one she'd got used to. She heard a faint whimper and opened her eyes. It sounded close by. Then she remembered. Lizzie. She threw back the eiderdown and sprang out of bed.

'Lizzie?'

Lizzie was sitting on the edge of the bed struggling to put her shoes on, still with her nightdress on.

'Are you all right?'

Lizzie nodded. Even that was a response, June thought, a flicker of optimism passing through her. Things were going to improve, she was certain. And the barrier Lizzie had built through no fault of her own would surely soon come tumbling down. Alan had said something very wise yesterday evening: that it wasn't right for Lizzie to be separated from the other children and that she should be allowed to play and eat with the others like a normal child. If a twelve-year-old could see it, then why was it so difficult for Matron to do so?

June helped Lizzie get dressed and made a decision. She would risk Matron's wrath and take Lizzie down with her to have breakfast. Matron liked a lie-in in the mornings and didn't usually appear until nine o'clock. She could easily get

Lizzie back to the nursery by then, and have another go with Matron. She'd have to tell her about Hilda even if it meant getting Iris into trouble. Perhaps she should speak to Iris first. She'd hate to lose Iris as a friend by saying the wrong thing.

Iris chuckled when June had a word with her. 'Say what you want to the old biddy,' she said. 'I'm here to look after the children when they get sick or have an accident – not just one child, much as I'd love to. But you could do the two things easily because Lizzie's natural place is with the others so you wouldn't have to split yourself in two.'

'Thank you for that, Iris. I've now got to face her again. She gets so angry with me.'

'Do you want me to come with you?'

'That's nice of you, but I don't want it to look as though I can't stand up to her.'

But June didn't get her chance. She was just on her way to Matron's office when she heard the crunch of bicycle tyres on the gravel path. There was a screech of brakes and a boy wearing a uniform jumped off and leaned his bicycle on the kitchen wall. Moments later Bertie came out of the kitchen.

'Telegram for Matron,' she said. 'I do hope it isn't bad news.'

'I'm going to see Matron right now,' June said, 'so I can take it.'

She knocked on Matron's door.

'Come in.' Matron's voice was coated with cigarette smoke.

'Good morning, Matron.' June tried hard to sound pleasant. 'The telegram boy's just this minute delivered this. It's for you.'

123

Matron took the single paper out of the envelope. Seconds later she rolled her eyes, and blew out her cheeks. Then she heaved her sturdy shoulders before letting them drop in resignation.

'I hope there's nothing wrong, Matron.'

The woman shook her head as though in disbelief. 'It's my sister. She's always having accidents. Never looks where she's going. She's taken a fall down the steps outside her cottage and struck her head on the path. Says she's got concussion. Wants me to look after her. Well, she's written: "Please come" so that's what I'll have to do.'

'I'm sorry to hear it,' June said, and she was. She didn't like to think of anyone who was injured or ill. But the sneaking thought came into her mind that this would be a perfect opportunity to help Lizzie.

'I shouldn't be away more than three or four days,' Matron said, as she stopped June after the morning break. She was carrying a small brown suitcase and a string bag with tins of food and vegetables poking out. 'I'll definitely be back well before Christmas. I'd made up my mind to have Christmas here this year for a change. You know the routine now. Don't start making new rules.' She glared at June, a suspicious look in her eyes. 'It's hard enough having them obey the ones we have. Unfortunately, my sister's not on the telephone.'

Even better, was June's immediate uncharitable thought. Matron wouldn't be telephoning a dozen times a day.

'I'm sure we'll cope, Matron,' June said. 'There's no need to worry. I hope your sister will soon be on her feet again.'

'You're sure you'll be all right?'

'Yes, of course,' June said quickly. Oh, why didn't the woman just leave? 'I'm not alone. The teachers are here every day and Kathleen and Iris and Cook are here at night to help. We'll all manage perfectly.'

'Hmm. That's as maybe.' Matron pursed her lips and her steel-grey eyes pierced through June. 'Is there anything else you need to tell me before I go?'

June's heart almost stopped. Could Matron have heard that Lizzie had been missing last night and been found in one of the barns? But surely if she had she would have sent for June immediately. June gave her a steady look.

'I don't think so, Matron. You really mustn't worry about us. It's your sister who is relying on you now.'

'Are you ready to go, Ma'am?' It was Harold. 'Let me take that case.' He took it from her. 'I've brought the car round for you.'

'Have a safe journey,' June said, thinking if Matron had been nice like Bertie she'd have kissed her cheek. But you didn't do that sort of thing with Matron.

With a last look round as though she was trying to catch someone out, Matron allowed herself to be led out of the front door and into the staff car, remarking as she went that her sister had been most inconsiderate to have an accident when there was so much work to be done at the orphanage, and didn't her sister realise how busy she was. How important she was to the children. That it couldn't possibly run properly without her.

June breathed a sigh of relief. It was as though someone had given her the best present possible, to have what she fervently hoped would be more than three or four days' peace from Matron's ever-watchful eye. With a bit of luck Matron wouldn't return until after Boxing Day. Hard-hearted though Matron was, surely she wouldn't leave her sister alone over the festive season. The children would have the best Christmas they'd ever had and just be normal children, instead of constantly hearing the words 'orphan' and 'evacuee' that Matron was so fond of using.

To June's utter disappointment Lizzie slipped back into her curled-up position in Bertie's kitchen that afternoon, her fingers once again in her mouth.

Poor little mite. It's her only comfort. If only she'd trust me.
And then she had an idea.

'Pamela,' she called as the child hopped on one leg through the Great Hall, little Betsy laughing as she followed behind, trying to emulate the older girl, just as Clara used to do with June. Both children began to giggle when Pamela lost her balance and fell in a heap. They were already taking advantage of Matron's absence, June thought, hiding a smile.

'Pamela, can you go and find Alan? Tell him I'd like to see him.'

'Yes, Miss.' Pamela jumped up, turned, still with Betsy at her heels, and disappeared along the corridor leading from one of the classrooms.

Alan was beside her in next to no time.

'Is Lizzie all right?' he asked immediately.

'Yes, Lizzie's fine. She's in the kitchen. You know Matron has been called away for a few days?' Alan nodded, a big grin plastered over his face. 'I'd like to have a word with all the teachers, so you might miss class this morning.'

'Oh, that's a shame, Miss.' His grin became even wider.

'I want to plan Christmas with them,' June said, noticing the boy's eyes sparkle with approval, 'and then we'll ask the older children, including you, to help make it the best Christmas ever.'

'We'll have to get a tree. A big one. Last year it was only this high.' Alan raised one hand in the air, indicating that the tree had been only about four feet tall.

126

'We'll have a lovely big tree,' June promised. 'And *all* the children will help to decorate it.'

'That'd be fun, Miss. It's better here now you've come.'

'That's a bit unfair to the others who work hard to take care of you.'

'I didn't mean to be rude, Miss, but Matron's always angry with us. I can't talk to her or any of the teachers like I can you.'

'Get away with you.' But secretly June was pleased. 'Anyway, enough of that. Do you think you could show Lizzie your fossil collection? Or anything you think she might like to see. I just want her to move around the house – get to know it – and I think she'd go with you.'

'Girls aren't ever interested,' he grunted. 'They'd rather play with their dolls.'

'I've never seen Lizzie with a doll. I don't even know if she has one. Why don't you ask her if she'd like to see your fossils anyway?'

'Okay.' Alan thrust his hands in his pocket as he walked with her to the kitchen. Lizzie hadn't moved.

'Lizzie, do you want to come and look at my fossil collection?' Lizzie shook her head at him and stared at the floor. 'They're very old.' He bent down to her so he was on her level. 'They're little animals that were buried in stones millions of years ago and we can still see the outlines of them today.'

Lizzie looked up, her eyes wide with disbelief.

'I think you'd like them.' Alan nodded encouragingly and held out his hand.

To June's amazement Lizzie got to her feet and took hold of Alan's hand. He turned and smiled triumphantly at her.

'She'll be safe with me, Miss. I won't let any harm come to her.'

'I know you won't, Alan. You're a good boy. Your mum and dad must be proud of you.'

At that, Alan's eyes filled with tears. 'I ain't got no mum and dad.'

June's eyes flew wide. 'But I thought you were evacuated here. That your parents wanted to keep you safe.'

'Nah. That's what I tell the other evacuated kids. I can't stand it when they talk about Mummy this and Daddy that.' He looked down at Lizzie. 'Come on, kid. Let's go and see the fossils.'

June looked after their retreating backs. She kicked herself for mentioning his parents. So he was an orphan after all, and she'd made things worse talking about his mum and dad as though they were still alive. If only Matron would let her see the files. Then she wouldn't have made such an awful mistake. But Iris had told her Matron locked the filing cabinet every time she left her office. Well, Matron wasn't here so maybe she could take even more advantage of the woman's absence. Have a snoop around. Perhaps she could find the key.

And then something else struck her. There was a spare bed in the girls' dormitory.

But first she needed to talk to the teachers. She wasn't sure she had the authority to put her plans into action but she was going to try. And she would need their agreement.

It hadn't been as difficult as she'd imagined. That evening, when the teachers and the two nurses were settled in the common room, June explained what had happened to Lizzie, and how Alan had found her.

'The wonderful surprise was that she spoke for the first time!' June ended, enjoying the gasps of surprise, and catching Iris's wink.

Miss Ayles's main concern was that it should be reported to Matron, but everyone agreed with June that as no harm had come to Lizzie it would be better to keep quiet about it.

'I don't want to risk Matron punishing Lizzie now she's broken her silence,' June said, anxiously looking around the group. She quickly outlined her plan for Lizzie to join in with the younger children for games and drawing and ABC lessons and be treated exactly like the other children.

'And there's one other thing,' June said. 'This is our only chance to get Lizzie down from the nursery and into a bed in the girls' dormitory. Once she gets used to it Matron can hardly make me take her to the nursery again. It would solve the problem of Hilda still being the one who is with her at night but not keeping a proper eye on her, and I think Lizzie will settle if she's with the other children.'

There were some murmurs of agreement.

'But June will need *everyone's* support,' Iris said. 'Hands up if you agree to help. To stand behind her if she has any problem with Matron when she returns.'

Everyone's hand shot up except Miss Ayles's. There was a silence as the others looked at her, waiting for her to respond.

Miss Ayles hesitated and sniffed again. 'I suppose I can't refuse.'

'Good.' June rushed in before any of them could change their minds. 'Alan's made a start . . . he's already shown Lizzie his fossil collection. And I'll go up and sort Lizzie's bed.'

June decided to spend Lizzie's first night in the girls' dormitory so the child wouldn't feel too strange, but she needn't have worried. As soon as Lizzie saw her rag doll that Pamela had given her the day before, propped up on the pillow with her nightie, she ran to the bed and looked up at June.

'Yes, Lizzie. You're old enough to be with the big girls. Do you think you'll like that?'

Lizzie caught her lower lip between her teeth and vigorously nodded.

There was not a peep out of her that night.

Chapter Thirteen

The next day Lizzie seemed quite content to join the other girls in the art room. She'd been good as gold in her new bed and June was hopeful that she'd soon join in with the others' chatter. June put her head round the door after half an hour, curious as to how her charge was getting on, and was delighted to see Lizzie dipping a brush into a little block of paint. But when she tiptoed up to the child June noticed the small piece of paper in front of her was covered in watery black swirls. She bent closer but Lizzie seemed oblivious. Then she recoiled as she saw that Lizzie had drawn a house with a chimney, and the black swirls represented black smoke. Three matchstick people were horizontal on the ground outside.

It was similar to Lizzie's scribbled drawing on the nursery wall. That vision must be going round and round in her head, June thought, her eyes growing moist.

Barbara gestured to her to come over. 'I'm letting her get rid of her nightmares by painting them out,' she said, 'to try to clear the way for her to start to speak again. But it's also important for her to paint nice happy things. I'm going to ask her to paint some flowers next.'

'I think that's a good idea,' June said, and left as quietly

131

as she'd entered. It was going to take time, and she mustn't rush the little girl.

'I'm on nit duty,' Kathleen grumbled next morning. 'Don't I hate that job.'

'Would you like me to do it for a change?' June offered.

Kathleen clapped her hands together in delight. '*Would* you?'

'Yes, of course. It will give me a chance to keep all their names in my head.'

The children lined up, the older ones shuffling and grumbling that they didn't need to be inspected – there was nothing wrong with their heads.

'It's all Jack's fault,' Alan told her. 'He's the newest. He brought them in.'

The younger ones sniffed back the tears, telling June how painful it was the last time. June had found a wraparound apron from the kitchen which swamped her, but at least she would have some protection from any of the little blighters, she thought grimly, as she nodded to the first boy, Jack, to sit on the hard chair. She took up the special nit comb and stood behind him and began.

'I ain't got no nits.'

'I don't have any nits,' June corrected him, hiding a smile. 'But you *do*, Jack. I can see two of them jumping.'

'Jack's got jumping nits,' Doris sang out.

'Shut up, you stupid girl,' Jack said, swivelling his head round to glare at her.

'Jack's got stupid nits,' Doris tormented, hopping round and round on one leg.

'Keep your head still,' June said, steering his head none too gently back into position. 'And it's very rude to call anyone stupid.' She gave his shoulder a nudge. 'It's also

132

rude to tell someone to shut up. So tell Doris you're sorry.'

'Shan't.' June raked through his hair more roughly than she would normally have done. 'Ouch! That hurt.'

'It will hurt more if you don't tell her you're sorry. And Doris' – June twisted round – 'stop that hopping. Stand quietly and don't torment Jack.'

'I wasn't.' Doris pouted her bottom lip. 'He's always horrible to me. And he's got horrible nits.'

'You're next,' June told Doris firmly. She caught the child's arm. Doris started to cry. 'Come on. Might as well get it over quickly.'

It took over an hour to find and kill the nits. Then she had to soak each child's head in vinegar. Some of the bigger children helped to dry the younger ones, and for that June was grateful. The sour smell of vinegar brought back memories of Clara when she used to fall and hurt herself. It seemed she was always having accidents. Their mother swore it was the best disinfectant for injuries but now it made June's stomach heave. A frightened little girl trying to escape a cruel father. Losing her footing . . . Her darling little sister with her neck at a funny angle. She forced herself to concentrate on the next child, with his thick mop of ginger hair, and took up the comb again. Poor Kathleen. She had to do this job every day. Perhaps she could relieve her once a week at least. If she could stand the vinegar smell, that is.

Murray's face strayed into June's mind too often for comfort. She could picture him clearly. His dazzling blue eyes. His wide, generous mouth that looked as though it would break into a smile at any minute. The cleft in his chin. The straight nose. Strong jaw. That crooked tooth. Yes, she could see him almost as clearly as if he was standing in front of her. Now would be a good time for him to telephone her with Matron away. Maybe if she willed it hard enough it would happen. Once she even screwed up her face in concentration, wishing hard. And every time the telephone rang her heart would start thumping furiously but no one called to tell her a gentleman was asking for her. Maybe he'd been sent on a mission and hadn't returned. A shudder ran across her shoulders. She mustn't think like that. He'd told her he was a good pilot and intended to get through this war unscathed. But how could he know for sure? How could anyone be sure?

Every day without Matron felt like a blessing to June. She hummed as she ironed the children's clothes, working out a story in her head for the children to learn and perform in the New Year when the excitement of Christmas was over. She worked hard to give as much attention as she could to Lizzie, but to June's deep disappointment the little girl remained silent. It was as though Lizzie had never uttered those few precious words when she'd stolen out of the house to check on the snowman.

'Miss, can I be in charge of the room decorations? Please, Miss.' Bouncing up to her, his eyes alight with enthusiasm, was Alan. He'd caught her just as she was leaving the classroom where she'd helped some of the children with extra reading.

'You can,' said June, beaming at the excited boy. 'Have all of you finished making the paper chains?'

'Hours ago.' Alan dug his hands in his pockets and gave her a sly sideways look. 'And I've been helping Mr Gilbert to choose a tree. He doesn't bother at all about the shape – only the size. But I think shape's just as important, don't you, Miss?'

'I certainly do, Alan.' June gave his arm a playful tap. She

134

knew she was flouting the rules of the home in two ways. First in calling him 'Alan' – she always addressed the children by their Christian names – and secondly in laying an affectionate hand on his arm. She wouldn't have got away with either if Matron had been on duty, she thought grimly. But it wasn't favouritism: it was simply acknowledging that each child was an individual – and appreciating their qualities. What was so dreadful about that?

She remembered when she was little and had fallen off her tricycle. Her mother had gathered her up in her arms, and June's head had rested on her bosom, drawing in the spicy perfume her mother always wore. She could feel this very minute her mother's fingers running through her hair, and her mother saying, 'Hush, Junie, everything's fine. You'll soon be back on it again.' June wanted the children to have that kind of love from her. The others at Dr Barnardo's were too busy nursing them or teaching them. She was the one who had a more flexible job and time to hug them and comfort them. But Matron had warned her more than once that the boys would grow up cissies with such behaviour.

'Where's Lizzie?' June asked. 'Is she where I left her an hour ago?'

'She's forgotten all about me.' Alan shrugged. 'As soon as Doris and Daisy said she could play with them she stuck to them like glue. If anyone can get her to speak, they will.'

'I'm glad they've taken her under their wing. They're all girls together.'

The doorbell jangled, making her jump. June glanced at the hall clock. Half-past eight. It would be the milkman and he'd want paying. She heard one of the maids open the door, and was about to tell her that Matron would be back shortly and sort out his bill when she stopped in her tracks.

135

'I've come to see Miss Lavender.'

She knew that voice. Strong. Masculine. Warm. Her pulse quickened. She'd tried so hard to dream him up and here he was. She put her hands to her hair, pulled out her tortoise-shell comb and pushed it in again as she tried to catch some stray wisps, but it wasn't easy without a mirror. Oh, well, he'd have to take her as she was.

'Hello, Murray.' To her ears, her voice didn't sound quite steady.

'Junie.' Murray's eyes crinkled as he smiled at her. 'I wanted to see you. I've got something to show you.' He took his cap off. 'Is it a good time to come in for a few minutes?' He stepped in the hall without waiting for her answer.

She heard a tiny sound coming from Murray's chest. He opened his coat and tucked inside was a shiny brown bundle. She gasped as two golden eyes opened.

'Murray?' Her voice came out in a squeak.

'Yes, it's what you think it is,' Murray laughed. 'But it's not for you – it's for Lizzie.'

'Lizzie? But we're not allowed animals in the home.'

'I'm hoping your dragon will make Freddie an exception. It's Lizzie's Christmas present. I think it will help her. He'll be her special friend. I was an only child until my parents gave me a puppy and from there on I had the best friend in the world.' He grinned. 'I told you I'd come up with something – so I have. What do you think?' He opened a few more buttons and put a trembling little creature in her arms.

'Oh, Murray, he's gorgeous.' June's eyes were misty as she stroked the puppy's silky head and floppy ears. 'But I'll have to hide him.' She looked at Murray, her eyes anxious. 'I presume it's a him.'

'Yes, it's a boy. The last in the litter. He's come from the landlady in our local pub – she asked if anyone would take him but no one volunteered. I suddenly thought of Lizzie. He's rather small but he's a bright little fellow. I think he and Lizzie are going to get along just fine.'

Footsteps made June turn round guiltily. It was Iris. June breathed a sigh of relief. She knew Iris would keep a secret. But how could she hide a puppy?

'Oh, it's Murray Andrews,' Iris said, extending her hand. 'Nice to see you again.'

'And you,' Murray said, smiling, shaking hands.

'What have you got there? Oh, don't say it's a puppy. Matron won't have it, you know.'

'It's for Lizzie,' June said defensively. 'Murray thinks it will help her if she has a companion. His name is Freddie.'

'I don't hold out any hope of Matron allowing him to stay,' Iris said, 'but it's a nice idea.' She glanced at the puppy again. 'He *is* sweet though.'

'Maybe he'll soften even Matron's hard heart,' June said tentatively.

'I think you're pushing your luck there' was Iris's reply. 'Anyway, got to go. Hope to see you soon, Murray.' She threw the words over her shoulder. 'I've got three children who've all come down with a suspicious rash. I need to telephone the doctor.' She dashed off.

'Will Iris keep a secret?' Murray asked as Iris disappeared.

'Iris will, but sooner or later someone's bound to mention it to Matron.' June put the quivering warm bundle back into Murray's hands. 'I'll see if Bertie has a scrap of chicken or something we can give him. And I need to find a box. Can you wait here for a moment? I shan't be a minute.'

'Where is Matron at the moment?' Murray said as he tucked Freddie back under his coat.

'Right here,' said a harsh voice from behind June.

June swung round, her heart in her throat. Where had Matron sprung from? How much had she seen and heard?

'And I'd very much like to know who this young man is and what he's doing here.'

'Matron, may I introduce Flight Lieutenant Andrews. He's a pilot from the RAF station at Speke.'

Matron's expression immediately changed. She let her eyebrows drop back into position and her mouth relax, and almost made a curtsey. June bit back a smile. The woman was obviously a little in awe of his rank. She only hoped Freddie would keep perfectly still and not make a sound.

To her delight Murray treated Matron to his most charming smile. 'I'm very pleased to meet you, Mrs—'

'Mrs Pherson.' Matron held out her hand. 'So you're helping to win the war?'

'I'm doing my best,' Murray said, shaking her hand. 'We all are.'

'When's all this trouble coming to an end?'

'No one knows. But we're going to do everything we can, and now the Americans are coming it should speed things up a bit.'

'Not before time.' Matron's lips pursed. 'I don't know why we got ourselves into it in the first place.' She tutted, raising her eyes to the rafters. 'Well, I must be getting along. I've been away and I expect everything's in turmoil. Rules not kept, children running wild' – she turned to June and glared – 'but I'm back now, in good time for Christmas, as I told you.' She gave Murray a nod, then said to June, 'Please bring me a cup of tea in my office in five minutes.' She glanced at her watch. 'No, give me ten. Then you can tell me all the news since I've been away.'

The moment she left the hall June whispered, 'Freddie can't stay here. I'll never be able to keep a puppy quiet.'

138

As though Freddie heard her, June saw a twitching under Murray's coat and a small muffled whine. Poor little thing must be almost suffocating. And doubtless hungry. She noticed a small trail of liquid dribble out of the bottom of Murray's coat.

'I think Freddie's just made a mistake,' she said, her teeth gripping her bottom lip as she tried not to laugh.

'What?' Murray laid a comforting hand over the contour where the puppy was hidden. 'Oh, I think I know what he's done.' His grin faded. 'June, I can't take him back. He's too young. Needs attention like a baby. And I'm hardly ever there these days. He'll be safer and happier with you and Lizzie.'

June stood still for about thirty seconds. 'All right,' she said. 'But if I get the sack you'll have to find me a job at the camp.' She kept a straight face. 'Washing up or something.'

'Delighted to,' Murray said, grinning, but looking visibly relieved.

'I'd better take him upstairs to my bedroom.' June held out her arms and Murray put the quivering creature in them again. Freddie licked her hand.

'I'll be off then, so I'll wish you a Merry Christmas.' Murray put his cap on, then raised it, winked at her and said under his breath, 'I'll write to you.' He hesitated. 'Oh, I nearly forgot. I knew there was something else. May I?' He pointed to her overall pocket.

June nodded, wanting him to disappear before they got into serious trouble.

He placed a small lumpy package wrapped in Christmas paper in her top pocket and left by the door he'd come in. June rushed upstairs with Freddie in her arms as quiet as a toy dog. Thankfully, there was no one on the stairs. She arrived at her bedroom door puffing with nerves rather than exertion. Glancing swiftly round her room she spotted an apple box that had held the tree decorations. That would do. She would put some earth in it for Freddie and try to sneak out a couple of tin bowls from the kitchen when Bertie wasn't looking. Maybe she could get away with it. Take Lizzie to her room to introduce her to Freddie. Her heart quickened as she imagined the child's excited expression.

June glanced up at the clock, the only sound in her room. Five minutes had gone already. She needed to leave the puppy while she went to get him some water at least. And Matron would be demanding her tea.

She had to line the box with something. Desperate, she opened the wardrobe and pulled out the newspaper which lined the bottom of the inside of the cupboard. She spread it in the box, all the time trying to hold on to Freddie, who by this point was frantically trying to jump down and investigate the room. She set him down on the newspaper but he immediately scrambled out and whined.

'I'll have to get you something from Cook,' she said to him, feeling a little silly knowing he had no way of understanding what on earth she was talking about. 'But you must be patient. And quiet. No one must know you're here. It will be our secret – and Lizzie's.' She lifted the puppy and sat on the edge of the bed with him on her lap, stroking him. He was such a dear little chap she could have sat with him all morning.

'Be a good boy and I'll be back with some food very soon.'

She put him back in the apple box, and again he struggled out on his little legs, whining. Worried as to what she'd let herself in for, she shut the door quietly behind her.

Swiftly June went to the kitchen and made a pot of tea, poured out a cup for Bertie, who was looking red and harassed, and took a tray into Matron's office. She placed a cup on the desk in front of Matron, who was leaning back in her chair reading the *Daily Express*, not bothering to look up. June sat down and stirred her tea, reading the headline on the front page of the newspaper:

NO NAZI COLLAPSE BEFORE WE KNOCK HITLER OUT.

She was trying to work out what it meant when Matron finally smoothed the newspaper and folded it, then put it to one side. She looked up with her perpetual frown of disapproval.

June took a deep breath. She'd have to tell her Lizzie now slept in the girls' dormitory. 'I hope you don't mind, Matron, but I thought we might take more than a few minutes and I was just on my way to the kitchen to make a cuppa for myself when you came in.'

'I see.' Matron's lips pursed. 'Well, now you've brought one for yourself I can hardly tell you to take it away.'

June kept silent. It was only a cup of blooming tea, for goodness' sake. Honestly, when the boys up there were risking their lives every second . . . She put her hands around her cup to still them, picturing Murray and his pals trying to see where they were going in the dark; trying to spot enemy aircraft before *they* were spotted. It was too horrible to imagine. She gulped down some tea and Matron frowned harder but didn't comment.

June broke the silence. 'You wanted to see me, Matron.'

'I certainly did. I'd dearly like to know what your – that young man was doing inside our home – without an invitation, I presume. Or did you invite him?' She bent forward over her desk, her face only a foot or so away from June's.

June swallowed. She could smell the acrid smoke on Matron's breath and something stronger underneath.

'No, Matron, I didn't invite him here. He came to bring

141

me something.' The words were out of her mouth before she could stop them.

'And what did he bring you, Miss Lavender?' Matron's lips were parted with a strange mixture of anger and curiosity. June decided the woman couldn't bear it that something had gone on since she'd been away that she had had no control over.

'Oh, it was n-nothing really,' June stuttered, wondering what on earth she was going to say. Then she remembered the little gift Murray had put in her pocket.

'I demand you tell me immediately.' Matron's nostrils flared as she pounded her fist on her desk. 'The rule is that no young man is to set foot on these premises unless I give permission. There's no telling what trouble the girls could get into. I've already had to dismiss one such girl – a kitchen maid – who was intimate, shall we call it' – she looked at June with cold grey eyes – 'and left with a bellyful of baby. I won't have our reputation spoilt by a slip of a girl.'

June blushed bright red. 'I'm *not* a slip of a girl, Matron. I've taken full responsibility since you've been away. Flight Lieutenant Andrews came to bring me a small gift, that's all.' She took the packet wrapped in Christmas holly paper out of her pocket and showed it.

'Hmm!' Matron eyed it with suspicion. 'You haven't opened it.' Her tone was accusing.

'I'm saving it until Christmas morning.' What a bully the woman was. June tried to change the subject. 'Have you seen the tree? The children are having a wonderful time decorating it.'

'Yes, I've seen it. I nearly fell over a branch that had fallen on the step. It should have been cleared away. Jones and Draper could have seen to it – they're old enough now. Any

142

one of us could have tripped on it.' She looked sharply at June. 'Are all the decorations finished?'

'Yes, the children spent some happy hours yesterday making paper chains and stringing them up,' June said, thankful Matron had gone along with her. She usually hung on like a terrier if she was determined to know something. 'You should go and see them. And we've got a small tree in the dining room that you might not have noticed when you came in. They've worked ever so hard. Especially the girls.' She hesitated, then plunged in. 'Even Lizzie joined in.' Matron frowned but for once made no comment. 'Do tell them they've done a good job,' June rushed on. 'They're so keen to let the boys see they can do things just as well. Megan was showing off—'

'I don't need telling how to handle the orphans,' Matron said, her lips in a thin line. 'And by the way, I notice everything and don't you forget it, my girl.' She staggered to her feet and for a moment she almost overbalanced. June shot up and put out a steadying hand but Matron brushed her off as though she were an irritating fly. 'That's all, Miss Lavender. You may go.'

June picked up both empty cups and put them on the tray, her thoughts racing. Matron never stayed late after supper; never checked on the children in bed. She needn't say anything to her about Lizzie moving to the dormitory. Maybe the least said the better. But before she got to the door she turned, feeling emboldened. 'Matron, may I ask one thing?'

'What is it?'

'Why do we have to call the boys by their surnames? It seems so cold, somehow. I really think they'd flourish more if we used their Christian names and gave them some individual affection. Most of them long for it, I can tell.'

'Aren't you the clever one?' Matron rolled her eyes. 'How long have you been here?' She glared at June, not looking as though she expected any reply. 'They should think themselves lucky we use their surnames. When the homes were first opened the children were just known by their numbers.'

June stared at Matron in horror. That was awful. To be a number rather than a child with a name. A child with parents. A normal child. A feeling of sadness swept over her. These children *weren't* normal. And they didn't have normal lives or normal homes. Little Lizzie, who'd never spoken since her whole family had burned to death, except for those few words in the barn. Beth and her brother Lenny, who refused to be separated. They went everywhere together, clinging on to each other's hands. At first June had thought it was sweet until she realised how much they craved motherly affection and were having to give comfort to each another. Then there was Alan, who'd behaved like a grown-up when Lizzie disappeared, but had lied to the other children about what had happened to his family. All he needed was encouragement. To be made to feel important and special. They all did. So why couldn't Matron see that each one was unique with a different set of problems? She wanted to hug them all – the naughty ones as well as the good ones. Especially the naughty ones, who were only difficult because of their circumstances, some of them still trying to feel their way into a place they were forced to call home. But she'd never be able to explain to Matron as she could hardly find the right words herself.

'Will your sister be on her own for Christmas?' June asked, hoping to change what seemed to be a touchy subject.

Matron's eyebrows met in a frown. 'What's that supposed to mean? That I've not done my duty by her? My God, if anyone hasn't done their duty . . .' She trailed off, a bitter expression on her face.

'I didn't mean it like that,' June said quickly. 'I didn't want to think of her on her own, that's all. Or anyone, for that matter.'

'My sister doesn't celebrate Christmas, if you must know.'

'Oh.' June met her glare with a clear gaze. 'Well, I hope you left your sister a little better than you found her,' she said finally. 'If that will be all, Matron, I'll take the tray back to the kitchen.'

But Matron was already diving into her desk drawer for her cigarettes.

Chapter Fourteen

Murray lit a cigarette and leaned back in his chair in the dispersal hut. It didn't seem possible that the day after tomorrow was Christmas Eve. Dawn hadn't even broken and the dozen or so pilots were mostly dozing or reading the newspaper. They looked relaxed but he knew for himself the tension was constantly running under their skins. The instant the signal came for the next scramble they would spring up and hurl themselves towards the aircraft no matter what time of day or night.

His mind dwelled on his last sortie. He'd nearly had it with a Messerschmitt. The Hun were flying much lower these days to target the docks, seeming prepared to risk getting a wing sliced off in the cables of the barrage balloons. He swallowed hard, reliving the nightmare. He'd been in his beloved Spit and had only looked up and seen him in the last fraction of a second, already bearing down on him and firing. With the aid of another Spit they'd managed to chase him, but it had been a bloody close call.

His fellow pilots had asked him to join them for a drink in the bar, to celebrate not losing a single aeroplane this time, but he hadn't felt like it, though he should at least have bought a beer for the chap in the other Spitfire. Murray closed his eyes for a few seconds. Pilots always said they were simply doing their job and became embarrassed if you thanked them. But what about the next mission? And the one after? He shook himself. Mustn't get into that train of thought.

Johnnie, in the chair beside him, crackled his newspaper shut, closed his eyes and breathed a long sigh of exhaustion. Murray knew exactly how he felt. They were all exhausted. But you had to keep going no matter how little sleep you'd had.

He stole a glance at Johnnie. Such a decent bloke. They'd become good pals. His wife had just delivered their first child – a girl – and Johnnie was desperate to be given some leave to see them. What a world to bring a baby into.

His thoughts turned to June as they did constantly these days. He felt sorry for her having to work for that dreadful Pherson woman – she was completely the wrong person in every sense to run an orphanage. Opinionated and obviously had no compassion for the children. And what a bully, the rude way she spoke to June. How did Junie put up with it? But he knew why. She genuinely loved the children – he could tell that a mile off.

His thoughts turned to Helen, so different from June. She'd shocked him with her declaration in the summer that she never wanted children. It would ruin her figure, she'd told him, and they would be a tie, with her trying to juggle a career on the stage that she'd worked so hard for. He hadn't blamed her one bit, but it didn't fit in with his dream of a family. They'd parted with only a few tears from Helen, and even those, he'd suspected, were an act. He was sure she'd been as relieved as he.

But June was different.

He wondered what she'd think when she opened the little

package he'd tucked into her pocket when Matron wasn't looking. He smiled. He'd bought the sweetheart brooch on a whim, knowing it was too early to tell her . . . His heart warmed with the image of her, a baby in her arms . . . stop . . . he mustn't . . . but with that image in his mind, he fell asleep.

Murray jerked awake at the sound of the telephone ringing. Didn't matter how many times he heard it, he always jumped. As he was the nearest he grabbed the receiver to hear the voice of an orderly shouting in his ear.

'Scramble – base – angels – twelve!'

As one, his fellow pilots, familiar as brothers, surged towards the door, strapping on their parachutes and Mae Wests, cursing and shouting, only seconds behind Murray, who was racing towards his Spitfire, the engine already firing.

Freddie had kept June awake on his first night with his squeaking, and every so often rustling the newspaper in his box, and tonight was no exception. Somehow he'd managed to claw his way on to her bed and begun to lick her forehead with his tiny pink tongue.

'Oh, don't, Freddie, that tickles,' she'd said, but he'd taken no notice and licked her cheek. She couldn't help smiling. Christmas time was for the animals too, after all. She pulled the blanket closer around her. After a few minutes Freddie settled further down the bed, and it was warm and comforting to feel his small silky body tucked into the crook of her elbow, remembering how Murray had hidden him underneath his huge coat. How thoughtful he'd been to bring little Freddie to help Lizzie. And how wonderful that he loved animals. A fuzzy feeling nestled around her heart as she gently stroked the puppy and whispered to him that he was a good boy. Finally, she put her frozen arm underneath the blanket as he dropped off to sleep.

As soon as June awoke from a final disrupted sleep Freddie climbed down from the bed and began to whine. He was obviously asking for his breakfast. She'd have to creep downstairs before anyone was up and get him some scraps from the kitchen. She glanced at the clock. Quarter-past five. She'd beat Bertie if she was quick.

'Keep quiet, Freddie,' she whispered. He wagged his tail, the length and breadth of a large garden worm. 'I'll be back in a jiffy with something for you to eat.'

She wrapped his droppings in newspaper and ran downstairs to the kitchen where she stopped short. Ellen, one of the kitchen maids, was already at work scrubbing boards for the vegetables to be chopped for today's dinner. The girl threw her a suspicious look.

June glanced round. 'Where's Bertie?'

'She don't come down till six at the earliest – just when we've prepared for her and she's ready for a nice cup of tea.' Ellen regarded June with interest. 'You seem at a loss, Miss . . .' She broke off, still watching her. 'Is there anything I can do?'

June hesitated. Could she trust the maid? If she took her into her confidence and Ellen went running to Matron . . . Ellen's blank stare met hers. Iris had told her nothing about Ellen but there was something about her . . . She daren't risk it. Lizzie hadn't even set eyes on Freddie. She had to give it a chance.

'No, no, thank you, Ellen. I was thirsty, that's all. I thought I'd make myself a cup of tea and wouldn't disturb anyone.'

'Be my guest,' Ellen said, propping the clean boards by the sink. 'You know where everything is. I'll take my cuppa into the playroom where I can have a few minutes' peace.' She threw a glance at June. 'I'll leave you to it, then.'

June couldn't have asked for anything better. As soon as Ellen's back was turned she rushed to the pantry. There was a bowl with a plate over the top. She lifted the plate, careful not to make a noise, and there were the insides of several chickens. Livers and kidneys and hearts. Just the thing. Except everything was raw. Well, Freddie would have to get used to everything she gave him. She certainly couldn't stop and boil up his breakfast. Stomach heaving, she put a tablespoon of offal onto a plate, grabbed a knife from the kitchen table drawer and a small chopping board and practically ran out of the door, hoping against hope that Ellen wouldn't suddenly decide to come back to the kitchen.

But there was no sound at all except for June's harsh breaths as she raced up the stairs with the plate of raw meat. She was greeted by a very excited puppy.

'All right, Freddie. Keep quiet,' she whispered. Freddie let out some excited squeaks. June chopped the pieces finely, feeling ill at the raw meat smell every time she made a new cut, only glad she hadn't scooped up a heart. She took a saucer from under the plant on the windowsill, making a mental note to bring up another one from the kitchen. For the time being this would have to do. She set the saucer on the floor. 'Breakfast, Freddie.'

He eyed it with scepticism for about two seconds and dived in. Two minutes later there wasn't a scrap left. She filled the saucer with some water from her jug on the wash-stand and he lapped up every drop, then raised up on his hind legs and promptly fell backwards. Surprised, he shook himself. June picked him up and nestled him against her. How was she going to stop him from whining when she was gone? What could she give him to play with? Her room contained nothing that would interest a puppy. She'd just have to rush up and see him for a few minutes every couple of hours. And one of those times she'd take Lizzie.

It was Christmas Eve. At morning Assembly, which usually took place in the chapel, Matron made an announcement from the lectern.

'We have a new boy coming to the home today. His name is' – she glanced down at a sheet of paper in her hand – 'J-o-a-c-h-i-m Woolfes.' She raised her eyes and gave a small grimace. 'I'm not sure how to pronounce it. Anyway, we're taking him in until we can find suitable foster parents. He's a German Jew.'

She gave a slight emphasis to the last word and June caught Iris's eye. Iris raised her eyes to the ceiling, then shook her head in warning.

There was an intake of breath in the chapel. The teachers all looked at one another, Miss Ayles shaking her head, and Barbara Steen raising her eyebrows. The children were muttering his name, getting it completely wrong, and poking one another.

'German! The Germans are trying to kill us! They want us all dead.' Thomas's voice was loud with accusation. 'He's an enemy.'

Immediately Betsy began to cry.

'Stop shouting immediately, Mason!' Matron glared over the top of her spectacles at Thomas who looked sulky.

Matron had told Thomas to stop shouting, but not reprimanded him for calling Joachim an enemy, June thought in surprise. She would have a word with the boy herself at the first opportunity.

'How old is he?' another boy called out.

'About the same as you, Barrow. Well, it's Christmas Day tomorrow and we will all do our best to make him welcome.'

Matron stated the last part with one of her quick smiles that never reached her eyes.

If it hadn't been so awful, it would have been comic, June thought.

'Where's his ma and pa?' Bobby asked.

'No more questions,' Matron snapped. 'He'll be here after dinner.'

But less than an hour later a motor car pulled up outside the entrance. One of the maids unbolted the door and a young man limped into the hall. Another war victim, June thought sadly. Then a boy of about nine or ten trailed after him, carrying a cardboard case and, slung over one shoulder, a box containing his gas mask.

'I've brought Joachim Woolfes,' the young man said, as he limped further into the room, edging the boy forward. 'I'm Mr Clarke's assistant at Dr Barnardo's – Dennis Fuller.' He smiled at the silent group. 'Is Matron here?'

June noticed Joachim's eyes were red and puffy as though he'd been crying since he first woke up this morning. He probably had, she thought bitterly, her heart going out to the boy, whose eyes darted to and fro, trying to take everything in. She glanced around. Both teachers and children had congregated as soon as they'd heard the motorcar crunching to a halt on the gravel drive, and June was just about to fetch Matron when she clattered across the hall.

'Ah, there you are. We didn't expect you this early.' Matron glowered at Mr Fuller whose smile instantly faded. 'Have you brought the boy's papers?'

Dennis Fuller handed her a file. 'I think you'll find everything there,' he said. 'We don't have an awful lot of information, owing to the circumstances.' He lowered his voice on the last few words.

Matron sniffed. 'Thank you.' She paused, then said in a

different tone, 'Will you be wanting anything to eat . . . or a cup of tea?'

'No, no. I'd better get moving. If I hurry I can catch the next train back to London.' He turned to Joachim. 'Be a good chap and remember what I told you.'

'And what would that be?' Matron demanded.

'We were just having a chat on the way here,' Dennis Fuller said, his smile returning. 'I'll be off then.' He nodded and disappeared.

'A German,' Miss Ayles hissed under her breath. 'In our lovely home.'

June would have to take the situation into her own hands. She frowned at Miss Ayles and went up to the child.

'Hello, Joachim. Is that how you pronounce your name?' The boy shook his head vehemently.

'Can you tell me the right way?' She tried to smile her encouragement.

Joachim remained silent although he kept sliding his boot back and forth on the polished floor.

'Matron said you were coming to stay with us for a while. You've had a long journey, haven't you?'

There was no response at all. Just a flicker of suspicion from the dark eyes.

'You've got a funny name,' Thomas said, going up to him and looking at him closely. 'I hope we bombed your house down. Then you know how *we* feel.'

'That's enough, Thomas,' June cut in, her voice sharp. She took hold of Joachim's hand but he immediately snatched it away and looked straight ahead. 'I'm sure you're hungry, aren't you, if you've been travelling a long way?'

Silence.

'Cat got your tongue?' Jack taunted. 'Don't say we've got another kid here who don't speak.'

June looked over her shoulder swiftly although she knew Lizzie was in the kitchen with Bertie and wouldn't have heard Jack's remark.

'That's unkind, Jack, and it's not "don't speak", it's "*doesn't* speak".' June turned to Joachim again. 'Would you like to come with me? I'll ask Cook if you can have a glass of milk and a piece of her cake.'

There was still no response. Suddenly June had a thought. 'Joachim, do you speak English?'

The boy nodded.

'Right.' Matron's expression was grim. 'If that's the case, all of you in class now. The new boy will be known as "Woolfes". I'm sure that won't present any problem.' She gazed at Joachim. 'We must decide what to do with you.'

As though he were a parcel. June pressed her lips together in anger as Matron stepped forward and put a hand on his arm. A moment later he disengaged himself.

There was more chattering and Matron raised her hand and clipped one of the boys nearest to her over the ear.

'He needs a drink and something to eat first.' June swung round to Matron, daring her to argue, but her heart beating fast since she was taking command without being asked. 'Come with me, Joachim,' she said, ignoring Matron's icy glare because she was taking no notice of her instruction to call the boy by his surname. 'I'll take you to the kitchen to meet Cook,' she told him. 'She's bound to have done some baking this morning.'

She tried to take the boy's hand again, but once more Joachim snatched it away. With an about-face, his cheeks red with fury, he pointed to himself and shouted to Matron, 'Not "*Woo*". It's "*Voo*". *Voolfes. Voolfes!*'

June bit back a smile. Joachim certainly wasn't frightened

154

of authority, though he'd need careful handling. She was gratified to see Matron's face colour.

Several boys giggled.

'*Woolfes, Woolfes*,' they chanted, and with the mispronunciation of his name ringing in June's ears, she grabbed Joachim's hand firmly this time and marched him towards the kitchen.

Even under Matron's scrutiny the children seemed more carefree than June had seen them before. As it was Christmas Eve there were no classes and they made up games. The girls finished decorating the tree, although the boys insisted on showing them where to place each bauble. June was glad to see the twins sticking up for themselves and taking no notice.

'Where's Lizzie?' Suddenly June felt panicky. She realised she hadn't seen the child for the last half-hour.

'Miss Graham's taken her to the toilet. She's wet herself again,' Megan called out.

Poor little thing. She could almost understand why Matron insisted upon keeping Lizzie separate from the others. It would be so embarrassing for the little girl if she wet her knickers in front of them. They'd never stop jeering.

At that moment Lizzie appeared with the English teacher.

'Can you keep an eye on her for a little while?' Athena asked June as she caught sight of her. 'I've caught my stocking on a rough piece of door frame and I want to darn it before it gets worse.'

'Of course,' June said, smiling. 'Come on, Lizzie. I want to show you something.' She took the child's hand and the two of them trotted up the four flights of stairs. She could hear Freddie scuffling around in her room and Lizzie looked up at her questioningly. But she kept her little rosebud mouth closed and June cautiously opened the door. Immediately, a small brown bundle shot by her feet. Lizzie let go of June's hand.

'Freddie. Come back!' June hissed.

For two seconds Freddie stopped and looked round, then shot off.

'Doggie.'

'Yes, a little doggie,' June said automatically. 'We must go and rescue him.' She glanced down at Lizzie's face, full of wonder and delight. It wasn't until that moment she realised Lizzie had spoken again.

June managed to scoop Freddie up before he'd got to the first landing. She ran back up the stairs, Freddie in her arms with his tongue hanging out as though he was laughing at the trick he'd played. Lizzie stood at the bedroom door, her eyes brilliant with excitement.

'Naughty Freddie,' June admonished as she set him down.

Freddie immediately went to Lizzie and sniffed her ankles. Lizzie sat down on her bottom and patted him. He looked up at her and gave a little whine.

'He's saying he's pleased to meet you,' June said, smiling at the child. 'Can you tell him your name? You know he's Freddie and he wants you to tell him yours.'

'My. Name. Is. Lizzie,' piped the little girl leaving a space between each word. June wanted to pinch herself with delight. To shout to everyone that Lizzie was talking again. But she couldn't say a word because that would mean Matron would find out about Freddie and he'd have to go.

'Lizzie, can you keep a secret?'

Lizzie stared.

'We mustn't tell anyone about Freddie just yet because we might not be able to keep him here. We have to hide him for the time being. Until he gets a bit bigger. Can you do that for me?'

Lizzie nodded, her little face serious. She bent over to stroke Freddie who was looking up at her with adoration, his tail wagging like mad.

'Can I see him tomorrow when it's Christmas?'

June could have wept with joy. Lizzie had said a whole sentence with no hesitation between the words. Maybe Lizzie would carry on talking naturally this time. She smiled at the little girl who was waiting for her answer.

'Yes, of course you can, darling. But we must leave him now or else everyone will wonder where we are.' June bent down and put her arms underneath Lizzie's and picked her up. Lizzie nuzzled in the crook of her shoulder and June sat on the bed with her.

'Want my mummy.'

June blinked back the tears. 'Mummy's gone to heaven with Daddy and your brother.' She'd forgotten his name and hoped Lizzie wouldn't realise. 'They want you to stay here with us and all the other children. Do you think you can do that?'

Lizzie nodded very slowly, her bottom lip trembling.

'And now you have seeing Freddie to look forward to. He'll be really pleased to see you too. We'll have to think of some games.'

Lizzie struggled to get down. Immediately Freddie snuffled into her arms.

'Be a good doggie,' she whispered in the little animal's pointed ear. 'Lizzie come back tomorrow.'

Chapter Fifteen

There was great excitement at Bingham Hall doing the last-minute Christmas preparations. Bertie had got extra help from two girls from the village and had made a special supper that evening. Joachim was very quiet after his outburst about how to pronounce his name. He watched everyone with a slight curl to his lip, although he followed June wherever she went. She felt desperately sorry for him. In the library she'd picked up a book about how people in other countries celebrated Christmas and found that in Germany Christmas Eve was more important than Christmas Day itself.

Poor little chap, she thought, wondering how he came to be at the home. Matron obviously hadn't wanted to go into too much detail in front of the other children, who regarded any Germans as the enemy. Even the older children couldn't be expected to understand that German Jews were plainly victims of Hitler's terrifying regime. June dreaded to think what had happened to his parents. He was going to feel terribly alone and different. Really it was more than any child should have to bear.

That evening in the library, which was decorated with the paper chains the children had made, she sat Joachim near her and Lizzie while everyone sang carols around the giant Christmas tree, lit with candles and coloured balls, with the Star of Bethlehem at the top. When they ended with 'Silent Night' June gave Joachim a sidelong glance. She could tell by the way he'd closed his eyes and was very gently swaying the top part of his body that he was engrossed. Then to her amazement she heard him hum the tune. She hardly dared breathe in case she disturbed him but he went right through the next verse, quietly humming. She suddenly remembered how both the British and the German soldiers sang carols from the trenches on Christmas Eve in the last world war. Maybe 'Silent Night' was one of them. She wanted to give Joachim's hand a squeeze but didn't dare spoil the moment. The children finished the carol but to her astonishment Joachim began to sing, quietly at first in German, and then with more confidence. His voice was as pure as any choirboy's. It was the first time June had ever heard the language and to her surprise she found it quite beautiful.

'Stille Nacht, heilige Nacht . . .'

And when Joachim's angelic voice rose on the last notes a shiver traced along her spine.

There was a deathly hush. All the children's heads were turned towards him, awestruck, but his eyes were still half closed when he'd finished.

June began to clap and some of the children joined in, and then the staff. All except Matron, who was watching him with a curious expression, as though she was astonished this foreign boy could make such a beautiful sound. Joachim opened his eyes and looked around as though he wasn't aware the clapping was for him.

'You sounded just like a choirboy,' June told him, but he only stared at her. 'It was wonderful,' she tried again, smiling encouragingly, but it made no difference except that he merely shrugged and his face closed up again.

'Come on, it's time for you younger ones to go to bed,' Kathleen broke in, 'so you're asleep when Father Christmas comes. Come on, children. I'll help you get ready.'

There were a few weak protests but June could tell by the way they were yawning that they were tired out. Even the older children began to half close their eyes, so it was only twenty minutes later that Iris rounded up all of them. June gave Joachim a gentle push.

'Iris will give you a stocking ready for Father Christmas,' she told him with a smile.

'We do not celebrate Christmas.'

She took a step back at the contempt in Joachim's tone.

'Oh.' Now was not the time to find out what his people celebrated instead, but she would ask him when the time was right. 'Why don't you think of it as a holiday and join in?'

He nodded. That was good enough, June thought tiredly.

After the children had made sure their stockings were easily spotted at the end of their beds ready for Father Christmas to find them, and had settled down for the night, Iris, Kathleen and June tiptoed through the rooms filling each of them with an orange, an apple, a little bag of nuts, and some crayons or other small gift. They placed a toy, which had been donated by the kind villagers, at the foot of each bed.

'Ouch!' Kathleen banged her shin on one of the iron bed railings in the girls' dormitory.

'Shhhh!' Iris pressed her finger to her lips. 'Don't wake them,' she whispered. 'We mustn't let anyone see what we're doing. Look at Lizzie with her thumb in her mouth – sound asleep. They're so excited about Father Christmas coming down the chimney.'

'Bertie's left mince pies and a cup of cocoa for him,' June whispered back.

'Bet Harold would rather have a beer,' said Iris, chuckling softly.

'Why, is he going to be Father Christmas?' June asked, smiling at the image.

'Ooh, I couldn't possibly say.' Iris sent her a wicked grin.

They put their hands to their mouths to supress their giggles. Pamela stirred and turned over. They waited until she began to breathe rhythmically again, and then they swiftly filled the last of the stockings and left the room, closing the door quietly behind them, ready to go on to the boys' dormitory.

It was hard to contain the children in the morning. A few of them had woken up as early as five o'clock and were tearing open their stockings and presents, mostly calling out with delight, though there were some moans of disappointment.

'I wanted a dolly,' Betsy grizzled. 'I haven't got a dolly and I asked Father Christmas to bring me one.' She thrust out a rag clown to June and burst into tears.

'Let's see if we can swap him with one of the other presents,' June said, as she helped her get dressed.

'I don't like the clown,' Betsy sobbed. 'He's got a horrid mouth. I hate him.'

'We'll get him changed after breakfast,' June soothed, running her fingers through the child's black curls.

The maids had decorated the breakfast table with coloured streamers and paper bells, and there was a balloon by the side of each child's plate.

'Not to be blown up at the table,' Matron said firmly. 'There are no classes today so you can play with them in the playroom. Anyone who wants to paint pictures can go to the art classroom and Miss Steen will be there to help you.' She swivelled her head around all the tables with her usual fierce expression.

She can't even smile at the children on Christmas Day, June thought sadly.

'Off you go then!' Matron waved her arm towards the door. 'And make sure you make your beds and tidy round your space first before any games.'

The children didn't need to be told twice. With a cacophony of scraping chairs and scuffles they raced out of the dining room and took the stairs two at a time.

June did her best to make it a happy day for the children. Harold looked the part in his Father Christmas suit and outstanding curly white beard, although Lizzie kept clear of him and spent most of the day curled in her corner of the kitchen with Bertie. June gave Joachim more attention than the others, trying hard to get him to join in the games. She saw Matron frown in her direction several times but took no notice. Thomas muttered loudly enough for Joachim to hear that German was a stupid language, and received a severe telling-off from Alan to stop being so nasty, but other than that, the children ran off to play and left Joachim to fend for himself.

June took him to the art classroom. It seemed the safest place and she thought he might enjoy doing some painting. She noticed his face brighten at seeing the pictures the children had recently painted stuck on the walls with drawing pins. The twins came in with Lizzie trailing behind, followed by Barbara.

'You can leave me with them, June,' she said, smiling at

the children. 'I'll set them some work and you can come back later and see how they're getting on. I know you worry about certain ones,' she added in a low tone.

June smiled back with relief. She wanted to have a quiet few minutes in her room after supper, just to gather her thoughts. Think about Clara. Open the card and present she'd had from Stella, and her cards from Iris and Kathleen and Athena. She wondered how Murray was spending Christmas and hoped they'd been given the day to rest.

As she got to her bedroom door she saw an envelope sticking out at the bottom. Someone had pushed it in while she'd been at supper. Another Christmas card, she suspected, from one of the staff. She felt a little guilty. She'd only bought cards for Iris and Kathleen, and signed a card to Matron from everyone. She'd have liked to have bought one for Murray but hadn't known exactly where to send it, and anyway he'd probably think her forward. He hadn't sent her one, after all.

June opened her door and picked up the envelope. Freddie rushed to her, wagging his tail and giving little barks of delight.

'Shhhh, Freddie. Someone will hear you.' She sat on the chair and Freddie jumped on to her lap, trembling with joy that she was here. She noticed he'd chewed the corner of the envelope but had obviously given up. He licked her all over her face and whined. She'd have to feed him or she'd never be able to read her letter in peace. She nipped down to the kitchen and once Freddie was wolfing down his evening meal she opened the envelope.

The writing was unfamiliar. Inside the envelope was one sheet of notepaper. Her heart leaped as she read the name 'Junie'.

Dear Junie,

I'm sorry I've not been out to buy you a Christmas card so I'm afraid this note will have to be in place of one. One of the chaps offered to bring it over as I can't get away, and I've entrusted him to give it to you or one of the staff <u>but NOT Matron,</u> so I hope you receive it.

It doesn't feel like Christmas to me but we're all keeping cheerful. At least we're not going skywards today or tomorrow.

How is Freddie getting along? Has Matron discovered him yet?

I hope it's not long before I see you again.

Yours,

Murray

PS I hope you liked the little gift.

With a start she realised she'd forgotten all about it. What with attending to Joachim and Freddie and then hearing the shouts and screams from the children extra early this morning, it had gone right out of her mind. She patted her overall pocket, relieved the little packet was still there, pulled it out and unfolded the holly-printed paper. Something small and lumpy, wrapped in cotton wool. Carefully she lifted the top layer and gave a gasp of delight. It was a silver brooch, a miniature copy of an RAF pilot's wings.

She picked it up and laid it in the palm of her hand. It took on the warmth of her skin and winked up at her. It was beautiful and instantly it became precious in her eyes. He must like her a lot to give her something so lovely, so . . . well, special, knowing how much flying meant to him. The brooch and the sentiment behind it struck her as somehow intimate. She flushed at the word, remembering the feel of his lips touching hers, so briefly yet so unforgettably. If only he could have been here when she opened it. Maybe he would have told her what it meant for him to give her such a gift. And she could have told him what it meant to receive it.

She bent her head and gave the brooch a kiss before she wrapped it back in its cotton wool and holly paper and tucked it into her drawer. It would never do to wear it in the home. Matron made a point of no jewellery, but she would pin it on her jacket the very next time she saw Murray. She only hoped she wouldn't have too long to wait.

Until then she wouldn't tell anyone – not even Iris.

Chapter Sixteen

Joachim's angelic rendering of 'Silent Night' was deceptive. After only a few days he quickly became one of the ringleaders in drawing the other children into mischief. He didn't need to speak much English. He just did exactly what he wanted and the others followed. It took all June's patience to deal with him. At first she tried reasoning but he fought back. She knew this was partly bravado but she had to take action. He was disruptive at mealtimes, refusing to eat the food put in front of him, once actually spitting it back onto the tin plate, to the other children's delight. They copied him and it was lucky that Matron wasn't there on that occasion as June could see him being punished.

This suppertime he seemed more difficult than ever.

'I don't like it,' he said.

'It's lovely. Don't you have it in Germany?'

Joachim just stared at her under long dark lashes.

'Bring your plate and come and sit by me,' June said, but he didn't budge.

'What's the trouble?' came a strident cold voice.

June's stomach sank. Matron. Normally she ate at a separate table, occasionally with Miss Ayles, whom she considered intelligent enough to confer with, but here she was, standing over June's shoulder.

June looked up into the glare of Matron's cool grey eyes.

'It's all right, Matron – just that Joachim has never had junket. I was just explaining what it was.'

'Hmm.' Matron pressed her lips together. 'Woolfes is a bad influence.' She didn't say it quietly, and the children nearest to June who were old enough to understand began to snigger.

June shook her head at them and put her finger to her lips. She waited for Matron's next move, praying that Joachim would start eating the junket, but when she glanced over she noticed he'd put his spoon down and was looking at the white pudding in disgust. She couldn't help feeling sympathetic towards him. She didn't like it much herself, and she remembered when Clara had refused to eat it. Her mother had told her it was good for her and she would have to stay there until she ate it.

'I'll be sick if I eat it,' Clara had said, tears welling in her eyes.

'Well, you'll have to be sick, but first you are going to eat it.' Her mother placed the spoon in Clara's hand again.

Clara had sat for an hour without touching it, but when she saw her mother meant business she ate the junket in rapid swallows. A minute later it had all come up again, all over the tablecloth. Wordlessly her mother gathered the material and put it in the scullery to deal with later. She never again forced any of her children to eat something they plainly didn't like.

June squeezed her eyes tight at the memory, not just of the junket episode, but of when they were a complete family – without Dad, of course. He'd spend most of his spare time in the pub or at the greyhound stadium after he'd finished his milk round.

When June opened her eyes Matron was bending over Joachim's shoulders.

'Come on, boy, eat up. You're keeping everyone waiting.'

All eyes had turned to Matron. Joachim didn't bother to acknowledge her, and a stubborn expression crept over his dark features. Matron apparently decided to take matters into her own hands and grabbed his spoon, plunged it into the white pudding and attempted to push the heaped spoon into Joachim's mouth. He gave a shout and knocked the spoon out of Matron's hand, whereupon she clipped him over the ear. Howling in protest, Joachim shot to his feet and said something to her in German before he rushed out of the room.

After supper, and still upset with Matron and even more with herself for not dealing with the situation quickly enough, June felt at her wits' end. Iris was too busy to talk to her as she and Kathleen were working solidly in the sick bay because of an outbreak of mumps, brought in by one of the village girls who occasionally helped out. Five children were already down with it and they'd had to call for the doctor before it became an epidemic.

June resolved to find out more about Joachim's background – and why it had been decided that he should be sent to Dr Barnardo's in Liverpool in the first place when it was likely he had family in Germany.

She thought she would see if Bertie could add anything about Joachim's past. She often knew snippets the others didn't. But Bertie shook her head.

'I did enquire but Matron changed the subject. I don't think she's too keen on having a German boy – Jewish or not.'

'So what do you think I should do, Bertie?'

Bertie put down her teacloth and thought for a few moments.

'I reckon you have to speak to the other children. Explain

to the older children how it's our responsibility to look after him. Keep him busy. And have Athena give him extra English lessons so he catches up with the others.'

June followed Bertie's advice, but it didn't make much difference. The more she tried to help Joachim, the more he played up, and sometimes her patience would wear thin. Every morning she would catch him looking out for the postman, but there was never a letter for him. He would walk away, his neck thrust forward, his shoulders slumped, and her heart would go out to him. She wondered again what had happened to his parents, and imagined they'd sent Joachim to England for safety – but had they escaped themselves?

It was New Year's Eve and not one of the staff stayed up to celebrate. Iris was all for it, but in the end even she was tired out.

'I must be getting old,' she told June, to her amusement. 'Twenty-five and still on the shelf.' She glanced at June. 'You know we were invited to a New Year's party by the RAF but the weather is so bad I can't be bothered to make the effort.'

'Not even for Paul?' June asked.

'Paul who?' Iris said with a laugh. 'Don't know who you're talking about.' She wrinkled her brow. 'Oh, *that* Paul. That cocky little squirt.' She laughed again. 'No, not interested.'

'And Chas?'

'I told you . . . he only has eyes for you.'

'But I don't think of him in that way at all,' June said.

'Yeah, it's Murray *you've* got your eye on, isn't it?'

'He's a lovely dancer,' June said, going a little pink. 'And he's a nice friend. But that's all.' She didn't add how disappointed she was not to have heard any word from him since the letter he'd sent at Christmas.

'I'll believe that when I see it,' Iris said, grinning.

Privately, June would quite like to have gone. It would certainly have been a reprieve from Joachim's playing up. But she wouldn't dream of going on her own. It was just that Murray might be there.

'I'm so sorry you haven't heard any news from your parents, Joachim,' June said when he mooched along the corridor on New Year's Day, the despair on his face set hard. 'I'm sure it won't be long before you hear something.'

He stared at her and for the first time she saw tears trickling down his face. Then he flung himself into her arms and sobbed.

'Dear child.' June held him close, stroking his head. 'Let's go somewhere quiet.'

She led him to the chapel and sat him down in one of the pews at the back. The bright morning sunshine streamed through the stained-glass windows but now was not the time to admire them. Joachim needed her attention. Thankfully it was a Thursday and there was no one in sight.

'Have you had bad news?' she asked him. Matron opened all the children's letters before handing them over, and if she disapproved of the contents she wouldn't give it to them. Something else June was determined to alter unless the contents were particularly sensitive.

'*Ich will meine Mutti.*' His blue eyes were wet with tears.

She guessed *Mutti* must mean 'mother'.

Joachim glanced up at her, chewing his lip. 'I want *Mutti und Vater und meine Schwester, Heidi.* Where did they go?'

'Oh, my love.' She leaned forward and rested her head on the back of the bench in front. 'Can you talk to me about them?'

He shook his head.

170

'What about Heidi? Is she older or younger than you?'

'She is eight.'

'What does she like to do?' Now June had got him to start talking she didn't want him to clam up again.

'She is clever. She likes mathematics. And music. Sometimes we do music together.'

'That's wonderful, Joachim.' June imagined the two children singing together and maybe the mother playing the piano, accompanying them. She needed to say the right thing to him now he'd calmed down a little.

'You believe in God, don't you?'

Joachim nodded.

'Then God will keep your mother and father and sister safe – I am sure of it.'

All of a sudden the boy's eyes filled with hope. June gave him a handkerchief and he blew his nose.

'Are you ready to go back?'

The boy nodded. '*Ja* . . . yes, I will go. She took his hand and this time he gripped it as they walked back to the main part of the house.

'Which class are you supposed to be in?' June asked him.

'Geography.'

'Then that will be in Room 3. So off you go. Learn all you can. Do what Miss Ayles tells you. And Joachim . . .?'

'Yes, Miss?'

'Your English is improving every day. Try to talk to the other children. Don't wait for them to talk to you. And only speak in English. It's important while you're in England. Do you understand what I'm saying?'

He turned to June and looked up at her. 'Yes, Miss.'

'And do you promise to do as I ask?'

He hesitated, then to her relief he said, 'I will try.'

Chapter Seventeen

January 1942

June had just returned from feeding Freddie, whose new home was in the stable block. The children were drinking their eleven o'clock milk, when she heard what sounded like thunder.

In a flash of horror she realised it was a bombing raid in Liverpool. But this one sounded louder than usual. Her heart beat hard. They should vacate the house – just in case it came closer.

At that moment Matron appeared at the dining room door.

'To the shelters,' Matron shouted. 'NOW!' She was flinging on her coat and, to June's horror, diving for the front door.

How can she be saving her own skin when the children were still in the building? June shook her head in disgust.

Other members of staff picked up the younger children. Alan shot by, Lizzie in one hand and the twins, Jimmy and Norman, hand in hand, in the other.

'I'll take Lizzie,' June said, rushing over, 'so you can hold on to the twins.'

Seeing their chance, Jimmy and Norman pulled away from Alan and raced along with their arms flapping up and down making aeroplane noises. June hushed them but they took no notice. Then to her amazement Joachim appeared, the only child with his satchel on his back, and grabbed hold of them, admonishing them sternly in German. It took them completely by surprise and they simmered down immediately. June, clutching a white-faced Lizzie, cast her eye over the last of the children.

'I'm scared,' Betsy wailed.

'Hold on to me,' June said, offering her other hand. 'We've got to run to the shelter.'

Everyone rushed to the door and dashed across the lawn at the rear to the two shelters, where they scrambled down the steps. Matron was already there, busying herself putting folding chairs up for the teachers and laying out blankets.

All very well, June thought grimly, but not much good if there were no children to lie on them.

More heads appeared and soon June's shelter was full. She was relieved to see Harold helping some of the smaller children, and only hoped everyone else was safely in the second shelter. She took a deep breath to calm herself and wished she hadn't. There was an overriding smell of stale sweat which seemed to be coming from Gilbert's direction. She tried not to think about it as she and Kathleen and Harold managed to get the children occupied with singing songs and the older ones to tell stories, but there was little for them to sit on, only the few blankets and a couple of groundsheets and some cushions – not nearly enough to go round.

'Have you ever had to come down here before?' June asked Kathleen nervously.

'We used to practise once a week, but nothing happened for months and we stopped doing it. We didn't know it, of course, but that was the Phoney War. After that we only practised occasionally because the bombs fell directly on

Liverpool and the docks. We always felt safe this far away from the city.' Kathleen's voice shook as she looked around the shelter. 'But it sounded nearer this time.'

Matron was still busy doing little. June caught her frowning at Gilbert, who'd taken one of the chairs and was watching the goings-on in the shelter with a sharp, malevolent eye.

'You can hardly count on those two for all the help they've been,' Kathleen added, lowering her voice. 'We could do with a couple of the teachers in *this* shelter instead of Gilbert, who's no use whatsoever.'

'Do you think they'll bomb us?' Hilda whispered, her face paler than usual.

'If they do try we're safe in here,' June said to the trembling girl, hoping it was true. 'Why don't you help Kathleen? It will take your mind off it.'

She'd barely uttered the words when there was a series of explosions above their heads and the noise of shattering glass, so loud she instinctively put her hands to her ears, then took them away quickly before anyone noticed. A child screamed for her mother and she rushed over to see Beth sobbing her heart out and clutching onto her brother, Lenny.

'You're safe with us,' June soothed as she picked up the little girl and sat down on one of the chairs, drawing her onto her lap. 'Don't cry.'

'She's still a baby,' Lenny said, but his words were drowned in another explosion.

June felt her flimsy chair shudder with the vibration. She heard Gilbert curse.

'Mother of Mercy . . .' Matron said, her hands folded together as if in prayer.

Dust fell like a shower on them. The children started choking and coughing, and several began to cry. When the children had finally quietened down and Lenny had reclaimed his sister, Lizzie sidled up to June to be cuddled. Eventually the little girl's breathing was rhythmic, her fingers firmly in her mouth. Kathleen who was sitting nearby handed around a bottle of water.

'Just take a few sips,' she told Alan, 'and pass it to the child next to you.' She turned towards June. 'We haven't got much in the way of provisions, and this could go on for who knows how long. There ought to be some food down here. And more water and drinks. But there's hardly anything. A tin of broken biscuits and some bottles of orange juice. Not much of a survival kit.'

'It's better than nothing,' Matron snapped, suddenly towering over the two young women and seeming to take control again. 'I want everyone to get in a line so I can do a count. Children first.' She took a piece of paper and handed it to June. 'Write their names down when you've seen them with your own eyes,' she added craftily.

So I take all the responsibility, June thought, now thoroughly annoyed.

'I'm hungry,' called out one of the boys.

'So'm I.'

A burst of chatter followed, but it was soon broken by a sharp voice.

'FIRE!'

It was Hilda screaming out. Everyone leaped up, and Lizzie awoke, her eyes wide with fear. She clung on to June and began to sob, the exertion racking her little body. June could smell burning.

Children were grabbing one another, ready to make a beeline for the steps, but Harold caught hold of two of them. 'Get back inside! All of you. There's no fire.' He caught June's eye and jerked his head towards Matron.

June turned and was quick enough to see Matron stub out a cigarette on the wall, leaving a trail of smoke. June and Kathleen looked at one another and Kathleen lifted her eyes heavenwards.

Everyone huddled together. June's arms felt numb with the weight of holding Lizzie, and the younger children became more fractious by the minute, calling 'Miss' incessantly.

'I hope it's over,' Kathleen said, 'but I don't understand why they would bomb an orphanage. Why would they want to kill innocent children?'

'It's probably a lone plane,' Harold answered grimly. 'We wouldn't be a normal target out here in the country. I'm going to stick my head out and have a look.' He was back in a few moments. 'He must've been driven off by our boys and dropped the last of his bombs over us on his way back to Germany. I doubt if there'll be any more action today but maybe we should stay where we are for another half an hour or so to be on the safe side.'

But Matron, it seemed, wasn't going to have anyone else make such a decision.

'Back to the house all of you!' she ordered. 'And back to your classroom.' She glared over at June. 'Have you everyone's names, Miss Lavender?'

'Yes. I've got them all.'

'Good. I'll check that everyone else is present in the other shelter.' Matron pulled herself up the steps to survey the scene. 'Here they come.'

There was plenty of shouting and talking from the second shelter, and June watched as each new head appeared. Even though Matron was counting them June kept her eye out for the rest of the children. The children were shouting and pushing one another. Now it was over they could show their bravery, though one of them was crying. Joachim.

'Come on, snap to it,' Miss Ayles admonished him. 'We've got no time for dawdling – and definitely no time for tears.'

'All of you back to the house and line up in the Great Hall,' Matron barked. She gazed long and hard at June, her lips hardening. 'And stop being soft with Woolfes, Miss Lavender. You'll make him lily-livered.' She turned and marched off.

June shook her head as she stared after her. Matron really didn't have any idea. Neither had Miss Ayles, come to that. She hurried over to her and Joachim, who was sniffing and wiping his eyes with the back of his hand.

'What's the matter with him?' she asked the teacher under her breath.

'He says one of the children has stolen his satchel but I doubt if he took it into the shelter. None of the other children picked theirs up. It'd be the last thing they'd think of.' Miss Ayles sniffed her disapproval.

'Well, I can vouch for him that he definitely took the satchel into the shelter,' June said, 'because I noticed it on his back when he was running over.'

Joachim looked up at June with a beseeching expression.

'I keep telling everyone that. They don't believe me. And they don't believe anyone's stolen it.'

'Why would anyone want to steal your books and homework? They've got enough to do themselves without doing yours.' June was trying to make light of it but fresh tears poured down Joachim's cheeks.

'I hate this place! And everyone. They've taken my satchel. I want it back. It belongs to me.' He thumped his foot on the grass.

'I'm sure it's a mistake,' June said. 'Or one of the other grown-ups must have seen it and didn't know whose it was.' She gave his arm a quick squeeze, thankful Matron wasn't there to witness the gesture. 'Come on, Joachim, wipe your eyes. It'll be in the house.'

What on earth was going on? The boy was acting as though it was his most precious possession. All it would have in it would be a couple of schoolbooks and his exercise book and pen and pencil. It didn't make sense, the fuss he was making.

'Where've you two been?' Iris said, when they were inside. She looked at Joachim. 'You've been crying.'

'He's lost his satchel,' June said. 'He had it on his back and must have taken it off in the shelter' – she looked at Joachim, who nodded – 'and then after it was over and everyone left, he couldn't find it.'

'I expect one of the teachers picked it up,' Iris said. 'Why don't you join the other children in the dining room? Bertie's made some cake and there's tea and lemonade. By the time you've finished it will have turned up, I'm sure.'

'Where's Matron?' June asked when Joachim had disappeared.

'Checking the house to see if there's any damage.'

'I need to check on Freddie,' June said, guilty that she'd forgotten him since they'd been in the shelter. 'He'll have been terrified with all that noise.'

'Let's go and see him first and then take a look at the greenhouses. I bet they've taken a blow with all that shattering glass sound we heard.'

Inside the stable block it was black as a cave and smelled of ammonia and dusty straw, but even though there were no longer any horses, it was easy to imagine the warm smell of their flesh, and hear their breathy snorts of welcome.

'Freddie,' June called. 'Freddie!'

A small silky head pushed up from a pile of straw on the

back wall. Even in the gloom the puppy's brown eyes gleamed. The next instant he'd emerged, tail wagging, and trembling with excitement as he thrust his head into her hand and licked it.

'Freddie. Oh, Freddie.' June picked him up and hugged him. 'You must have wondered what on earth was happening. You can come with us and get some exercise. It's all over now.' She set him down and took his lead from a hook. 'Keep still, Freddie. Let me get your lead on. And don't bark. They still mustn't see you.'

The two young women hurried round the side of the house and through the kitchen garden gate to where the enormous Victorian greenhouses stood. Or at least they had that morning. June and Iris stared in dismay. One of the greenhouses was barely standing.

The door had been blown off and most of the window panes smashed. There was glass everywhere. Inside, slate worktops and pots of flowers and trays of vegetables now looked like heaps of rubbish.

'They'll be expensive to rebuild,' Iris said. 'Damned Jerry.' She grimaced. 'We'd better have a look at the cottages.'

They half ran along the drive to where the three terraced cottages stood, one of them being Matron's and the other two for Miss Ayles and Bertie. They were untouched. The two women, Freddie happily scampering along with them, rushed over to a small cottage a few hundred feet away belonging to the gardener and his wife. They pulled up sharply. The front of the cottage was half blown away.

'Oh, no.' Iris's face was white. 'We'd better try to find out if they're hurt.'

She gingerly stepped through the gaping hole and June watched her friend vanish into the swirling dust and debris.

'I'm not sure it's safe to go far in,' June called out, but

she followed her friend, her heart hammering with fear, and Freddie whining as he pulled on the end of his lead.

It was almost dark and she felt the dust would suffocate her. She put her hand up to her nose to try to keep the dust out, and heard Iris trip over something. Her friend swore. Moments later she heard Iris cry out – then silence.

'Iris. Are you all right?' June called. 'Where are you?'

'I'm here.' Iris stumbled back into the space which had once been the front room, 'but Mr and Mrs Sumner . . . oh, it's awful, Junie . . . they're still sitting at the dining table—' She broke off.

'Are they hurt?'

'They're both dead.'

June flew back to the house leaving Iris to stay with the couple – just in case. In case what? June thought. In case they suddenly came back to life? Oh, what a waste all this was. She'd only bumped into Mr Sumner a couple of times and they'd had a short conversation, mostly to do with Bingham Hall, and Mrs Sumner had had her and Iris and Kathleen for tea one afternoon. They seemed such a sweet couple. And now they were gone. It didn't seem possible, but June couldn't quell the guilty thought that she would rather it be them, who were older, than one of her precious charges. As though there'd been any choice.

Chapter Eighteen

'There's a Mr Clarke from Stepney Causeway to see you, Madam,' Ellen said as Matron marched past her on her way to the kitchen.

June, who was about to have her morning meeting with Matron, was intrigued to see Matron flush. She knew Stepney Causeway was Dr Barnardo's Head Office, where her letter had come from, offering her the appointment.

'Miss Lavender, would you show him into my office.' Matron ran her finger inside the neck of her dress and pulled the material away as if it was too tight, and stretched up her chin. 'Wait with him while I go over tomorrow's menus with Cook.' She turned her head. 'Ellen, make him a cup of tea. I'll be there shortly.'

'Very well, Madam.'

June led Mr Clarke into Matron's office. She looked at him curiously. He was a tall bony man of middle age wearing a heavy overcoat which he removed to reveal a faded pin-striped suit. He took off his hat and set his briefcase down on Matron's desk, then clicked open the two brass locks and pulled out a lined pad and pencil.

Matron would not be at all pleased to see her files, pens, ink bottles, blotting paper and the telephone on her desk being pushed to one side by some man's briefcase, but it wasn't

June's place to say anything. She bit back a smile, observing the way he kept shifting position and looking at his watch. Obviously, his time was precious and he was patently annoyed that Matron did not appear to be aware of it.

By the time Matron appeared, looking thoroughly flustered, Ellen had brought in three cups of tea. Mr Clarke stood up as soon as Matron appeared but she waved him back in his seat. June was not sure whether she should stay or go and rose to her feet, not wanting to embarrass anyone.

'Yes, you may go, Miss Lavender. Take your tea. I'll see Mr Clarke on my own.'

'I'd like Miss Lavender to stay, if you please, Mrs Pherson,' Mr Clarke broke in. 'I've come in answer to your report on the recent bombing which we must discuss.' He nodded towards June. 'And Miss Lavender, being your assistant, should take full part in the discussion.'

Matron pursed her lips and gave June a curt nod.

'Your report was rather brief so I would like to know in more detail exactly what happened. I did notice the gardener's cottage as I came down the drive. Terrible business. When is Mr and Mrs Sumner's funeral?'

'Wednesday. In the village. Two o'clock.'

Mr Clarke adjusted his spectacles, which hung on the end of his nose even more precariously than Matron's on hers, and made a note. He nodded for Matron to continue.

'One of the bombs came very close to the house and destroyed one of the Victorian greenhouses, as I said in the report.' Matron shook her head, her mouth disappearing into a thin line. 'Most unfortunate. Thank goodness they didn't get my cottage.'

June looked at her in bewilderment. How could she make such a remark? As long as *she* was all right, that was all that mattered.

Mr Clarke frowned. 'I'll send someone to assess the damage of the gardener's cottage to see if it can be saved, and also we need another man for the head gardener's position.' His eyes fastened on Matron. 'Any damage to the main house?'

'Not really – a few cracked windows and some tiles off the roof. That's about it. I have someone coming next week to do the repairs.'

'Hmm. And where were the children when this happened?'

'Oh, down in the shelters, of course. I got them all safely away from the house and into the shelters. They have training every week so when it's a real emergency they know exactly what to do.'

June looked at her in amazement. Matron was taking all the credit for something she'd had no part in, and she'd stopped the training a year ago, so Iris had told her. Mr Clarke scribbled a few lines on his notepad.

'And then what happened?'

'We waited until Harold told us it must have been one of the last pilots escaping, so I decided it was safe for the children to return to their classes.'

'You didn't wait a bit to make sure? Hear the All Clear?'

'Being that far from Liverpool there was no way of knowing if the All Clear had gone.' Matron didn't hesitate. 'I used my common sense.'

'Hmm.' Mr Clarke looked directly at her. 'How many children have you at the moment?'

'Um . . .' Matron cleared her throat. 'I believe it's getting on for forty now.'

'It's actually forty-one with Joachim Woolfes,' June said, wondering if it was wise to correct Matron but feeling that she must.

Mr Clarke nodded. 'The German refugee was the last boy to join you, was he not?'

'Yes, that's right. It's been extremely difficult, I might say, to integrate a German boy with the other children. Most disturbing for them.'

'Is that right?' Mr Clarke's eyes narrowed as he turned his head to look at June.

'It was a little difficult at first because he didn't speak much English,' June admitted, aware of Matron's eyes like steel, boring into her. 'But he's turned out to be a decent lad when you think of what he's been through. The other children are getting used to him and Bobby at least apologised to him for taking his satchel – as a joke.'

Mr Clarke leaned forward in his chair. 'What do you mean?'

'It was just a childish prank,' June said. 'It's all blown over now. You know how children are when they're showing off.'

'This is another point I want to talk to you both about,' Mr Clarke said, looking over the top of his spectacles. 'It's come to my attention that someone here is calling the boy names – a "dirty Jew", to be precise.' Matron opened her mouth but Mr Clarke put the palm of his hand up in the space between them. 'No, let me finish, Mrs Pherson. I won't tolerate this kind of language. We pride ourselves at Dr Barnardo's that every child is equal no matter what his colour or his religion. Every child is to be protected in our homes, and is fed, watered, housed, and receives an education.' He voice rose with passion. 'And name-calling is not allowed under any circumstances by those in charge of the children – or indeed the children themselves.' He glared at Matron. 'But in this case it was one of the staff. What do you have to say on the matter, Mrs Pherson?'

June sat horrified. She stole a sideways look at Matron, whose face had turned to stone. There was a deathly silence only broken by Mr Clarke taking up his teaspoon and stirring his tea, which he'd already done. A few more seconds went by and June began to feel distinctly uncomfortable, as if he might be accusing either of them of saying something so awful.

'One of the staff?' Matron repeated his words, a flush creeping over her face. 'Are you absolutely certain?'

'Absolutely certain.'

'How do you know?'

'The boy wrote to Dennis Fuller, my assistant, who brought him here, if you remember. Apparently Mr Fuller, who is himself Jewish, was worried about the boy being a German Jew and told Joachim that if there was ever any problem that the matron couldn't sort out, he was to write to *him*.'

'But he didn't say who the person was?' Matron fidgeted with her hands while she waited for Mr Clarke's reply.

'No. He just said Matron would know because she knows everything, or words to that effect.'

'Well, Matron *doesn't* know,' Matron said through clenched teeth, 'But whoever it is, I shall be giving her her notice.' She opened her drawer, removed a packet of cigarettes and offered one to Mr Clarke, who shook his head and instead took out his pipe and proceeded to light it. 'I hope you don't mind if *I* do.' She removed one from the packet and allowed Mr Clarke to light it for her.

'I have no idea why the boy didn't come to me first.' Matron drew in some angry puffs. 'There was no need to bring you all this way.'

'May I speak, Mr Clarke?' June waited for him to nod before she carried on. 'I've never heard anyone say anything of the kind. There must have been some kind of misunderstanding.'

185

'That's as maybe, but I decided to come to Bingham Hall and speak to Matron myself.' He directed his gaze at Matron again, his lips round his pipe making little popping noises. 'I insist you must have a meeting with everyone here and warn them of the serious nature of their words. The person is not setting the kind of example we would expect in a Dr Barnardo's home and I want your assurance this will never happen again.' He gave her a sharp look. 'By the way, what is *your* view on having a German boy here, Mrs Pherson?'

'I've made no bones about the difficulty,' Matron flashed. 'The other boys taunted him at the beginning for being the enemy and I immediately put a stop to it – I'd warned Head Office this would happen. But so far as I know, no member of my staff ever calls him such names. And I believe the children have settled down well together now, haven't they, Miss Lavender?' She looked over her desk at June, her eyes warning her to agree.

'Yes, Matron,' June answered.

Mr Clarke looked unconvinced. 'How did the boy react when some of the children accused him of being the enemy?'

Matron drew her eyebrows together and glanced at June. Mr Clarke waited, tapping his pencil.

'Miss Lavender would know more than me,' she said, 'as she sees them at closer quarters.'

Mr Clarke nodded at June.

'He was upset at first and retaliated,' June said, 'but we all talked to the children and explained it wasn't his fault just because he'd been born a German. And that only some Germans were Nazis, or bad people. We told them he'd come to England to escape from these bad Germans. The boys were quite in awe of his adventure and it seemed to put a stop to any more nonsense.'

Matron sent June a look of gratitude.

'And as far as you know, no one called him the name he claims?' Mr Clarke persisted.

'Certainly not.' Matron appeared to have found her voice again, but June noticed her hand tremble as she took a gulp of her tea. She was obviously furious that she should be so questioned.

Mr Clarke wrote a few more notes, then looked up at Matron. 'Well, I'm sorry if I've taken up your time unnecessarily, Mrs Pherson,' he said, putting his pad and pencil back in his briefcase, 'but you'll understand I had to investigate the issue. And I thought it best if your very worthy assistant stayed as she might have something to add – which it turns out she did. I will say no more on the subject' – he gave a tight smile – 'but if I find out this sort of thing has not been curtailed I will take severe action. I hope you understand my position.'

'Of course,' Matron said stiffly.

'In the meantime I would appreciate it if someone could show me into one of the shelters. Is that possible? I'd like to inspect them.'

'Of course,' Matron repeated. She threw June a cool glance. 'Would you like to show Mr Clarke, Miss Lavender?'

'I'll be pleased to.'

Mr Clarke scrambled to his feet and extended his hand which Matron barely touched, reminding June of her first meeting with this formidable woman. There'd been the same lack of warmth.

'Good day, Mrs Pherson, and thank you for the tea.' He put his overcoat on, picked up his hat and turned to June with a smile. 'After you, Miss Lavender.'

June led the way to the shelter she had gone to yesterday. Once inside, Mr Clarke let his gaze fall on every corner, shaking his head, his lips pursed in dissatisfaction.

'The shelter looks adequate enough, but there are virtually no provisions here at all.'

'We were only in here an hour or so,' June remarked.

'And how do you know the next time that you won't be stranded here for longer?' Mr Clarke said sternly. 'It's just not good enough. You must get this kitted out, and the one next door, so you're ready for anything Jerry throws at us.' He pulled his scarf a little tighter. 'Isn't there a cellar underneath the house?'

'Yes.'

'What's it like down there?'

'I don't know,' June said. 'I've never been down.'

'Surely it's quicker to get there than running outside and into the shelter?' Mr Clarke's eyes sharpened. 'Particularly at night. Presumably the children sleep upstairs.'

June nodded. 'Yes, they're on the second floor and the nursery on the fourth.'

'They'd be a lot safer if they slept permanently in the cellar. You seem a sensible girl.' He looked at her as though for confirmation. 'Don't you agree?'

'It's a good idea,' June said. 'I'll mention it to Matron.'

June had broached the subject only the following day after the bombing, proposing that they should use the cellar if there was a bomb scare at night. They'd heard in the distance some heavy night raids recently and even felt the vibrations, though Harold said it was usually the docks that caught it. But the children were getting jittery, especially since they'd recently had such a close call. As usual, Matron had not agreed, but then she disagreed with almost any suggestion June made, often before June had finished making her point.

'Ridiculous idea,' Matron had said. 'It's too damp and cold down there for the children.'

Now, facing Mr Clarke, who was staring at her, she had the feeling he knew she'd already suggested it to Matron.

'Thank you, Miss Lavender. I'd be most grateful if you pursue the matter.'

June hesitated. Mr Clarke had come on a long train journey and Matron had made no mention of his staying for dinner. They couldn't send the poor man away with no food inside him. But Matron would be furious that June had taken such initiative. Good manners and thought for the poor man won.

'Mr Clarke, would you like to join us in the dining room for dinner at one o'clock? It can be a bit rowdy with the children but—'

She was rewarded by a warm smile.

'Thank you, Miss Lavender. I would be delighted.'

The service for Mr and Mrs Sumner took place two days later in Bingham village church. There was a small crowd of their family and friends, together with several of the staff from Bingham Hall. A thought flashed through June's mind when she was kneeling in prayer. What if Murray was dead too? That's why she hadn't heard from him. A shudder went through her whole body and she almost overbalanced as she pulled herself back on to the church pew.

Whatever it looked like – even if she appeared 'fast' to him – she didn't care. Life was fragile and she needed to know if he was safe. She would write to him this very evening.

After Mr Clarke's visit Matron had announced that both shelters must be equipped with food and water, blankets, books and games for both the children and the adults, and improvised bedding should there be any more alerts.

'The way she tells everyone it's her idea.' Kathleen raised

189

her eyes to the ceiling. 'Full of her own importance, which doesn't help us to do what we're all trying to achieve, but she can't see it.'

June, Iris and Kathleen were having their late night cup of cocoa in the common room after the teachers had disappeared. The three young women had got into the habit, desperate for some privacy for a chat at the end of each day when they were all worn out and needed to relax a little. It was also the hour the nurses had together before they changed shifts, leaving one of the maids to keep an eye on the ward.

'Well, it doesn't matter as long as we do something,' June said. 'We can get the children to help. Even the little ones, so it's not so frightening for them the next time we have to go down there. They'll be more used to it.'

'Good idea.' Kathleen propped her legs up on a stool. 'Oh, that's better.' She let out a long sigh of relief. 'My feet are killing me and my legs ache like billy-o.'

'It's all that standing on a stone floor, I'm sure of it,' Iris said, stretching out her own legs and kicking off her lace-ups, which she'd already untied.

'So do *we* organise getting the shelters ready or do we wait for our dear Matron?' Kathleen said.

'If we do that it will never get done.' Iris glanced across at June. 'I think we'll have to take our orders from Matron's assistant, Miss Lavender.'

They all chuckled, but June soon became serious. 'We should do it tomorrow morning. It's urgent and I think if another inspector came round and saw how little prepared we are we'd be in trouble. Matron would blame us for shirking our duties. So let's get cracking early before classes, and we can finish in between times.'

'Sounds like a sensible plan,' Iris said. 'If we all muck in with the children we should be finished in two or three days without interrupting their lessons too much.'

'You'll have to tell Matron what we're planning,' Kathleen said slyly in June's direction.

'I know,' June said, smiling. 'And I know I'll have to do it on my own as you two are so terrified of her. Two women taller and stronger than little frail me, making me do all the dirty work.' She broke into a wide grin. She loved the banter between the three of them. She'd never had that with Stella, although Clara had had a lovely sense of humour even though she was so much younger.

Iris looked at her watch. 'I know it's early but I'm off upstairs. I need to wash my hair. I'm out tomorrow evening. Paul's back on the scene.' And with that she shot up and disappeared.

'Paul?' Kathleen said, looking at June questioningly. 'I've not heard about him.'

'He was at the dance that first night I went, but with another woman. Poor Iris was furious. She asked Chas, an American, to dance with her to make Paul jealous, but it seemed he only had eyes for the woman in his arms. And when he finally caught sight of Iris she said he just gave her a sheepish grin.'

'That would be it for me,' Kathleen said, decidedly. 'No second chance as far as I'm concerned. I just hope she doesn't get her heart broken.'

'I don't think it's true love even though she was pretty upset that night and said she'd never forgive him – I don't think it's the first time he's gone off with someone – but it seems she's giving him another chance.' June smothered a yawn. 'It's been quite a day, so I think I'll turn in early as well. I've got a good book I'm reading – *Rebecca*. It's a bit creepy at times, especially when I read it at night.'

She couldn't help it – at the very mention of books Murray's image rose in front of her. She'd promised him she'd lend him Monica Dickens' autobiography.

'I'm going, too.' Kathleen jumped to her feet. 'It's a long night for me. Let's hope Jerry doesn't make it any worse.'

Against all Matron's disapproving looks, the children turned the furnishing of the shelters into a game. Miss Ayles and Athena remained in the house with Hilda and Bertie, but most of the staff joined in, and by the end of the week the shelters were transformed.

'I think we all deserve a medal.' Barbara looked around with satisfaction. 'We've got food and drink for at least a week, just in case; we've got a decent first-aid kit, plenty of warm bedding and extra clothing, kettle and Primus stove, and enough books and games and crayons to keep the kids occupied.'

'Well done, kids,' Iris said. 'Bobby, thank you for taking charge of the younger ones.'

'It was nothing, Nurse.' He went off whistling.

'I'd better get them back for their lessons,' June said. 'But I'm pleased we've got this job done. If there's another raid at least the children have got some proper provisions.'

'Don't forget the grown-ups, Junie,' Iris put in. 'We'd quite like some proper provisions too.'

Chapter Nineteen

'Hello, Junie.' Murray's voice was warm over the telephone wires. 'I'm so sorry I haven't been in touch, but this is the first time in ages I've had an opportunity to ring you.'

'I wrote to you the other day because I was worried I hadn't heard.'

'Oh, Junie, I didn't get your letter. You must have thought me a cad not to have replied but the post isn't as reliable as it used to be. Please don't ever worry about me – I'm all right. How's Freddie settling in?'

'That's what I need to talk to you about. But the worst thing – we had a bombing raid the week before last – that's why I wrote to you.'

She could feel the tension over the wires.

'Oh, my God. Is anyone hurt?'

'Yes, two people dead – the couple in the gardener's cottage. They were sitting at the table and the cottage took a direct hit. They must have died instantly.' Her voice shook.

'Anyone else?'

'No. No one else was injured. Luckily Bingham Hall was unscathed but it was very frightening.'

There was a pause and then she heard Murray's voice sounding far away.

'Oh, I'm so sorry. It's dreadful for the poor couple but thank goodness they were the only casualties.' The line crackled and she held the receiver tighter to her ear as though that would help keep the contact. 'Thank God you're all right, Junie. I had no idea you'd had a raid. They usually target the cities.'

'Harold said it was a lone pilot dumping his bombs on his way back to Germany. I suppose it could have been worse.'

'It certainly could.' There was a pause. 'You said Freddie is another thing. Has the dragon discovered him?'

'Yes,' June said miserably. 'I'd managed to hide him so far in one of the stables but Freddie was already getting restless locked up in there. Anyway, Hilda, one of the girls, was taking the twins outside for a runaround while I was in church and they heard barking. Freddie's bark used to be so small, but he's getting louder by the day. They looked in the stable and there he was, all excited to see them, thinking they were going to have a game with him.'

'Poor little chap.'

'I know. He's the sweetest little dog in the world. I love him to bits. But Hilda went running straight to Matron as soon as she came back from church, and of course Matron came out to inspect the stable for herself. Luckily Iris overheard some of the conversation and got hold of him beforehand and took him into her own room, but Matron found out she had him and demanded that he's sent back to where he came from. "No dogs allowed, and that's an order," she was bellowing to anyone in her sight.'

'I suppose it's surprising we got away with it as long as we did,' Murray said. 'Do you want me to come and get him – take him back to the station?'

'I think it's the only answer, and at least he knows you.'

'Don't worry. He'll be our mascot. It won't be so difficult

taking care of him now he's a little older. I'll get over there tomorrow and collect him. Can you bring him to the bottom of the lane at . . . let me see . . . eleven o'clock? That be all right?'

'Yes.' She swallowed and looked around the hall to see if Matron was waiting to pounce. There was no one. She breathed out. She was going to miss the little chap. But Lizzie was going to miss him even worse. 'Oh, Murray, Lizzie comes to see him in my room twice a day. She's started talking to him – just like you thought she would. She's a changed child. She's sleeping in the girls' dormitory now. But she still won't speak if she sees Matron. And even if Matron knew, it wouldn't make any difference. It's no pets and that's it. Lizzie will be devastated when she finds he's gone. I don't know what to tell her.'

'Tell her he's having a holiday with Uncle Murray,' he said, and she could hear the reassuring smile in his voice. 'We'll work something out. Is there anything else I can do?'

'No, nothing. Just look after Freddie. And give him a hug sometimes. He likes that.' The pips went. 'I'll bring him tomorrow at eleven.'

She put the receiver down. Freddie's fate had been decided.

At a quarter to eleven the next day she put the quivering bundle of puppy into a basket with a cloth over it and shot out of the door as the children and teachers had their morning break. She hurried down the lane wondering how she'd feel when she saw Murray. It was silly but every time she saw him she wondered if it would be the last. His job was so dangerous. But she also knew that if anything should happen to him nobody would think to tell her. She was just another girl he knew. With a sickening feeling she reached the top of the lane and exactly five minutes later a lorry pulled up and a uniformed man jumped out. Heart in her throat she ran towards him. But it wasn't Murray.

'Flight Lieutenant Andrews couldn't come, love,' a twinkling young man said. 'There was an emergency and he asked me to pick up a dog, but I don't see him.'

Trembling with disappointment that it wasn't Murray, and feeling sick with guilt, she wordlessly handed over the basket with Freddie's nose now pushing through the cloth she'd half buried him in.

'Gosh, he's just a puppy,' the young man said. 'But he'll be fine with me. The boys will look after him until Flight Lieutenant Andrews comes back.' Freddie whined as he realised he was going off with someone he didn't know and June's heart contracted. 'It's all right, love.' The young man smiled at June. 'Don't you worry at all. He'll be quite safe with us.'

Chapter Twenty

'Only one letter today, Miss Lavender,' the postman said as he swung his leg from the bar of his bike and jumped off. 'And it's for you.' He threw her an appreciative glance that sent June a little pink and breathless. 'Lucky beggar, whoever he is.'

He was a good-looking young man, and cheeky with it. She couldn't help smiling. It was nice to be noticed. She looked at the envelope, now recognising Murray's handwriting. It was postmarked 23 January 1942. With trembling hands she pulled out the sheet of notepaper.

My dear Junie,

I'm so sorry not to have made it to pick up Freddie. Don't worry about him. He's settled in and the chaps are spoiling him rotten.

My news is that I've been given a whole two days' leave this coming weekend and would love to spend it with you. I know you won't be allowed two days but can you try to arrange with that cantankerous old matron of yours that you would like to have next Saturday off? It would be 31ˢᵗ January. I'm hoping to get tickets for the theatre in Liverpool as we've never been out anywhere nice for the evening. We can have supper before or afterwards – whichever you prefer. One of the chaps has offered to lend me his motor – and I've managed to get some petrol! – so I can pick you up as early as you can get away. What about 10 a.m.?

I'm longing to see you again. It seems ages. Please write and let me know as soon as possible so I can look forward to seeing you.

Yours,
Murray x

Her heart leaped. How wonderful to spend a whole day with him. And then in the evening a play. The last time she'd been to see a play was with dear Aunt Ada. And now she'd be going with Murray. Her mind rushed on ahead. What should she wear? It would have to be the same black skirt she'd worn for the dance, but maybe there was time for her to make a new blouse. She had five days. Yes, there'd be time – that is if she had the chance to buy some pretty material.

June desperately tried to see Matron to ask permission about Saturday but every time Matron shook her head and said, 'I can't stop. Come and see me tomorrow.' Then tomorrow would come and the woman would say the same thing. If she didn't get hold of Matron soon, Murray wouldn't get the letter in time to tell him she could or couldn't go. And she was determined she would see him. Who knew when there would be another chance?

To calm her frustration she decided she would start making her blouse. It was getting too close to the date for any shopping in town, but maybe there was some material she could have in the Sewing Room. She'd ask Barbara.

'I don't think there's anything suitable for evening wear,' Barbara said. 'What's the occasion, if I might ask?'

'It's a date, actually,' June said, blushing.

198

'Ah. With that dashing pilot of yours.' Barbara gave her a knowing wink.

'I wish everyone would stop calling him *my* pilot. We're just friends.'

'Mmm. That's what everyone says when there's a lot more going on – which I want to hear about.' Barbara grinned. 'Anyway, this isn't getting us anywhere. Let me have a look in the cupboards and I'll see if there's anything I've forgotten about.'

'Thanks, Barbara. I'd be really grateful.'

'Just as long as he's worth it.'

'Oh, he is. He definitely is.'

But later that day, June was disappointed that Barbara wasn't able to find anything remotely suitable.

'It's because the girls mainly sew things like aprons and embroider tablecloths. And at the moment we've only got seven girls and they're all too young to do any proper sewing. I'm really sorry, June.'

'Never mind. Maybe something will turn up.'

'Has the Fierce One given permission for you to have next Saturday off?' Iris said under her breath as the two of them left the dining room after tea the following day.

'I can't pin her down. She always has an excuse as to why she can't see me.'

'Maybe she thinks you're going to ask her something awkward.'

'I don't know what that might be.' June looked at her friend. Should she tell Iris what she was worried about? She'd be the best person to confide in. 'Can we go somewhere private?'

'Come to my bedroom,' Iris said, taking her arm. 'You sound quite serious.'

Iris's bedroom was exactly as it was that first time, possibly even worse. How on earth did Iris look so beautifully groomed every day?

'Sorry as usual for the mess,' Iris said, casually acknowledging the state of the room. 'Take a pew. Perch on my bed, why don't you? Now, spill.'

'Did you see that man, Mr Clarke, the other day, from Stepney Causeway?'

'Oh, Dr Barnardo's Head Office?'

June nodded.

'No, but Ellen mentioned it. She seemed anxious, but the staff always are when we have a visit from the top nobs.'

'It's just something rather disturbing.' June took a deep breath and told her quickly that someone at Bingham Hall, and it wasn't one of the children, had called Joachim a 'dirty Jew'.

Iris's eyes widened in shock. 'Dear Lord, what a thing to say! When you read of all the horror that's being dished out to those poor Jews in Europe. How awful. It has to be someone who's anti-Semitic.' She closed her eyes, frowning in concentration. 'So it's not one of the children, you say?'

'No. And I had the distinct feeling that he suspected Matron. But although I think she's not the right person to be put in charge of an orphanage, and she wasn't keen on having a German child, she's too clever to do or say anything which would put her job at risk. Well, that's what I believe, anyway.'

'I think you're right,' Iris said slowly. 'Do you know who reported it to Head Office?'

'Apparently, Joachim himself. He wrote to Dennis Fuller, the chap who brought him to us, but he won't name the person.'

'Who on earth could be saying such disgusting things to a child?' Iris said.

'Well, it won't be any of the teachers, I'm certain, nor Kathleen or Bertie . . .'

Iris shook her head.

'. . . and I doubt if it would be the maids as neither of them would say boo to a goose,' June finished.

'What about Hilda? I hate to say it, but she's quite a spiteful person and always feels hard done by. She's got it in for Matron ever since she ordered her to work in the kitchen instead of the nursery. Quite right, too. She might have wanted to get Matron in trouble by reporting her. And who knows – maybe it *was* our beloved Matron.'

'I don't think it was,' June said. 'And I don't think Hilda would have telephoned Stepney Causeway and reported anything. She'd be too scared.' June frowned, trying to imagine who might have been so cruel. Mentally, she ran through all the teachers, the staff in the kitchen, the maids, the nurses, sure none of them would be so cruel. And then it dawned on her. Matron had said whoever it was would be given *her* notice, but if she didn't know who it was, she couldn't be certain it wasn't a man. There was Harold, the chauffeur. No, not him – she just couldn't picture it. He was a real gentleman, reserved but cheerful, and he'd been so good with the children that time in the shelter. Besides, she'd never heard him make snide remarks to the boys. In fact, the opposite. If one of the boys misbehaved he would tick them off, and even give them a clip over the ear, but they still liked and respected him. But there was one who could never command respect. She shuddered. One who made her blood go cold every time he came near her.

'What's the matter, Junie?' Iris was looking at her with concern.

'Gilbert.'

Iris raised both eyebrows. 'What about him?'

'I think he might be the one who called him that. Maybe I'm being unfair but the way he was about Lizzie when I first came here, and how rude he's been to me on several occasions, I just don't trust the man. And I'm going to find out if I'm right.'

'You might well be right,' Iris said, thoughtfully. 'Only the other day I heard him call Thomas a little sod. I actually told him off and he gave me such a dirty look I practically shrivelled up in front of him. He didn't dare retaliate, of course, but he is a nasty piece of work. Don't know why Matron keeps him on. I expect he's cheap labour.'

'That's not a good enough excuse.'

'Well, we'll keep an ear pricked for Gilbert, and if he comes out with any other bad language towards the children we'll damn well report him.'

'Horrid little man,' June said fervently. 'I just wonder what his background is. Be interesting to find out.'

'Have you actually asked Joachim who the person is who called him such a horrible name?'

'Yes, twice.'

'And . . .'

'He refuses to tell me,' June said. 'When I asked him the second time he clammed right up.'

'If it *is* Gilbert, maybe he threatened him that if he ever told anyone he would – oh, I can't think what he might do, he's such a dreadful little man, but I bet he's frightened him silly.' Iris ran her hands through her curls.

'I just wish Joachim would be brave enough to tell me.'

'Yes, because if Gilbert, or whoever it is, has done it once he'll say it again and I don't want the children to hear it. Joachim is damaged enough already. We need to keep our eyes and ears peeled.'

'And tell one another if we hear anything suspicious.'

202

'Yes, of course. Anyway, let's talk about happier things.' Iris threw June a sly look. 'What will you do if Matron refuses to give you permission to go out on Saturday?'

June frowned. 'I've thought of that. I wouldn't want to go against her as she can be really nasty if she thinks anyone is disobeying her, but I intend to go.'

'Ooh, you look quite determined,' Iris teased.

'I am.' June smiled. 'I didn't have a day off for the last two Mondays with Miss Ayles ill in the ward with influenza—'

'Just a cold,' Iris interrupted. 'And what a difficult patient she turned out to be.'

June smiled in sympathy. 'Anyway, I think I deserve a few hours off now she's back on her feet again. I'll just have to insist on asking Matron for two minutes of her precious time. But first' – she looked at Iris and grinned mischievously – 'I need your help!'

Every hour dragged for June until the Saturday came round and she would see Murray again. She loved her job and the children but her heart practically did cartwheels when she thought of their meeting. Maybe he would kiss her again. For longer, this time. He must like her to want her to spend the day with him. She bit her lip with annoyance as Matron's words sounded in her ear. The woman had refused to allow her the whole day off.

'You may not leave the home until six o'clock,' she'd said, her lips in a tight line.

'But that won't give us . . . I mean me time to . . .' June stuttered.

'I expect you're going with that pilot,' Matron said, a crafty expression flitting across her features. 'So don't try to say different.'

'It's my personal time off, Matron,' June said, forcing Matron to look her in the eye. 'I'm merely asking for at least the afternoon and evening.'

Matron was silent for a few moments. 'Just this once,' she said finally. 'You may leave at four. But mind he brings you home before eleven.'

'I'll start back as soon as the play's finished,' June said. She had no idea when it would end but she was determined not to miss one moment of it because of having to rush back to Bingham Hall.

Matron nodded and June took it to mean that she had agreed.

Chapter Twenty-One

'No, you definitely can't appear in that same skirt and blouse you wore at the dance,' Iris said. The two of them were in Iris's bedroom. She'd told June she'd do her hair, so to come by an hour before Murray arrived.

June had puffed some powder on to her nose and even added a little rouge, then wiped it off again as she'd hated the artificiality of the colour. She'd touched her lips with a very soft red which instantly gave her a quiet air of confidence – totally different from how she really felt at the moment; just thinking about meeting Murray, let alone seeing him in person, was making her quake. Now, with Iris's comment, she felt herself coming unstuck again.

'I'll put a bit of make-up on you,' Iris said firmly. 'You're much too pale. But let's get your hair done first as that will make all the difference.'

June didn't bother to tell her she'd already tried some rouge and wiped it off. You didn't say no to Iris when she wore that determined look.

Somehow she'd cleared a space of sorts and sat June down at her dressing table, which was piled high with bottles and jars and brushes. To June it looked like something off a film set, yet Iris was a nurse and was only allowed to wear the very minimum of make-up.

'Right. We'll put it up like this.' Iris got hold of a hank of hair and pushed some pins in. The hair immediately fell out. 'You've got beautiful thick hair,' she commented, 'with a will of its own. But I shan't let it beat me. In the meantime I'm going to turn you away from the mirror so you don't see what I'm doing.'

Fifteen minutes later June's hair was swept away from her face and caught up at the neck in a thick twist, the long hairpins and Kirby grips holding it so firmly in place they were beginning to dig into June's scalp, but she dared not say anything. She felt Iris slide a comb into one side of her head.

'Why don't you try my black dress.' Iris looked June up and down. 'You're about the same figure as me, though it will be a bit longer on you as I'm taller.' She stepped through the debris in her bedroom and opened her wardrobe door.

From the angle where she sat on the edge of Iris's bed June could see her friend had triple the amount of clothes she had. And although her bedroom was a mess as usual, the inside of the wardrobe was beautifully neat, everything colour coordinated, hats on the top shelf, pairs of shoes on the floor. Iris had obviously not come from any working-class family. June tried to repress the ripple of envy as she watched Iris slip a dress from one of the wooden coat-hangers and hand it to her.

'See what you think.'

Slightly embarrassed at stripping in front of her friend, June removed her work clothes and stood in her plain knickers and brassière.

'Not much of a show-stopper there,' Iris said, chuckling. 'You need some pretty lingerie, girl.'

'I'm not exactly getting married.' June grinned back. 'It's a casual meeting – remember?'

206

'If Murray's got any sense he won't allow it to be too casual for too long.' Iris tossed a cream petticoat over. 'Here, you need this first.'

June slipped it on. Carefully, so as not to disturb her hair, she drew the black dress over her head and smoothed it down over her gently rounded hips. Except for the length, which came to her mid-calf, it fitted perfectly. It was a slim-fitting little number of fine wool, with a scooped neck and silver belt.

'It's perfect,' Iris said admiringly. 'Luckily mid-calf is still fashionable. Come and look in the mirror.' She grabbed a load of beads and belts and a couple of evening bags which she'd slung on the edge of the mirror.

June took in a sharp breath. 'Is that sophisticated lady really me?'

'No one else here,' Iris said grinning. 'You look simply gorgeous.'

June stroked one of the sleeves. They were sheer black organza showing tantalising glimpses of the firm flesh of her arms. The silver comb matched the silver belt accentuating her trim waist. The effect was stunning. She would have liked to fasten the little silver RAF brooch to the dress but was worried that the pin might damage the fine material. And if she was honest, she wasn't quite ready to show the brooch to anyone, not even Iris, just yet.

'Shame you haven't any evening shoes, and your feet are so tiny they'd be lost in a pair of mine . . . but I suppose those will do.' Iris nodded doubtfully at June's feet. They were plain court with a little heel and June privately thought they looked fine.

'You need a bag.' Iris went to her wardrobe again and removed a black-beaded evening bag with silver handles.

'I don't know how to thank you.'

'You don't have to thank me. I've loved being part of the transformation.'

'I shall feel like Cinderella when I come home and take everything off and look in the mirror and see just an ordinary girl staring back at me.'

'You're far from ordinary, June. You just haven't given yourself a chance. And now you're ready to meet your pilot, looking sensational.'

'I don't know about that,' June said, laughing, for once not correcting her friend on the 'your pilot' bit. 'But I do feel the most glamorous I've ever felt in my life.'

'Good. It will give you confidence. He'll wonder what's hit him.'

The blackout curtains had already been pulled at the windows of Bingham Hall when June heard the car on the gravel at five minutes to four. It had been a crisp sunny day and June had tried hard not to be too upset with Matron for forbidding her to leave any earlier. Why was Matron so intent on spoiling anything nice? But now he was here. She'd been waiting for this moment; she didn't want him to ring the bell and have the maid answer with Matron lurking in the background.

June quickly pulled the heavy door open and stepped out, feeling a little strange in Iris's dress underneath her coat. She could feel the silky petticoat next to her skin and it was an odd sensation. But wonderful. She'd decided not to wear a hat as it might spoil her lovely hairdo. The silver comb would have to be the only ornament. Her heart beat fast. Would Murray like the new Junie? Then a thought struck her. Would he think her forward for not waiting until he rang the bell – that she was too eager by being outside already?

It was too late. He'd already spotted her.

In a flash Murray had jumped out of the car, leaving the engine running, striding towards her, a grin splitting his face in two, his eyes sparkling with anticipation. It was the first time she'd ever seen him in civvies and her heart jumped. He looked incredibly sophisticated in his dark-grey coat and black hat, a white silk scarf casually tied at the neck.

'You look lovely, Junie,' he said, taking her arm, his gaze upon her. 'The hairstyle suits you – very elegant.' He nodded his approval. 'I'm going to feel proud to have you by my side.'

It was as though they'd suddenly moved several steps forward in their relationship, and she felt her cheeks grow warm. He opened the door of his friend's motor, waited while she swung her legs into the car, and slammed the door shut.

'Ready?' he asked.

June nodded.

'Right, we're off.' He tossed his hat in the rear seat. 'Freedom at last' – he turned to her soberly – 'except when you're in the forces you're never free, even on leave.' His serious look turned into a ready smile. 'But we'll make the most of it.'

It sounded as though they were colluding and she returned his smile.

He drove in an easy way, and she imagined him high up in the clouds, those same hands controlling a Spitfire. It gave her a delicious frisson of excitement until she remembered what a dangerous place he'd be in. She shook herself. It was no good giving in to wild imaginings. The excitement was replaced by a feeling of fear and worry.

'Penny for them.' Murray momentarily turned his head. 'You look very thoughtful. Is everything all right?'

'Y-yes.' She couldn't help stuttering; it was as though he'd tuned into her mind.

'Sure?'

'Very sure.'

'So what were you thinking?'

She said the first thing that came into her head. 'Actually, I was wondering how you managed to get some petrol.'

Murray chuckled. 'Not easy. You have to know the right people. Let's say it's been a long time since I had any time off, and I think they felt I deserved a gallon or two for good behaviour.' He gave her a swift glance. 'I haven't stolen it or done anything wrong, June, in case that's what you're thinking.'

'Oh, no, not at all,' she said quickly, even though she could tell by his grin that he was only teasing. 'I know you wouldn't do anything like that.'

'And how do you know such a thing about me?'

'Because I do.'

He gave her such a sharp look it made her blush, and then they both laughed.

She suddenly remembered something. 'I've never thanked you for my little brooch. I love it. I'm not wearing it on my coat as I didn't want to lose it. I wanted to pin it on my dress but I was worried the pin might leave a mark.' She wouldn't mention it was Iris's dress she was wearing so she needed to be extra careful. 'It's a military brooch, isn't it?'

'Yes, but it's a special one for ladies. Sometimes the boys buy one for their mother – or if they have a girlfriend,' he added.

There was a pause. She wondered if he wished he hadn't said that. Then he turned to her and she saw his smile – the same slightly mocking one he'd given her on the train that time.

'How's Freddie?' she asked, her pulse rapid, pretending she hadn't given any importance to his words.

'Full of beans. The chaps love him. He's got plenty of food, he can go outside when he wants, and he's never without some pats and cuddles. You don't need to worry at all about him.'

'How soon they forget,' June tried to joke, but she was still upset she wasn't there to laugh at his antics with Lizzie.

'You can bring Lizzie to see Freddie any chance you get,' Murray said, taking his hand off the wheel for a second and touching her arm. 'Even if I'm not around, I'm sure someone will allow you to see him, but it's best if I'm there, of course.'

'I was hoping you'd say that,' June said, giving him a quick glance. She liked his profile. His straight nose, eyes concentrating ahead, and his mouth smiling. He returned her glance and chuckled.

'It'll be a good excuse to see you again.'

They drove along in silence but it was a comfortable one. Finally Murray broke it.

'As it's later than I'd hoped, I suggest we eat first and see the play afterwards. Then Matron won't give you a hard time. Does that sound okay?'

'It does. I have to admit that Matron only gave permission for me to be out this evening if I came straight back after the theatre.'

'That's what I thought.' Murray kept his eyes ahead. 'But we're going to make the most of every minute.'

'Am I allowed to know what we're going to see, or is it meant to be a surprise?'

Murray's blue eyes, full of laughter, caught hers for a second before he fixed them on the road again.

'It's an Oscar Wilde play – *The Importance of Being Earnest.*

John Gielgud and Edith Evans are in it. I've been wanting to see it for ages.'

June had barely heard of Oscar Wilde, much less his plays, though she'd vaguely heard Aunt Ada talk of John Gielgud and what a wonderful Shakespearean actor he was. She had to say something so she didn't look too much of an idiot.

'John Gielgud – isn't he a Shakespearean actor?'

Murray grinned appreciatively. 'He certainly is. Famous for his Hamlet and Macbeth. But I chose tonight's play because I felt we needed something lighter and this is supposed to be one of Wilde's finest comedies.' He paused and gave her another quick glance. 'You haven't seen it already, have you?'

'No, no, I haven't, though I've always wanted to.' She crossed her fingers as she uttered the fib, telling herself if she'd known about the *Being Earnest* play, she was sure she'd have wanted to see it. Thank goodness at least she now knew it was a comedy.

'Phew! I was a bit worried for a moment.' He chuckled, and she realised he was teasing her again. It was a good feeling. 'Tell me about your job,' he said, giving a wide berth to a bicycle which looked as though it was about to wobble right into them.

'Are you really interested?'

'I am. I love kids and feel sorry for those little ones at your orphanage. Dr Barnardo was a great character, and it was incredible how he got even the first home going in those days, let alone the ones he now has all over the country.'

June secretly stored the information away that Murray loved children.

'He must have had a lot of money,' she commented, 'as well as a big heart.'

'I don't know that he was particularly wealthy, but he must have had some money . . . and then apparently he got people to donate to his cause. I believe in the end he set up Dr Barnardo's as a charity. He's certainly done a marvellous job with homeless children.'

'How do you know all that about Dr Barnardo?'

'Did him at school. I remember thinking how even one person can have such an extraordinary effect on society. Bit like Dickens.'

June glowed. What a kind and compassionate man he was.

'Speaking of Dickens – how are you getting on with his granddaughter's book?'

'I finished it. She's a really interesting person. I should have brought it with me.'

'Maybe next time.' He pulled up at a set of traffic lights. 'Tell me about Lizzie,' he said. 'Was she terribly upset?'

'She was.' June bit her lip. 'Freddie helped a lot to get her behaving like a normal child. He was the one who really got her talking again, though one of the older boys, Alan, has been very good with her, but she wouldn't speak again for days after Freddie left. She still keeps asking when you're going to bring him back.' She paused and glanced at him. 'Is he happy with all of you?'

'Perfectly.' Murray laughed. 'He's always got someone to play with.'

'I'm glad. It wasn't the best for him to be shut in my room all day. Or in the stable. But he's a dear little dog and used to make me laugh. I miss him much more than I thought I would.'

'Yes, that matron of yours is a harridan, isn't she?'

'She just has no understanding of children. Thinks they should be seen and not heard. She's much too strict – when they haven't done anything that bad. She was horrible to poor Lizzie and threatened to send her back to the nursery if she didn't stop crying, which only made Lizzie cry harder.'

'Poor little kid. We'll try to fix something up soon so she can see her puppy. Because Freddie is still hers and I'm determined she'll have him back again one day.'

'It would be a miracle if Matron has anything to do with it,' June said with feeling, 'but it would be wonderful.'

They chatted some more about the goings-on at Bingham Hall. June longed to know more about Murray's job but of course she knew he couldn't talk about it. Everything was hush-hush.

As they drew into Liverpool she was shocked all over again at the damage – whole streets destroyed, just the occasional house left standing intact. But who would want to remain there when all they had for neighbours was a pile of bricks and masonry, and what were once family pets now confused and searching desperately for food?

'It's pretty dire, isn't it?' Murray said, reading her thoughts. 'You can't imagine the misery those folk are going through. Not just their homes but losing loved ones. Some of them not even finding their bodies.'

June could only nod in agreement. They'd come a different way from the route Harold had taken her and Iris before Christmas. This side of Liverpool was nearer to the docks, which the Luftwaffe had bombed night after night in the Liverpool Blitz a year ago. The German planes were still constantly reminding the residents of their power.

'I think here is as good a place as any to park.' Murray eventually turned into a small side street that so far had escaped any major damage. He turned off the engine and the lights, and June saw it was already quite dark outside.

A dozen children clamoured round before he'd even got the door open.

'What motor is that, Mister?' one of the grimy little lads asked.

Most of them looked no more than ten or eleven years old.

'It's a 1933 Austin 7.'

'Cor. Can I have a ride in it?' one of the older boys asked.

'Sorry, lad. Not this time.' Murray climbed out and went round to the other side to open the door for June.

The boy shrugged and swaggered off on his own.

'Miss – you got any sweets?' from a girl with ginger curls and a runny nose.

June brought out a small bag of toffees to offer her a couple; quick as a dart the child grabbed the whole bag and made off with it, shouting with glee at her prize.

'They were for us to have in the theatre,' she said ruefully.

'She needs a treat more than we do,' Murray said, slamming the car door shut. He held out his arm and June took it.

It was only a short walk to the Royal Court Theatre and she never wanted it to end. It felt right walking along with Murray, her hand lightly hooked into his arm, his face peering down at her and smiling. Once he gave her hand a little squeeze and she felt the tingling pressure of his fingers, even through their gloves.

'There's a good little restaurant near the theatre,' Murray said. 'They do a pre-theatre supper. Would that be to your taste, Madam?'

He was teasing her again.

'Very much to my taste – though I'm not always sure what my taste *is* these days.' She grinned.

He opened the door for her and she stepped in. It was

dimly lit and the blackout curtains were already drawn for the evening. It was still early with only a few diners and they were shown a table tucked away in a corner. A waiter came along immediately, took her coat and pulled out her chair so she could be seated.

'That's a beautiful dress you're wearing,' Murray said, looking her up and down, a smile tugging at the corners of his mouth. 'You look like a mannequin.'

'Like a plastic doll, do you mean?' It was her turn to tease.

'No, no, I didn't mean one of those you see in a shop window – I meant a fashion model. Something out of *Vogue* magazine.'

'How do you know about *Vogue*?' June asked him.

'My mother. She takes it every month.'

It was obvious from the way Murray spoke that he came from a good family, June thought. She tried not to dwell on the difference between his family and her own, and was relieved when the waiter returned and lit a candle for them.

'Tell me about your mother and father.'

'My father was killed in the last war,' Murray said, looking up from the menu.

'I'm sorry. He couldn't have been very old.'

'Not thirty.' Murray's eyes were moist and June was sorry she'd started such a conversation. 'But let's not talk of anything sad tonight. Let's just be selfish.'

'What about your mother? You said she likes *Vogue* magazine.'

'She does. Mother always looks immaculate. She's still a lovely looking woman.'

'Has she ever met anyone else?'

'No one she's got serious with. My brother and I used to vet them all – tell her they weren't any good for her, just after her money.' He smiled. 'Now, do you see anything you

216

fancy on the menu? I want you to choose whatever you'd like. Something you wouldn't ordinarily get at the home.'

'Like porridge and bread and jam,' June said, chuckling.

'I'm sure your cook does better than that,' Murray said with a grin, looking at the choice again. 'The menu's not quite like it used to be before the rationing, but apparently they still put on a few decent dishes.'

June couldn't help her eyes straying to the prices. She blinked. My goodness, she could get a week's groceries with just the price of the main meal.

'I'll have the macaroni cheese, if that's all right,' she said, picking the cheapest meal on the menu.

'You're not having anything of the kind,' Murray said, once again seeming to read her thoughts. 'I don't do badly on pay and this is our treat – to see something of the normal world instead of all this chaos.' His eyes gazed at her intently. 'I suggest the baked cod, if you like fish.'

'Yes, I do, very much.' She didn't tell him that was the very dish she had had her eye on. 'All right, then, I'll have that.'

'I'll join you.'

Murray seemed so familiar as he sat opposite her, talking and laughing, not taking those brilliant blue eyes off her for more than a few seconds at a time. She'd never felt so comfortable with anyone before and wondered if he felt the same. If only she could glimpse inside his head. But she was absolutely certain that he felt just as happy in her company as she did in his. Maybe there was no need for questions. They should just be in the moment. That's what everyone said with this war on: 'Live for the moment – you never know if it's your last.'

She looked across at Murray from under her lashes, knowing she was flirting a little for the first time in her life.

Taking a sip of the delicious wine and feeling very much a woman of the world, she was rewarded when he placed his hand warmly over hers and sent her the most magical smile.

June was reluctant to break the spell by getting up to leave the restaurant, but as soon as Murray paid the bill and helped her into her coat she began to feel excited at the thought of seeing a play. It had been a while since she'd been to one with Aunt Ada, and this one sounded fun.

Several of the buildings surrounding the theatre had been badly damaged but the Royal Court stood like a beacon of hope.

'One Jerry didn't get in the Blitz,' Murray said as he guided her through the entrance door, 'though it did catch fire a few years ago – they completely refurbished it with a nautical theme in the Art Deco style. It's beautiful, isn't it?'

'I love it,' June said, looking around admiringly.

'The lounge is supposed to be modelled on the lounge of the *Queen Mary*. We should take a look.'

Couples were already gathering in the foyer. Many of the women wore fur, either the full coat or a fox fur around their neck. June hated the idea of an animal slung round her own neck, but she couldn't help admiring all the glittering jewels on fingers, throats, ears, wrists, arms and elaborate hairstyles, and long strings of necklaces plunging downwards to show off cleavages. Compared to these exotic-looking creatures the gentlemen looked quite plain, June thought, although she noticed many a sparkling cufflink. There was constant chatter, which sounded like the twittering of birds, and around the foyer wafted a delicious smell of expensive perfume. June wanted to gaze at the women longer, but she felt the lightest touch of Murray's hand on her back and they followed more couples down a curved staircase to the lower floor.

It did indeed feel like the interior of a ship, June thought smiling, as though she'd been on one and could tell. Everywhere she looked twinkled and flickered, from the candelabra shining in the mirrors, the waiters' silver trays, the light catching on the crystal champagne glasses, and the candles adorning the small tables where people sat. Even the tinkling laughter from the women seemed to match the fairy-like atmosphere.

Murray looked at his watch. 'Would you like a drink before we go in, Junie? We have a few minutes.'

'Oh, no, thank you. I couldn't eat or drink another thing.'

'Neither could I, really. So shall we go in then?'

The auditorium was just as glamorous as the entrance. Murray had chosen circle tickets and a uniformed lady showed them their seats. He took her coat and put it on top of his own.

'I'll put everything on the seat next to me and hope no one comes,' he whispered.

The theatre began to fill and soon practically every seat was occupied, including the one next to Murray. He gave her a rueful grin and patted the pile of coats on his knees.

The lights dimmed and the chattering audience instantly hushed. The curtain went up and in the darkness Murray felt for June's hand and entwined her fingers with his own. He glanced at her, and before it went completely dark she saw a kind of question in his eyes that she couldn't read. It didn't matter. She let herself sink into the velvet chair and couldn't remember ever being so happy.

It was later than Matron had ordered by the time they arrived back at Bingham Hall.

'I've had the most wonderful night,' June told him. 'The play is still making me smile. Some of those lines from Lady

Bracknell were hilarious. The one about losing one parent being a misfortune but losing both is carelessness.' She began to giggle all over again and Murray joined in.

'It was the first time I've heard you laughing so much.'

'I couldn't help it. And the rest of the audience enjoyed it too, didn't they?'

They stood close, smiling at each other. Then, as their gaze held, their smiles faded. The air shimmered between them. Her eyes dropped to his mouth and she longed for him to kiss her again – a proper kiss, a lover's kiss. But it wasn't to be – he made no move. Her eyes stinging with disappointment, she turned to go, but to her surprise he stayed her with his hand on her shoulder, and gently brought her face back towards him, his other hand cupped around her cheek.

'Junie,' he whispered.

Before she could answer he'd taken her in his arms and she felt his lips on hers, demanding, seeking . . . she knew not what. Instinctively, and with her whole being, she curved her body into his, her lips parting softly under his mouth, and kissed him back. He kissed her cheeks, her eyelids, her nose, the lobes of her ears, until he found her mouth again. He said her name against her lips and drew her even closer. By the time he released her she was dizzy, but he held her until she regained her balance.

'Are you all right?' he said huskily.

'I think so.'

But she knew she would never be all right again if he wasn't by her side.

'I must go in.' Her voice shook and she hoped he wouldn't notice. 'Matron will find out how late I am and she'll never allow me out again.'

'I know.' He kissed her on her forehead. 'I'll wait here until you're safely inside.'

'You don't need to.' The words sailed on the cold air of her breath, but Murray stood where he was, waving her objection away.

Iris had told her she'd wait up and let her in. She was just about to gently tap on the heavy oak door when it creaked open and there was Iris, standing to one side, pulling her in.

'You're lucky,' Iris said, blowing a kiss to Murray and shutting the door. 'Matron had a headache and went to bed early. I'll make us a cup of cocoa and you can tell me all about it.'

Chapter Twenty-Two

The next day being Sunday, there were no classes and the day began half an hour later. June puffed up her flat pillow, trying to give her head a modicum of support. There was no point in pulling back the curtains – it would still be pitch-dark. She stretched her legs under the blanket and let herself drift as she relived her evening with Murray. It couldn't have been more wonderful . . . and she would always cherish every moment. A vision of his dear face crowded her brain, making her smile. She wondered when they might meet the next time. It wouldn't be easy. He'd told her his job was getting busier by the day.

How did she feel about him? She forced herself to ask the question in a rational manner. She hadn't known him long. Had spent hardly more than a few hours in his company when you added them up. She knew very little about him as a person or his background. But she didn't need to, her heart sang out. She could ask all the rational, sensible questions she liked. She could tell herself to be careful. She could say it was too soon to even *think* about falling in love. But whatever she told herself, her heart told her differently – that with every heartbeat she loved him.

Last night over cocoa Iris had been burning with curiosity, but June hadn't gone into any detail about the evening. It was too precious and she wanted to hug it to herself. She didn't want to tell anyone in case it was only a few kisses with a nice girl as far as Murray was concerned. But somehow she didn't think so.

Climbing the flights of stairs to her room, she'd immediately missed him. Hearing his voice, feeling the touch of his hand, his mouth . . . oh, his mouth on hers. Her knees almost gave way on the last flight. Her room would be completely silent – lifeless. With a sigh she'd put her key in the lock.

All this thinking and worrying wasn't getting anywhere. June swung her legs out of bed, drew back her curtains and padded over to the washbasin, where she had a quick wash, then dressed and ran downstairs. Her mouth was terribly dry and she was in dire need of a cup of tea.

Dear Bertie was already bustling around in the kitchen preparing breakfast. She'd filled an enamel basin with eggs, ready to boil, and was slicing bread for the toast.

'Don't know where Hilda is,' she grumbled as June came into the kitchen. 'Girl's always late.'

'Can I do anything to help?'

'Yes, you can put the plates and eggcups and cups and saucers out . . . oh, and the salt and pepper . . . and the marmalade.'

June carried the crockery out to the dining room and laid it all out on the three tables, thinking how strange she'd felt only a few weeks ago and how familiar everything looked to her now. She loved her job, she loved the children, and she was completely rewarded when Lizzie uttered a few words, or one of the other children gave her a hug against all the rules. Iris was already a dear friend, and Kathleen and Athena and Barbara were lovely girls to chat to, and Bertie was almost like a mother to them all. There was only

223

Matron's and Gilbert's bad temper to contend with, and she wouldn't let them get the better of her. She strengthened her resolve to try harder with those two.

But it was the thought of Murray, seeing him again, reliving every hour they'd spent together, how he'd murmured during the interval that she looked more beautiful than any other woman there. She'd been sipping a glass of wine and whether it was the alcohol she wasn't used to or Murray's compliment, it had gone straight to her head. Anticipating their next meeting made her light up inside with happiness.

'I would like the teachers, nurses and Cook to be in the library this evening at seven-thirty sharp,' Matron announced after the children had eaten their supper and had a short playtime period before the younger ones went to bed. She turned to June. 'And you, too, of course, Miss Lavender. I have some news.' She spun importantly on her heel, leaving June and Iris to give one another a lifted eyebrow and quick grin. Matron always made everything a small drama. It couldn't be that earth-shattering, their glances said.

When they all trooped into the library Matron was already there, standing behind the main desk, and at her side sat a reserved-looking middle-aged gentleman, his dark hair greying at the temples, dressed in a navy pin-striped suit and striped tie, with shiny black shoes. He was a plain-looking man with a strong nose but a mouth that looked as though it might smile at you at any moment. But it was his dark eyes that caught your attention. June could tell by the way his glance fell on each person that he was intelligent and completely absorbed in the surroundings and the people who gathered. She noticed his gaze rested on Iris a few seconds longer than anyone else and allowed herself a small

224

smile. Paul was playing up again. It wouldn't hurt him to have some competition.

'Be seated, everyone,' Matron instructed in her usual dictatorial way. 'I'll come straight to the point. Marjorie Ayles, as I'm sure you all realise, is not so young any more.'

'Few of us are,' Bertie quipped to subdued laughter.

Matron frowned. 'She has given me her notice and will retire at the end of the month. I'm sure we will all wish her a long and happy retirement, and also thank her for the years she's been at Dr Barnardo's.' She directed her look at Miss Ayles, who sat on the other side of June with her hands folded in her lap. 'I believe it's close to twenty years, isn't it, Marjorie?'

Miss Ayles gave an almost imperceptible nod as though she regretted her decision.

'To show our thanks I would like to give you a small present.' She picked up a square box, already gift-wrapped. 'Would you care to come up, Marjorie?'

Miss Ayles struggled to her feet and made her way to the front. Matron handed her the box, whereupon Miss Ayles nodded again and must have said 'thank you' though June couldn't hear any words from where she was sitting. A little flushed from the attention, Miss Ayles tottered back to her seat to the sound of restrained clapping, and set the box on her lap.

'I want to introduce you to David Cannon,' continued Matron, gesturing needlessly towards him. 'He's going to take over from Miss Ayles. That means history and geography, but he's adding music. Yes' – Matron paused and looked at him coquettishly – 'we are very lucky in that he is a musician. We haven't had a music teacher here for some years, so we will look forward, I'm sure, to many evening concerts.'

Mr Cannon sent a gentle smile across to his new colleagues.

'So please give him your support and make him feel at home. He'll settle in this evening and be ready to start work tomorrow. We don't give anyone time to change their minds.' Matron looked at him and actually laughed.

'Seems as though having a man around has cheered up the old dragon,' Iris whispered in June's ear.

June grinned. 'Maybe Mr Cannon will join us in the common room later,' she whispered back mischievously as everyone politely clapped.

'Speech,' Iris called out cheekily.

Mr Cannon glanced at Matron who nodded her permission. He got stiffly to his feet and June noticed his long fingers held on to the edges of the desk.

'Thank you, Matron, for the introduction. Just for clarity, I'm not fighting in the war. Too old, they tell me.' A few polite smiles. 'But I fought in the last war and got a bullet wound – in the leg. Unfortunately it put paid to my career as a violinist in the BBC Symphony Orchestra. Couldn't sit for those long rehearsals. So what would be the next best thing? I came to the conclusion that it must be teaching. As Matron said, I'll be teaching history and geography, but I want to instil a love of music in as many children as I can, so I intend to introduce classical music appreciation.'

There were some mumbles from Kathleen and Bertie that they wouldn't be interested. 'It sounds grand,' Mr Cannon went on, as though he'd heard, 'but I can assure you it's not. You don't need to know anything about classical music at all. Matron has given permission for me to hold a weekly concert here in the library. She's going to organise a gramophone' – he paused and Matron nodded and smiled – 'and I hope to see you as often as possible. We've also agreed that children over twelve can attend these weekly evening concerts if they have a special interest in music and have made their interest known to me in advance. Also, if they come in with one of the teachers or nurses. I say this not because I want to make it difficult for them to attend, but I want them to be serious. I'll be giving them music lessons and appreciation in their school time anyway.

'Lastly, I thank you for welcoming me to this marvellous Dr Barnardo's home.' He glanced around the library again and sat down to more clapping, this time a little more enthusiastic, thanks to Iris, who, June was amused to see, had started it off loudly.

Throughout his speech June had glanced at her friend more than once, noticing Iris was listening attentively to every word. All attention was on Mr Cannon, and then Matron, with some difficulty, stood up.

'To mark Marjorie's retirement and to welcome Mr Cannon, I've organised a little celebration. Cook's made some cakes and biscuits . . . *and* we're going to have a glass of wine,' Matron added unexpectedly. She moved towards the window where a smaller desk stood, and with a flourish like a conjuror, whipped a white sheet away to uncover three bottles of wine, glasses, and Bertie's wonderful treats. She expertly uncorked the bottle, poured a glass of red wine and handed it to Mr Cannon, who was still quietly seated. He took it and thanked her, shyly looking over at the others who were queuing for cakes and drinks.

I wonder what's going on in his head, June thought, getting up to join the others. I hope he doesn't think he's made a terrible mistake. She looked round for Iris and to her surprise saw her friend hadn't moved from her seat. She went over to her.

'Iris? I thought you'd be first in the queue,' June teased.

'What? What are you saying?' Iris looked dazed, as though she'd had too much sleep and had just woken up.

'So do all introduce yourselves to Mr Cannon.' Matron bustled around, being the hostess.

'Come on, Iris. I'll join you for a glass of wine,' June said, holding out her hand to pull Iris to her feet.

'Oh, yes . . . all right.'

Having David Cannon amongst all the women has put a sparkle in their step, June thought, highly amused, as she watched Barbara, Athena and Kathleen gather round him, glasses in hand, chattering and laughing as though they were at a party. Matron was smiling and circulating as though she were hostess in her own home. June was disappointed to see that Iris had left. She was sure her friend had enjoyed Mr Cannon's speech and would go over to talk to him. So where was she?

'I couldn't bear watching all that simpering over the new man,' Iris confided later to June in the common room – now empty because the small party in the library was still going on.

'Matron's certainly gone very girlish all of a sudden,' June said, poking the fire to try to whip the glow into some proper flames.

'It makes you sick.'

'He does seem very nice though,' June said, giving Iris a sideways glance.

'I'm sure he's nice enough,' Iris conceded. 'But I don't have any confidence in his chances here. Soon as he gets the measure of us he'll see just what it's like facing all us women every day, every evening. It won't be easy. He'll need to be a strong person and not allow himself to be bullied. But at the moment Matron seems to be showing another side of herself – flirtatious, if you ask me.'

'Oh, do you think so?' June immediately became fascinated at the change Mr Cannon might bring to all those at Bingham Hall.

'I do. Anyway,' she said, her back to June as she boiled the kettle for the cocoa, 'I'm not interested in the sort of music he's talking about. It's jazz for me. So I shan't be looking in on any of his music appreciation classes.' She turned round and her eyes met June's. 'How about you, Junie? Will you go?'

'Definitely.'

'Really?' Iris sounded surprised. 'I didn't put you down as a music buff.'

'Not sure what you mean by that,' June said with a smile, 'but I love classical music. Aunt Ada introduced me to it when I lived with her and was doing my nursery training. We'd go to concerts quite frequently, and I must say I miss them.' June gave Iris a knowing smile. 'This might be a good substitute. Why don't you come with me, Iris? You might just learn something.'

Chapter Twenty-Three

'Miss Lavender?'

'Yes, Joachim?'

'I would like to listen to the music with Herr Cannon this evening.'

June looked at his eager face, his eyes shining. She remembered how he'd sung 'Silent Night' in German on Christmas Eve, in perfect tune, his clear young voice making her almost want to weep, it was so moving.

'You are supposed to go to his class in the daytime. The evening is for the staff members and older children.'

'It's baby music in the day. "Peter and the Wolf". Learning the different sounds of the instruments. I know already the name of all instruments and their sounds.'

June looked at him in surprise. He was tall for his age and she had to remind herself that he was only nine. She glanced at her watch. 'It doesn't start for another hour and a half and you'll be getting ready to go to bed. *And* Mr Cannon said you had to be twelve.'

'Just this one time.' Joachim's eyes were pleading. 'It is a Beethoven concerto and I would very much like to hear – but Mrs Pherson say – says I cannot attend.' He refused to use the term Matron no matter how many times Matron admonished him.

'Why? Did she give a reason?' June said.

'I told him it's not for children, unless they're twelve or more.'

June felt the heavy presence of Matron behind her. How did she have this uncanny knack of coming up behind you just at the very moment you didn't want her to hear what you were talking about?

She reluctantly turned to find Matron giving her the usual glare. She'd begun to get used to them by now – not take them to heart. It was just Matron's way, she told herself, excusing the woman. But this time she had to bite back her anger.

'He can't study every minute of the day, Matron. Sometimes one has to do something for the soul, like reading poetry or painting . . . or listening to music.'

'*One* has to do no such thing,' Matron said, her eyebrows drawn together in a heavy frown. 'There's no possibility for him to do music when he hasn't grasped all the other subjects – English in particular. He needs to catch up with the others. When he's passed his exam, we'll see.' She said the word 'music' in a contemptuous tone, quite different from the one she'd used when she'd first introduced Mr Cannon.

'*Ich hasse Ihnen.*' Joachim threw Matron a fierce look and stormed off, hands deep in his pockets, leaving June alone with her.

'I'm sure Mr Cannon – if you agreed,' June hurriedly added, 'would make an exception for Joachim. I believe he does have a special interest in music and—'

'And I'll thank you to keep your opinions to yourself, Miss Lavender. I'm not at all certain you're a good influence on the children. I'm not sure what Woolfes just said but his tone was most disrespectful. You are *not* to take him into the library this evening. I'll be keeping an eye on you, so don't disobey me.'

231

She marched off leaving June staring after her.

Matron was ordering him not to have a little bit of enjoyment with all he'd been through. And June was determined that he would.

Over the next hour, she began to form a plan that might solve Joachim's problem and engage in a little bit of subtle matchmaking. She smiled. It ought to work if everyone was willing to play their part, except she couldn't actually give them their lines.

'Iris, are you doing anything this evening?' June asked her friend when Iris emerged from a long afternoon in the sick room.

'No, why do you ask?'

'I've got to catch up with some letter-writing or I'd go with him myself,' June added a little slyly, hoping Iris wouldn't notice.

'Go with whom?' Iris demanded. 'And where to?'

'Mr Cannon is going to play – or rather, put a record on of one of the Beethoven concertos this evening. It starts at seven and Joachim wants to listen to it. He's asked Matron if he might attend, but she's put her foot down as usual and forbidden me to take him in. But she hasn't forbidden *you*.' June looked steadily at her friend. 'Would you take him in?'

'What, and listen to some German composer for two hours? Haven't we got enough trouble with them in this war?' Iris said.

June was about to protest when Iris threw her head back and laughed.

'Caught you well and truly, didn't I? You fell for that. Yes, 'course I'll take him and try and maybe pick up a bit of culture myself at the same time.' She threw June a sharp glance. 'That's what your aim is really, isn't it, Junie?'

Their gaze flicked one to the other, and then they both collapsed into laughter.

'And you're not doing any letter-writing,' Iris said, still chuckling, 'so you can jolly well come with me. *I'm* taking Woolfie, and you're just going along for the ride.'

June went to find Joachim and tell him the news. She was rewarded by a smile so wide it nearly split his face in two.

'Nurse Marchant is taking you in with her so you need to tell her about your special interest in music, and explain to Mr Cannon. Tell him although you're not twelve you are very serious about music.'

'Are you coming too, Miss?' Joachim's eyes were anxious.

'Yes, I'll be there as well, but Nurse wants to listen to the concert with you close by. It's the first time she's ever heard any classical music and I think she feels a bit nervous. She thought it might help if you were there with her.'

Joachim looked surprised but didn't say anything more. He just nodded.

'*Danke* – I mean, thank you, Miss.'

'Don't go in until the last minute. Nurse will be in the hall waiting for you. And don't tell any of the other children.'

'Yes, Miss – I mean, no, Miss.'

He dashed off like a normal schoolboy who'd been given an unexpected tuckbox. Maybe to him that was exactly how it felt, June mused, as she watched him run.

As arranged, June went into the library a few minutes before seven. It was empty except for David Cannon, who looked up from searching through his records and gave her a smile.

'Thank you for coming, Miss Lavender,' he said.

'Oh, do call me June.' June returned his smile as she chose a seat. 'We use Christian names when we're off-duty.'

'Then I'm David,' he said. 'I hope there'll be a few more

233

people.' He glanced at his watch. 'I like to start punctually.'

'It's not yet seven,' June said. 'I'm sure there'll be some others.'

'Do you have any particular favourite composer, June?'

'I like so many,' she answered sincerely. 'My aunt used to take me regularly to concerts when I lived with her in London. She was a real classical devotee and taught me how to enjoy them. I miss the music, so I'm really looking forward to this evening and am quite happy with anything you choose.'

'I'm delighted you've already been introduced to some of them,' David said. 'What about opera? Have you—?'

He was interrupted by Barbara and, to June's amazement, Hilda.

'Good evening, ladies,' he said. 'Do take a seat. We'll be starting in just a couple of minutes.'

'Don't start without us,' Iris's voice came from the doorway. She nipped in, followed by Joachim who was looking suitably serious.

June noticed the boy had changed clothes and was wearing his best trousers and shirt.

'You're looking very smart, Joachim,' she said.

'It is an important evening for me,' Joachim explained. 'I have been many times to a concert with *Papa* and *Mutti* when I am young. Is it all right for me to listen, Mr Cannon?'

'I'm delighted to see you both,' David said, his eyes lingering on Iris. 'Take a seat and we'll get started.' He bent over the gramophone and guided the needle to the edge of the record.

'I'm afraid you won't be doing anything of the kind, Mr Cannon, until Joachim comes out.'

All heads looked round at Matron, standing in the doorway, red with temper.

'I specifically told Miss Lavender she was not to take Woolfes into the library tonight. He has English homework to do.'

'Perhaps you could make an exception for the boy for once,' David Cannon said, a wary look coming into his eyes.

'I'm sorry, I cannot.' Matron flounced in and turned to Joachim. 'Come with me this instant, Woolfes. You know very well I told you not to attend this evening.'

Joachim looked from Matron to David Cannon, a beseeching expression in his brown eyes.

'I'd like the boy to stay,' David said firmly. 'He's had a rough time, I imagine, and music is a balm for the soul. I think it will help him more than studying English at the moment.'

Matron's mouth twisted. 'I'm sorry, I can't agree. Maybe when he's further along with his studies.'

'Matron, just this once.' Iris stood up and faced her.

'I'll ask you to mind your own business, Nurse.' Matron gave her a withering look. 'And you, too, Miss Lavender. I'll be speaking to you both later.'

'June had nothing to do with this,' Iris said. '*I* took Woolfie – Joachim in with *me*.'

'Then he should have told you I did not give permission.' She turned on her heel and swept out of the door.

'I will come.' Joachim gave Iris and June a sorrowful look and got to his feet.

'Perhaps another time, Joachim,' the music teacher said.

Barbara and Hilda had sat quietly all this time but now Hilda spoke up.

'Are you or aren't you going to play the record?'

David Cannon gave her a steady look. 'You know, I don't feel much like listening to Beethoven after all.'

'I'm going then.' Hilda stalked off.

'I'm getting tired of Matron's dictatorial manner,' Barbara commented, flushed with annoyance. 'The sooner we can put a stop to this nonsense, the better. Anyway, I'm off. Shame, as I was looking forward to a relaxing evening but it seems impossible under her roof.' She turned and smiled. 'Goodnight, everyone.'

'I feel embarrassed on your behalf,' Iris said to David as he put the record carefully back in its paper sleeve. 'But I'm afraid it's typical of Matron. She rules with an iron rod.'

'Don't worry about me. I'll see the boy on his own tomorrow. Find out where his interests lie in classical music.'

'I suddenly feel tired,' June said, stretching up and pretending to smother an exaggerated yawn. 'I think I'll go to bed early and read.' Iris got up to follow but June waved her down. 'You stay, Iris. Maybe David will play you a record and you can listen to it quietly.' She sent her friend an innocent smile, and softly closed the library door behind her.

'You left us alone on purpose,' Iris said to June accusingly, but the amused light shining in her sapphire-blue eyes was plain to see.

It was Monday, June's day off, and Iris was due to work the night shift. The two had decided to go to Liverpool and even maybe have a quick look at the docklands. Iris said it was important to keep up with all the damage – that Bingham Hall was so institutionalised that they were cushioned from the outside world.

They were sitting in the same café Murray had taken June to. It was the first time they'd had a chance to talk since Joachim's dismissal from the library.

'Oh, I wouldn't say that,' June said with a laugh.

'*I* would.' She threw a mock glare at June. 'If I didn't

'know better I'd go so far as to say the whole thing was a set-up.'

'That's a terrible thing to say.'

They both giggled.

'But he *is* rather sweet, June.' Iris had gone misty-eyed. 'And he's talked to Woolfie. Told him he would play a record especially for him today – this afternoon, after lessons. Matron can't possibly grumble at that.'

'She'll find something,' June said. 'I'm getting tired of Matron saying no to everything.' She looked at her friend and smiled. 'But it's wonderful that David's taking such an interest in him. It's exactly what he needs.'

'David's learned quite a lot about Woolfie in his chat with him.' Iris looked up, her eyes now moist. 'I feel so sorry for him. He came over from Germany on the *Kindertransport* – you know, the children's train. I read about it in some newspaper ages ago. David says they sent several thousand Jewish children to England for safety but the train's stopped now. Probably because it was run by Jews and they've been arrested.'

'Are they putting other foreign children in similar homes?'

'Yes, but it's not an easy transition, if you ask me.'

'Where are Joachim's parents?'

'Nobody knows. His sister is still in Germany. Matron said she was too young to come with her brother but he's hanging on to the fact that she might be old enough in another year or so.'

June shivered. From what she'd heard about the Jewish people in Germany – and they might be rumours but somehow she didn't think so – there wasn't much hope. People were being sent to camps; made to do hard labour with little food in their stomachs. She'd heard that people were literally starving to death. It was imperative that

237

Joachim shouldn't hear these stories and maybe they were exaggerated anyway. Even if they weren't, he was upset enough as it was.

'He's been in England over a year,' Iris continued, 'with foster parents, but they wouldn't allow him to eat with the family. He had to have his meals in his room and they treated him like a servant. From what he said to David, he didn't get enough to eat so no wonder he's so thin. He ran away and was picked up off the street by – would you believe? – a Dr Barnardo's inspector. And here he is. Bingham Hall. For better or worse, poor little blighter. I feel sorry for him.'

'He's passionate about music,' June said, thoughtfully. 'Let's hope our lovely new music teacher will be able to overcome Matron's decision and let the child listen next week, when maybe he'll be able to play his records without her interfering.'

'I think David's going to go one further than that,' Iris said, her blue eyes sparkling mischievously, and a faint flush on her cheeks.

'Really?' June looked across at her friend. 'You seem to be in the know all of a sudden. What's he planning?'

'Wait and see,' Iris said, smiling. 'Just wait and see.'

Chapter Twenty-Four

June hadn't forgotten her suspicions that it was Gilbert who'd called Joachim that terrible name. She kept a strict eye on him, and she and Iris had a quick chat every evening in the common room to see whether he'd slipped up when he thought no one was in earshot by calling any of the children distasteful names.

'He's such a slippery character,' Iris said, stretching out her legs. Kathleen was reading a book and David was making notes, which he'd told them were for the following day's history lesson. They'd agreed they wouldn't speak about their suspicion to any people they considered 'possibilities', but really there was only a handful – Matron, Hilda, Miss Ayles, who hadn't yet left and had made her view known on several occasions that she disapproved of having a German child in their midst . . . and Gilbert.

'Why does Matron still have him here?' June said under her breath. 'You don't think they're in cahoots at all?'

'I wouldn't put it past them.' Iris fumbled in her bag for her packet of cigarettes. She found them and flipped open the lid. 'Anyone?' She vaguely waved the packet in the air. 'No takers? Then, thank you, I'll have one myself.'

David looked across at her and smiled. He rose to his feet and striking a match he ambled over. He bent to light Iris's cigarette and June was amused to see how Iris closed her hand around his as though to steady it and looked up into David's warm brown eyes. The cigarette took hold and Iris pulled in a deep breath and exhaled a blue stream of smoke.

'Oh, that's better,' she said, her face visibly relaxing. 'I've had quite a day. Woolfie seems to have stomach trouble. I'm a bit worried about him.'

'I think his stomach is adjusting to proper food and more of it,' David said, sitting down near the two girls. 'From what I gather, his family were very short of food in Berlin – most of the shops refuse to serve Jews – and then coming here, well, I'm ashamed to say we haven't treated the boy much better. We English, I mean – his foster parents specifically. The body takes time to adjust and he's had one shock after another.' He winced as he stretched out his legs. 'Did Iris tell you I came down in the early hours one morning and heard a Chopin nocturne? I honestly thought I'd somehow left the gramophone on in the classroom. It was Joachim playing it on a violin. It sounded just as wonderful as on a piano. I was amazed, I can tell you. I asked him where he'd got the music from and he said he'd brought several pieces from Germany in his satchel. He told me they were his most precious possessions.'

'No wonder he was so worried when he couldn't find his satchel that time we had a bombing raid,' June said.

'Quite.' David nodded. 'So I'm going to see he gets all the help he possibly can.'

'In what way?' June was genuinely interested.

'Well, I've probably got enough experience and knowledge to teach him for a year. By then he'll be ahead of me. The inspector for Dr Barnardo's didn't know when he picked him up off the street that he was doing a good turn for a child genius.'

240

'Good gracious.' June's mouth fell open. 'Is he really a genius?'

'He seems to be. As I was telling Iris yesterday, I've saved a fair bit of money from my years in the orchestra, then when my wife died four years ago I sold the house – couldn't bear to stay in it any longer without her there. I decided to rent, but now I'm here I don't even have to pay that. I want to help the lad and I've already made enquiries for him to go to the Royal Academy of Music in London. If they accept him he'll be set for life.'

'My goodness, what an achievement if he gets in,' June said. 'I'm sure he will – he seems so dedicated.'

'Does he have to have an audition?' Iris asked.

'Oh, yes. And an extremely tough one. But I think he'll do it standing on his head. Well, not quite standing on his head, but you know what I mean.' David's dark eyes twinkled.

'That would be the way to grab their attention,' Iris said with a grin.

'I'm leaving you lot,' Kathleen suddenly called across to them as she snapped her book closed. 'Very difficult to read when you're all yakking.'

'Sorry, Kathleen.' Iris threw her an apologetic smile. 'Truth is, I think we all forgot you were there, you were so quiet. Were we being awfully loud?'

'Not really.' Kathleen was deathly pale. 'It's me. I'm just sick to death of this damn war. Sick of never getting letters from Robert. Sick of worrying about him – if anything bad's happened, if I'll ever see him again. I heard on the wireless this morning that another one of our ships has been sunk by those damn U-boats. It's not his this time, but who knows when it'll be his turn? It's just too horrible for words.' She got up, tears streaming down her face.

June jumped up as well. She put her arm round Kathleen. 'Do you fancy having a cup of cocoa in the kitchen, just you

241

and me?' She touched the girl's arm and winked, gesturing with her head towards Iris and David.

Kathleen nodded and gave a weak smile. 'I'd like that very much,' she said.

The following morning before going into Assembly Iris said she wanted to talk to June in private. Could they meet after dinner and go for a walk down the drive and back? Immediately June said yes, she could do with the exercise.

Well wrapped up with scarves and hats and gloves, the girls met outside the house and began to walk briskly down the drive towards the lane.

'You sounded very mysterious,' June remarked when they'd gone only a couple of hundred yards.

'It's just that I didn't want anyone within earshot, but you know when you and Kathleen left us last night?'

'Yes.'

'Well, David said he thinks we're right. He thinks it *is* Gilbert calling Woolfie names. When David passed him yesterday morning he heard Gilbert muttering under his breath about damned Jews.' She stopped and turned to June, her blue eyes fixed on her friend's. 'You've probably guessed that David is a Jew?'

'No, I hadn't,' June replied. 'And even if I had, what difference does it make?'

'That's my point. It shouldn't make any difference to anyone. But it seems to badly get up Gilbert's nose. If he could say that in David's hearing, I'm sure he could say it straight out to a child.'

June shuddered.

'And there's another thing,' Iris said as they continued walking. 'I don't know why I've never noticed it before. David pointed it out. The way Gilbert looks. Have you ever seen him in anything different? Anything coloured, like a bright jumper, for instance?'

June gazed at Iris in surprise. What on earth was she getting at?

'No,' Iris answered her own question, 'he always wears the same black trousers and black shirt like he's just going or just coming from a funeral. And who else wears a black shirt?' June blinked. 'Someone who was quite famous,' Iris prompted.

And then it dawned. June froze. 'Oswald Mosley – leader of the Fascists,' she said, shivering not from the cold but from her words. She swallowed hard. 'But I thought that had all broken up ages ago.'

'It might have,' Iris said. 'But just because a movement breaks up, it doesn't mean to say the members don't think the same as they always did. If you have the mentality to join a Nazi party, then just because you no longer go to rallies and meetings doesn't mean you've altered your opinion on Jews or gypsies or anyone else Mr Hitler deems not worthy to be called human beings.'

'Oh, Iris, it's just too horrible. What are we going to do?'

'We're going to talk to Matron. We're going to get rid of him.'

June and Iris sat in front of Matron in her office. Matron leaned back in her chair, blowing out clouds of smoke. June got her handkerchief out and pressed it to her nose, trying not to cough.

'So what is this all about?' Matron demanded.

'We wondered if you've found out who the person was who called Joachim horrible names.' June watched Matron's expression intently.

Matron shook her head. 'No, nothing. I've come to the conclusion it's all a fabrication.'

'I don't think so,' Iris said firmly. 'Mr Cannon's had much the same indirectly said to *him*.'

'Oh.' Matron tapped the ash into the saucer of her teacup. 'Well, go on.'

'Because you know Mr Cannon's Jewish, don't you?' Iris practically threw the words across the desk.

'Well, no, I hadn't realised until I met him . . . and guessed he was.'

'Would it have made any difference if you'd known?'

'I will not lower myself to answer such a question.' Matron glared at Iris through her spectacles, her confidence seeming to return.

'Because the Dr Barnardo's creed is that we accept everyone – every child, whatever the colour of their skin, or their religion,' Iris went on. 'And that must go for the members of staff as well.'

'Please do not tell me what the creed is,' Matron snapped. 'I'm only too well aware.'

'You haven't asked Iris who made the remarks to Mr Cannon,' June said.

Matron drew her mouth into a straight line.

'It was Gilbert!' Iris banged her hand down on the desk, making Matron jump. 'Gilbert muttered something about damned Jews when he went past David yesterday. That's pretty close to naming someone a dirty Jew, I would have thought. Wouldn't you, Matron?'

Matron's face whitened. When she finally spoke, her voice was like ice.

'I would expect you to keep your observations to yourself. You have no proof. And I will not have the staff upset with such allegations, do you hear?' Her broad chest rose and fell with the thrust of her fury.

'No, I don't hear,' Iris said unwaveringly. 'I don't intend to let this drop.'

'If you dare say one thing more, I can assure you, Miss Marchant, your position here will be terminated immediately. You, too, Miss Lavender. Now go – both of you. I have work to do.' She got up and walked to the door, opened it and practically pushed them out. 'Not another word. And I mean it.' The door slammed behind them.

'She's worried,' Iris said. 'And so she should be. I will not be threatened by that woman. In fact, I'm going to telephone Mr Clarke straightaway.'

Chapter Twenty-Five

March 1942

'Letters,' Kathleen said, coming into the common room before lessons began. She was waving a thick bundle of post, and June's heart lifted in hope that there might be something for her.

It had been over a month since June had heard anything from Murray. She was beginning to worry. Of course he was busy and she knew he often went without much sleep for days at a time, but why hadn't he even sent a postcard? Every time she heard the roar of an aeroplane going over, her heart would stand still with terror. She would strain to look up, picturing him at the controls, concentrating with all his might – she daren't think about the enemy firing at him, damaging his aeroplane . . . or worse. She closed her eyes and immediately the image of his aeroplane was in front of her, cartwheeling out of control, plunging into the sea in flames. It happened so many times these days it was becoming almost normal and she'd had to learn to let the image fade and not give in to tears. If only she had a letter from him this awful worry would stop, she was sure of it.

'Athena.' Kathleen gave the teacher a couple of envelopes. 'Oh, there's actually one for me here.' She glanced at the address, pulled a face before tucking it into her pocket, and continued sorting the rest of them. When June had given up hope Kathleen handed her the last envelope.

'For you,' she said, with a knowing smile and a saucy wink.

June tried to look perfectly composed as she took the letter without even glancing at the writing. She didn't have to. It was the same military envelope he'd sent her a letter in before. Heart pounding, she excused herself, saying she needed to collect something from her room.

Dear Junie,

Sorry I've not been in touch lately. Been really busy here. But I do need to talk. Can we go somewhere? Maybe supper and a film afterwards if you fancy it?

What about this coming Monday on your day off? Could you do six o'clock at The Barn restaurant? It's just before you get to Brown's Books.

Yours,
Murray

June read the note again, slightly puzzled. She went to her 'special' drawer – the one with precious items such as Clara's photograph, one with her mother and Stella together, both smiling, and Murray's two letters with the brooch. She picked up the last letter from him and spread them out side by side, comparing them, knowing she was being foolish but not being able to help herself.

Yes, she was right. He'd put a kiss on the previous one and said how he was looking forward to seeing her again. There was nothing of the kind on this one. She frowned. Maybe it was because he'd written it in haste. Yes, that would be it. She had nothing to worry about. Those kisses when they'd last said goodbye gave her all the reason in the world to think he was beginning to fall in love with her. She gave herself a little hug of excitement. He wanted to talk to her.

She couldn't wait to hear.

She'd arranged to take the bus into town. Petrol was short and, if the note was anything to go by, Murray's time was tight. As soon as she'd arrived in Liverpool she was reminded again of how lucky they all were at Bingham Hall. Except for that one raid, so far the home had escaped the wrath of the Luftwaffe the past year. Her heart went out to a cat and two dogs, all with their ribs showing, sniffing for any signs of food in the heaps of rubbish. How she wished she had something to give them. The wind was bitter and she tightened her scarf and pulled her hat down a little more. She was early, as she'd planned to be. It was just that she wanted to see him first. Watch him from a distance, and gradually let him become clearer as she moved towards him.

Suddenly, there he was, looking in the other direction. He was back in uniform. She was thinking how different he looked in civilian clothes – she liked either way – when he turned his head more fully in her direction. He was looking serious, even when he caught sight of her and waved. She began to panic again but inwardly gathered her courage; he obviously had something important he wanted to discuss. Then he smiled and kissed her cheek, and her heart melted as he took her arm and they walked to the restaurant chatting about nothing in particular. She wouldn't get agitated. He'd tell her in his own time.

All through the meal June was aware that he kept glancing at her, a thoughtful expression on his face. She thought she would burst if he didn't tell her soon.

'Can we go to the later showing of the film?' He ran his hand through his hair making the front stick up in a tuft.

She wanted to lean over and straighten it but he might think her too forward, and anyway the waiter was hovering, ready to give them the bill.

'Yes, of course.' June put her knife and fork neatly together, trying to appear calm, though inwardly her heart was hammering.

There was another silence.

'Is everything all right?' she asked, really concerned now.

Maybe he was being sent away. It would be more difficult for them to stay in touch, if so. She worried about him. He'd been lucky so far but he could go up today or tomorrow or next week or next month and never come back.

'Yes, as right as it *can* be. Defending Liverpool is a darned sight better than taking off for Germany at night with a load of bombs.' He gave her a rueful smile. 'Not that it's without its moments.'

Her stomach lurched as it always did when she imagined him flying his aeroplane and fending off the Germans at the same time. To her, it never seemed humanly possible, and certainly not the easy option.

'Anyway, I don't want to talk about work, even if I was allowed to.' Murray put his hand out and covered hers. Instantly, she felt a bolt of electricity rush up her arm. 'I'd like us to be somewhere private but it's so difficult these days.'

June gave a quick glance round the room. 'I don't think anyone's taking any notice of us.'

'Still . . .' Murray sounded uncertain.

June waited. After a long pause he finally spoke.

'I bless the day we met on the train and then by wonderful chance in the bookshop.'

Her heart lifted. 'Me, too,' she faltered.

'You're also the prettiest girl I've ever known. And the sweetest.'

A warmth and longing flooded through her. It was going to be all right. She looked straight into his bright-blue eyes, crinkling at the corners. Then she took a mental step backwards. His eyes weren't full of love but filled with anxiety. What was the matter? She told herself not to be a fool. Of course. He was worried what she might say. He wouldn't want to commit himself and embarrass her if she didn't feel the same. Yes, that was it.

'June, you know how very, very fond I am of you?'

Fond? That wasn't the word she was hoping to hear. But she nodded. And waited.

'I do love you, you know.'

Oh, Murray.

He was right. They needed to be private. She was aware of the couple at the next table clattering their cutlery and clinking their wine glasses. She could see out of the corner of her eye the man lean across and kiss the woman's lips. They were obviously madly in love. They certainly didn't care about privacy. But she did. Though what did it matter? She and Murray loved each other and soon the whole world would know. She opened her mouth to tell him she loved him too.

'But not in the way you deserve.' He squeezed her hand gently.

She tried to clear her head. Couldn't understand. What was he saying? She couldn't have heard him properly. He loved her. He'd just told her so.

'You're a darling girl and you deserve someone to love you with no holds barred.'

He didn't love her after all. He was letting her go. No warning, no nothing.

Her bottom lip quivered and she put her hand to her mouth to stop it. He couldn't be saying what she thought he'd said.

'But—' She couldn't speak.

'I should have made it clear sooner. I was very wrong not to. Maybe I didn't know myself.' Murray took his hand away and it was as though he'd dealt her a blow.

How she wanted to rerun the last five minutes. Have him tell her he'd fallen in love with her and ask would she do him the honour of becoming his wife. She didn't dare look at him because if she did she'd break down. He loved her only as a friend and if he had an inkling that she felt differently, he'd be terribly upset that he'd hurt her. No, he mustn't see her face crumple. Her brain took in his words, and her heart mocked her for being so foolish. Her insides racked in turmoil. She pulled in her stomach and tried to take in a strong breath to keep from throwing herself at his feet, begging him to love her as she loved him.

She willed the tears not to fall and swallowed, wondering if the lump in her throat would ever go away.

'You don't have to say anything more,' she said, her voice low and flat.

Please don't say anything more.

'Can we still be friends?'

She raised her eyes to him, not knowing, not caring if he saw the tears gather.

'Of course we're friends,' she managed to answer.

Murray leaned towards her and grasped her hand again. His eyes were bright and if she wasn't mistaken, they looked moist, almost with regret.

'I'm glad,' he said. 'I would have hated it if you'd begun to get serious about me. You know I wouldn't hurt you for the world.'

251

June took up her glass of wine, still half-full. She tipped it back and gulped it down as though she were in a desert gasping for the last glass of water. Her insides were collapsing and she felt the heat of embarrassment pulsing through her whole body. He must never know the truth. She looked at her watch, more for something to do, trying to think of an excuse to get away before she broke down completely.

'I should get back. They're short-staffed at the moment. It was a bad time for me to leave. And I know you're busy too.' She knew she was gabbling.

'What about the Bette Davis film we were going to? You wanted to see it and I invited you. I'll feel bad if we don't go – and there's still time even to see the early show if we hurry.'

No, it was a comedy and she didn't feel like laughing.

She rose to her feet. 'Let's plan to go another time.'

'All right. But I'll see you home.' He got up from the table.

'There's no need.' She picked up her bag and gloves. 'The bus will be along in a few minutes and if I hurry I can just catch it.'

'If you're sure . . .' Murray's tone was doubtful.

'Perfectly sure.' She even managed to smile but her eyes felt cold.

He came round to her side of the table and kissed her cheek.

'Goodbye, Murray.'

'It's not goodbye. Don't say goodbye.'

She was aware of him calling her name, softly, almost as though he didn't want her to hear him. It was all she could do to hold herself together, the wine she'd drunk too quickly making her stumble across the floor of the restaurant. She had to get out of the door before it was too late and she would break down and sob her heart out.

Bloody insensitive stupid idiot.

If he was honest he knew he'd gone too far with her. He should never have kissed her the way he had that evening. Felt her warm soft lips under his. Hugging her to him, stroking her hair, laughing at silly things with her, watching the way her face lit up when she caught sight of him, dancing with her, holding her close, feeling the lines of her slender body . . . He shook his head in despair. It was all his fault. He'd let her think he was becoming serious. And it was true – he had been. And then the planes that didn't come back. He'd counted them one by one, feeling sick in the pit of his stomach. Two more still to come. He'd almost given up when a lone aeroplane had come limping home. But it was their newest pilot – a young inexperienced one. Yet he'd survived.

'I saw him go down,' he'd told the waiting pilots, his voice shaking, his eyes wide with shock.

As soon as Murray had had a chance he'd gone to the men's and vomited into the pan.

And then the agony of losing two more of his friends in the space of the next two days, and Shorty's face, once so damned good-looking, now so badly burned that they told him he'd have to go to a special burns unit in Sussex. This bloody war. No, he couldn't allow June to fall in love with him and then have something happen to him like it had Shorty. June was such a loyal person. She'd say she would stay with him. Look after him. Ruin her own life. Not get married and have a family. His mind felt as if it was bursting – shooting in all directions like fireworks. Must back off. Not get close. Better to let June carry on thinking they could only be friends. But he hadn't bargained for how deeply hurt she'd been. She'd looked at him disbelievingly, and tried to say that of course they were friends, that she understood, but he'd heard her voice tremble. He'd hoped she wouldn't believe him. But she had and he'd had to let her go – let her walk away. She hadn't turned round. And now he'd lost her.

Chapter Twenty-Six

'You're wanted, June,' shouted Athena, putting her hand over the receiver as June was hurrying by on her way to the classroom.

Barbara had been taken poorly with a chest infection and Matron had asked June if she would take the scripture class. All she knew was what she'd learned in her regular attendance at Sunday school, but she reasoned if she could keep at least a couple of lessons ahead of the most informed child, she'd manage somehow.

June's heart raced. Who could be calling her? Murray, she thought instinctively. She glanced at her watch. It was already twenty to nine. She wanted to be in class well before the children appeared at nine so she could decide what story she was going to read from the Bible and how she would lead the discussion. Feeling irritated at Matron's casual way of telling her at the last minute she was to teach twelve boys and three girls religion, she wondered how she'd answer him. She must keep it light.

A fortnight had gone by since that horrible evening and Murray hadn't been in touch since. She'd tried to carry on normally but inside she was weeping. Only yesterday Iris had asked her when the wedding was going to be announced. She knew her friend was teasing but she'd rounded on her.

'Please stop talking such nonsense, Iris. There's never going to be one.'

June felt a stinging behind her eyes and blinked. She'd been horrible to Iris, who hadn't deserved it. What was the matter with her? Poor Iris had been mortified when June told her she and Murray were only friends and would never be anything more. That it was what Murray wanted.

June swallowed.

'Come on, June,' Athena said impatiently, 'the pips have gone twice already.'

June grabbed the receiver. 'June Lavender here.' But to her surprise there was no answering name, no smile in the sound of 'Flight Lieutenant Andrews this end,' as he usually said. In fact there was a dead silence. June shook the receiver and repeated her name. There was a grunt and a groan. Then cursing. She was just about to put the telephone back on its cradle when a voice said: 'Is that you, June?'

The jolt of surprise nearly knocked her off her feet. It was the last person she wanted to speak to. Her stomach crawled with apprehension and loathing. She gripped the receiver.

'I want to speak to my daughter, June Lavender.' Now the voice was clearer over the telephone line.

A sick feeling started in the pit of her stomach. Why? Why was he calling? How did he know where she was? She hadn't left him any address even. Just somewhere near Liverpool. Only one person. Aunt Ada. Oh, how could she?

'It's June,' she mumbled, hating to own up that that was indeed who she was.

'Ah, there you are.' Her father's tone softened just a little. 'How you doing, girl, up north, so far away from all of us?'

'I'm very happy here.' She'd long made up her mind she would never call him 'Dad' again. He had no right to expect it.

'I've missed you, girl.'

June felt a slick of bile at the back of her throat. Dear God, what did he want? Money, she supposed. Well, she'd have to send him some though he'd only go out and spend it on beer.

'What do you want?' she forced herself to ask. 'I have to go into class now and teach religion.'

She would have liked him to think about that, but she knew it would be lost on him.

'My, my. My little girl a teacher.' He gave a throaty chuckle. 'Well, now, I'm right proud of you.'

The words trickled off her like a summer shower. In a moment, if he didn't say what he'd rung her for, she'd put the receiver down on him. She would. He couldn't do anything to her now. Couldn't hurt her. She was hundreds of miles away. But his next words caused her to nearly fall to her knees.

'I've had a bad accident, girl. Your poor old dad can't walk. Won't walk never again. You see, I'm numb from me waist down. I fell off a roof trying to look out for the bleeding Hun. Fighting for king and country, I was. Now I'll spend the rest of me life in a chair.' She heard a strange sound she'd never heard him make before. He was crying. Sobbing. There was a loud sniff, and she heard him blow his nose. 'I need you to come back, June, m'girl. There's no one else. I need you more than those little wretches. Come back and look after your poor old dad.'

No. It can't be. June dropped the receiver in her anguish, and watched it dangle on the end of the grey plaited cord. Dear God, it couldn't be true. She heard his voice calling out and without hesitating she banged the receiver back on its cradle. Falling into the nearest chair she sank her head in her hands. She couldn't do it . . . she couldn't. She'd be sick looking after that creature. As though her stomach reacted to her thoughts, nausea rushed to her throat. She got up and ran to the cloakroom and put her head over the toilet, retching with the violence of her anger, the perspiration pouring off her forehead. Slowly she rose and turned on the tap and put her mouth under the gush of water, greedily swallowing mouthful after mouthful. She turned off the tap. She daren't look at herself in the mirror above the basin. She knew she must look a fright.

Somehow she had to compose herself. She couldn't explain to anyone what had happened. What she'd been asked to do – to give up her life for someone who didn't give one iota for her. Someone she hated. Someone she had to acknowledge was her father. She cringed, and more tears trickled down her cheeks. Suddenly she missed Stella. She was the only one who would understand. Stella might be a little selfish at times but she'd had every right to snatch some happiness, especially since she'd lost Nigel in the war. She only hoped Stella's new man would treat her kindly and, if it was serious, be a good father to those boys.

Lost in her thoughts she shut the cloakroom door behind her and almost bumped into Iris.

'I wondered where you were, Junie. God, you look awful. Have you been crying? Who was that on the telephone?'

'I've just been sick.' June looked at her friend, her voice dull. Iris was the only one here she'd trust to tell. 'He's just made the longest speech I've ever heard. He wants me to go back and look after him.'

'Who does?'

'My father.'

'You're not going back to that bastard,' Iris said firmly, 'and that's an order.'

'You don't understand,' June said, her vision so blurry she could hardly see straight. 'I've got to.'

'Why have you got to?'

'Because I'm all he has.'

'Don't be ridiculous.' Iris pulled up a chair and took one of June's hands in her own. 'He's a bully and he's violent. Why should you devote your life to him? Do you think he'd do the same for you?'

June shook her head. She was trembling with the force of her anger at him placing her in such a position.

'What about Stella? And your aunt. Ada, isn't it? Is she his sister?'

'No. She's Mum's. She hates him. Says he's good for nothing.'

'Sounds like a good description from what you've told me.'

'Stella's got enough to manage with her three boys,' June said, struggling not to let any envy creep into her voice. She'd never been envious of Stella, but she wished at that moment she could have changed places with her. 'And she lives in Cambridgeshire so she's much too far away.'

'Well, you're even further in Liverpool,' Iris said reasonably. 'He can't expect you to drop everything – the children and your job.'

'He doesn't see it like that. I don't have my own children or a husband. So I'm free to look after him.'

'And Murray? You were a bit sharp the other day when I joked about the wedding date, but I also happen to know you're in love with him.'

June's heart contracted so sharply it was as though a clamp had squeezed it.

'Murray and I are friends – that's all.' She tried to laugh it off.

'Friends, my foot.' Iris looked at June sternly. 'I don't care what he told you. The two of you are crazy about each other.' She ignored June's shake of her head. 'You're not going and that's final.'

But the following morning June was on the bus to the railway station with a ticket in her pocket for London.

Everyone at the home had told her not to worry. She'd find someone to care for her father and she'd soon be back to Bingham Hall. But June wasn't convinced. Her father had once again reached out a long arm and dragged her away from something she loved, something she felt she might even be good at – and she was too much of a coward to tell him to go to the devil.

She refused to think that she'd also been dragged away from Murray.

Chapter Twenty-Seven

After June's mother died, her father had moved from their old house in Cambridgeshire to London, saying he was going to start afresh. June had had to bite her tongue to stop a bitter reply. The room he'd rented wasn't that far from Aunt Ada's house, but she failed to understand why he'd chosen it. Aunt Ada wouldn't look after the brute, as she called him, in a million years and why should she? He'd been responsible for her sister's broken heart after Clara died, and that in turn had led to her death.

It was another tedious journey but thankfully there were no bad hold-ups and by mid-afternoon she was outside the house where her father now lived.

June put her hand up to the knocker on the front door, wondering how her father could manage in a wheelchair. She'd only been here once before, to tell him she had a job near Liverpool, hoping it would be for good, and at that time he had been on the third floor. 'Good view up here,' he'd said. There were no steps up to the front door but it was likely to be difficult, once you were inside what she remembered was a narrow hall, to fit in a wheelchair.

A woman with too much make-up, and grey hair tied back in a wispy scarf, opened the door.

'Yes?'

'Is Mr Lavender at home?'

'What would you be wanting with Billy Lavender?' The woman narrowed her eyes with suspicion.

'He's my father.' Oh, how she hated to admit it.

'Your father, eh?' The woman's tone softened a fraction. 'I feel sorry for you, love. Not an easy man, I'd say. He's up in number 8. Third floor.' She jerked her head towards the stairs.

June frowned. It was the same number. How on earth could he manage? He'd be like a prisoner. She took a deep breath as though to prepare herself, and climbed the three flights of stairs, twisting round and round until she reached the top landing. There was number 8 facing her. She knocked, her heart beating hard in her chest.

The door opened immediately as if he'd been waiting for this moment. She drew back as the smell of beer hit her nostrils. And then the stink of his unwashed body enveloping her, the pretence of a smile hovering on his too-thick mouth. He moved a walking stick to one side. Where was the wheelchair? Where were the paralysed legs? A bolt of rage swept through her. She should have known. Why had she believed him? She made as though to escape but he caught her arm in a vice-like grip and pulled her inside.

'There you are, girl. Come in, come in. Make yourself at home. It's a bit untidy, mind, but you'll soon have it ship-shape, I'll be bound.'

She thought she would gag. The stench reached right inside her lungs, making her gasp.

He shut the door behind her and immediately she felt trapped. His huge bulk seemed to take up the whole sitting room, if you could call it that. June's disbelieving eyes scanned the room. The furniture looked worse than she remembered it. A rag-and-bone man would probably turn it down. Stuffing was protruding from a sofa which tipped down at one side, the front of it well-shredded by what looked like a disobedient cat. What was once a matching armchair had a greasy patch the size of a dinner plate on the upright where her father, or someone, had constantly rested a Brylcreemed head. There was a table with a wad of paper under one of the legs, presumably to balance it, and stacked with newspapers and several stained cups. A rug that hardly covered the worn and cracked green lino beneath, and windows and frames that were filthy. Cobwebs draped in corners and over the curtain rail, and anywhere they could cling. Damp and urine and smoke permeated the atmosphere. Her father had obviously never attempted to do any cleaning at all since he'd lived here and evidently took little notice.

'Cup of tea for you, girl?'

She'd rather die than accept anything from him. She only had to glimpse through an open door to his kitchen to see what a disgusting mess it was in. It looked as though a week's worth of dishes was piled on the draining board, and she could see cigarette butts and empty beer bottles thrown in a heap in the corner with some old clothes tossed on the top.

How could this man be anything to do with her, let alone be her father? She shuddered. And then her rage boiled over.

'You've got me here under false pretences. There's obviously nothing wrong with your legs. "In a wheelchair. Can't walk. Completely numb for life."' She turned on him, not caring, spitting out the words.

He actually moved back a step in surprise.

'Now, girl, don't be like that to your poor old dad.'

'You're *not* my dad.' June raised her voice to make sure he heard every word. 'You've never been a dad to me, never acted like one and you never will. I hate every bone in your rotten body. I don't know why my mother married you. You disgust me. I'm leaving – right this minute. And I never want to set eyes on you again.' She turned and made for the door, suitcase still in her hand.

'Just hear me out, young lady, with your high-and-mighty talk.' Her father sat heavily on the armchair. 'I think you need to know something before you go mouthing off. I was the one who rescued your mother from the gutter.'

What was he on about? Her fingers were already on the door handle. She kept her back to him as she said, 'Don't you dare talk about my mother like that.'

'It's the truth. She would've ended up a doxy if it hadn't been for me.'

June swung round, her eyes ablaze. 'I don't believe you.'

'It's true. She already had Stella. Yes, you can look. Stella was three when I took her in. Married your mother to give the little bastard a name. Make an honest woman of her. So don't make me laugh, girl. Your mother owes me, and more.'

'Well, she can hardly repay you for your *kindness*' – June emphasised the word – 'when she's no longer alive.'

'That's it. You've hit the nail on the head. She can't – but *you* can. Because you see, June, dear' – his lips formed a sneer – 'not only was Stella a little bastard, but so were you!'

It was difficult to stand there in the claustrophobic stench and take in what he was saying. Her mother had had *two* illegitimate babies? Not just one, but two. It didn't make sense.

'That's shut your gob up for a bit.' Her father gave a mirthless chuckle. 'I thought that might bring you up short.'

'What about Clara?' June whispered, dreading what he would say next.

His lips formed a smile. 'She's your mother's. But she

264

ain't mine neither. None of yous are mine. Three of you. So what do you think of that?' A bubble of spit gathered in the corner of his lips, but his eyes were alight with triumph. June realised he was actually enjoying telling her these secrets about her mother. How he must have hated her too. And how her mother must have hated him to have sought comfort elsewhere. A sliver of admiration crept into her heart. June was glad her mother hadn't completely cowed under her bully of a husband. She hoped, whoever the man was, he'd treated her mother with kindness and love.

'Yes, she carried on with him even after I married her. She couldn't never have him 'cos he already had a wife. And like a fool I stuck with her. She tried to pass you and Clara off as mine. But I knew different and after I gave her a good hiding she admitted it in the end.' He paused and his mouth twisted. 'And in case you're wonderin', it's no good going looking for him. He's dead and buried – long ago.'

June couldn't take her eyes off him. Instinctively she knew for once he was speaking the truth. And the light dawned, big and bright. She wanted to shout with joy. Not one drop of his bad blood was in her. It was as though a huge weight lifted from her. She wouldn't have to ever worry again about whether she'd inherited any of his rotten traits. They had nothing whatsoever to do with her – or with Stella, or with Clara. No wonder his treatment of his so-called three daughters was so cruel. He had no love for any of us, she thought. We weren't his. We were simply three little bastards who lived under the same roof.

'And Clara—'

'Don't you dare mention Clara's name to me ever again.' June's voice shook with fury. 'I will never forgive you for what happened.'

'I agree, that were unfortunate.'

265

'*Unfortunate*?' June screamed at him. 'How *dare* you call my sister's death "unfortunate"?'

'It were an acci—'

Hardly aware of what she was doing June dropped her case in one movement and grabbed the nearest object and threw it straight at him. The vase bounced off his skull and smashed into the fireplace. He placed his hands on the arms of the chair and half rose, his eyes wide with terror, and then he slowly slumped back in the chair without a word, blood pouring from his head.

She ran over to him and shook him but he didn't respond. Blindly she found the toilet and grabbed a dingy towel off the door handle and clumsily wrapped it round his head. He didn't stir.

'Speak to me.' The word 'Dad' stuck in her throat.

But there was nothing.

What had she done? Dear God, what had she done? She must have killed him.

She didn't stop to think. She turned and raced out of the door, taking the stairs two at a time. Then ran back up, heart pounding with exertion, and without looking at the lifeless figure in the chair, snatched up her case and ran back down the stairs again.

As she flew along the hallway the grey-haired landlady came out of one of the rooms and shot an arm out to stop her.

'Just where are you going in such a hurry, Miss Lavender?'

June shook the arm off. She was in a daze. Couldn't think. Was he dead?

'Please telephone for an ambulance,' she shouted as she flung open the front door. 'My father's had an accident.' She pulled the door behind her, slamming out the landlady's call for her to come back this instant.

Oh, the relief to be out in the street. She took three seconds to gulp some air, and then she ran and ran and ran. She had no idea which direction she was running in. If she'd killed him she was glad. If she hadn't she hoped he'd have a sore, throbbing head for the rest of his life. Then she stopped and caught her breath, her heart thundering like mad in her chest. If she'd killed him it would be murder. She'd be up for murder. Hanged. Oh, dear God. Even if they didn't hang her she would go to prison for the rest of her life. Everything she'd worked for would be gone – her job at Dr Barnardo's which meant the world to her, Lizzie and all the other children she'd grown so fond of, and who she was sure had begun to rely on her, Aunt Ada's loving support, her friends, Iris and Kathleen, and most of all . . . a man in a greatcoat with twinkling eyes the colour of a summer sky. How could she confess to him she'd killed her own father? Who wasn't her father. Oh, this was a nightmare.

She closed her eyes as the whole horrible truth took hold. Tears squeezed through her eyelids and slid down her cheeks.

Still panting hard, she put her hand on a bus stop to steady herself. Sweat was pouring off her forehead. She should have stayed until the ambulance arrived. Instead she'd left the landlady to deal with a dead body. Bile rose in her throat. She was glad. He deserved it. But she knew she was only trying to persuade herself. No one deserved to die. Except maybe Hitler and all the wicked men around him, carrying out his revolting orders.

She looked around to see where she was. She knew she wasn't far from Oxford Street. But that was the last place she wanted to be, among crowds of normal people doing their shopping. There was a large church in the distance that didn't look too far away. Maybe she could just go in there for a few minutes – try to think what she must do. Her head felt as if it would burst. Should she go and see Aunt Ada? She bit her lip so hard she tasted a trickle of blood. Aunt Ada would probably say, 'Good riddance to bad rubbish.' She started to hurry towards the church, head down, not wanting to catch anyone's eye and have them wonder what this mad woman was doing, rushing along. She only knew she must find somewhere to stop and think. Sit quietly. Think what she should do.

She felt the force of knocking into someone who put out a hand to steady her.

'Well, I'll be darned – it's June Lavender, isn't it?' Charles Lockstone grinned down at her. 'Where are you going in such a hurry?'

Now she'd stopped she couldn't catch her breath. She tilted her neck back, just to make sure. Chas. Easy-going Chas. Could she tell him? Would he understand? Would he believe her? If only it was Murray who stood in front of her.

'You look as though something's upset you mighty bad,' Chas said, still holding her arm firmly. She was thankful. She'd begun to feel quite light-headed. Feeling she would choke and swallowing hard, she tried to dislodge the lump in her throat.

He looked down at her intently. 'Do you want to tell me about it? I'm a good listener.'

She shook her head. She didn't want him to go with her and sit in church.

'I'm on leave for a few days and my buddy wasn't inter-ested in any sightseeing.' He hesitated. 'Look, why don't we go and sit on a bench in the park?'

She nodded. He took her hand as they crossed the road.

'Come on, tell Uncle Charles what's the matter,' Chas said when they were sitting on the bench.

'I think I've just killed my father,' June blurted.

There was a sharp intake of breath beside her. She ventured to take her hands from her face and look at him. His cheery grin had faded and a look of horror had taken its place.

'You don't know what you're saying.' The horror had faded to disbelief.

'I-I do know what I'm saying.' She was sobbing openly now. 'I shouldn't have told you. I'm sorry.' She drew in a huge breath and Chas handed her a handkerchief. She blew her nose.

'Yes, you *should* tell me.' He took hold of her hands and turned her towards him. 'This is serious, June. You must start from the beginning.'

He sat there silently while she told him everything.

'You poor girl. But you need to go back to his lodgings and find out what happened. If the ambulance came. If he really *is* dead – which he probably isn't.'

She looked up at him, despair in her eyes. 'I'll come with you, if you like,' he added.

She leaned against him gratefully for a few seconds, then pulled away. He might misinterpret her action when she was feeling vulnerable.

Chas got hold of her arm and tucked it through his, and together they quickly retraced the steps to Billy Lavender's. This time the front door was slightly ajar and there was no landlady in sight. They rushed up to number 8 and that door, too, was unlocked. They went in. Her father was no longer there. The vase was still in fragments in the fireplace and there were bloodstains on the lino and on the back of the chair he'd slumped against.

She felt sick again and had to rush to the toilet, where she brought up a stream of bile. She rinsed out her mouth.

'Are you okay?' Chas sounded concerned.

'I don't know what to do. I suppose they've taken the body to hospital to find out how he died.'

'Which is the nearest?'

'I don't know. We'll have to find the landlady.'

But she was nowhere around. The whole house seemed to be empty.

'We'll get a cab,' Chas said. 'The driver will probably know which one he'll have gone to.'

A quarter of an hour later the taxi dropped them off at the front door of a plain sprawling building with a hospital sign. Chas marched straight up to the reception desk and asked if Billy Lavender had been brought in as an emergency.

The young girl shuffled some papers and ran her pencil down the list.

'A William Lavender was admitted about an hour ago.'

'That's him.' June joined him at the desk. 'I'm his daughter' – her voice shook – 'and I—'

'One moment.' The girl picked up the internal telephone. 'I've got Mr Lavender's daughter here.' There was a pause. 'Yes, she's here in reception. Oh, I see . . .' Her voice trailed off.

He's dead. I'll be hanged. I'm a murderess. I'll go to hell.

To her surprise the girl turned towards her and smiled. 'Would you like to see him? He's in Ward 9. Down the corridor and turn left. Then through the swing doors. You'll see it marked.'

'He-he's not dead then?'

'Apparently not,' she said, and laughed. 'He's sitting up and demanding his dinner.'

Chas roared with laughter too and squeezed her arm. 'Say, that's swell. Shall we go and see the old so-and-so?'

The young girl frowned. 'It's a quiet area all over the hospital.'

'I'm sorry, Ma'am.' He gave her his charming smile and she simpered. Then he bent down and whispered in June's ear, 'So you're not a murderess after all. Shame. I was looking forward to some excitement.'

June glanced at him doubtfully. His American ways would take some getting used to. He caught her eye and held out his arm. 'Let's go find him.'

'No,' June said, her teeth on edge. 'Let's not.' She took his arm. 'I want to get out of here – right now. Get some air. I feel I'm suffocating.'

'We'll go have a coffee first.' Chas sent an apologetic glance to the young girl behind the desk.

It was after they'd left the café that June saw the puppy. Chas had said he wanted to go to back to Oxford Street, to Selfridges, to buy something for his mother's birthday, and when they were walking along Regent Street, June feeling a little calmer, she saw the puppy in Hamleys' window. He was amongst a few dozen other toys, but he stood out. He was so like Freddie with his brown head and spark of white above his nose. His red felt tongue was hanging out, and he looked for all the world as though he might bark with happiness at any moment. She had to have him no matter how much he cost.

'Chas, I'm going to ask the price of the puppy over there.' She pointed to it.

'You girls with your stuffed toys,' Chas said with a laugh, guiding her into the shop.

She didn't bother to tell him it was for Lizzie.

A thin pasty-faced boy stood behind the counter wearing a tin hat. June looked round to see two other staff in tin hats. Silently Chas pointed up to the ceiling which had been recently damaged.

'We wear the hats all the time,' the pasty young man said as he followed their glance. 'We've already been caught three times.'

'Do you mean the shop's been bombed three times?'

'Yes, that's right.' His lips were almost white with fear and he gave a nervous giggle. 'Can I help you with something?'

'I'd like one of the brown-and-white puppies like the one in the window.'

'I'm afraid they've all been sold, Miss. They've been very popular.'

'But what about the one in the window?'

'That's for display so we can sell the whole boxful.'

'But if they're all sold now you don't need the one in the window to help with any more sales,' June persisted.

'It's against the rules to take anything out of the window.'

'Then I'd like to speak to the manager.'

'He's on a break.'

June tapped a foot impatiently. 'When will he be back?'

The boy looked over at the wall clock. 'Maybe half an hour. Maybe longer. No saying with Mr Barber. He's often late . . .' His voice trailed off and he went bright red. 'Oh, Mr Barber, can you help this lady? She's asking for you.'

'I'll talk to you later, young man.' Mr Barber sent him a stern look, then turned to June and Chas with a bright smile.

June repeated her request.

'I'm afraid young Robson was right – the window has to stay as it is until the dresser comes next week and re-does it.'

'But I won't be here next week,' June protested. 'It's for a child who's had her real puppy taken away from her. She's lost her whole family in a bombing raid and she didn't speak – until she had Freddie. Then she had to give him back because Matron at the orphanage wouldn't allow it. The toy puppy looks so much like Freddie, I think she'd talk to him.'

'Well, in that case I suppose we can make an exception,' the manager said, his voice softening a little. 'Robson, will you get that brown-and-white puppy out of the window and wrap it up for the lady?'

'How much is it?' June asked, getting her purse out while the young man was leaning into the window to remove the toy.

The manager glanced at the price tag. 'One guinea.'

'A guinea,' June squeaked. 'I'm not sure—'

'I'll be glad to buy it for the lady.' Chas stepped up to the counter. He got out his wallet and removed a bundle of notes. He peeled a pound note off the top. 'A guinea' – he turned to June – 'it's another shilling, isn't it? But I'm afraid I don't have any change.'

'I've got a shilling.' June's face flushed with embarrassment. She should have asked how much it was right at the beginning. A guinea. She'd guessed about five shillings.

'I'll pay you back, Chas,' she said when they were outside, the brown package safely under Chas's arm.

'No sweat. Consider it a present.'

'But it's for Lizzie.'

'It's a present for Lizzie, then. She sounds as though she's had a rough time.'

'You're really kind, Chas. Thank you.' She looked up at him and smiled.

'I want to be kind to you, June. You're so lovely. Don't you know by now I'm crazy about you? Say, what about having a spot of tea, as you Limeys say, at the hotel where I'm staying? It's not far from here. We can walk.'

Immediately June felt uncomfortable. She put it down to his American-ness but she didn't want to hear those sorts

273

of declarations. They didn't make one jot of difference to her feelings. She knew by now he really liked her, but in her eyes he'd never be more than a friend – a *good* friend, after the way he'd helped her today, but sooner or later, if he carried on like this, she'd have to tell him her heart belonged to someone else.

Chapter Twenty-Eight

Feeling embarrassed that her clothes weren't posh enough for such a grand place, June followed Chas through the elegant revolving doors of the Strand Palace Hotel. He seemed perfectly at ease as he walked up to the reception desk, exchanged a few words and nods, and collected his key.

She looked around the foyer. It was a stunning space, beautifully designed in the art deco style, reminding her of the theatre in Liverpool where Murray had taken her to see the Oscar Wilde play. She ran her tongue over her lips, almost tasting his kiss when he'd brought her back to Bingham Hall. Her eyes stung with the memory. She was sure he hadn't had friendship on his mind that evening.

Chas followed her gaze. 'It's rather marvellous, isn't it?' he said.

It was teeming with American soldiers, all of them in uniform, drinking and laughing loudly, some of them sprawled on comfortable-looking sofas around the fireplaces, or gathered at the tables, or standing in groups smoking around the bar.

'I'm afraid we Americans rather took over the place,' Chas said apologetically. 'It's now an official rest and recuperation place for US soldiers. But I'm glad it's so popular. For some of them it'll be their last night – ever.'

A shiver ran down June's back. She was in no doubt as to what he meant.

'I'm glad, too,' she whispered.

Her attention was caught by one lady, beautifully dressed with a fox fur folded over the shoulder of her cream coat, a hat perched at a dangerous angle, being led by a small white poodle amongst the crowds. She was walking to and fro with undisguised impatience, glancing at her watch, strapped over the top of her glove, every few seconds. June wondered who she was waiting for.

'They're going to bring us tea and cakes to my room,' Chas said. 'We can be more private there.'

There were very few vacant seats, June decided, so it seemed a sensible suggestion. She brushed aside the thought that she'd be going up to a man's bedroom – a man she barely knew. He'd been so kind to her and it would make her look as though she was worried he had an ulterior motive. She drew in a shaky breath, too tired to argue.

The lift took them to the third floor. Chas put the key in a door next to the lift and gestured her inside. To her relief the room was huge, although the first thing to face her was an enormous bed, draped in cream bedcovers and cushions. She averted her eyes and stood wondering what she should do.

'Do sit down, June. The waiter will be here shortly and we can have that cup of tea. I think we both need one. Here, let me take your coat.'

Thankfully she eased into an armchair by the side of a desk under one of the windows, putting her bag and her parcel on the floor beside her. Everything was beautifully and softly lit, and there was a faint smell of rose in the air. Still, she felt self-conscious in Chas's bedroom. The bed was so dominant she couldn't feel at ease. Maybe she was being too sensitive. She thought of the lady in the foyer in her fox fur stole. *She* would know how to handle the situation, no doubt about it. June took a few deep breaths and felt a little calmer, but she was still glad of the interruption of a gentle tap on the door. Chas went to open it and the waiter came in pushing a chrome art deco tea trolley with the tea service set out on top, and a plate of cream cakes and small sandwiches with the crusts taken off on the shelf underneath.

Chas took the upright chair and moved it opposite. He handed her the plate of sandwiches and she took one. He nodded for her to take more but she couldn't, even though she realised she was hungry. The sandwich was egg and cress and delicious, but she was too nervous to enjoy it. Chas took one, swallowed it in a couple of bites, then reached for another.

'Are you warm enough?'

She nodded.

'And comfortable?'

'Yes, thank you.'

'Shall I be mother?' He smiled at her. 'Isn't that what you English say?'

She nodded and smiled back. He was obviously trying to put her at her ease and she was grateful. Without asking, he put two lumps of sugar in her cup. She took her time stirring it for something to do, now that she'd finished the sandwich. She couldn't face one of the cream cakes, though Chas wolfed down a couple.

'Thanks, Chas. I don't know what I would have done without you,' she said fervently.

'It was nothing.' Chas leaned towards her, smiling encouragingly.

'It was everything.' The image of Billy Lavender sinking

277

back in the chair, blood pouring from his head, flashed through her mind. She realised how close she'd come to doing a most fearful deed, which would without doubt have ruined the rest of her life. She gave a shudder. The tears started again and she couldn't stop trembling. With a shaking hand she put her cup and saucer down on the desk. The cup rattled in the saucer and she tried to steady it but she only made it worse. Without warning she put her head in her hands and began to sob.

Immediately, Chas leaped to his feet and was by her side, his arms around her.

'Come on, honey. You've had a terrible shock but it's all over. You're safe here. Why don't you lie down on the bed for a few minutes. Take a nap if you want. I don't mind. I just want you to feel better.'

He gently pulled her to her feet and led her to the bed where he sat her on the edge and pulled off her shoes. Then he lifted her legs on to the bed and tucked an extra pillow behind her head.

'There. Do you think you could close your eyes for a little while? You've been through so much today, and I think it's the shock coming out now.'

The bed was the most wonderful, the most comfortable she had ever lain upon.

Without effort she shut her eyes and immediately drifted. She didn't know how long she'd been lying there – how long she'd slept – when she was aware of someone lying by the side of her . . . then on top of her . . . someone crushing her . . . kissing her . . . saying her name over and over . . . She was dreaming – it couldn't be . . .

'June. Oh, June.' There was a groan. 'I can't help myself.'

Her eyes flew open and she felt his hand, dear God, it was Chas's hand pulling up her skirt . . . pressing down on her . . . something unfamiliar pushing between the tops of her legs . . . what was he doing? She made to scream but his hand came over her mouth.

'Don't call out,' he said. 'Just let me do it. Oh, June, let me do it. I'll be careful. I love you. Don't you know how much I love you?'

She tried to pull herself away from under him. 'Take your hand away – let me—'

'June, don't you know how much I want you?' Chas groaned.

'Please! I'll call the police if you don't stop.' She thought she was shouting but her heart was hammering in her ears, muffling her voice.

'Why, you little tease. Why did you agree to come to my bedroom if you didn't want it?' His eyes flashed with anger above her, challenging her, frightening her with his fury.

She barely knew what he was saying. All she knew was that she had to get out. But she was trapped by his heavy bulk on top of her, pushing the breath out of her.

'Chas' – her voice was reduced to a whimper – 'please let me go.'

There was a roaring noise like a train. Chas shot up, releasing his hold.

'What is it?' June's eyes were wide with fear as she scrambled from beneath him and pulled down her skirt.

'I don't know, but it doesn't sound right.' His tone changed to fear as he turned his back to her and zipped up his trousers.

As he spoke an alarm went off. Loud and clanging and insistent. The next moment they heard pounding footsteps rush by the door.

June looked up into Chas's startled eyes. 'C'mon, June, we've gotta get outta here. It sounds like a—'

He never finished the sentence. There was a deafening sound of an explosion and the shattering of glass.

'Get your shoes and coat. We gotta go! NOW!'

Quickly, she pushed on her shoes, and grabbed her coat and bag. Chas pulled open the door and they flew along the corridor, meeting dazed-looking guests who didn't seem to know what to do.

'Be careful. A ceiling could cave in at any moment,' a man's voice shouted.

'Don't use the lift,' someone else called.

June was swept along with a herd of panicking guests, one or two of whom were trying to take some kind of control. She thought Chas might be one of them but he was three or four people ahead of her now.

She tried to push through, to catch up with him, and it was then that she remembered – she was only carrying her coat and bag. She didn't have the precious parcel. The toy dog. She had to get it. It was the only thing that might bring Lizzie to speak again. She'd never be able to find another one like it. Drawing back and turning on the stairs she faced a man, red with anger.

'What the hell are you doing? Get going. You can't turn back. You're upsetting the line.'

'I must,' she said. 'I've left something.'

'June!' It was Chas's voice calling her. 'Where are you?'

But she ignored him and somehow managed to push her way through the people pouring down the stairs. She rushed along the corridor, back to Chas's room. The door was still open and she dashed in. The parcel was still there by the side of the armchair where she'd left it. Heart racing, she grabbed it up and made for the door again.

A tremendous crash made her jump. Another and then another.

The hotel's been struck.

She stumbled as she tried to grab the door handle. Her fingers slipped. A scream rang in her eardrums. Lumps of plaster showered her and she felt something fall on her . . .

Her world went dark.

'June, June, please open your eyes.'

An American voice. Her eyelids fluttered and she saw a tall figure bending over her. She closed her eyes again. It was too much effort. The pain in her shoulder . . . or was it her arm? She couldn't tell. Sleep. If she could just sleep through it she'd be all right.

Chapter Twenty-Nine

'June, wake up! The building's been hit. There's smoke. We gotta get out of here.'

She opened her eyes. It was Chas. What was he doing? And then she remembered. She'd been in his room having tea. She'd been in shock . . . her father . . . it all came flooding back. Chas had lain her on his bed and she'd immediately gone to sleep . . . until she felt him on top of her doing things he shouldn't.

Heat from her neck rose to her face. What a fool she'd been. He'd planned the whole thing. She'd heard of men seducing women and that's what would have happened to her if it hadn't been for the alarm going off in the hotel . . . yet he'd come back for her.

'Don't touch my arm,' she cried out as Chas tried to pull her up.

'Come on, June.'

'The parcel,' she moaned.

'NOW!'

Her head swam. *Why was he so loud? Why couldn't he leave her alone?*

'Where's Freddie?' She burst into tears.

'June, listen to me. We have to go. Do you want us both killed?'

With his help she struggled to her feet. Leaning on him, his arm around her waist, she stumbled along as fast as she could, coughing as the smoke caught in her lungs. There was a strange heat which made her gasp and pull away from Chas to lean a few seconds against the passage wall, desperate to breathe. Her eyes stung with grit as she peered through the swirling dust. Where was he? He'd left her. She must run after him but the muscles in her legs refused to work.

'June?' His voice was urgent.

'I'm here.'

She felt his hand grasp hers, pulling her from the wall.

'Come on. It could collapse at any minute.'

'I can't breathe.'

'Pull your scarf over your mouth.'

She did as she was told but the flimsy scarf made no difference. The dust was so thick she could barely see where she was stepping. She could feel the heat burning into her nostrils. There must be a fire somewhere.

Chas rushed her down the second flight of stairs and they were into the foyer, where smoke was pouring in. No voices. It was eerily quiet. It seemed they were the only two in the building. There was no sound except their harsh breathing.

She heard Chas bump into something and swear, but the next moment he'd got her outside, where they both took in great gulps of air. A crowd of people had already congregated and were standing on the other side of the road looking dazed and dishevelled. Members of the hotel staff and some of the soldiers were attempting to comfort several women who were crying.

'There was no siren,' June heard someone say. 'Why didn't it go off?'

'Come on, June, let's go.'

At least the air had cleared her head. She looked at Chas

283

and was shocked at his appearance. Gone was the immaculate officer. His face was as filthy as a tramp's and both his eyes were bloodshot. Even his eyelashes were coated in dust. She must look the same.

'Shouldn't we stay and let them know we're safe? They'll be checking our names off a list, I should think.'

'No, no, we don't want to get caught up with these people.'

'But—'

'No buts.' Chas grabbed her hand but he'd caught the wrong one. She practically screamed out. He stopped. 'Here, let me look at that arm.'

'No, no, it's all right.'

The last thing she wanted was for Chas to touch her.

They started walking again.

'I'm sorry, June. I should have told you why I wanted to get away quickly. I was on my way back to the hotel to collect my things as I was checking out this afternoon. Now I'm left with no change of clothes or toilet bag or any goddamned thing. Just my camera – and my wallet in my jacket. Thank God I have some money. Oh, and this, of course.' He handed her the brown parcel.

'It was all my fault,' June stammered. 'I can't believe I did something so foolish that nearly got us both killed. But I so badly wanted it for Lizzie to start her talking again. Thank you for bringing it.'

They were both silent. Chas seemed almost as embarrassed as she was. He took her good arm as they walked along the road and kept glancing at her and asking if she was sure she was all right. That she was not in too much pain. Did she want him to take her to the hospital? Would she come back to Liverpool with him?

'I'm going to Aunt Ada's,' she said. 'I only hope she's there because she's not on the telephone.'

'I'll get a cab and come with you to make sure.'

'No, Chas. You must get the next train back. If she's not home her neighbour will know where she is. I just want to be with her. She's like a mother to me.'

'What are you going to do about your father – who we now know is not your father?'

'I made my decision as soon as I set eyes on him – when I saw there was only a walking stick, when he said he'd be in a wheelchair the rest of his life,' June said. 'He's lied once too often. I'm washing my hands of him. I'm going back to Bingham Hall. The children need me far more than he does. I'm not going back to that bully. Ever. But I wish I hadn't lost my temper. I could easily have killed him.'

'He would've deserved it. And maybe it taught the son-of-a-bitch a lesson he should've learned long ago.' He abruptly stopped walking. 'Taxi!' he shouted, halfway in the road, waving his arms. One slowed down and pulled to a halt.

Chas opened the door and June dropped thankfully into the seat. She was just about to lean over to say goodbye to him when he jumped in.

'I want to see you safely with your aunt,' he said. 'Then I'll carry on to the station.'

Outside her aunt's house, June knocked at the door and waited. Moments later the door opened and her aunt was framed in the doorway.

'June, dear, what—?'

'I'll explain everything,' June said, turning towards the waiting taxi. Chas had already wound the window down and was peering out.

'She's here,' June said unnecessarily. 'You go on, Chas. And thank you for helping me with . . . Billy.'

It was only when she was safely indoors and her aunt was

putting the kettle on that she realised Chas had never apologised for what he'd attempted to do.

'What's the matter with your arm, dear?' Aunt Ada set the tea tray on the dining table as her eyes followed June, who was rubbing her shoulder and grimacing.

'Nothing much. It's just a bit painful. Something fell on it. I think it's just bruised. I'll tell you about that in a bit, but it's Dad.' She swallowed, trying to compose herself. 'He wanted me to see him. He said he'd had an accident, but he lied. He—'

'That's nothing new,' her aunt interrupted. 'You don't want to pay any attention to him.' She looked at June. 'I wondered what had brought you to London without letting me know.' She poured June a cup of tea. 'Take your time. Just tell me slowly. I want to know everything.'

'And then he told me he wasn't my real father or my sisters',' June finished. Something struck her and her head shot up. 'Aunt Ada, did you know he was only our stepfather?'

'I always knew Stella was Tom's,' her aunt said, 'because she had her before she met Billy Lavender. But your mother didn't tell me about you and Clara until after Clara was born. I happened to mention that neither of you looked anything like Billy, and she said, "I'm not surprised." When I asked her what she meant she told me she was still in love with Tom, the man she'd loved since she was about the same age as you are now – and that they'd never stopped loving one another.'

'What happened to him?'

It was strange asking questions and hearing about her own true father for the first time in her life.

'He wanted to marry your mother but his family had

286

other ideas. Your mother wasn't classy enough for their son, and they did everything they could to keep them apart. But then she fell for your sister Stella, and Tom told his parents that was it, they'd have to get married now. He had a good job in his father's company and was on his way to promotion when his father, your real grandfather, said he would make sure he was penniless if he went ahead. He'd be cut out of the will. And there'd no longer be a position at Carter & Sons. And he'd make sure every other law firm in Cambridge closed their doors on him too. If he thought anything of Maisie, he'd let the family give her some money to keep her quiet, and to promise never to try to see him again.'

June's mouth fell open. 'I can hardly believe it. Poor Mum. What happened then?'

'She took the money – she had to because Stella was on the way and she didn't have a husband. Then Billy came along and promised her the world and that he'd look after Stella as his own. Hard to imagine, but he was a handsome brute once and could charm the birds off the trees. She believed him. At first things weren't too bad. She was relieved she had a husband and a home to bring the baby into. Stella would have been three then. It wasn't until her fourth birthday that he started knocking my sister about. By then she knew she'd made a terrible mistake but she thought so long as he didn't hit her child she'd put up with it. You see, she'd read in the paper that Tom had got married to a society gal. She was heartbroken.'

All the time her aunt was talking, June's eyes never left her face. It was impossible that she was hearing such things about her own mother and Billy and now Tom.

'Do you want me to carry on?'

June nodded. 'Yes, please.' Her voice was thick with tears.

'By this time Billy was drinking. He was pickled more

often than he was sober. Your mother and Tom began to meet. Just as friends at first. Until they both admitted they still loved one another. Tom confessed he'd made a mistake. Got married on the rebound to an empty-headed spoilt brat. It wasn't long before your mother fell again. This time it was you. She didn't dare tell Billy, and he didn't find out until Clara was conceived. Then he nearly went mad as by then they hadn't had any husband-and-wife relationship so he knew Clara couldn't be his. I kept telling her to leave – told her to come here – but she said it wasn't fair on me and there was only one spare single bedroom. She had no money – nowhere to go. That's how it was.'

'So that's why he was so cruel to Clara.' June's voice was hardly above a whisper. 'I couldn't ever understand it. She was such a beautiful child with such a sunny nature.' She dropped her head in her hands and began to sob her heart out.

'Don't cry, love. You don't ever have to see him again if you don't want to.'

'You don't understand,' June said, looking at her aunt through eyes wet with tears. 'You see h-he started to say something about C-Clara. About it being an accident.'

Aunt Ada poured her another cup of tea. 'Come on, love. Your tea's gone cold. Have this while it's hot. Nothing can be that bad.'

'But it is.' June looked up at her aunt with red-rimmed eyes.

'Shhhhh. Drink your tea.'

She gulped it down but it didn't make her feel any better. 'I feel a bit dizzy.'

'When did you last have a proper meal?' Aunt Ada demanded.

'It was . . . oh, I can't remember. Hours ago. Chas and I were about to have tea and cakes at his hotel' – she broke off and blushed furiously – 'and then – then bombs fell on the building and we had to make a run for it.'

'Oh, dear Lord . . .' Her aunt paled. 'Was that how your arm was injured?'

'Yes. Something fell on it. A piece of flying timber . . . I'm not sure.'

'Let me see it,' her aunt said.

June removed her jumper and blouse and Aunt Ada gently fingered it.

'The bruise is already coming out. I think you might have sprained your shoulder and you should have the doctor look at it. We'll see how you are in the morning. But at any rate you're going to stay with me for a few days. Rest it before rushing back to Liverpool.' She paused and looked at June, concern written all over her face. 'You were lucky not to have been killed. Thank goodness you had a young man looking after you – Chas, did you say?'

'Yes, he's just a friend,' June said, not able to say his name without going pink.

Her aunt raised an eyebrow but didn't comment. Instead, she jumped up from her chair saying, 'Before you tell me Billy's latest tomfoolery, I'm going to heat up the soup I made this morning. You need something substantial inside you, by the look of things.' She bustled into the kitchen.

From where she sat, June could see her putting the saucepan on top of the stove and cutting up some thick slices of bread. 'You just stay right where you are,' her aunt called.

Two minutes later she reappeared.

'Have this while you're waiting.' She put a plate in June's lap with a hunk of bread and cheese. 'You must be starving.

No wonder you feel faint. Don't say another word until you've got this down you.'

Aunt Ada waited until June had taken a few mouthfuls.

'I want to finish the story so you know everything. What a terrible person I am,' June said.

'I'm quite sure you're not.' Her aunt sat on an opposite chair. 'All right, love. Tell me what happened then.'

'As I was telling you,' June took a quivering breath, 'he said Clara's accident was unfortunate. *Unfortunate.*' She heard Billy say the word as clearly as though he were in the room. 'I saw red and picked up a vase and threw it as hard as I could at him. It hit his head. He went white, then slumped down and I thought I'd killed him. But I found out at the hospital he'd been brought in and was all right.'

'Pity you didn't finish him off,' her aunt said bitterly. 'My sister was tortured by that evil monster.'

'The only good thing out of this is that I don't have one cell of his in my body, nor do my sisters.' She squeezed her eyes shut at the memory of him, lifeless in his chair, the blood . . . She gave a sharp intake of breath.

'What is it, love?'

'I just wish Mum had told me the truth about my father. I wouldn't have felt so bad hating him so much. I think Stella would have felt better too. And Clara . . .' She broke down again and wept. 'I wish you'd told me, Aunt.' She raised her face to her aunt's, tears streaming down.

'I couldn't. I swore to your mother. She said she'd tell you one day – she didn't expect to die so young.'

June broke into fresh sobs.

'There, there. Don't take on so. I'd have thought Billy not being your father was a good piece of news. Come on, my love. Let's get to the table. The soup should be heated through by now.'

290

Aunt Ada's soup of potatoes and leeks was delicious. June ate two bowlfuls as well as more bread and cheese. When she'd finished she helped clear the dishes against her aunt's protests.

'Here, love. This'll do you good.'

Aunt Ada handed her a small glass of deep-red liquid, but June shook her head. The colour reminded her of Billy Lavender's blood.

'N-no, I couldn't.'

'You can. It's port. The best. Just sip it and I guarantee you'll feel better. Then it's early to bed for you, my girl. And I'm giving you a couple of Aspros for your arm. You'll see that after a good night's rest things will look a lot better in the morning. And if your arm's no better we're getting you to the doctor's.'

June tossed in her aunt's guest bed all night, visions of bombs falling on Bingham Hall, killing the children, blood and screaming and . . . She awoke in the morning, water trickling off her brow and down her nose, her breath coming in loud rasps, and feeling as though she'd been put through a wringer. She was thankful to hear her aunt knocking at her door and quietly opening it. She had a cup of tea in her hand and two digestive biscuits.

'How are you, dear? Did you sleep?' She set the cup and saucer on the bedside table.

'Not much, even with the port and Aspros.' June gave a rueful grin. 'My arm was quite painful, though it does actually feel easier this morning.' She pulled up the sleeve of her nightdress to show her aunt a black and blue patch on her upper arm.

'Oh, my dear . . . you poor thing. But at least it's come out. I'll put some witch hazel on it. And you're to rest today.'

'Thanks, Aunt, but I'll be fine after my cup of tea.' She looked up into her aunt's grey eyes that so reminded her of her mother. 'What would I do without you?'

Her aunt shook her head in protest and smiled. 'You're family, love. That's what I'm here for.'

June picked up her cup. 'I'll get up right away when I've drunk this.'

'There's no need to rush. You went through a lot yesterday.' She kissed June on the cheek and shut the door quietly behind her.

If her aunt knew the full story she'd be horrified.

June drank her tea and let the hot sweet liquid flow through her, warming and soothing her a little. Then she threw back the eiderdown and blanket and stumbled out of bed. She washed and dressed quickly and as soon as she opened her bedroom door she could smell toast and bacon cooking. Suddenly hungry, she hurried down the stairs.

'You must have used up all your coupons this week to have bacon,' she said, savouring every morsel.

'I like to give myself a little treat once a month,' said her aunt, smiling and showing her uneven teeth.

Dear Aunt Ada. She so reminded June of her mother before the drinking started . . . *Oh, no, don't think of that again.* She blinked back the tears. Whatever happened to her, nothing in the world would ever be as bad as losing her beloved Clara. At that moment an image of Lizzie danced in front of her eyes. She swallowed. Lizzie would be asking for her.

'What will you do today, dear?' her aunt broke into her thoughts.

'Get my ticket. I want to go back to Dr Barnardo's tomorrow. There's nothing for me here – except you, of course.' June attempted a smile.

'And everything for you there.' Aunt Ada collected the breakfast dishes. 'Don't worry,' she said when June opened her mouth to protest. 'I understand. You must go back. They all need you.'

Everyone except Murray, June thought, and her face became flushed as she saw him in her mind's eye. Now, in the gentle comfort of her aunt's home, a solitary tear slid down her face. How could she have misread the signs? She remembered his kisses, his murmured sighs, his fingers through her hair. They were not the acts of friendship. So what had changed? Her stomach tightened.

'You have to put this all behind you.' Her aunt's voice broke into her memories. 'It's a shock about your mother but she definitely had cause, the way he treated her.'

June tried to bring herself back into the present.

'It's good, really. I've spent my whole life, always on the lookout for any of his traits that I might have inherited.' She gave a feeble laugh. 'Now I don't have to worry any more, though it would be nice to know about my real father. And if I'm anything like him.'

'You'll be a mixture of him and your mother.' Aunt Ada began to brush the crumbs off the tablecloth into a small clean pan kept especially for the purpose. 'Like we all are.'

'There's something I'd very much like to know,' June said almost to herself as she leaned her head back on her aunt's hard upright chair. 'I wonder if my real father knew I existed. I would so love to have met him.' A thought occurred to her. 'Did you ever meet him, Aunt?'

'Several times.' A glow came over her aunt's face as she stopped brushing the table and looked at June. 'Your mother must have been about six months gone with you at the time when I first saw them together.'

'What was he like?' June turned eagerly to her aunt.

'He was a lovely man. A wonderful man. They were perfect together. It was the saddest thing how their lives turned out. And if I hadn't known how much your mother adored him, I'd have gone for him myself!' She gave a girlish giggle. 'No wonder it took her so long to introduce me to him.'

A sudden thought came to June, so strong it almost knocked her sideways. Her aunt had called her father 'Tom'. And in that instant she had an image of a tall, fair-haired man smelling of lemons, with a wide smile and strong loving arms, who swept her up and kissed her. He'd taken her to the zoo. To the circus. To her first ballet. He'd never forgotten her birthday or Christmas. Uncle Thomas. Was he her father?

'Are you all right, dear?'

June realised her eyes were closed. She opened them and smiled at her aunt through tear-filled eyes.

'Tom was my lovely Uncle Thomas, wasn't he?'

'Yes.' Aunt Ada paused, her loving eyes searching June's.

Of course he was. She *had* known him, but as an uncle. Slowly June's smile turned to a beam of sunlight. She didn't have to ask questions any more. She had known her father, even though she must have only been six when she'd last seen him. She remembered his last visit; he'd come to look at the new baby. She supposed Billy had been at work and her mother must have sent for him. She could see his smile now, as he looked down on the cot at her new baby sister, Clara. She remembered asking her mother when was Uncle Thomas going to come and see them again, and how upset her mother became. She said he'd gone away and might not be back for a long time.

'I wondered if it would occur to you. What did Billy say about him?' her aunt asked.

'That he'd died.'

'Unfortunately, this is one of the only times he's told the

truth. Tom jumped into the river after a young lad who'd fallen in, and ended up . . .' She blinked several times. 'Well, the boy was saved but Tom didn't survive. Your mother never got over it. And then Clara . . .' She looked at June. 'But we mustn't be sad. Your father died a hero. He'd have been so proud of you, looking after those children at Dr Barnardo's. And he'd want you to live your life to the very best. It's all in front of you, my love. And rest assured, your dad knew and loved all three of you. His daughters were his pride and joy.'

Chapter Thirty

'What's wrong, Junie?' Iris said, appearing at the library door one evening three days after June had returned from London.

June glanced up and tried to smile. 'Nothing. I just needed some time on my own, that's all.'

Iris came into the library and stood over June. She put her hand gently under June's chin and tilted it up. 'You've not been your usual self,' she said. 'Your face is pale and your eyes are dull. You're not sickening for anything, are you?'

'No, Nurse Iris,' she attempted a wan smile. 'I'm all right – honestly.'

'Sorry, Junie, I'm not swallowing that.' Iris took the old leather armchair opposite. 'You've been very quiet ever since you came back from London. I know it must have been pretty awful what happened with your father, who isn't your father, thank God, but as far as I can see, he deserved every bit of it. So there's no need to feel a shred of guilt over *him*. And you said you'd bumped into Chas after you thought you'd committed murder' – Iris broke into a grin – 'and he'd been marvellous, and also when the bombs dropped on the hotel. Sounds like you might not have even been alive if it hadn't been for him.'

June swallowed hard but the lump in her throat wouldn't dislodge.

'He *was* marvellous.' She chewed her lip.

'Well, then.'

June unconsciously rubbed her shoulder.

'Is that still painful?'

'A bit,' June admitted, 'but nowhere near like it was.'

'Let me have a look.' Iris quickly examined her arm and shoulder. 'It's already much better. Are you still putting the cold compresses on like I showed you?'

'Yes, regularly.' June was thankful Iris had changed the subject, but she hadn't bargained on Iris's tenacity.

'So what is it? I'm not going to be fobbed off.' Iris looked at her sternly. 'We're friends, aren't we? You can tell me anything and it won't go any further.'

'You're the dearest friend,' June said, her eyes swimming with tears. 'I just didn't want to say anything. I'm so ashamed.'

'*You* – ashamed?'

'I didn't tell you the whole story,' June said in a low voice. 'What happened before the hotel was hit. After we'd had our tea.'

'Oh, don't tell me – I can guess.' Iris leaned forward and gave June an admiring grin. 'He had his wicked way with you. He was a good lover and you enjoyed it. And now you feel guilty because of Murray. You're worried if Murray should ever find out.'

June gave a humourless smile. 'Not quite, Iris, but close.'

'Go on.'

June told Iris in a rush.

'What a cad,' Iris said, when June had finished.

'So now you know the whole story, and why I've been so quiet,' June said.

'All I can say is, forget about Chas. He was behaving like a typical male when the opportunity presented itself to him.

297

I know full well it's Murray you're madly in love with.' She caught June's eye. 'I'm right, aren't I?'

June bit her lip as hard as she could bear, to stop herself breaking into sobs, and nodded. The next moment she felt Iris's arms wrap around her.

'Come on, Junie, it'll all turn out okay. I promise. But you need your food and rest or you'll get ill. And then I'll have to look after you in the sick bay. And you won't want that. I'm very strict, you know. Ask any of the kids who've been under my care.'

June smiled.

'That's more like it,' Iris said. 'Now come on to the common room and I'll make us a hot cocoa for a special treat!'

Murray hadn't been that taken with Chas from the first time he'd set eyes on him, even though Chas had volunteered to come to England several weeks before his fellow Americans. He had to admit that the Yank had a cheerful personality, was always polite and turned his hand to anything. And he seemed fearless every time he took his plane up. Murray shook his head. He couldn't quite put his finger on it but he distrusted him. Maybe Chas was a little bit too nice . . . too smiley . . . too eager to be popular. Or was Murray simply envious of the other pilot's easy charm?

A lot of the time the Americans stuck together and didn't mix with the British, yet Chas always found time to stroll over after a British sortie and talk it over with the crews. The other chaps in his crew seemed happy to do this but Murray always kept his own counsel. He didn't want to share experiences afterwards. Just wanted a breather before the next time. But Chas almost relished reliving the action. Not Murray's idea of fun at all.

This evening was no different. Most of the officers had gathered in the bar and the chattering assaulted his ears. He wasn't in the mood. One of the pilots had been shot down: a new one and desperately young – 19, he believed. It was too depressing for words. He felt like bursting into tears when he thought of all the young men sacrificing their lives – the women, too, of course – because of that bastard Hitler.

He needed a drink. He strolled over to the bar, and was several times stopped by his pals tapping him on the shoulder, gesturing to him to join them at their tables, but he merely nodded and hovered behind a row of officers already ordering drinks or waiting their turn. He noticed Chas was back from leave that morning and at the front of the bar. You couldn't miss him. He was head and shoulders above nearly all the men and commanded attention. Murray saw Chas buy several beers and carry the tray to a nearby table.

With curiosity he looked to see who Chas was going to entertain with his yarns this time. It looked like they were all Yanks. Interesting to hear what they talked about, Murray thought. Were they moaning about being over here in our freezing weather – March had been particularly cold and dismal – and drinking warm beer, or were they boasting how they'd come to save the British? They certainly pinch our girls, Murray thought sourly, with their dashing uniforms, showering the women with silk stockings and chocolates, showing off with their crazy dances, flinging their money about, having better food and more of it . . . He berated himself. They were doing a good job on the whole, and if he was truthful they weren't a bad bunch.

Not taking any time to reason why he was so interested he decided to sit at a table in a darkened corner. Only one chap occupied it. He had his head in his hands, his shoulders drooping, the picture of misery, and didn't even look up when Murray approached. All the others had probably thought he should be left alone, Murray guessed, as he took the chair opposite so he could keep Chas in view. A deep sound like a sob emanated from his table companion.

'You okay, pal?' Murray asked, laying a sympathetic hand on the man's shoulder.

The man looked up, eyes red and watering. 'Does it look like it?'

Murray was about to make a snappy reply when something stopped him. 'Do you want to talk about it?' he said instead.

'Not really.'

'I'd leave you in peace, but there's not many spare seats going,' Murray said, gesturing towards the crowd.

'It's all right. You're not bothering me. It's just that I' – he made another awful smothered sound – 'I've had a Dear John letter from my girl today.'

'I'm really sorry,' Murray said. 'Trouble with this bloody war is that it's happening all the time. But you'll find someone else – someone more deserving – and you'll wonder why you got so upset,' he added, not meaning to be flippant, but it came out rather that way.

The man looked at him with dull eyes. 'It's not a matter of finding another girl. She's my *wife*. You don't expect that from your wife, do you? Mother of my children.' He held his head in his hands again.

Murray patted him on the arm and was about to offer some kind of platitude when he heard Chas say something that caught his attention.

'I adore women and they usually seem to find me – well, let's just say they like me,' Chas was boasting. 'Why, only the other day I bumped into a great little English gal in London who I actually knew. We had tea in my room at the hotel – do y'all know it? The Strand Palace Hotel that the US of A have officially taken over for R and R? You should go if you've not been already. They do great afternoon teas. That's how I enticed the little gal in. *Tea*. Can you imagine?' He chuckled. 'And after our *tea* . . . there we were on the bed, and would you believe a bomb fell on the goddamn building just at a son-of-a-bitch inopportune moment.'

The four Americans at the table laughed and pumped his arm. Chas looked round and smiled.

'So what happened next?' one of the men asked, swallowing half a glass of beer in one gulp.

'We had to hightail it out of there. She nearly got us killed because she'd forgotten a toy dog I'd bought for her for some kid who'd had to give up her puppy. Nice thought, but not in a goddamn air raid. She rushed back and I had to rescue her.'

Murray froze, straining his ears to hear more.

'I'm worried about what happened to the toy dog,' another said, chuckling. 'Did he get rescued too?'

'Oh, yes,' Chas said, grinning. 'I grabbed her *and* the dog. She thanked me very prettily and said Lizzie would be thrilled.'

Chapter Thirty-One

Weeks had slid by since June returned to Bingham Hall from her disastrous trip to London. It was only the first week in June and temperatures had shot to almost 90°F by the Friday. Some of the children were fractious in the sticky heat of the classrooms, playing up the teachers, and Matron's temper became even more impossible.

June had heard nothing from Murray. She tried to remember they were only supposed to be friends, but something didn't feel right. Why had he kissed her that time? Over and over. That surely wasn't done in friendship. The more she thought about it, the more she felt there was something Murray wasn't telling her. Something maybe he was afraid of telling her. It flashed through her mind that he might be married but she shook it away immediately. She was sure he was not the kind of man to live such a lie.

She'd finally finished carrying out all her duties this morning, getting hotter by the minute from sweeping and mopping floors, dusting, cleaning out the children's bedside cabinets, stripping half a dozen of the beds whose small occupants were still wetting them every night, and collecting dresses and shirts that required mending. That would be her afternoon chore, she thought, as she stood up and pulled back her shoulders to ease her aching arms. She grimaced as she felt a twinge of pain in the one that had taken the knock, and immediately she was back in the London hotel. She shook her head to get rid of the image of Chas.

After dinner, when she'd put the younger ones to bed for their afternoon nap, she strolled along the avenue of lime trees clothed in their summer green, forming an arch over the drive. The birds were singing their messages to one another and it was so beautiful and peaceful that for several minutes she forgot the war was relentlessly going on.

She came to the road at the top of the drive. The sky was a bright blue dotted with a fluffy cloud here and there, but moments later she heard a roar of planes high above. She put her hand to her forehead to shield the sun from her eyes and craned her neck, biting her lip in her fear. Was Murray one of the pilots? Or was he dead? Was that why she hadn't heard? Of course it was possible but her heart told her he was definitely alive and for reasons of his own he hadn't been in touch.

She decided to write him a letter that very night. Just friendly. Just as he wanted. But to let him know she hoped he was well and giving him some news from the orphanage. She'd tell him about David, the music teacher, and how he'd discovered one of the children was a talented violinist whom he was going to help, and that Lizzie still missed Freddie but she had at last begun to speak again. She'd tell Murray she'd found Lizzie a toy dog in London who looked a lot like Freddie and she was going to give it to the child on her birthday next week.

She posted the letter the following morning.

Lizzie's birthday preparations would help to take her mind off him. At least that's what she told herself.

Lizzie was still quieter than most of the other children when she was in their company but she listened to everything they said, and occasionally came out with her own amusing observations. June was astonished at Lizzie's sense of humour when she thought how much the child had gone through. As her birthday approached, June was delighted to see the little girl was beginning to get excited, and even asked Bertie if she was making her a cake.

Bertie had made not one but two pink iced birthday cakes and was putting on the finishing touches when June entered the kitchen and sat down for a minute.

'I've had to use mostly marg,' she told June, wiping her hands on the kitchen roller towel 'What with all the rationing, butter's become a real luxury.' She gave the roller towel a yank.

'Lizzie won't know the difference,' June assured her. 'She's too excited for words.'

The two women broke into laughter as they realised what June had just said.

'It's the most wonderful thing to see Lizzie speaking and acting normally,' said June and she smiled happily.

'You had everything to do with such a change in her, June,' Bertie said, giving her a fond pat on the shoulder.

'No, it was Alan. He was the first child to take her under his wing. She needed that contact with another child, even if he was much older. He's been exceptional with her. And Freddie, of course. He was really important in getting her to speak. I told her he'd lost his mummy and daddy too, and she had to help him. She took to that role immediately. It's such a shame he had to go back to the camp.'

'Well, Alan's certainly a changed lad.' Bertie stuck four bright-pink candles in little white holders and pushed them firmly in the top of one of the cakes. 'There. I think that's it. Now the sandwiches. I've made the jellies and they're in the larder setting.'

'Can I do anything?'

'You can help me with the sandwiches, hen, if you insist. I've made the fillings, but first just sit here and keep me company while I get off my feet – they feel like rats are gnawing at them, they're that sore. We'll sit for a few minutes and have a cup of tea.'

'I'll make *you* one for a change, Bertie.'

The dining room was filled with children's excited shouts and giggles as they watched Lizzie open her presents. David had made her a doll's crib out of an apple box and Barbara and Athena had lined it and made the covers and even embroidered the pillow. Lizzie immediately jumped down from the table and ran up to her bedroom to fetch Lady, her rag doll with knitted hair and dress to match, and came rushing back. She carefully placed the doll in the crib and tucked the covers around it. Satisfied, she climbed back on to her chair and opened the few remaining gifts.

June's heart was in her mouth when the little girl picked up the bulky package and started pressing it. June had only been able to find some ordinary green paper which the local chemist used to wrap bottles of medicine. She'd begged the man for a sheet and he'd given it to her for nothing when she'd explained what she wanted it for.

'Guess what it is before you open it,' Alan called from a few chairs further up the table.

'I don't know what's inside,' Lizzie's voice piped up.

'Go on, try.'

June nearly stopped breathing. Lizzie shook her head and began to unwrap the parcel. She carefully unfolded the last section and laid the paper out fully to reveal the toy dog. It looked up at her with a red tongue hanging out as though he were laughing. He was even more like Freddie than June remembered. She was almost as excited as little Lizzie was going to be. It had been worth the risk of rushing back to Chas's room to rescue it. A warm feeling stole round her heart as she waited for Lizzie's next move.

Lizzie looked at it, her eyes wide. The children suddenly became quiet as they watched her. Then Lizzie turned bright red. She snatched the dog up and threw it as far as her little arm would allow. It landed in front of Doris.

'It's not Freddie,' Lizzie sobbed. 'I want Freddie back!'

Doris caught hold of the toy dog and held him to her chest, squeezing him tightly.

'Can I have him if you don't want him?' she asked.

'NO!' Lizzie screamed as she shot up from the table and ran sobbing from the room, shouting that she hated the dog.

June sprang to her feet and flew after Lizzie into the hall, where she practically had to grab her to stop her running up the stairs.

'Lizzie, come back. It's your birthday party and all the children want to have some of your lovely birthday cake.'

June bent down so she was on the same level as the child. 'I thought you'd love him, Lizzie. He was in a shop window in London, looking at me. He wanted a home and I had to buy him. I thought you'd love him,' she repeated lamely as she looked into Lizzie's red eyes, the tears still trickling down her flushed cheeks.

'I want my real Freddie,' Lizzie said, and flung herself into June's arms.

June held the trembling body close and stroked her hair.

'If you come back with me to the dining room and finish off your birthday which everyone's been looking forward to – even the grown-ups – then you can blow out your candles and make a wish – any wish you like.' She smiled at the child.

'Can I make a wish to see Freddie?'

'Yes, you can, but don't tell anyone else or it won't come true. Do you promise?'

Lizzie nodded, her face serious.

June kissed her cheek. 'Let's go back, Lizzie. Hold my hand and we'll go back in the room together.' She paused and looked down at the child. 'What are you going to do with the toy puppy? Will you let Doris keep him?'

Lizzie shook her head vehemently. 'No, me wants him till Freddie comes back. Then Doris can have him.'

June wondered at the child's working out of what should be done. If it wasn't so upsetting it would be amusing. She bit back a smile and made her face as serious as Lizzie's, praying she'd be able to make the little girl's wish come true.

'That sounds a very good idea to me.'

The children took up all her attention when she was on duty, but in the short periods she was off, she couldn't get Murray out of her mind. Maybe he hadn't written because he didn't think she would want to hear from him again. Yet he'd been adamant that he still wanted them to be friends. She could only hope that he was too busy to find time to write. All she could do was pray he was safe and well.

Twice she'd picked up the telephone to try to contact him, and twice she'd put the receiver down before the operator put her through, not wanting him to think she was chasing him and be embarrassed.

'June,' Iris called outside her bedroom door as she was

cleaning her teeth after breakfast, 'Matron's told me there's a telephone call for you.'

Please, not Billy. Her stomach clenched with the idea that it might be him hounding her again. Slowly, she walked down the stairs and picked up the receiver in the hall.

'June, is that you? It's Chas.'

She sighed. Apart from Billy, Chas was the last person she wanted to hear from. He'd caused enough trouble.

'June?'

'Hello, Chas.'

'June, I know you're still mad at me and I don't blame you. I'm sorry for my behaviour in the hotel. I should have told you how sorry I was at the time. I don't know what came over me. But you looked so lovely lying there and—'

'Please don't go on any more, Chas. I want to forget it ever happened.'

She heard him suck in a breath.

'I'm afraid I've got something more important than that to tell you . . .'

Alarm rushed to her throat. She knew what he was going to say but he mustn't say it. If he didn't say anything, everything would be exactly as she wanted it to be. *Don't say anything, Chas. Don't tell me. Please.*

Chas's voice came over the line, but it was faint so she had to press the receiver close to her ear. 'Flight Lieutenant Andrews transferred to Bomber Command two months ago, somewhere in East Anglia. I shouldn't really be telling you this but I got the idea you were sweet on him.'

June hardly heard Chas's last words. All she could think of was that Murray had wanted to get far away from her. Why would he do that? Was it so she got the message loud and clear that they were only friends? Maybe he hadn't asked for a transfer – maybe it had been decided for him and he'd had no choice. But why hadn't he written to tell her? She took in a deep breath and felt her heart calm down. For a moment she'd thought Chas had been about to say something dreadful. She'd ask him if she could have his address so she could write to him.

'It's a pretty dangerous job in Bomber Command,' Chas was saying.

Yes, but so must it have been as a fighter pilot. She closed her eyes, thinking of the risks all the boys had to face every time they took off.

'. . . and I hate to be the bearer of bad news but I thought you should know that Murray's Lancaster was shot down over a week ago. He's been reported as "Missing, presumed dead" along with the six others in the crew.'

What was that? What was he saying?

'D-d-dead?'

She felt the blood drain from her face. She put her hands up as though to stem the flow, dropping the receiver. More than a week. All the time she'd been thinking about him, wondering why he hadn't written, he was already dead. So of course he couldn't write. He was dead. She hung on to the telephone table.

'June.'

She could hear Chas calling her name – shouting now – and numbly took hold of the receiver again. 'I'm here.'

'It says "Missing, *presumed* dead" – it doesn't say he *is*. There's always hope.'

She shook her head. 'Thank you for letting me know, Chas. I appreciate it.' Was this really her speaking? Calmly, normally? She felt as though she wasn't herself any longer. Her voice was coming from far away. She bit the inside of her mouth, tasting blood. 'I must go – the children – they need me.'

'Gee, I'm sorry I wasn't able to call you sooner but I was away. Only just got back and heard the news and knew you two were good buddies.'

'Thank you for letting me know.'

'If I hear anything more I'll call you.'

June put the receiver slowly back on its cradle and stumbled up the staircase. Hilda passed her on the first landing, looking at her curiously, but June kept her head down and rushed up to her room. She sat on her bed and put her head in her hands, making small, stifled whimpers. She didn't care whether Matron was looking for her or not. She couldn't face anyone. She needed to be by herself in this funny little room she'd begun to call hers. To think. To remember him. She tried to picture his face. It was as though she was looking through a veil. She tried to remember the warmth of him. His warm hands. His warm lips. But no matter how hard she tried to remember, she couldn't.

She sat there rocking herself, shaking her head, her body tense with disbelief. Her heart seemed to have slowed to nothing. She put her hand to her chest wondering if it had actually stopped. But there it was, a steady rhythm, still beating. Why was *her* heart beating when Murray's no longer was?

There was a light tap on her door. She froze. She wasn't going to speak to anyone. Why wouldn't they leave her alone? The tap was louder this time.

'Go away.' She thought she was shouting and was surprised her voice didn't reverberate around the room.

Someone called her name. She didn't want to see anyone. Didn't want to speak. The voice called again. Who was it? Couldn't they understand she wanted to be left alone? Whoever was outside was now trying the doorknob. Slowly June pushed herself off the bed, feeling the room tip. She half fell against the wardrobe with a thud, and, desperately trying to steady herself, she managed the few feet to the door. With effort she opened it.

'Iris.' Her voice was hardly above a whisper.

'Oh, my God, Junie, you look like you've seen a ghost. Have you had some bad news? Was it the telephone call?' As she was talking she led June over to the bed and sat down next to her.

June turned her head. Her face was wooden. 'Murray transferred to Bomber Command, somewhere in East Anglia – he didn't tell me – and his aeroplane was shot down and now he's dead.'

'Oh, Junie.' Iris folded her into her strong arms.

It was only then that June wept.

Minutes passed until June finally raised her head from Iris's shoulder. 'I'm sorry,' she said.

'Don't be silly. It's what friends are for. It's horrible news. I don't know what to say to give you any comfort, but you know I'm here.' Iris gave her a gentle squeeze. 'Who was on the telephone?'

'Chas. He told me that Murray had been reported m-missing for over a week,' June choked. Her eyes, red with weeping, rested on her friend. 'I'll never see Murray again. Oh, Iris, how shall I bear it?'

'You just said Chas told you Murray was reported missing.'

'P-presumed d-dead,' June finished.

'But it's not definite. There's always hope that he might have been picked up.'

'That's what Chas said. But if he had, they'd have found him by now. It happened *over a week ago*.' Her voice rose. 'Oh, why didn't someone let me know sooner?'

'Because they only tell wives and mothers that sort of news,' Iris said.

311

'And I'm just a friend – is that it?' June's voice was raw and challenging.

''Fraid so, love – as far as the military's concerned, anyway.'

'I'll never be able to tell him I love him.' She broke down again.

'All you can do for the time being, Junie, is hope. Don't give up. Here . . .' Iris wiped fresh tears from June's eyes. 'Come and splash your face with cold water and go and see Bertie. She'll make you a cup of tea. It's what you need. You've had an awful shock.'

June didn't think she would have made it down the stairs if it hadn't been for Iris keeping a firm arm around her waist, talking to her, encouraging her.

'I don't want any tea,' June kept repeating.

'Well, go and sit with Bertie anyway,' Iris said. 'We've got Bobby in the sick room with a bad case of diarrhoea. Kathleen will be wanting me to take over so she can get some sleep.'

'You go on,' June said. 'Don't worry about me. I'll be all right.'

But Iris insisted. The girls made their way to the kitchen, and when Iris pushed the kitchen door open, June was thankful to see that Bertie was on her own, cutting up some meat.

'Making a stew for dinner,' Bertie said with a smile, glancing over at the two women, 'and waiting for some help. Hilda's late as usual.' Her smile faded. 'June, what's the matter, love?' She put down the knife and washed her hands at the sink.

'Look after her, Bertie,' Iris said, giving June a little push onto one of the kitchen chairs. 'She's had some frightful news.'

'Leave her with me.' Bertie wiped her hands on her apron. 'I'll put the kettle on. If you want to, hen,' she looked at June and smiled, 'you can tell me all about it. But only if you want to. I promise you whatever it is, I'll understand. And it won't go any further.'

Iris shut the door quietly behind her.

June carried out her duties in a daze and when she attended to the children they occasionally made her forget – sometimes as long as an hour or two. But when she was alone, cleaning their bedrooms and doing all the other tasks Matron had set her, it would sweep over her like a storm. At first she tried to hang on to the word 'missing' but every day her sliver of hope faded a little more. Most nights she'd cry herself to sleep, hugging herself into a tight ball of misery. She'd wake after a restless night and open her eyes and for a few wonderful seconds her world was normal. Then everything came tumbling down on top of her. Murray was no longer in her world. She'd drag herself out of bed, her head throbbing, trying to put on a brave face.

Even Matron patted her arm awkwardly. 'I'm sorry to hear about your young man.'

June didn't have the will to tell her Murray wasn't, after all, *her* young man. She just nodded and miserably hunched her way to the laundry room with a bag of dirty washing from the children. She had to keep going – for their sake.

'Junie, I've got something to tell you, and I want you to know before anyone,' Iris said as they were taking a brisk walk after supper – a new habit Iris had insisted upon so that June got out in the fresh air.

'Something good, I hope,' June said, her eyes red from last night's sobbing. It was getting to be a habit, crying herself to sleep every night. She knew she had to stop it. Nothing was going to bring him back. She tried to pull herself into the present. What was Iris saying?

'It happened the same evening you heard about Murray,' Iris said. 'And I couldn't say anything then – obviously.' She stopped.

June glanced at her friend's anxious expression. 'What is it, Iris?'

Iris stretched out her left hand and June gasped. On the fourth finger was a sapphire ring, the exact colour of Iris's eyes, gleaming up at her in the last of the day's sunshine.

June swallowed. A stab of envy shot through her and she forced herself to smile as widely as she could.

'Oh, Iris. You and David?' June caught hold of Iris's hand. 'It's beautiful. I can't believe it. Well, of course I can,' she added hurriedly. 'Talk about anyone being Mr Right. David is a darling and just perfect for you. When is the wedding?'

'We're not going to wait. This war could go on for months – years – no one knows. We're going to snatch some happiness while we can.'

'What about Dr Barnardo's rules? Are you allowed to work here as a married couple? I know it's selfish but please say yes, you are.'

'I'm not sure,' Iris said. 'It might suit us for a while, but we want our own home and David has always longed to live in Scotland, so that's where we might end up.' Iris's voice was dreamy. 'Now you know why I couldn't tell you until now. Couldn't even wear my ring. You were in such shock that I had to let some time go by before I felt you could be happy for me.'

'Oh, Iris, I *am* happy for you. So very happy.' June threw her arms round Iris and hugged her tightly. 'I like him very much.'

314

'I feel really lucky to have found him,' Iris said.

'I believe it was *me* who found him for you,' June quipped, hardly aware that for the first time since Chas had made that terrible telephone call, a sense of quiet resignation was stealing into her own heart. 'I had to persuade you to go and listen to his classical concerts. "Oh, no, I shan't go",' she impersonated Iris, '"I only like jazz."'

Iris giggled. 'Did I really say that? I must have been mad. I'm getting very knowledgeable about all that serious stuff.'

'Oh, Iris, I *am* happy for you. I just wish . . .' June blinked back the ready tears.

'I know, Junie. I'm so sorry you haven't heard anything. I suppose we have to come to terms with the idea that he did die in the crash.' She put her arm around June. 'But one day, love, you'll meet someone and be happy again.'

June didn't reply. Whatever she said would take the edge off Iris's happiness and she wasn't going to spoil that for anything in the world.

Chapter Thirty-Two

The following morning June heard a report on the wireless that there was always a chance a missing soldier could turn up. It had happened many times. Just hearing that possibility gave her fresh hope. Maybe he'd been found and taken to some hospital. Maybe lost his memory. Maybe his identification papers had been mislaid or burned in the accident. Maybe he'd come down on enemy soil and was in prison. Then she told herself not to be so foolish and brushed the hope away, along with fresh tears, telling herself she had to face up to it. He'd have been found by now.

That afternoon June and some of the older children decided to go on a long walk in the grounds while the younger ones were taking their nap. Fresh air would do everyone good, June decided. She wouldn't even ask Matron, whom she'd seen totter down the path to her cottage. June enjoyed pointing out the names of the trees she recognised, displaying all the beautiful greens of midsummer, and they were in high spirits until the children charged into the Great Hall and stopped short when they saw Matron's frowning expression, her pudgy hands pushing hard on the bulk of her hips.

'Wipe your shoes this minute!' Matron's lips were a grim line. 'No wonder the library floor is such a disgrace,' she added, her voice echoing her irritation. Her steely eyes raked over the group. 'Woolfes, Jones, Crossland – you three can set to and polish it before supper.'

'But we're tired, Matron,' Alan said, 'and starving hungry.'

'You don't know what starving is,' Matron growled. 'Now get moving!'

Why did the woman seem to get such satisfaction out of being so horrible to the children? June wondered. Never had a smile for them or a word of praise. She just stood there, her arms now folded. She had to be obeyed.

'Come on, you three. I'll help you,' June said. 'The sooner we do it the sooner you can have your supper.'

Upstairs in the library June noticed Joachim wasn't with them. She was just about to go and find him when he appeared at the door, smirking, holding several dusters. He silently handed two each to the others, then sat down and tied a duster round each shoe, fixing it with a rubber band. The others grinned and moments later even June had joined the children and was sliding up and down the parquet floor, laughing for the first time since her awful news.

They didn't hear the door open.

'What do you all think you're playing at?' Matron barked.

As though they'd committed some terrible crime, ran through June's mind. She was just about to make light of it when Bobby Crossland pointed to Joachim. 'It was him, Matron. The German.'

'And what do you have to say for yourself, Woolfes?'

'I think it is a good quick way to get a nice shine on the floor,' came the boy's quick reply.

'Please, Bobby, will you stop calling Joachim "the German",' June admonished.

'Well, that's what he is,' Bobby said sulkily. 'Don't mean to say I don't like him.'

'You still do not call him anything but his own name,' June said firmly, 'I mean it. Do you hear?'

She didn't care that she said this in front of Matron. If she didn't say anything, Matron certainly wouldn't.

'Bobby?'

Bobby kicked an imaginary stone. 'Yes, I heard. Won't do it again, Miss.'

'And tomorrow, Woolfes,' Matron resumed, 'you can polish the library floor the proper way.' She turned to June. 'And I'll see *you* in my office after supper, Miss Lavender.'

She spun on her heel and June stared after her. Matron always had to have the last word.

Day after day dragged by. Murray was on June's mind no matter how busy she was with the children. Could he possibly still be alive? Sometimes he felt so close to her it seemed he must be. She gave a deep sigh. Not knowing for certain was almost worse.

It was supper time and as usual she wasn't hungry. The children were still filing noisily into the dining room when the telephone in the Great Hall rang. She hesitated. She should be helping the teachers with the children but it might be important. She hurried over and picked up the receiver.

'Bingham Hall. June Lavender speaking.'

'Oh, June, I'm so glad you answered. It's Chas.'

Chas. Why didn't he just give up? If he was the last man on earth, she didn't want him. She was just about to tell him so in the politest way she could, when she heard him say:

'Andrews has been found!'

She must be hearing things. She pressed the receiver closer to her ear. There was a silence. She'd dreamed of hearing those words so often she must have imagined that's what

318

Chas had just said. She was about to put the receiver down, thinking she must be hearing things, when his voice came over the wires again.

'June? June, did you hear me? Murray Andrews is alive!'

She began to shake. She couldn't speak . . . daren't ask if he was badly hurt . . . if he was asking for her. She ran her tongue over her lips. It couldn't be true.

'June, say something. Are you there?'

She swallowed. 'Oh, Chas, I can't believe it. I'm sorry – I was just – I'm . . . I don't know what to say, only thank you so much for taking the trouble to tell me.' Thank God she'd found her voice. 'When did you hear the news?'

'An hour ago. It seems his plane was shot down and the crew bailed out over Holland. I don't know any more than that except Johnnie Upton didn't make it. The others are injured in different ways. I'm so glad for your sake that he's been found. Wish him luck for me when you see him, won't you? We didn't always agree, but he's a good guy.'

'Do you know what his injuries are?'

'Burned arm – one of his eyes got it. That's about all I can tell you.'

'Do you know where he is?'

'Queen Victoria Hospital, East Grinstead – special burns unit.' There was a pause and then she heard him say, 'Look, June, I gotta go. Look after yourself.'

She heard the click of the receiver.

Her brain felt numb, as though it couldn't take in any more information. Murray was injured. That was all she knew. His arm and his eye. She only prayed he hadn't lost the sight of his eye, because if he had, they'd never allow him to fly aeroplanes again. And that was what he loved doing more than anything. It was his life. But that was it – he was alive. Against all odds he was alive . . . and she was

319

going to see him . . . wherever East Grinstead happened to be. Her face broke into a broad smile of joy.

She needed to see Matron. Ask if she could have some leave to go and visit Murray in hospital. June pressed her lips into a determined line, even though she felt like bursting with happiness that he was alive. He'd get better – she'd see to that.

After supper Matron was not to be found in her office.

'Has anyone seen Matron?' June asked whenever she saw one of the staff.

'She was here fifteen minutes ago,' said Kathleen. 'I know because I asked her if I could have a lift with Harold tomorrow morning. I need to restock the medicine chest.'

June searched everywhere she could think of in the house. She looked out into the gardens, but a heavy rain was falling. No, Matron wouldn't go out into the grounds in this weather, and she didn't usually retreat to her cottage quite this early. June suddenly had a thought. The cellar. Maybe Matron was finally inspecting it to see if it was dry enough to bring the children's beds down now that the summer was here.

Step by careful step June descended the ladder-like staircase towards the cellar floor. Someone sneezed just as her foot was about to reach the last step.

June listened, hardly breathing. It might not be Matron, she suddenly thought. It could be an intruder.

There was a strange popping noise.

'Is anybody there?' she called.

Silence.

Then, 'Who's there?'

The voice was definitely Matron's.

'It's me – June. Is that Matron?'

A tall figure appeared in a white overall. June gave a

startled step backwards. It was like seeing a ghost gliding through the murky gloom.

'What do you think you're doing frightening me like that?' Matron demanded.

'I'm sorry, Matron, I thought you were a burglar.'

'Of course I'm not a burglar. I was just looking at the possibility of bringing the children down here at night. It might be safer for them.'

June looked at her with irritation. Matron had declared it as though it were *her* idea – as if June had never mentioned it all those months ago. June caught the gleam of dislike in Matron's eyes. Better say nothing. It wouldn't do to slip further into her bad books.

'I think that's a very good idea,' June said limply.

'Good, I'm glad you think so,' Matron said crisply. 'Now, if you'll just leave me to get on with what I was doing, trying to decide where the beds could go, et cetera. Goodnight, Miss Lavender.'

'I do wish you'd call me June.'

Matron pursed her lips and put her hand up in a dismissive gesture. 'That will be all, Miss Lavender.' She turned on her heel, her shoes clopping loudly on the flagstone floor.

June stared after the determined figure. Matron's hand had been shaking. Why? As far as she knew, Matron wasn't sickening for anything. And she couldn't have been that angry just to see her assistant come down to the cellar. Was she embarrassed that she'd been caught doing something that June had suggested? Or was it something more ominous?

If she went back upstairs she'd never get the chance to have a quiet word with Matron about seeing Murray. Drawing herself up to her full height and squaring her shoulders, she decided she would speak to her there and then.

321

But Matron had turned her back to June and already marched off.

Give her a few minutes, June thought. Matron had stirred her curiosity.

She counted to a hundred, then counted again, and walked through the cellar, noting various alcoves and rooms leading from the main area where the stairs were. She heard Matron sneeze again. She must be coming down with a cold.

The sneeze came from a room on her left. Quietly she opened it. From the smell it was a wine cellar. Of course. It would be where Lord Bingham had kept his wine. He wouldn't have had time to crate it all up if he and his family had left in a hurry. Yes, there was Matron sitting on an upright chair by a table on which stood a bottle of wine – the cork already out. That must have been the popping noise she heard.

'How dare you come here spying on me!' Matron leaped up, knocking over her glass. Red liquid spilt out, running into rivulets down the table leg.

'I'm sorry, Matron.' June took a step forward. 'But I came down to the cellar to find you to ask you something and you didn't give me a chance. It's nothing to do with spying on you.'

'Well, now you've seen I like the odd glass of wine.' Matron glared at her.

'What you do is none of my business,' June pursued. 'But there's an emergency and—'

'One of the children?' Matron barked.

'No, no. Nothing with any of the children.' June looked pityingly at the figure across the table. Matron was obviously most uncomfortable with June finding her in such a position.

'Then what is it?' Matron drew her shaggy eyebrows together suspiciously.

'My friend, Murray – you know, the pilot – he's been found alive but badly injured. I wondered if I could have a few days off to go and see him.'

'What's the extent of this injury?'

'I don't know exactly.'

'Where is he?'

'In East Grinstead. Special burns unit. I would dearly like to see him. They say he's in a bad state and won't talk to anyone. I'd be back in no time if you'd allow it.'

Matron's eyes were on June's face and June felt she could see the workings of the woman's mind. If she didn't grant the girl some leave, there was no telling what she'd get up to. June might report her to one of the directors of Dr Barnardo's – tell them Matron was a secret drinker. No, that would never do.

'East Grinstead, you say? Do you know where that is?'

June shook her head.

'It's Sussex. Hundreds of miles away.'

'I'd still like to go and see him,' June said obstinately.

'I suppose we can manage for a few days,' Matron finally conceded, allowing her lips to form a smile which didn't even attempt to reach her eyes. 'I suppose you'd like to go tomorrow?' She reached in her apron pocket and took out a handkerchief and blew her nose.

'Yes, if that's all right,' June said. 'I'm really grateful. I don't think he'll ever fly again and that's why he's in such a bad way.' She paused. 'I heard you sneezing,' she began tentatively. 'Are you coming down with a cold?'

'Of course not. It's all this dust. For goodness' sake, go back upstairs and get on with your work.'

'Thank you, Matron. I'll get back to work right away.'

When June returned to the main house, she didn't tell anyone about discovering Matron in the cellar. It was too delicate a situation. But she was sure, after her experience with Billy Lavender and her own mother, that Matron's shaking hand was connected with drinking too much. She remembered how nervous Matron had been when Mr Clarke came to see her from Stepney Causeway. How her hand that held the teacup trembled. She'd thought at the time that Matron was simply angry, but now she had more worries than ever that the woman was not fit to be in charge of an orphanage.

Chapter Thirty-Three

'The train for Euston Station is about to leave on Platform 3. Will all persons not travelling please step down from the train.'

The journey took the best part of the day. As usual the carriages were packed, and because the weather was so warm, June felt smothered in the small space. She had to make several changes but finally her last train pulled into East Grinstead.

She asked the porter how far the hospital was from the station.

'Bit over a mile, love,' he said. 'Unfortunately, you've just missed the bus and there won't be another one along for an hour. You should probably get a taxi.'

Finding one was not so easy. She stood in the taxi rank in a long queue. It was beginning to drizzle and she pulled her sou'wester down, hoping it wasn't going to be much of a shower.

The queue didn't move for several minutes, until finally a taxi drew up and she was grateful to see four people immediately take possession, but still it was another fifteen minutes before she reached the head of the queue.

'Where to, Miss?' the driver asked. He looked as dismal as the rain, which had become heavier.

She gave him a smile. 'Queen Victoria Hospital. I'm sorry I'm so wet. I'll probably drip all over your seat.'

'Don't worry about that, love,' the driver said, smiling back. 'Jump in.'

East Grinstead seemed to have escaped any bombing, June thought, as she peered out of the taxi window. It was almost more unusual to see a town intact than one which had had large areas smashed to pieces.

'Are you visiting someone in the burns unit?' the taxi driver asked.

'Yes.' June hesitated, but he gave her such a kindly smile it seemed rude not to say something more. 'I'm visiting a pilot who was shot down.'

'Sorry to hear that, love. There's quite a few of our boys in there with terrible burns but they've got a surgeon who performs miracles, so we're told. I hope you don't find your young man too bad.'

June swallowed. 'Thank you,' she managed as he nodded and drove off.

Once inside she made her way to the reception desk. Two tired-looking middle-aged ladies stood behind it chatting to each other.

'Good afternoon,' June began. 'I've come to visit Flight Lieutenant Murray Andrews.'

One of the ladies flipped through some papers. 'He's in Ward 5.' She gestured toward a pair of swing doors. 'Through those doors, down the corridor, turn left and it's the first door on the left. You can't miss it.' She looked up at June. 'Good luck, dear.'

June's heart was in her throat as she walked along the corridor, the smell of polished lino in her nose, her shoes making a clacking sound at every step she took. The nearer she got to Ward 5, the more worried she became. If Murray was terribly injured maybe they wouldn't allow her in. After all, she wasn't family – or his wife.

What kind of condition was Murray really in, inside his head? she wondered. He was bound to be feeling low and she only hoped she would be able to cheer him up. Let him know she was thinking of him. One moment she felt confident that all would be well, and the next that she had no business to be here after all.

A nurse passed her and smiled and nodded, followed by a tall, thin, white-coated doctor who didn't acknowledge her at all but simply hurried by, his mind obviously on more important things than a young woman visiting a burns patient.

A smell of disinfectant mixed with a strong carbolic soap greeted her. Probably used to disguise all sorts of other worse smells, she thought grimly, though the general appearance of the hospital, though shabby and in need of decorating, was spotlessly clean. Her heart began to pound as she saw the sign: Ward 5. She opened the door and stepped up to the desk.

'Name of the person?' asked a nurse with dark curly hair escaping from under her cap. She reminded June of Iris, but it was soon evident that this was in appearance only.

'Flight Lieutenant Murray Andrews.'

'Relationship?'

'Um – friend. A *close* friend.'

'Hmm. Let me check.' She flipped through a file. 'As I thought,' she said, almost triumphantly. 'No visitors.'

'B-but I've come—'

'I'm sorry.' The nurse picked up a telephone and began to dial, an expression of dismissal clear on her smooth, healthy features.

June fought back her frustration. She chewed her lip,

wondering what to do next. Perhaps something to eat and a cuppa.

A visitor pushing an old man in a wheelchair told her where she'd find the canteen. She chose an egg sandwich but as soon as she took the first bite she felt she would choke. Surely she hadn't come all this way for nothing. Murray would be so upset to think she'd been right outside the ward and hadn't been allowed in. A wave of determination swept over her. No, she wouldn't give up. She'd explain the distance she'd travelled and that she was sure it would help Murray if he could see someone he knew.

She managed another bite of her sandwich and finished her cup of tea, and fifteen minutes later she was back in Ward 5. To her delight there was a different nurse on the desk who looked up and gave her a welcoming smile.

'What can I do for you?'

'I've come to see Flight Lieutenant Murray Andrews.'

'Wait one moment,' the new nurse said. She checked the list and her smile faded. 'It says, "No Visitors". I'm so sorry.'

'But I've come all this way,' June said. 'Is he so badly hurt that he's not allowed to see *anyone*?' She tried to brace herself for the answer.

'He's had major surgery,' the nurse frowned, reading the notes. 'But I can't see why—' She broke off. 'Oh, I see.' She looked up at June. 'It's not that he's not *allowed* visitors, because he is.'

'Then what is it?' June tried to keep the impatient note out of her voice.

'*He* doesn't want to see anyone.'

'No one at all?' June couldn't help her shocked tone.

'It doesn't say specifically . . .' The nurse looked directly at her. 'I suppose you're his girlfriend. I could give you ten minutes. Would that do?'

June didn't correct the nurse's assumption that she was Murray's girlfriend. If only she was.

'Yes, that would be wonderful,' she said, managing a smile.

'Go through that glass door. He's in the far corner by the window.' The nurse waved her hand. 'If he's asleep I'd prefer you to come back later.'

'I will.'

She wouldn't. She'd wait for however long it took for him to wake up.

The figure at the far end of the ward was lying flat with a couple of pillows under his head. One of his arms was resting on the top of the bedcover, heavily bandaged. When she was close enough June noticed there was dark bruising under his eyes, which were closed. She was aware of the nurse's last words but she wasn't going to heed them. This might be her only opportunity. With beating heart she tiptoed to the near side of his bed.

'Murray, it's me – June.'

Murray's eyelids fluttered open, but not before she saw the thin red wound, like a vertical slice, on one of them. For an instant she thought she saw a flash of joy on his face, and she smiled at him encouragingly. But his next words made her flinch.

'No, don't want . . . how did you get in? I said I didn't want any visitors. Please go.'

June watched the increased rise and fall of his chest as his breathing grew agitated. She felt sick. She'd made an awful mistake thinking Murray would be pleased to see her. She had to explain before it was too late.

'I'm sorry I haven't been before but it's taken me ages to find out even where you were stationed,' she said in a rush. 'And then everyone was reluctant to tell me where you were. I was shocked you'd been injured. As soon as I heard I asked

Matron if I could have a few days' leave to come and see you. She didn't want to at first and I almost had to beg her.' She knew she was running on, trying to fill the awkward silence.

She willed him to speak to her but there was no reaction at all.

Then he said, 'June . . .' His voice didn't even sound like him. It was dull and resigned.

She bent over him. 'Yes, Murray,' she said softly.

'It would be better for you to go.' His eyelids flickered down, the right one with the wound almost reproaching her.

So that was it. He didn't want anything from her whatsoever. Tears stung her eyes and she turned away, her hope shattered.

A sigh escaped Murray's lips. 'It was a long way to come for nothing. I'm sorry.'

She barely heard the words but his tone was enough to stop her in her tracks. She spun round and was by his bed in an instant.

'It's me who should be sorry,' June said. 'I should have telephoned the hospital. Made sure you didn't mind me coming to visit. I didn't even think.' She blinked to stop the tears. He mustn't see her upset. He was already upset enough himself. 'I've misjudged everything.'

'No, no. It's me. It's this bloody war.'

'Do you want to talk about it?'

'No.' Murray turned his head away.

'It might help if you do.' This was awful. She wasn't getting through to him at all. Her heart ached with wanting to reach him.

'I won't be able to fly again,' he suddenly blurted. 'And worse – I've lost so many friends, I've given up counting. One of them's in the next bed. Shorty.' He hoisted himself up and jerked his head over to the left where a figure with a heavily bandaged face lay quietly. Then he fell back on to the pillows, his chest heaving with exertion.

'Oh, Murray, I'm so sorry.'

He turned his head. 'Could you prop me up?'

'Of course.' She busied herself with his pillows, keeping her head turned from him so he couldn't see her tears welling.

'Can you give me some water?' He jerked his head. 'Over there.'

She watched as he held a beaker of water with his good hand and drank thirstily.

'*What* do you think you're doing in here?'

June looked up startled. The nurse who'd reminded her of Iris was glaring at her with open dislike.

'I thought I'd told you Flight Lieutenant Andrews specifically requested that he does not want any visitors – at all. And that means you too, Miss.'

'I think he wants to see his fiancée,' June said quickly, pressing Murray's shoulder surreptitiously.

'His fiancée? You didn't tell me you were his fiancée. Why didn't you say so?' The nurse's tone softened a fraction. 'I'll give you two more minutes. Not a second longer. And that's an order.' She spun on her heel.

'She can be a dragon, that one, but she's got a good heart.' Murray looked at June curiously. 'My fiancée?'

'I wouldn't have got in if she hadn't thought I was someone in the family,' she said, bending her head and smoothing the sheet, hoping he wouldn't notice her red cheeks. 'It was the first thing I could think of. I was determined she wasn't going to send me away again.'

Murray didn't say anything for a few moments. Then he said, 'Where are you staying?'

'At a bed-and-breakfast, not far.' Should she say more? The two minutes would be up soon.

'Will you come tomorrow, Junie?'

She couldn't tell whether he was looking straight at her, as his injured eye was terribly bloodshot and didn't seem to be focusing properly. But he'd used his old name for her. Warmth flooded her whole being. 'That's why I've come,' she said. 'To see you as often as I can before I have to go back. Matron's let me off for a few days.'

'I'm glad.'

June leaned over and kissed him lightly on the cheek. She was rewarded with the hint of a smile.

'I suppose we have a lot to talk about,' he said quietly.

Chapter Thirty-Four

He shouldn't have let her go like that without saying anything important. He could tell by her voice, her trembling hand when she'd touched him, that she was terribly hurt he'd treated her so off-handedly when she'd first arrived. Letting her know in no uncertain terms that he'd specifically asked for no visitors – although he'd never in his wildest dreams imagined she would be his first.

What a dear girl she was. He loved her for telling the nurse she was his fiancée so she could get in to see him. What a wonderful wife she'd make for some lucky chap. But it wouldn't be him. He wasn't the man she'd first met on that train to Liverpool any more.

He'd never thought he'd see her again. He'd had no idea where she was headed for, that day. Hadn't thought to ask, he'd been in such a spin by her beauty. He'd tried to find her when they'd reached Liverpool but she'd been swallowed up in the crowds and he'd had to tell himself it was just one of those things. A chance encounter. Yet he'd never been able to get her out of his mind.

Seeing those green eyes flash in indignation when she'd tried to get by in the corridor of the train. He'd deliberately blocked her way so he could look at her for a few more moments. And then she'd stepped into the very bookshop where he'd been trying to get hold of a map. And as far as he was concerned, that was it. He never ever wanted any other woman.

But he could never tell her he loved her. Not in that way. Not in the way he wanted. That he loved her with his body, heart and soul. He couldn't bear her pity even though he was making a fair recovery. If she said she loved him in return he would always wonder if she only stayed with him because she was sorry for him.

Tears ran down his cheeks and he didn't bother to use his good hand to brush them away. He remembered every one of their kisses, tentative at first but how quickly they'd changed to passion . . . loving, tender kisses they'd once shared when he'd honestly thought she was falling in love with him and might one day become his wife. It was what he'd dreamed of. And he'd been sure she'd shared his dream. Until he'd told her they could only be friends. What a damned fool he'd been.

Chas had nearly ruined everything for him. When he'd overheard Chas in the bar that night bragging about an English girl buying a toy dog for a child called Lizzie it was as though his heart was being sawn in half. Even that poor devil who'd just received a Dear John letter from his wife had asked him what was the matter. He'd told the poor bloke it was none of his bloody business, tipped back the rest of his beer, got up and strolled over to where Chas was sitting. Chas had his head bent listening to one of the other pilots and jerked his head in Murray's direction. Murray swung his arm out and gave him a surprise blow on his jaw.

He was delighted to watch Chas rub that handsome face of his, a look of disbelief in his eyes.

'What the hell was that for, buddy?'

'I'm not your buddy and never will be,' Murray growled.

'That was for June. The next one won't leave you in your seat. I suggest you leave her alone, you cad.'

He'd turned and marched out to a few chuckles from the table where Chas still sat. He didn't care if he got court-martialled. All he knew was that it had given him the greatest satisfaction.

A bolt of pain now shot through his eye making him screw up his face against it. His good eye. Dear God, don't let anything happen to his good eye. If only he could get back into his Spit and help his friends beat the Germans. But it wasn't to be. They would never allow him to go up again. He closed his eyes to ease the pain.

But of course he was no longer flying Spits anyway. He'd moved into Bomber Command to get away from Liverpool – to forget June. But it had been the biggest mistake of his life. Fighting one pilot, one to another, both with an even chance, was one thing; dropping bombs on innocent civilians – worse, on women and children – was another.

Somehow when he'd transferred he hadn't thought of individuals. They'd had it drummed into them that they were to drop bombs on the cities to crush the people's morale. But he'd crushed so much more. To think he was responsible for ending hundreds, maybe thousands, of lives, even in the few weeks he'd been on those grim missions. Children who would never grow up to have careers and families. Children left with one or both parents killed. Some of them would end up in a home like Dr Barnardo's – plucked away from everything and everyone who was familiar to them. As if that wasn't bad enough there were the beautiful buildings – cathedrals, churches, houses, hospitals – and the railways: all smashed to smithereens. It made no difference that they were German buildings, German architecture. They were icons of beauty whoever had designed them and built

335

them. His stomach churned as he thought of the misery he'd inflicted, night after night, upon German civilians who probably didn't want this war any more than the British. In a way it was almost a relief knowing he wouldn't be able to continue in Bomber Command. But because he'd been part of it, though only for a short time, how could someone as dear as Junie ever forgive him for the horror he'd brought upon innocent people? It didn't help that many of his pals felt exactly the same.

He gave a despairing sigh and more tears trickled down his cheek. Life wasn't really worth living if June wasn't there by his side.

Chapter Thirty-Five

The landlady at the bed-and-breakfast could not have been more welcoming. She was a plump lady with her hair mostly covered by a hairnet, and wearing a pink flowered overall with lipstick to match.

'I hoped you wouldn't be too late, dear, as I need to pop to the shop and get a few bits, but I wanted to be here when you arrived. Come in, come in. I'm Elsie Sutton. But call me Elsie.'

She led June along a corridor to the sitting room.

'Sit down, my duck. I'll make some tea and then I'll leave you to it while I go and get the groceries.' She scuttled off.

Elsie was not the best cook. The macaroni cheese hadn't been cooked long enough and tasted more of mustard than of cheese.

'It's not my best effort,' Elsie apologised. 'What with the rationing we don't get enough in the way of cheese and butter – and the amount of meat I manage to get is laughable, even though they know I'm trying to run a business.'

'It's lovely, Elsie. Honestly.' She smiled at the landlady. 'Do you have children?'

'Two sons.' Elsie chewed her lower lip. 'Both of them fighting for king and country.'

'You must be very proud of them.'

'Oh, I'm proud, all right. They look right handsome in their uniforms – they're soldiers, both of them in the army – but I'd rather *not* be proud and have them home safe with me. Every time I see a telegram boy deliver something in the road I think, "Please don't come any nearer. Don't stop at my door. Go past. Go to anyone's door but mine." And then I think how horrible I am because some other poor boy's been killed or injured and some other mother is heart-broken. I just don't want it to be one of *my* boys. I don't want to read a telegram with bad news. It'd kill me, what with my husband dead from influenza after the last war, poor bugger, when he fought in the trenches and never got a bruise. It don't seem fair.'

'Oh, Elsie, I'm so sorry. This dreadful war.'

'When will it end? That's what I'm asking every day. When will it end?'

June felt far more confident when she went to the hospital the following morning, but she was disappointed to see the stern nurse on duty again.

'I've come to see Flight Lieutenant Murray Andrews,' she began.

The nurse looked up. 'Oh, yes, his fiancée.' She empha-sised the last word.

June caught her eye and felt there was a suspicious glint. But the nurse gave her a nod. 'He's just having a bed bath. It'll be about ten minutes. Take a seat.' She gestured with her head.

'You may go in now.'

June made the short walk to the bed at the far end, which still had the curtains pulled round. She hesitated, but a plump nurse appeared and swung the curtains back, and there was Murray, propped up against a pile of pillows. He smiled as he saw her and June, a little self-consciously, kissed the nearest side of his face.

'Hello, Murray. How are you feeling?'

'Better now I've seen you.'

A glow spread through her. Even if she'd lost him as her boyfriend – was he ever that? – he was too precious for her to lose as a friend, and to her relief he seemed to feel the same way. She sat down on the metal visitor's chair.

'How do you really feel?'

'Not so bad. They say I should be out of here in a week.'

'That's wonderful news.'

'By the way, who let you know I was missing?'

His question came out of the blue and June swallowed. The last thing she wanted to bring up was Chas. But Murray was looking at her, waiting for her to answer.

'Chas Lockstone. He rang me at the home. He said he knew we were friends – "buddies", he called us,' June said, deliberately ignoring Murray's frown at the mention of Chas. 'He said he was sorry not to have let me know earlier but he'd been on leave, and that you'd now been missing for a week or more. I was distraught. Then after I'd almost given up hope he telephoned to say you'd been found. Oh, Murray' – she let her eyes linger on him and allowed herself to smile – 'it was the best telephone call I've ever had. But Chas was hazy on what had actually happened to you.'

'We were hit and bailed out but the plane caught fire,' Murray said, his eyes now fixed on to the ceiling. 'Luckily we were over Holland. Our luck held when we were picked up by a group of Dutch resisters who'd seen us come down. My arm was in a bad shape so they had to get a doctor to patch it up but he said I should have an X-ray and it would need to be operated on. It must have been a week or more before they managed to get me back to England.'

'What happened to the rest of the crew?'

He closed his eyes as though his answer was too painful for him to tell her. 'Four others injured, one of them seriously, one almost unscathed except for a few cuts and bruises . . . and one . . .' He opened his bloodshot eyes and turned to look at her, his eyes wet. 'My pal Johnnie. One of the best navigators. They couldn't save him.' She heard him swallow before he spoke again. 'They were such super chaps, Junie. I'll never forget any of them – especially Johnnie.'

She took his good hand and gave it a gentle squeeze. She was desperate to ask him why he'd moved into Bomber Command – was it anything to do with her? Had he had any intention of seeing her again? Did he miss her? But it wasn't the time or the place. Murray was upset enough already.

The stern nurse gave her longer than yesterday, but she appeared after half an hour and warned June she only had five more minutes.

Knowing they would soon be saying goodbye again made them awkward with one another. They were both silent for quite one minute until June broke it.

'Where will they send you from here?' she said.

'Back to Speke, I imagine.' Murray kept his voice low, even though no one was around to hear him. Shorty was still lying peacefully in the next bed. 'The doc likes to get you rehabilitated as soon as possible and there's no job for me now in Bomber Command.' He looked directly at her. 'It was the wrong decision for me anyway.'

She decided this wasn't the time to question him about why he'd put in for the transfer.

'What about your eye—' June started.

'They've operated,' Murray interrupted, 'and are hopeful, but I'm not banking on anything.' He sighed and lowered his voice. 'You get used to anything in here. Even poor old Shorty will get used to his face in time. He's had two operations since I've been in – six in all, poor devil.'

She didn't know what to say.

'They won't let me fly again,' Murray continued, his voice hard with resentment. 'I'll have to do office work, I expect.'

'I know it's not what you really want,' June said, remembering how his eyes used to light up when he talked to her about taking off into the air, even though she knew he hated the actual fighting and having to witness another pilot go down, whether he was British *or* German. To Murray it was simply another young man, a skilled pilot like himself, spiralling to his doom. She smiled at him. 'But at least you're safe and getting well. And I'm sure they won't keep you in office work forever.'

'I don't want to talk about it. What about *you*, Junie?' He watched her closely. 'Are you still happy at Dr Barnardo's?'

Her heart turned over at his use of her name.

'It's where I belong,' she said, simply.

Murray caught her eye and smiled. 'Yes, you *do* belong there. I can see it now. That's where you're happiest.'

No! she wanted to scream out. I *am* happy there, it's true, but I want to share it with you, Murray. I'm happiest with you. I want to be with you when this war's over. Can't you tell? But she remained silent. The last thing he'd want was for her to feel sorry for him. But it wouldn't be that at all. She loved him. She always would. But she could never tell him because he'd made it plain, even before his accident, that he would never love her in that way.

'Sorry to butt in but time's up, I'm afraid.' A nurse new to June stepped briskly towards them. 'Lieutenant Andrews has got to go for an eye examination.'

Just as she'd done the day before, June leaned over the bed and kissed Murray's cheek. Then to her surprise he brought his hand up to her face and stroked the contours as though he wanted to fix the memory of her deep within him.

'Thank you for coming. You've cheered me up.'

'I haven't done anything for you to thank me for,' June answered shakily. 'I just wanted to see you, but tomorrow's the last day. Then I have to go back.'

'Maybe you can tell me what happened when you went to London that time.' His eye closed as he leaned back on the pillows.

'What do you mean?' Had he heard about what she'd done to Billy Lavender? She steeled herself.

'When you met Chas in London.' His words were mumbled but she still heard him. Her heart did a sickening turn and she went pale. Chas – when she'd bumped into him in London after . . . What had Chas told him? Suddenly the image of Chas on top of her flooded her pale cheeks with fire. He must have boasted to Murray that he'd made love to her. Her hand flew to her mouth and she was thankful Murray still had his eyes closed. How could Chas? Was it because she'd tried to push him off, told him to stop, *before* any bomb went off? She remembered his humiliated expression. He couldn't even use the excuse that they were interrupted by a bombing raid. That must be it. Chas had bragged to Murray that she was a willing partner. Had gone happily up to his bedroom of her own accord.

Once again the feeling of deepest shame swept over her. Why had she been so stupid as to go to his room, just because he'd said she was in shock and needed a cup of tea, and then why not take a nap on his bed? She'd been gullible and nothing could make the clocks go back. She'd have to live

342

with this guilt forever. And whatever she said to Murray, how could he believe her?

No wonder he'd specifically said he didn't want any visitors. He was terrified she'd come and torment him. He must have been devastated when Chas told him his version. Had Chas also told him about what she'd done to her father? What must he think of her? That it would serve her right if she was put in prison, no doubt. You might be able to forgive the person you loved one terrible thing, but two? That would be impossible.

Murray's breathing became regular. June tiptoed out of the ward. Tears stung the back of her eyes but she was determined not to cry. The thought had never crossed her mind that she was doing something wrong. 'Little tease', she seemed to remember Chas calling her. Before all that she'd genuinely thought he was being kind and understanding after what she had just gone through with her father.

June took comfort that she would see Murray tomorrow, and perhaps have a chance to explain.

Chapter Thirty-Six

Murray had tried hard to drift off to sleep when June left. He kept seeing Chas inviting June up to his hotel room with one idea only in that Yank's mind. Murray swallowed hard, praying she wasn't taken in by Chas. The thought sickened him. No, June was too level-headed. But what if she really liked Chas? There was nothing he could do: she was a free woman. He could only hope that Chas had been his usual swaggering, boastful American self, showing off to his buddies that he could get any girl, and there was nothing in it.

In his irritation Murray began to cough. He raised himself to reach the jug on his bedside table. He drank thirstily but pulled a face midway through. It was lukewarm water and he craved cold.

'Everything all right?' A young nurse with bright ginger hair and freckles smiled at him. 'Can I bring you a cup of tea?'

'Yes, please,' he said, mainly to get rid of the girl, nice though she was, to be left alone with his thoughts. 'And some fresh water, thanks.'

'Coming up.' She grinned and disappeared.

'Lockstone got what he deserved,' Murray said out loud, thinking of the feeling of hitting Chas in the face. There was a mumble from the next bed, and immediately he felt ashamed.

'What is it, Murray? Speak up, you old bugger.'

'I was just thinking of this damned war and how we're both messed up and we've got to learn to live with it, and I don't want anyone's pity.'

'No, that's not what you said.' The voice was clearer now, and more urgent. 'I heard the name Lockstone. Presumably you're talking about the Yank, Chas Lockstone. What did he get that he deserved?'

Murray sighed. He'd always known the risks but he'd never truly thought he'd end up being treated for third-degree burns. But at least it was his arm. Not like poor old Shorty, whose face had caught the brunt of the fire when his Hurricane had gone down. He'd thought Shorty was fast asleep. As if the bloke didn't have enough on his plate without hearing Murray's woes. He was just about to say it was nothing and pretend to fall asleep when he suddenly realised he was treating Shorty like some kind of fool. Just because his face was burned didn't mean his brain had gone soft.

'A punch in the jaw. I gave him one.'

'Really.' Shorty sounded amused. 'Well, he's had it coming for some time. What was it for?'

'For telling his buddies, as he calls them, that he'd seduced June in his hotel bedroom.'

'You didn't believe it, did you?'

'I did at the time, but when I thought about it later I knew June would never do anything like it. If she went to his room, there'd be a reason why and it wouldn't be that.'

He broke off as the ginger-haired nurse appeared with his tea and water, and another nurse helped Shorty to drink some kind of liquid through a straw.

When they'd gone, Murray told him how his friendship with June had developed – even about Freddie and how he'd brought him to the home for Lizzie.

'So what's the problem now?' Shorty said. 'I ask that as I couldn't help overhearing a bit of your conversation. I can't see her but she sounds a lovely girl. And I could tell she loves you. It's in her voice every time she speaks to you.'

Murray's eyes filled with ready tears. Shorty seemed to understand more than *he* did. His voice was not quite steady as he answered his friend.

'Not any more. She might have begun to love me once, but then I told her we could only be friends.'

'Why the devil did you tell her that?'

Murray was silent. How could he explain to Shorty of all people that he didn't want Junie to waste her life on him? It would sound as though Shorty would have no hope whatsoever of finding happiness. And didn't he have a girlfriend? Murray tried to rack his tired brain. Yes, Shorty had definitely mentioned a girl when they were at Speke. Come to think of it, she was a nurse. But he'd never seen her visit him. She must have ditched him right away when she'd heard how badly he'd been injured.

'I was falling in love with her,' Murray went on, 'and then so many pilots didn't come back and I didn't want to end up so badly injured that she'd only stay with me out of loyalty – she's that sort of person. And that was *before* the crash. Before all my fears came true.' A self-pitying tear ran down his cheek.

'You were worried you'd end up like me, you mean,' Shorty said quietly.

'I'm so sorry, old pal. I didn't mean it to come out like that, but I didn't want June to waste the rest of her life if anything happened to me.'

There was an awkward silence between them. Finally, Shorty broke it.

'Do you know what's keeping me going?' he said.

'No.'

'My girl, Connie, still loves me. She says she doesn't care tuppence about what my face looks like. It's me *inside* she loves. And that's how your June will be. You're a bloody fool, Andrews, to let her slip away like that. And you know damn well she loves you. But she's hurt, and I don't blame her.'

Murray lay there for several minutes taking in what Shorty was saying. He recalled the love shining in June's eyes each time she came to visit him. He'd wanted to tell her there and then that he loved her. What a bloody fool he was. But maybe it wasn't too late.

'Shorty,' he finally called across to the next bed. 'Thanks, old boy. I think you've put it all into perspective.'

'Mind you tell her next time,' Shorty grunted.

'Tell her what?'

'That you're crazy about her, you idiot. And you intend to marry her – before anyone else gets there first.'

Before he could reply the ginger-haired nurse appeared again, followed by a smiling young woman with chestnut hair.

'He's over there, love,' the nurse said, gesturing.

Murray watched in astonishment as the young woman made straight for Shorty's bed and bent over him.

'Darling, it's me – Connie.'

June was in for a shock when she arrived at the hospital the following day.

'I'm afraid we needed the bed so we released him as he was doing so well.' It was the nurse who had reminded her of Iris.

347

'Where did they send him?' June asked.

'Back to RAF Speke.' She regarded June with narrowed eyes. 'You're not his fiancée, are you?'

June blushed to the roots of her hair. 'I'm sorry,' she stuttered, 'but there was no other way and I—'

'It's all right. I wouldn't dream of standing in love's way.' The nurse unexpectedly grinned. She took out her watch fob and glanced at the time. 'You should have told me as much when you first came in two days ago. You just said you were a friend – a *close* friend, is how I believe you described it. Then changed your mind next time and said you were his *fiancée*.' She laughed. 'He's a lovely chap. Somewhat bitter at the moment but who can blame him? I'd go for him myself if he didn't already have a fiancée.' She gave June a wink and laughed.

June smiled politely back but she felt sick at the thought that through her own stupidity she'd lost Murray – lost his heart forever.

Chapter Thirty-Seven

She dreaded the long journey back to Liverpool. Every nerve was on edge, thinking about Murray and how bad he must be feeling, all this while imagining she'd gone to bed with Chas. That she was a good-time girl. Not the girl he'd thought she was. No wonder he hadn't wanted any visitors – her especially. She clung on to the fact that he'd come round a bit at the end of their first visit, but he hadn't been the same person. Of course the accident was terrible and it was bound to make you feel depressed and worried about the future, and that's what she'd thought had wrought such a change in him, but now she knew the truth. Chas was at the bottom of it all. She swallowed hard. Surely Murray must be feeling bad that he hadn't given her a chance to explain before now – now that they were moving him. If only he'd left a note for her.

June arrived in Liverpool two and a half hours later than was scheduled. They would have had supper at the home by now but she wasn't hungry. Already Murray's face was blurred in her mind. Maybe it was because she was tired. So much had happened in the last few days that her brain felt as though it would burst.

The taxi dropped her outside the front door of Bingham Hall. The driver hopped out and put her suitcase on the drive, then helped her out of the taxi. June couldn't help tilting her head back to take in the magnificent house – just as she had the very first time she'd caught sight of it. She'd made it her home as far as she could, and now she'd made the decision that this was where she'd stay as long as they needed her. She rang the bell.

Gilbert opened the door to her – the last person she wanted to see. His black eyes seemed to pierce right through her and she flinched. If looks could kill, I'd be dead, she thought, as she stepped into the hall.

Shuddering under Gilbert's malevolent stare she was grateful to see Iris come running towards her.

'Junie. You're back. I've missed you. We've *all* missed you.' She hugged her friend and whispered, 'Meet you in the common room for a cup of tea.' She looked at her friend. 'You look terrible. Have you eaten?'

June shook her head.

'I'll make you a sandwich. See you in a few minutes.'

With an effort June dragged her case up the stairs, feeling Gilbert's eyes still on her, watching her every movement until she finally turned the corner out of his sight. She set her case down, too tired to unpack it, and stepped over to the washbasin to splash her face. She looked up into the mirror and couldn't recognise herself. Her hair, which she'd tucked into a snood that morning, had half escaped, and there were long strands falling away at the sides and the back of her neck. Her face was flecked with smuts that must have blown in when she'd stuck her head out of the corridor window in the train to catch a breeze; her skin looked sallow and there were deep shadows under her eyes.

She sat on the bed and wept. She cried for her father she'd lost when she was still a child; she cried for Lizzie and

Joachim going through so much worse, losing their families; she cried for the way Chas had tried to take advantage of her, which had destroyed Murray's trust in her; she cried for poor Shorty in the next bed to Murray – he would have to undergo many more operations but he was so cheerful; but most of all she cried because Murray only wanted her as a friend. He didn't love her. He never would.

Finally, when she had no more tears left, she dragged herself up and took a handkerchief from her drawer and blew her nose. This wouldn't do. She mustn't wallow in self-pity. She had so much here – Iris, who'd become such a dear friend, and Kathleen and Bertie, and even Barbara, Athena and David were kind and friendly, and she had the children. They were the whole reason she was here. To help heal her broken heart from when Clara died. And although she would never forget Clara, never stop loving her, her heart had begun to mend. She'd made a mistake, that's all, thinking Murray might become part of her healing. Well, it wasn't to be. She must face it head on.

She sniffed and dried the last of her tears. A cup of tea. That's what she needed, with her dear Iris. Resolutely, she made her way down the staircase and into the common room where Iris sat waiting for her.

'Get this down you.' Iris sprang up to give June a plate with a thickly cut cheese sandwich. 'And here's your tea. Hope it's still hot.' She handed her a cup and added wickedly, 'I've put in half a teaspoon of extra sugar. You looked like you needed it.'

'So long as Matron doesn't find out,' June said with a small smile, gulping down half the lukewarm contents. 'Or Cook, for that matter.'

'Talking of Matron, I have news.' Iris's eyes were a sparkling deep blue and a grin spread over her face.

'Oh?'

'She's gone!'

'Who?'

'Matron.'

'Do you mean she's gone for good?'

'Yes.'

June's mouth dropped open and she put her cup down with such force it rattled loudly on the saucer. 'How? When? What happened?'

'So many questions.' Iris chuckled. 'You missed all the fun. Mr Clarke came down and they were huddled together in Matron's office for at least an hour. Then he left and eventually Matron emerged in a cloud of smoke. She must have lit one after the other.'

'Do you think he persuaded her to leave?'

'Nobody knows but I bet that's what happened. And to save face she called a meeting of all of us right here in this room the day before yesterday and announced she was retiring with immediate effect. I had to bite my tongue not to shout out "Hallelujah".'

June couldn't help it. A smile spread over her face. 'You're sure it's not some joke?' she said, suddenly anxious after a few seconds, trying to take it in.

'No, it's no joke. She was gone at noon yesterday without even a goodbye. And Mr Clarke wants you to telephone him as soon as you're back. But before you do anything, eat your sandwich!'

June was almost glad she hadn't been able to see Murray. How embarrassing it would have been to try to explain – try to convince him of her innocence when the finger pointed straight at her. How could she have convinced him she was only taking a nap on Chas's bed and in her wildest imagination it had never occurred to her that Chas would take advantage of her vulnerability. She didn't think she could go through it all again to Murray. And why should he listen? He'd obviously formed his own conclusions.

One moment she desperately wanted to talk to Iris, ask her what she should do, the next moment she wanted to curl up into a ball like Lizzie used to in the warmth of Bertie's kitchen, and say nothing to anybody.

She found Iris watching her curiously, and once or twice her friend asked if she was all right. June told her Murray was in quite a state and she hadn't stayed long on either occasion, and now he'd been moved back to Speke.

'Well, at least he's been able to speak to you in the hospital,' Iris said cheerfully, when they were in the library that evening. 'He'll write when he's got settled. At least he's much nearer to us again.' She gave June's arm a little shake. 'Come on, Junie, it's not like you to be in the doldrums.'

'He won't write.' June rounded on her friend. 'He doesn't want anything to do with me any more.'

'What are you talking about?' Iris's blue eyes deepened with concern. 'You said he was pleased to see you.'

'I-I didn't want to tell you the truth,' June faltered. 'I thought at first when he'd got over the shock of seeing me that he was pleased – it must be lonely for him day after day with no visitors. And he was even better the next day. Until the end – as we were leaving. And then he said . . . he said . . .' She broke down, sobbing.

Iris jumped up from her chair and came to kneel beside June's. She put her arms round her.

'Junie, you must tell me. What did Murray say? It can't be that bad that you can't tell me.'

June looked up with weeping eyes. 'He said perhaps we can talk about what happened. When I asked him what he meant, he said, "When you met Chas in London."' She looked at Iris. 'How did he know about that?' she said, desperation coating her words.

'Chas must have told him,' Iris said, patting her hand. 'You know what men are like. Chas is American. They're quite cocky. He probably did it on purpose to make Murray jealous.'

'Well, he certainly succeeded,' June said bitterly.

'Why don't you write Murray a letter?' Iris suggested. 'It will be easier to put it on paper, then you won't have to see his reaction. He can take time to read it over and reflect on it. Maybe when he's got time to think about it he'll understand and believe you. And if he doesn't, then you don't want him anyway.' June threw her a look of misery. 'But he *will* believe you, because he's a good chap, Junie. You two are meant to be together.'

June stared at her friend for a few moments, then crumpled back into her chair and cried as though her heart were breaking.

'Junie, don't.' Iris was by her side in a flash again. 'Honestly, everything will be all right. Murray is not like Chas. He's decent and loyal and he loves you. You know he does, deep down in your heart. If he saw you like this he'd never forgive himself. And I'll tell you something – he's feeling much worse about you being tied to him with only sight in one eye and a permanently injured arm than about the Chas episode, which was a load of nonsense anyway. The problem is Murray himself. He doesn't want your pity or you to spend your life looking after him.'

'Do you really think so?' June looked at her friend, tears still streaming down her face. It was something she hadn't thought of. Could Iris really be right? And if her friend was, then why hadn't June been able to see this for herself?

'Of course I do.' Iris took a handkerchief out of her apron. 'I'm a nurse, aren't I?' June tried to smile. 'Here, take this. Wipe your eyes like a good girl and tell me you'll write to Murray this very evening.'

June dabbed her eyes, then blew her nose.

'Junie?'

'Yes, all right. Anything you say, Auntie Iris.'

Iris pretended to cuff her. 'And don't forget – tell him exactly what happened, and ask him to believe you – not forgive you. You've done nothing for him to forgive.'

'I'm sorry I've been such a misery when you must be bursting with excitement at being engaged to David.'

'We're not starry-eyed,' Iris said matter-of-factly. I'm nearly twenty-six and he's forty-three. It sounds old but it isn't with him. He's not a bit fuddy-duddy . . . and do you know what else?' June shook her head. 'You and I are going to have a discussion about Mozart and his operas one of these days.' Iris threw back her head and roared with laughter. 'Me. Can you imagine?'

'Yes, I can,' June said fervently. 'I think it's wonderful that he's converted you. As I said, he's exactly right for you – and forty-something is no age these days.'

Iris gave her a grateful smile. 'Wish you could say that to Mum and Dad. Mum keeps saying he's only a few years younger than Dad. But at least they've told me to bring him home when I get a chance.' She grinned and waved her ring finger in front of her face, peering at it as though she still couldn't quite believe it.

It was truly wonderful that Iris had found such happiness with someone who believed in her and loved her and wanted to make her his wife.

'They'll love him as soon as they see him,' June said, genuinely smiling. 'I've never asked you – does David have children?'

'Yes, a son and a daughter. They'd both been offered a place at university but that's all been scuppered for the moment. They've both gone into the navy. David's so proud of them but he can't bear the thought of bringing any more children into this crazy world.'

'Do you mind?'

'Not a bit.' Iris laughed. 'You know my opinion on that by now. I couldn't bear having grizzling smelly babies to look after. But we're going to sponsor Joachim with his music – act more like foster parents until we find out exactly what's happened to his real family. David says he's going to make that his mission, though it'll be impossible until the war's ended, no doubt.'

'Have you said anything to Joachim?' June felt a warm glow steal over her heart. He was one of her 'specials'.

'Yes, he knows and he's very happy. And he's had a piece of marvellous news. He's been accepted by the Royal Academy of Music in London. He starts in September.'

'Oh, Iris, he must be absolutely thrilled. I turn my back for a few days and all sorts of things happen—' She broke off.

'Your turn will come, June Lavender,' Iris said seriously. 'Just you see if I'm not right.'

The young women were silent for a few moments, June lost in her thoughts of Murray and what she should say in the letter – that is, if she wrote it. She glanced across at her friend, who positively glowed. It made June smile.

'Do you realise we've never toasted your engagement? And now you're going to have a child to love.'

'The best sort,' Iris grinned. 'A ready-made child. No dirty napkins, no wet bottoms, no sleepless nights – it's perfect.'

'So that's two things we have to toast – and I don't mean with a cup of tea, either.'

'Get you, begging for alcohol,' Iris teased. She jumped to her feet and put out her hand to pull June up. 'There's a bottle of wine in the pantry I've had my eye on – probably Matron's, but that's good. It'll be decent. Let's go and see if it's still there. Bertie and the girls will have finished clearing up the kitchen. We'll have a toast, even if it's out of a teacup. And if they're still there then they can help celebrate too.'

Later that evening in her room, feeling squiffy from the unexpected wine, which she still wasn't used to, June sat at the small table under her window and got out her writing pad and pen. It was only when she wrote '22nd June' that she realised today was her birthday. Her twenty-first. Supposed to be the important one. She brushed away the thought that it seemed like a bad omen that she'd forgotten her own birthday.

She stared at the blank sheet. Her head had begun to throb, gently at first, but now it was becoming more insistent. She hesitated. Maybe it was foolish to even try to explain. Maybe Murray would be more embarrassed to receive such a letter than she was feeling herself at this minute, wondering how even to begin.

Resolutely she began to write.

Dear Murray,

First I want to say how pleased I was to see you in hospital and that you are on the way to recovery.

June set the pen down a moment. That was the easy bit. She sighed and took up her pen.

Just before we left you mentioned Chas. I'd hoped I'd never have to explain that time, but you deserve to

357

know. I expect he told you I was in his hotel room, on his bed. But what he may not have told you was that when I bumped into him in Oxford Street I was in shock. I'd just had a terrible visit to my father's and I'd ended up throwing a vase at his head. It sounds melodramatic but I honestly thought I'd killed him. I'll tell you why I did this when or if I see you again. It doesn't matter at this moment. What matters is that Chas was kind at the time and made me go back to my father's flat. They'd called an ambulance and we went to the hospital and found out he was all right. I didn't go and see him. Chas invited me to his hotel for a cup of tea to calm down as I was still in a state, and because the foyer was crowded he invited me to his room. We had our tea, but I was exhausted. He suggested I have a nap on his bed and I lay on the top of the cover with my clothes on, not thinking anything of it, and actually fell asleep.

The next thing I knew was Chas begging me to let him make love. I screamed out but a bomb went off and the hotel's alarm straight after. Chas grabbed me and we ran down the stairs, but I ran back to the room to get a little toy dog for Lizzie's birthday that Chas had generously paid for when I didn't have enough money. I got hit by a piece of falling timber and luckily Chas had rushed up the stairs after me. He was angry and rightly so as another bomb went off and I could have got us both killed.

That's what happened, Murray. Then Chas got a taxi and we went to Aunt Ada's. He didn't even stop for a cup of tea – I think he was too annoyed with me and probably in a state of shock himself when he realised how close that bomb had been. I haven't heard anything more from him since he rang to tell me you'd been found and

I don't want to. I don't think he's a bad man – it was just the heat of the moment.

I hope after reading this you will find it in your heart to for—

She crossed out the last three letters and instead wrote:

. . . believe me as I never intended, nor did I ever do, anything wrong.
Your friend always,
Junie

She'd decide in the morning whether she would put it in the letterbox.

She didn't post the letter. It didn't read right when she skimmed it over the next morning. It was almost as though she was trying too hard to defend herself. She thought about making it shorter but in the end she felt it was pointless. She put it in the drawer next to the little winged brooch that Murray had given her. She was utterly drained. If only her real father had been alive and she could have talked it over with him. She needed his presence – needed him to tell her what she should do.

Chapter Thirty-Eight

Mr Clarke came to Bingham Hall three weeks after June returned.

'We'll go in the library, if you don't mind,' he told her. 'Mrs Pherson's office still smells of cigarette smoke. Quite turns my stomach. Give me a pipe any day.'

Once they were settled in two easy chairs facing each other, and Mr Clarke had lit his pipe, he leaned forward.

'Did Mrs Pherson ever call a meeting with the staff about the name-calling?'

'No,' June said. 'She kept saying she would but nothing happened.'

'Hmm. I thought as much, as I would have expected her to send me in a report as to any outcome.'

'In all honesty she wasn't keen to have a German boy here. She said the others would be upset too. We all protested but she wouldn't have it, though she didn't call him anything nasty as far as I know and we're all thrilled he's been chosen to go to the music academy. It's given him a real boost.'

'Well, Mrs Pherson was always a bit anti,' Mr Clarke said. 'It took some persuading for her to have the boy. And from what I've heard, I'm not at all sure about Mr Gilbert, though I admit we've never found any concrete evidence of his leanings. But I do know he's not the right person to uphold

Dr Barnardo's creed, and, like Mrs Pherson, he's at retiring age anyway.' He cleared his throat. 'To change the subject, have you found everything you need until we get a replacement for her?'

'I've had to go into her office a few times,' June admitted, 'but the filing cabinet is locked so I haven't always found what I needed. I was wondering if you had the key.'

Mr Clarke dipped into his pocket and handed her a small key, and another larger one. 'That one's for the office door,' he said. 'It should be kept locked at all times – Mrs Pherson was always meticulous about locking up, and rightly so.'

June put them in her overall pocket.

'Has she actually gone?' she asked. 'Because several of her personal things are there still.'

'She left in a hurry,' Mr Clarke said, rubbing the back of his neck. 'Seems she couldn't wait to retire. Can you see that her personal belongings are packed up and sent off to her? She's gone to her sister's. I have her address if you should need it.'

'I have it, thank you,' June said, mindful that she needed to get back to her job.

'Just one more thing.' Mr Clarke leaned forward in his chair. 'We need a matron, of course. And with this war on they don't come two a penny. We've been discussing the situation at Stepney Causeway, and decided the best thing is to offer *you* the job.'

June gave a start. This was not at all what she expected.

'Of course we'll give you a week to think about it,' Mr Clarke said, smiling. 'But we think you'd do a sterling job for us. We've had excellent reports about your work.'

'From Matron?' June couldn't stop the incredulous tone.

'No, not from Matron. I believe that would be more than she could bear to do. But from Mr Cannon and the two other teachers, from both nurses, and we even had a quiet word with Mrs Bertram.'

'Cook?'

Mr Clarke nodded. 'We don't offer these things lightly, you know. We realise you're very young, but you're a hard worker with the children's interests close to your heart. And that's the kind of person we're looking for – relying on. We'd give you a full job description and of course there would be a generous salary increase. As a newly appointed matron you would earn twelve guineas a month, all in, and Mrs Pherson's old cottage. So what do you think, eh?'

'I don't need a week to think about it,' June said, her face relaxing into a grateful smile. 'I feel honoured and I'd love to do it.' And then an idea struck her. The most wonderful idea. Her smile turned into a beam. It was what Mr Clarke had said about her having Matron's cottage.

'That's excellent news, Miss Lavender.'

'But I'd like to ask you just one thing.'

Mr Clarke nodded for her to carry on.

'You mentioned I would have Matron's old cottage.'

'That's right. Goes with the job.'

'I know animals are not allowed in the home and I understand why, but would you, or would Dr Barnardo's, object if I had a small, extremely well-behaved dog living with me in the cottage?' June's heart practically stopped as she waited for Mr Clarke's answer.

Mr Clarke took his glasses off and removed the handkerchief which peeped from the top pocket of his suit. He opened his mouth and blew on each lens with a short 'Huh', then polished each one. He held them up in front of him, gave a final polish, then a nod of satisfaction, and put them back on the rim of his nose, all the while not catching her eye.

Had she gone too far? Had she ruined this wonderful opportunity? She could have kicked herself.

'I'm sorry, I shouldn't have—'

'Shouldn't have what, Miss Lavender?' He raised a thin eyebrow.

'Asked you if I could break the rules. It was impertinent.'

Mr Clarke smiled. 'I've made a decision. So long as the dog has a proper pen in your bit of garden and can't run wild, I don't see a problem. Are you talking about the puppy that Mrs Pherson reported to me?'

'Yes. He's really Lizzie's and she loves him so much. It was Freddie who got her talking again. She's been terribly upset since Matron made me send him back to the RAF camp and she'll be thrilled she can come and visit him sometimes.'

'Well, you know our creed,' Mr Clarke said, throwing her a sly smile. 'If anyone needs a home, we at Dr Barnardo's will provide it. And you've persuaded me that this little chap Freddie is obviously an orphan and needs a home.' He stood up and put his hat on. 'I don't think we need to discuss it any further, Miss Lavender, only for me to say congratulations on your promotion. I'll get the paperwork sorted out right away. All you have to do is read it carefully, sign it and post it back to me.'

'Thank you, Mr Clarke.' June gulped, not quite believing what had just taken place in the library. 'I promise I won't let you down.'

'I don't think there's any chance of that,' he said with a smile. 'And, Miss Lavender, keep an eye on Gilbert, won't you? If he does or says anything out of turn I give you full permission to handle it, however you see fit. And that means giving him his marching orders if you deem it necessary.' He looked at his watch. 'Well, I'll be off now. I've another Dr Barnardo's home to see in town.'

'Thank you for everything.' June rose to her feet. She held out her hand and Mr Clarke took it in his thin bony one and shook it lightly.

He picked up his briefcase. 'Don't worry, Miss Lavender – I'll see myself out. Good day to you.' He touched the rim of his hat and this time his gaunt face actually split in two as he smiled broadly at her before he let himself out of the library door, closing it behind him with a determined click.

As soon as Mr Clarke left, June hurried to Matron's old office, giving a wry grin as she glanced at the sign saying 'Matron' on the door. She threw wide the window, welcoming the warm summer air.

First job was something she'd wanted to do ever since she first arrived at Bingham Hall – examine the backgrounds of the children. She unlocked the filing cabinet and took out half a dozen files marked with the names of individual children. She sat at the desk and slowly went through them, making notes of their backgrounds. There was so much to take in that she'd need to spend several mornings reading each child's notes carefully.

June had been sitting at the desk for almost an hour trying to decipher Matron's brief scrawled notes. Several of the case notes provided little detail on where the children had come from and what they'd been through. Thank goodness Iris and the previous nurses had kept updated details of the children's health and vaccinations. She toyed with the idea of having the older ones come into the office and maybe persuading them to tell her about themselves in their own words. They'd have to be carefully handled so as not to upset them, but, as well as the past, she needed to know what they hoped to achieve in the future so they could be steered towards such goals with the teachers. Also, it was important to note any improvements in their behaviour or, heaven forbid, any deterioration.

'Cup of coffee for you, hen?' Bertie poked her head round the door. 'And one of my pieces of shortbread, just out of the oven.'

'Oh, yes please, Bertie, that would be lovely.'

The cook was back just as she was reading about Lenny and Beth, brother and sister. Their mother had left them for another man, and their father couldn't cope and had committed suicide.

'Oh, Bertie, poor little Lenny and Beth.'

'Wait until you get to Betsy's file. That would make a grown man cry.'

June braced herself. 'Have you time to sit for a minute or two and tell me what happened to her?'

'She'd been beaten black and blue, though it was hard to tell all of them, being coloured.' Bertie shook her head as though she was remembering the day Betsy came to the home. 'She had cuts and lesions on her face, she was full of nits, she'd soiled her pants, she was as thin as a rake, and she had no shoes. When we took her dress off she screamed. There were weals and scars all over her back. If I ever found out who did that to her I'd kill him with my bare hands.'

June fell silent at Bertie's story. Poor little Betsy. But now she seemed a happy child although occasionally she had a bad tantrum. June had long decided the best way to pull her out of them was to talk gently and calmly to the child, not tell her off as Matron used to do, but simply ask what was the matter. Ask her why was she so angry. And sooner or later Betsy would say what was troubling her.

'Yes, there are some gruesome cases,' Bertie said, putting her hands on the arms of the chair. 'But at least we can provide a good home for some of them.' She struggled to her feet. 'Well, I must be off. Let me know if I can be of any more help. I've probably been here the longest so I might be able to answer your questions.'

When the cook had shut the door behind her, June slid the children's files back into the cabinet, knowing she couldn't put Gilbert off any longer. She walked over to the window and saw him taking the rubbish to the bonfire. She watched him for a few moments before coming back to the filing cabinet. What could she give as her reason? He'd simply deny saying anything to Joachim and say the boy was lying to get rid of him.

She sighed. She might have to call David in as a witness, as he'd heard Gilbert mutter the same name-calling under his breath. It would be good to have David's support. And then she changed her mind. She'd deal with this herself.

She was about to lock the cabinet when she saw a label sticking up from one of the files saying PRIVATE & CONFIDENTIAL. Curiously, she lifted out a thick file and laid it on the desk. Maybe it was Matron's personal file and she should pack it up and post it on to her. But something made her open it. There was a small stack of newscuttings. She picked up the top one.

A man stared back at her though the photograph was indistinct. She racked her brain. There was something about him that gave her the creeps. She picked up the next cutting to find a photograph of a crowd of people, all with their arms raised in a Hitler salute. Her blood thickened in her veins. The same man was marching with his troops. He was taller than most of the other men around him and there was something sinister about the way he was dressed – all in black, even his shirt. She'd seen this kind of rally in Germany on the news at the cinema. Then she remembered who it was. Oswald Mosley, the British Fascist and admirer of Hitler.

Black Shirts, they called them, though she thought they'd disappeared at the beginning of the war.

There was an envelope tucked into the next page. June opened it and a photograph fell out. She immediately recognised him. Unmistakeably Gilbert.

Gilbert. In his black shirt. Giving the Nazi salute. Iris had noticed he always dressed in black. How had a man like this ended up in a Dr Barnardo's home? June put the photograph face down on the desk, loathing the sight of it, and looked through the file again. There was a pile of leaflets advertising a Fascist meeting with a scrap of paper pinned to the top one. She recognised the scrawling writing immediately. *G – we should attend this one.*

June gazed at the note, her eyes wide. There was no signature but it didn't need one. She wondered why it was still in Matron's desk drawer. She must have forgotten to give it to him. But there was no doubting the message. They were Fascists, the pair of them.

Twenty minutes later she opened the office door and caught Rose scurrying past with an armful of ironed linen.

'Rose, could you please ask Gilbert to come to Matron's office immediately.'

'It weren't illegal to be in the BUF,' Gilbert said, an angry gleam in eyes as black as his shirt.

'Maybe not in the early days,' June said, swallowing her contempt, 'but when the war started any known Fascists in this country were arrested and put straight into jail, and there they'll stay until this war's over. I've a good mind to call the police.'

Gilbert paled. 'I ain't done nothing with them since I've been at Bingham.'

'Perhaps because they disbanded,' June returned coolly,

though her heart was hammering. 'And you *have* done harm with your name-calling' – she half rose from the desk – 'even though you knew perfectly well when you applied for this job that Dr Barnardo's creed was that every child of any colour or religion was accepted, and they would all be cared for and treated exactly the same. The poor man would turn in his grave if he knew we had a Fascist amongst us.'

'Poor man indeed.' Moving quickly for an older man, Gilbert shot to his feet. 'He made plenty of money out of it.'

'I don't care if he was a millionaire at the end,' June said. 'He was a wonderful man and thousands of children have had a chance for a normal life in his homes. As for you, I would like you to pack your things and be gone by Friday – earlier if you have somewhere immediately to go to. Harold will take you to the station at ten o'clock Friday morning – not a moment later. If you leave me your address I will see that your wages are paid up to date including the rest of this week. Now, please leave my office.'

'What d'yer mean, *your* office? You're only here till Mrs Pherson's back.'

'You must have missed the announcements. Mrs Pherson isn't coming back. Mr Clarke has promoted *me* in her place. And as Matron, I order you to be packed up and gone by Friday, ten o'clock, as I've just told you.'

Throwing June another furious look, Gilbert swung out of the door, slamming it behind him.

June sat down, her heart still thumping away. She wouldn't rest until Harold's motorcar, with Gilbert and his case in the back, had disappeared down the drive.

She opened one of the desk drawers and found an empty lozenge tin. When she lifted the lid, a waft of eucalyptus rose to her nostrils. She dropped the key to the cabinet inside with a rattle and shut Matron's drawer – or rather hers, now – though it still felt strange, as though she were intruding.

She'd continue going through the files of the rest of the children tomorrow.

Meanwhile she'd stroll over and look at the cottage – her new home . . . and Freddie's.

Lizzie would be able to visit Freddie every single day. She hugged herself at the thought.

Chapter Thirty-Nine

'Dr Barnardo's at Bingham Hall.'

'Junie?'

There was only one other person who called her that besides Iris. His voice melted her insides. She squeezed the receiver as though it might steady her.

'Junie – are you there?'

'Yes, I'm here, Murray.' Saying his name made her heart swell with love. 'Where are you?'

'I had to go to a rest home for a bit, but now I'm back at the camp. They've already got me busy, though only light jobs at the moment.'

'I'm so pleased for you, Murray.'

There was a pause. 'Junie, I need to talk to you. It's important.'

June clung to the sound of his voice. It was making her tremble. The line crackled and she thought she heard the word 'meet'.

'I'm sorry,' June said. 'I didn't quite hear.'

'Can we meet somewhere?'

'All right.' It was her turn to hesitate. Then she added, 'I'd like that.'

Was it her imagination or did she hear him sigh with relief?

'What about at Brown's Books?' he suggested. 'Then whoever's first can be inside, as they say there's going to be a storm. It's certainly a scorcher, so just right for one.' The pips went and she heard the clink of coins. 'Are you still there, Junie?'

'Yes, I'm here.'

'Can you manage tomorrow afternoon?'

A bomb would have to strike to prevent her being there.

'Yes,' she told him, her voice on the edge of shaking. 'What time?'

The pips went again as Murray said frantically, 'I haven't got any more change, Junie. Tomorrow at—'

The line went dead. It didn't matter. She'd be at Mr Brown's shop as soon as she'd helped clear away lunch. She'd wait all afternoon if she had to.

By a stroke of luck Harold stuck his head around the dining-room door, asking if anyone needed anything or would like a lift into town.

'Oh, Harold, yes, please,' June said, scrambling up from her chair.

Barbara, who was sitting a few feet away, raised her eyebrow but June pretended she hadn't noticed.

'Sorry I can't hang around – need to go in ten minutes.' Harold's head disappeared from view.

'Sounds as though you've got something important to do,' Barbara said, a gleam in her eye. 'And by the looks of that pretty dress I haven't seen before . . .'

June felt the colour rise to her cheeks. Trying to sound as casual as she could, she said, 'I just need a new library book and I hate it if I haven't anything to read.'

'We have a complete library *here*, in case you hadn't noticed.' Barbara sounded amused.

'Um, yes, I know, but . . .'

'It's obviously a young man' – Barbara grinned – 'and you're not letting on. All right, go on. I'll clear up for you.'

It was raining – not heavily, although the sky was black with cloud – but June put her umbrella up. She spotted him quite some way away, striding towards the bookshop from the opposite direction. She was sure he hadn't seen her yet as his head was slightly bent as though deep in thought. His left arm was in a sling, but it didn't seem to be any deterrent to several girls whose heads turned as he passed by.

'Cor,' June heard one of them say to her friend in a voice loud enough for the whole street to hear, including Murray, 'he's not half a looker. Been through the wars, too, by the look of him.'

June felt a stab of satisfaction that he hadn't even given them a glance. She pretended to be looking in the bookshop window, where raindrops were running down the panes so it was difficult to make out the titles. Her umbrella bumped against the window pane and her heart beat wildly against her ribs. This lovely man was coming to see her. What was he going to say? She remembered the letter she'd written explaining about Chas; the letter she'd never sent. It weighed heavily on her mind that she'd never spoken to Murray about him. She'd been going to on her third visit to the hospital, but he'd already been moved. Nor had she told Murray of her rage with Billy Lavender when she'd put him in hospital. What would he think of her doing such a thing? It was an act of violence. She shuddered. She'd often used that very word for Billy when he'd been cruel to her mother and Clara. Desperately, she tried to push such thoughts away. She'd face it when it came.

'Junie!'

She turned.

His smile lit up his face. 'I can't believe you beat me here. I didn't even tell you what time before the pips went.' He made to kiss her cheek but it landed somewhere above her ear as she slightly turned, and she suspected he felt just as awkward.

'We met once before at half-past two, so I went by that time.' She was stumbling with her words, not knowing what she was saying now that he was so close she could smell the fresh musky scent of his skin, the tang of mint and cigarette smoke on his breath.

'I hoped that's what—'

'I thought it was you two outside,' Mr Brown interrupted as he appeared in the doorway of his shop. 'Why don't you come in and shelter for a few minutes? It looks as though it's going to bucket down. And I've had something in which might be of interest to the young lady.'

As he spoke a crack of lightning lit up the High Street and a few seconds later a roll of thunder broke around them.

June instinctively jerked towards Murray and she felt his arm slide around her waist, drawing her in. She mustn't – no, she mustn't read anything into it. He was just being a gentleman, that was all. She was grateful for Mr Brown's interruption. What a nice man he was, offering them shelter.

'You've got me curious, Mr Brown,' Murray remarked when they'd dashed inside and June had put her dripping umbrella in the stand. 'You have something which might be of interest to Miss Lavender, you said.'

'Yes, yes, now where did I put it?'

While Mr Brown was busy opening drawers and cupboards at speed, June glanced around, surprised to see a couple of tables covered with gingham cloths along the right-hand wall, already set with cups and saucers and plates.

'Ah, here it is.' Mr Brown placed a book on the counter. 'Came in yesterday. I thought of you at once, Miss – Miss Lavender, did I hear your young man call you?'

'Yes.' June blushed furiously. 'But he's not—' she started to say. She was conscious Murray's arm was encircling her waist again.

Murray tightened his grip and smiled at Mr Brown. 'Do the teacups mean you're serving teas?'

'That's right, sir. The missus says people like to stop and browse and then they get thirsty so they go off for a cup of tea and don't always come back. She says we might as well make them a pot, and keep them in the shop.'

'Good thinking.' Murray grinned. 'And sell them an extra book.' He looked at June. 'Shall we have tea while we're sheltering and you can have a look at the book Mr Brown's been saving for you?'

'Um . . . yes, that would be nice.'

The rain swept the shop window viciously and a crack of lightning lit up the dismal shop for a few seconds, turning Mr Brown's face yellow. Another rumble of thunder made her jump.

'Here – give me your coat. I'll put it on the back of the chair,' Murray said, helping her out of the wet raincoat.

'Let me hang it up for you,' Mr Brown said, taking it. 'I shan't be a mo. Will that be a pot of tea for two? And what about two nice scones that the missus made this morning, with some of her homemade strawberry jam?'

'Junie?' Murray was gazing at her.

She allowed herself to raise her eyes directly to his. Although they were still the same intense blue as the first time she'd bumped into him on the train to Liverpool, his right eyelid was visibly scarred and the shape a little distorted. Still, the dark circles had practically disappeared and it was more difficult to tell from a quick glance that one of his eyes had been so badly injured. She wondered if she dared bring the subject up.

Mr Brown cleared his throat, reminding her she hadn't answered his question.

'That would be lovely, thank you, Mr Brown,' she said.

Mr Brown nodded and disappeared through a door at the back, and she heard him call out to his wife to put the kettle on.

For something to do, June took the book he'd saved for her and turned it over to see the title.

'Oh, it's another Monica Dickens book,' she said, pleased and touched that Mr Brown had thought of her. '*One Pair of Feet.*'

'That's two of hers I've got to read,' Murray said, gesturing to the table furthest away from the counter. 'Shall we?'

'How is your arm?' she asked, as he pulled her chair out with his good arm and took the one opposite.

'Healing well.' Murray gave her a rueful smile. 'It'll never be like the other one. It's very scarred and raw-looking. I can't remember if I told you but the surgeon at the Queen Victoria did a skin graft on it. It still doesn't resemble the old arm but it's a damn sight better than it was.' He straightened his back. 'Sorry, June, I don't usually swear in front of ladies and compared to Shorty I'm bl— I'm very lucky.'

'How is Shorty?'

'Still where I left him. He tells me he's in the Guinea Pig Club and seems quite proud of it.'

June's brow puckered.

'They call the burn patients' – he paused and momentarily closed his eyes – 'guinea pigs because the surgeon, Archibald

375

McIndoe, practically admits he's experimenting on them – rebuilding their faces. But the boys don't care about being guinea pigs. They love him. Apparently he works miracles on the most terrible cases.'

'I hope they can work a miracle on Shorty,' June said quietly. She couldn't bear to think of him and all those other young men who were so badly burned. Murray had once told her that some were unrecognisable even to their own mothers.

Murray put his hand on hers, which had been resting lightly on the table. His touch sent a tingle up her spine, so strong she thought he must have felt the same quiver of shock. His eyes sought hers and she noticed a smudge of anxiety.

'And your eye?' she blurted before she realised what she was saying.

'That's the main problem.' He lowered his eyelids to show her the red angry scar on the right-hand one.

'Can you see anything out of it?'

He covered his good eye with his free hand. 'Something hazy – like an outline.'

'Have they said it will improve even more?'

'Just that it needs time to heal properly. They're optimistic. But I do have some news. If it improves even just a bit more, and everything else goes to plan, I'll be allowed to teach fighter pilots. At least I'll be doing something worthwhile still . . . and what I love.'

'Oh, Murray, that's wonderful.' Without thinking she raised his hand to her cheek and held it there for a few seconds before she realised what she was doing. Overcome with embarrassment she abruptly let his hand drop from her fingers.

He must be thinking how forward she was. She was about to chide herself when his voice broke into her thoughts.

'How is everyone at Bingham Hall?'

'Oh.' She caught his gaze and smiled. 'I don't think I told you – Matron's left – for good.'

'Thank the Lord. Let's hope her replacement is someone more suitable, though anyone would be better than that dragon.'

'Well, I hope you'll consider that *I'll* be better than the dragon.'

Murray gave a start, then beamed. 'Junie, that's marvellous. I'm so pleased for you – proud of you. You'll be a fine matron. You're just what the children need.'

'Thank you, Murray. I'm going to do my very best but it'll be a challenge, no doubt.'

'You're a natural. You'll do an extraordinary job.'

She fell silent, and stole a glance at Murray. He was looking away and she was sure he was thinking of Chas. She'd have to explain but not in Brown's teashop, surely. Tears filled her eyes. He'd never believe her. She heard him clear his throat as though ready to ask her the dreaded question. He turned his head towards her, rubbing the back of his neck, and she made a play of peering at her watch.

'I don't have time for tea after all,' she said, not daring to catch his eye.

'June – Junie, why are you so upset?'

He got up too, and pulled her close but she resisted. A flash of lightning lit up the shop, and then an almighty boom. She clung to him and with one strong arm he pulled her closer. She felt the material of his tunic against her cheek, felt his mouth on hers . . . like that first time . . . no, it wasn't like the first time at all. This time his lips were firm and warm, his breath coming unevenly. Her lips parted under his and she could feel the solid beat of his heart. The kiss ended and Murray began to kiss her eyes, her nose, along her jaw, until he found her mouth again. She felt she was drowning and never wanted to come to the surface . . . to the real world.

'Well, if it takes a thunderstorm to allow me to kiss you, let it roll,' Murray said, and laughed.

She couldn't help laughing too. 'You must think I'm one of those pathetic women who are scared of storms, but I'm not. I like thunderstorms, but these days it always sounds like a bomb going off.'

'I don't think you're pathetic at all,' Murray said, not letting her go. 'If you really want my opinion, I think you're the most wonderful, sweetest, dearest girl in the whole world.'

She put her finger to her bruised lips. Her mind reeled.

'Junie, I—'

'Don't say anything, Murray.' She buried her head in his shoulder. The dear comforting feeling of being held so tightly against him she could smell the hint of spice on his skin. She'd stay here a minute longer. Just one more minute before she told him what she knew she must . . . She'd relish the closeness of him, feel his heartbeat for just a few more precious moments before she was forced to see the look of dismay on his face.

'Murray, I want to explain—'

'Junie, I think I know what you want to say. I should never have brought it up just as you were leaving the hospital. You want to explain about Chas. You don't have to. Chas was showing off, boasting he'd made love to you in his hotel bedroom, though he made out the bomb had fallen at the wrong time and interrupted everything. So, yes, I'm sorry to say that at first I believed him. But I still gave him a punch on the jaw. Told him to stay away from you. But later – later when I had time to think about it, I knew his version couldn't possibly be true, though I'll never forgive him for trying to seduce you.'

Her eyes went wide. 'You hit him? Over me?'

Murray gave a rueful smile. 'It was no more than he deserved.' He kissed her forehead. 'Did he tell you he had a fiancée back in the States?'

She took a step back. 'No, but I can't say I'm surprised. I think the English girls are a challenge to him. He told me they were very different from anyone he knew at home but if he's really got a fiancée I'm sure he'll settle when he goes back to America.'

'You sound as though you're sticking up for him.'

'Not really. But he did finally apologise for his behaviour, and he was the one who rang to tell me you were missing – presumed dead,' June added with a shudder. 'I would never have known, else. And he had the decency to let me know that you'd been found. That's not the action of a bad person.'

'Hmm.' Murray didn't sound convinced. 'The sooner he goes back to the States the better, as far as I'm concerned.'

'Is he good at his job?'

'He's an okay pilot, I suppose.' Murray sounded reluctant to give the American any sort of compliment.

'Then be grateful to have him at the station. He's offering his life as well as you and everyone else.'

It was easier to talk to Murray once she'd begun, but there was a burning question she felt compelled to ask.

'Why did you think it wasn't true that I'd been with Chas in that way?'

Murray lowered his eyes. 'I was sure . . . when I thought about it, that you couldn't love him.'

That word. It made her heart twist. 'Why were you so sure I couldn't?' June's voice dropped to a whisper.

He leaned forward and ran his finger over the little silver

winged RAF brooch she'd managed to pin on her dress before running down the stairs at Bingham Hall just as Harold started the engine.

'Because I knew how you felt about *me*.'

By the time Mr Brown struggled through the back door, levering it open with his foot as he wheeled a tea trolley, June and Murray had taken their seats demurely at the table, though Murray kept his fingers warm and firm around her hand as though he couldn't bear to lose contact with her.

'I'm afraid I have another confession,' she said, feeling a little less scared of his reaction.

'Oh, no.' His eyes were teasing. 'Well, you'd better tell me everything. Get it over with. I might as well know the worst about my angel.'

'You won't think me one of those when I tell you what I did.' She told him about Billy Lavender, quickly and without sparing herself.

'He deserved it, Junie,' Murray said. 'He should be behind bars. But the best news is – he's not your real father.'

'I'm not claiming him as anything, not even my stepfather. He was never any kind of father to me. I just wish I could see my real dad. Talk to him.' A tear trickled down June's cheek and Murray wiped it gently away with his napkin. 'But the funny thing is that when Billy told me he wasn't my father, I remembered a man whom my mother sometimes took me to meet. I called him Uncle Thomas. He used to pick me up and put me on his shoulder. And all the time I never knew he was my father. And he and Mum took me to the fair once. We went on a ghost train. Well, Uncle Thomas – I mean Dad – he and I went. Mum waited for us by the gate.' How strange to be calling someone who was so hazy in her memory her dad. 'I've

380

remembered other times when I saw him. He was always smiling.'

'You might remember more things about your father now your mind is clear of Billy,' Murray said. 'What about your name? Are you going to keep the name Lavender? It doesn't seem a good choice any longer.'

'Funnily enough, I always liked the name until recently. Now I loathe anything which reminds me of him. Mum's maiden name was Parker so I'll change it and be June Parker. I'm not so keen on it, but at least I shan't keep being reminded.'

Murray took her hand. 'I have a much better idea,' he said, kissing her palm, then curling her fingers around it. His eyes gazed into hers. 'How about changing Lavender to Andrews?'

June gave a start of surprise. It sounded like a proposal. If it was, what on earth had changed him from only wanting to be friends to suddenly wanting her to be his wife? A tiny spurt of anger bubbled up inside her. It was as though he thought he was in sole charge of their relationship. *His* decision to be friends only, even though he'd kissed her and made her feel special, and led her to believe . . . She felt the anger build. It was *his* decision now to ask her – in a strange, unromantic way – to marry him, in so many words. *Why* such a change? And where did *she* come into all this? He'd never even once said he loved her, except as a friend. She blinked back the angry tears.

'I've already decided on Parker,' she said in as calm a voice as she could muster, ignoring the flicker of surprise on his face. She glanced at her watch. 'It's time I was getting back. It's been lovely to talk and see you looking so much better than the last time I saw you.'

'Junie, what is it? What have I said?'

381

She rose to her feet. 'I really must go. Oh, and by the way, now I have my own cottage I'm allowed to have Freddie back.'

'Junie, you seem so different. What on earth's the matter? I know something's wrong. Please tell me.'

'Nothing's the matter at all.' She made her voice even. She wouldn't let him know how angry she was. 'I need to see where Mr Brown has hung my raincoat.'

She came back with both their coats. Murray was still sitting at the table flicking through the book.

'What's changed, Junie? I thought you were as happy as me a few minutes ago.'

'When would you be able to bring Freddie?' She ignored the hurt in his eyes, and pushed away a sliver of guilt that she had brought this upon him.

'All going well I can bring him this coming Friday.' He sprang up and helped her on with her raincoat. 'Would that suit?' He sounded drained.

'That would be perfect,' she said, feeling a tell-tale sting at the back of her eyes. She wouldn't let him know how much it had cost her to throw what she was sure had been a proposal of marriage right back in his face.

What a prize idiot he'd been. What a way to propose to the girl he loved with all his heart and soul – with every fibre of his being. She was the one he'd thought of every time he took to the skies, hoping and praying he'd make it back safely with the rest of his crew so he could feast his eyes on her again. And he'd had more than enough time to think these past weeks. Wielding a pen for a couple of hours a day, which was all his superior had allowed him to do, didn't exactly require the same level of concentration as flying a Hurricane or a Spit.

He rushed outside to glimpse the bus which June had likely caught vanish round the corner, and swallowed hard. If he didn't have June, if he couldn't have her, then he had nothing. He shook his head as if to get rid of such a depressing thought.

And he still hadn't told her that he loved her.

No wonder she obviously wanted nothing more to do with him.

He had one last chance. He'd be seeing her Friday with Freddie in his arms.

Chapter Forty

June swung from elation that she would see Murray in three days' time to despair at the thought of the way she had acted at their last meeting. If Murray really had been asking her to marry him she couldn't have told him any plainer that she wasn't interested. But then she'd feel angry again that he had messed her around so much: telling her they could only be friends one minute, then offering himself as a husband the next – without any kind of explanation of what had happened in between to make such a declaration – if that's what it was.

Yet he'd come to his own conclusion that she would never have gone to Chas's bedroom if she'd known what he'd had in his mind. She hadn't had to convince him at all. In spite of herself, she began to soften a little.

At least now when Murray came there was no Matron to deal with. She could talk to him freely in her own office without fear of being interrupted or told off. The knowledge of such freedom almost took her breath away. But every time she thought of this man she loved with all her heart she felt a stab of despair. She'd turned down what must surely have been a proposal for the sake of her pride, just when things had been so wonderful between them only minutes before.

'I don't know what Mr Brown in the bookshop must have thought of us,' June said, when she'd finished telling Iris that she'd left Murray and stalked out. 'He's such a nice man and has been so kind to me ever since I first went in that day.' She smiled. 'Thank goodness I went into the nice book-shop that first time, and not the mean, bad-tempered one you warned me against.'

Iris burst out laughing.

'The bad-tempered one *is* Mr Brown,' she said, almost choking with mirth, and pointing her finger at June.

'What!'

'I didn't tell you at the time because you were all wrapped up in your pilot. You must have brought out the best in the grumpy old geezer.'

June couldn't help smiling. Her friend was incorrigible.

'Let's hope on Friday you can bring out the best in Murray,' Iris said, having the last word as usual.

Days and hours and minutes dragged. Then, before she knew it, he was sitting on the other side of her desk drinking tea, with Freddie lapping his bowl of water in the corner, having given her a rapturous and very sloppy welcome.

It was hard to stop staring at Murray. He had put his cap on the desk, and although he appeared quite at ease, she didn't think he was. He tapped one foot restlessly and when he'd stopped that – Freddie had thought he was playing a game and kept rushing over and trying to bite his laces – he drummed his fingers on his thigh instead.

So he was not perfectly at ease.

She waited.

'Are you enjoying your new position?' he said finally.

'I'm working my way into it,' June replied. 'Luckily Matron was quite methodical with the files, but not so with the accounts. I was never at all sure she understood them and I'm going to have to ask Mr Clarke if he can send someone from Head Office to explain them to me. As far as the children are concerned I've changed a few things.'

'Like what?'

'Like not calling them by their surnames.' She stopped, wishing she could take back the words, thinking of the last time she and Murray had spoken about surnames. It was the last thing she wanted to bring up. She glanced at him and his expression seemed to collapse.

'Junie, I—'

'Can I get you some more tea?'

'What? Oh, no, thank you.'

He caught her eye. The air shimmered between them.

'I can't talk to you properly with this desk in between,' he said. 'Is there somewhere we can go where we won't be disturbed by anyone?'

She hadn't thought that far ahead. 'Maybe the library,' she said doubtfully. There was often one of the teachers in there, but at this time of the morning they should all be in class.

'Shall we have a look?' Murray got to his feet.

'We can't take Freddie into the library,' June said. 'He's not supposed to be in the house at all. I'm only allowed to have him because I have the cottage.'

'You're the matron. You can break the rules just this once. I'll hold him. He's a good little fellow and he usually obeys me.'

The library was deserted. She led him into an alcove where there was a round table and a few hard-backed chairs. Murray set Freddie in an empty box he'd spotted in the corner and told him, 'Stay', then arranged two of the chairs away from the table so they were almost opposite one another. June felt awkward, but she was determined not to let any anger rise the way it had in Mr Brown's shop the other day.

Murray took her hand and examined it, turning it over as though he'd never seen it before.

'So delicate,' he murmured. He looked up and June saw his eyes were moist. 'June, I have a confession to make.'

She sat very still. Was this the moment when he was about to tell her he was sorry he'd led her up the garden path. That it was only a few kisses in the bookshop but he was sure she'd understand that they were friends only, just like he'd told her before.

She couldn't go through all that again. Her nerve endings tingled with anxiety.

'Junie, I want you to hear me out before you judge me. I've treated you shamefully, telling you all that nonsense about wanting only to be friends. I don't know why I felt I couldn't explain. And then it was too late. You looked so hurt I didn't know how to take the words back. But I wanted to put the brakes on our relationship because I was beginning to get serious about you. And the odds were heavy that I might not make it and I didn't want to leave you a young widow, or worse – if I'd got badly injured and you'd felt obliged to look after me. I didn't want your pity. And I didn't want you to waste your life. You have so much to give – particularly to the children. And you'll want your own children one day.'

What was he talking about? Why should anything matter so long as he was alive? And if he were to die, well, they would have taken a chance for happiness, which was a whole lot better than doing nothing.

'And then I had the accident. Ended up with Shorty in the next bed. I told them I didn't want any visitors. But in you came. Shorty said—'

'What did Shorty have to do with it?' June demanded.

'I just didn't know how to get you back. Or even if you wanted me. Shorty said he'd only heard your voice when you came to the hospital those two times, but not being able to see, he said the expression in your voice told him that you were . . . well . . . that you . . .'

'That I loved you?' The words fell from her lips before she could stop them.

Murray nodded.

'But you left the hospital without any word,' June said, her voice unsteady. 'I went to visit you the following day and the nurse – that strict, dark-haired one – said they needed the bed, so they'd sent you back to Liverpool.'

Murray drew his brows together. 'I wrote to you to explain. I gave the letter to one of the other nurses and told her to be sure to hand it to you as you'd said you'd come again the next day.' He looked at her. 'You never received it, did you? Oh, Junie, I'm so sorry. But I *did* write.'

'Seems we've both had apologies and confessions to make.' June swallowed. She couldn't quite understand what was happening but she could sense some kind of change between them.

'Will you forgive me for being such an idiot?'

'There's nothing to forgive, Murray.'

He pulled her up from her chair. 'Shorty made me realise you have to live for the day. Not worry about the future. None of us knows what's going to happen, but if we don't live in the present we're not being true to ourselves.' He drew her closer and she could feel the tension in his good arm.

She pulled away a fraction, her eyes sparkling. 'I have a question.'

'Anything.'

'The little brooch you gave me. Since Matron left I wear it every day. It feels special to me.' Her hand went instinctively to the collar of her navy-blue dress where she'd pinned it.

'It *is* special.'

'Does it have a meaning?'

'Yes.' He looked deep into her eyes and she thought she would melt. 'It's called a sweetheart brooch. A chap in the RAF gives it to his girl – his sweetheart.'

'But you hardly knew me when you gave it to me,' June protested. 'I thought it must be a token of friendship, particularly when you later insisted we were only friends.'

'What a bloody fool I was,' he said again.

'Yes, I think I have to agree with you there,' she said, and sent him a mischievous smile but Murray's expression remained serious.

'I knew you were the girl for me when I first set eyes on you – that chance encounter on the train.' He smoothed the hair from her forehead. 'Tell me if this feels friendly,' he whispered, and bent his head so that his mouth found hers. He planted little kisses at the corners of her mouth and lightly brushed her lips with his. He kissed her eyelids, along her jaw, on the tip of her nose, and back to a butterfly kiss on her mouth, until she ached for him to kiss her properly. When he did, his kiss was gentle, tender, but then he groaned and his kiss deepened and became more urgent as though he could never get enough of her, until her lips tingled and she put her hands through his tawny-coloured hair, using her fingers to press him closer . . . until she couldn't tell if the wild beating was her heart or his.

'You haven't answered my question.' His voice was husky when they finally drew apart.

'I've forgotten what it was,' June teased.

'Did it feel friendly?'

'I'm not sure' – she laughed softly – 'but maybe if you do it again, I can definitely confirm one way or the other.'

This time his kiss was as searching, as passionate, as magical as she could wish.

Shaken, she pulled away and gazed into his eyes.

'I love you, Junie. I always have – now and forever.'

'I love you, too.'

As Murray went to draw her closer again, Freddie suddenly barked and they practically leaped apart.

'Trust him to spoil such a romantic moment,' Murray laughed, looking down at the eager little dog, who was now nuzzling at their ankles and giving yelps of excitement.

'I think he's telling us he's hungry,' June said. 'I'll have to feed him.' She opened the library door to running foot-steps and childish laughter. Freddie cocked his head for a second or two, then dashed out.

'Freddie! Here, boy!' Murray ordered.

June put a hand on his arm to stop him going after the excited little dog.

'Freddie's come home!' It was Lizzie, squealing with joy.

They watched as Freddie and Lizzie rushed towards one another, landing in a heap on the slippery floor. Lizzie threw her arms around the puppy's neck. 'Freddie's come back,' she shouted to a group of curious children who had gathered around her. She looked down at Freddie again. 'Don't you ever go away again.' She wagged her finger at him and he wagged his tail in return.

Murray's arm slid around her waist and pulled her to him.

'I could say the same to you,' he said, grinning and wagging his finger at her the way Lizzie had at Freddie. 'Don't you ever go away again.' He dropped a kiss on the top of her head.

'I never went away.' June looked up at him, her green eyes sparkling with happiness. 'I was always here . . . waiting for you.'

After . . .

Bertie said she'd never seen anything like this in all the fifteen years she'd been the cook at Bingham Hall. The orphanage was buzzing with giggles and shouts as children rushed from different corners of the house to the library, every child full of importance in the task he or she had been given.

June put her head round the door of the art class, and Barbara immediately looked up and beckoned her in, a smile lighting her plump face. June watched Barbara help Betsy, Pamela and Janet place the last three wonky triangles, which the children had cut from odd scraps of material and worn-out clothes, for Barbara to stitch on to a long piece of tape.

'Let me help. What can I do?'

'They always say that when the job's almost done,' Barbara said with a chuckle.

June grinned. 'I'll go and see how the library's going then,' she said.

'Give us a few minutes,' Barbara said, 'and you can help get this bunting up.'

The last month had flown in a whirl. June still couldn't believe she was actually engaged to be married to the dearest man on earth. She glanced at her ring as she did a hundred times a day to reassure herself it was really true – the beautiful ruby enclosed in a circle of tiny sparkling diamonds that had been Murray's grandmother's own engagement ring.

Iris had decided two engagements and a promotion were definitely an excuse to throw a party.

'We'd never have been allowed anything like this with the Fierce One,' she'd said, her eyes crinkling with laughter as she was making cocoa late one night in the kitchen, the day after June became engaged. 'Thank goodness you're now in charge. We can have a real knees-up, which is just what we need after all the awful news from the war.' She poured hot water into the cups and stirred vigorously.

The two women had taken their drinks and sat on one of the kitchen chairs. Bertie had retreated to her cottage some time ago and the maids had long departed. They were silent for a few moments. Then Iris drew herself up and smiled at June.

'We *will* win – we have to. But we're going to think of nice things.' She took a slurp of cocoa and caught June's eye. 'This place is so different now you're the matron, Junie. Even the children sense it. The Fierce One got it completely wrong, dishing out punishment all the time for the least little thing. As far as I could see, she positively disliked children. You know, if it wasn't for this damned war, life would be pretty near perfect.'

'Yes, but I would never have met Murray if it hadn't been for the "damned war",' June said, feeling a little daring as she repeated the mild swear word. She lifted her cup, the warm comforting smell of chocolate filling her nostrils.

'That's true, and you wouldn't have carried on meeting him if it hadn't been for me practically forcing you to go to the dance.' Iris threw her a saucy wink.

'I'll let you take all the credit,' June said with a grin. 'Even for Murray's proposal.'

'Maybe not that,' Iris said, laughing. 'But I'm so happy for you, Junie.'

'Oh, Iris.' June turned to her friend, her eyes moist. 'I'm going to miss you so much. You and David *will* come and visit sometimes, won't you?'

''Course we will. If it wasn't for Joachim studying his music we probably wouldn't be moving to London, especially as it's so risky these days, but we want to be near him so he feels he's got some support. David was adamant about it and I know he's right, but we'll have to put his dream of living in Scotland on the back burner for a while. It's worth it, though. Young Joachim certainly hasn't had it easy.'

'But things have turned around for him, thank goodness,' June said. 'It's a shame he can't be here this evening.'

'I know, but he's studying like mad for his exams.'

June hesitated. Should she say anything? But this was Iris – her best friend.

'What's the matter, Junie? You look like you've got something on your mind.'

'Oh, Iris, I must share a secret with you or I'll burst – Murray and I are going to officially adopt Lizzie once we're married. That is, if we have approval from her grandmother – whom we've not even met yet but who's invited us for tea next week.'

'Junie, that's wonderful.' Iris hugged her tightly and kissed her cheek. 'The best news ever. I'm sure granny will approve. Does Lizzie know?'

'Not yet.' June took a sip of cocoa. 'She did ask me if I'd still be here after I'd married Uncle Murray, as she calls him, and I assured her I would, so she seemed happy with that.'

'Little does she know she'll soon be calling him Daddy,'

Iris said with a grin. 'And if two engagements and now this latest bombshell doesn't justify throwing a summer party, I don't know what does. What do you reckon, Matron?'

June kept a straight face. 'I think that will be perfectly in order, Nurse Marchant.'

Bertie brought in the special cake she'd made and set it on one of the large tables on which the children had spread white cloths, normally only used at Christmas. She'd piped pink hearts on the edge of the cake and placed two tiny couples in formal dress standing opposite each other on the icing. Athena lit several candles, which flickered around the library, catching David's frown as he stood by the table with the gramophone and sifted through his record collection.

'Nothing too serious, David,' Iris warned as she and June carried trays of food in. 'This is a party, not one of your stuffy concerts.'

He looked up and gave her a smile of adoration. 'I thought you and June might like a little Bach this evening to make the party go with a swing,' he said, keeping his face straight.

'I'd be quite happy with Bach' – June laughed as she set her tray down – 'but I don't think your fiancée would be too pleased.'

A loud crackle emanated from the gramophone and George Formby's cheery voice broke through the chatter and laughter. Then footsteps June recognised came from behind and seconds later she felt an arm slip round her waist. She turned to look into Murray's eyes, his injured eye reminding her how close she'd been to losing him. Her heart fluttered as it always did when he was so near.

'Hello, darling,' he said, kissing her cheek. 'I hope I'm not late.'

'Miss.' Bobby came running up. 'Thomas keeps pinching cakes. There won't be any left at this rate.'

'I'll have a word with him,' June said. 'Will you go and help the teachers to count all the children, Bobby? Make sure they're all here.'

Barbara appeared with her small band of helpers and organised Murray and David to assist in putting up the bunting, then throwing a few balloons around the room for the children to catch. The only person who looked distinctly unhappy was Hilda. She was standing at the side, looking on with disapproval. If only she would join in, June thought. Hilda always gave every indication that she was not a happy girl. June was determined to talk to her as soon as she had the chance. Ask what was troubling her and let her know she was there to help.

June pulled her gaze away from the dejected figure, and allowed happiness to spread through her whole being as she watched Murray having a word with Kathleen and Barbara as they handed out the drinks. Who would have thought her decision to come to Bingham Hall would change her life so dramatically? There was her beloved Aunt Ada chatting to Harold, who somehow looked a little out of place as he rarely stepped beyond the hall, but he was tipping back his glass of beer and making the best of it. Aunt Ada caught June's eye and beamed, but as soon as she noticed Murray she made her excuses and bustled over.

'So this is your young man,' she said, her eyes twinkling up at him as they shook hands. 'I've heard all about you.'

'All good, I hope,' Murray grinned.

'Mostly,' June teased, smiling broadly at him. She banged a spoon on a glass and everyone grew quiet – except George, who was still leaning on his lamppost.

'Ladies and gentlemen, boys and girls,' she began. 'Before

the party begins, please all stand as we are now going to give three cheers for His Majesty, the King.' She paused until the children had stopped scuffling and shoving and they had turned their attention towards her. She beamed around at everyone who had become so familiar and dear to her. 'Hip hip . . .'

'Hurray!' The children's voices were raucous and shrill as they rose above the staff's in a fervent chorus. 'Hip hip, hurray! Hip hip, HURRAY!'

Read on for an exclusive extract from
the next Molly Green novel . . .

An Orphan's War

Coming May 2018

Chapter One

Liverpool, September 1939

Three days after war was declared, Maxine Grey walked slowly down the aisle. Her fingers nervously gripped her father's rigid arm, as they moved towards the man she had promised to marry – her best friend, Johnny Taylor. Despite the bad luck she'd warned him it would bring, Johnny had turned at her entrance, and now he gave her his wide smile and a cheeky wink. She knew it was meant to reassure her, but if anything it made her more conscious of the huge step she was taking. The strident organ notes of 'Here Comes the Bride' almost took her by surprise, making her pause, her ears hum. She pulled in a deep breath to slow down her heartbeat. Her father gave her a quick glance and patted her hand.

She could hear the swish of the satin-like material of her dress; feel it catch at the back of her legs with every stride. It had taken her a month of evenings and half days off from the hospital to make the simple cream dress that swept the floor and the little matching cropped jacket from a McCall's pattern – the same amount of time Johnny had given her when he'd persuaded her they should get married. There was definitely going to be a war, he'd said, and it would probably come sooner rather than later. She swallowed. How right he'd been.

Another step. She took a deep breath, but the scent of the flowers left over from last Sunday's service was cloying and she pulled her stomach in tight to stop herself from feeling faint. A final step. She'd reached him. Her father nudged her forward and a little to the right where Johnny stood waiting for her, watching her every movement. His smile had faded now as if it had finally dawned on him too that this was a serious event. How different he looked in his grey suit. Older. Not like her Johnny. Her fingers reluctantly left her father's arm and she was alone. But of course she wasn't alone. Johnny was here. They were going to be married. Every bride was nervous on her wedding day, so her mother had said when they'd shared a pot of tea that morning. It was to be expected. She wasn't to worry. Johnny was a good boy. He'd always look after her.

'Johnny's who we always wanted for you, Maxine. Your dad's so happy. He can die in peace knowing he's left you in good hands.'

It was no secret that her dad had a dicky heart. Oh, he had a couple of years left, Dr Turnbull had assured them – maybe more – but he'd encouraged the family to enjoy as much time together as possible. And now Maxine was leaving him in the hands of her mother who constantly fussed over him, making him feel closer to death's door than he probably was.

She took her place next to Johnny, her shoulder only inches away from his, and tried to draw his easy confidence into her own body which was taut with the thought of the unknown.

As the vicar started to address the congregation, Johnny turned towards her and Maxine noticed the same concerned expression he'd had only a few weeks ago, when they were sitting on their favourite park bench feeding the pigeons.

400

'I've got something to tell you, Max,' he'd said. 'I'm joining the army. I think I can be of use with my medical training.'

At his words her heart turned over. Johnny. Her dearest friend. If anything should happen to him . . . she daren't think further.

'So what say you and I get hitched?' He coated the words with a mock American accent. It had taken her completely by surprise. Yes, she loved him. More than anyone. He was the one she'd run to since she was a little girl, right from when he and his parents had moved in next door but one. Being a boy of eleven, he hadn't wanted to be bothered with an eight-year-old, and a girl at that, but she'd badgered him until he'd sometimes nodded and allowed her to accompany him when he went off bird-watching, or climbed trees in the nearby woods. Best of all she loved it when he'd take her down to the docks. She could have watched the ships come and go for hours. Luckily he was every bit as fascinated and would tell her where they'd come from and where they were going.

'You've been watching too many cowboy films,' she'd answered, trying to make light of his clumsy proposal, not wanting to hurt him by saying she didn't think she loved him in the way a wife should love her husband. She saw his face drop.

'You do love me, don't you?' As if he'd read her mind he grabbed both her hands and planted a firm kiss on her lips, then grinned at her. 'You always said you'd marry me when you grew up.'

'It's what children say to one another.' Maxine bit her lip. 'Why don't we wait and see what happens. If there really *is* going to be a war—'

'Not "if" but "when",' Johnny said, his grin fading. 'And if the worst should happen—'

'Don't say it!' Maxine jumped up. 'Don't tempt fate.'

'We have to be realistic.' Johnny took hold of her hand

401

and gently pulled her back onto the seat again. 'If it does, then at least you'll get a pension as a soldier's widow. And if you start a family – which I'd love more than anything in the world – you'll be glad of the extra money for the baby.'

She couldn't answer. Didn't want to think beyond Johnny becoming a soldier. He was more of a brother than her own flesh and blood. Her real brother Mickey had never taken any interest in her whatsoever, even though there was only thirteen months between them.

For a moment neither of them had spoken. Then he took her chin in his hand and turned her face towards him.

'I love you so much, Max,' he said, his voice thick. 'Right from when you were a snotty-faced kid. I'd do anything for you – you know that. And because I'm older you've usually left me to make the decisions – so I'm making *this* one for you. You'll make me the happiest man in town and the envy of all the lads if you say yes.' He looked at her, his eyes the colour of the conkers they used to play with. 'Maybe this will help make up your mind.'

He drew from his pocket a small navy blue velvet box.

And then she knew. Before he'd even flipped open the lid on its little spring with his thumb, she knew she couldn't turn him down. He was quite the dearest man she'd ever known. If there was a war and he died, she'd never forgive herself for not making him happy by telling him she would be honoured to be his wife.

The emerald shone back at her, as though to reinforce her thoughts.

She hadn't the heart to tell him that emeralds were considered to bring bad luck.

'Do you, Maxine Elizabeth, take John Laurence to be thy wedded husband?'

The words rang in Maxine's ears and she gave a start, pulling herself out of the past and back to the church. Forcing herself to be calm she repeated the words of the vicar as though in a dream, her voice low and trembling. She felt the brush of Johnny's hand, and when he said his vows she realised he wasn't quite so assured as he made out. Twice he stumbled on the words and sent her a rueful smile, but when it was over he grasped her hand and they stepped to the back of the altar where they signed the register.

She looked down at her signature. Strange how it was still Maxine Grey. But it would be the last time. From now on she would be known as Mrs Maxine Taylor. And on letters even worse – she would be Mrs *John* Taylor.

Would Maxine Grey be gone forever?

'Now we're married you won't have to work anymore.'

Maxine regarded her new husband with astonishment when he spoke to her later that day. Breaking away from the small party the two sets of parents had thrown proved more difficult than she'd imagined, but now they were in a comfortable bedroom in the Royal Hotel, which Johnny had chosen for their first three nights together. He'd already had his call-up papers and would be leaving in four days. Maxine's mind whirled with events that were racing ahead. He'd never mentioned her giving up work before. She hadn't even thought to discuss it as she'd never thought to marry him. During this past month she'd seen very little of her fiancé to talk about such matters, what with making the wedding dress in every spare moment she'd had from the hospital. Now that war had been officially declared she'd naturally assumed she'd carry on and finish her training.

Her parents had wanted her to become a nurse ever since

they'd watched her bandaging her dolls and talking to them in a wise and encouraging seven-year-old voice.

'You're a born nurse,' her mother had told her. And years later, when Maxine was secretly applying at the teachers' training college, her mother had announced, 'Your father and I are going to do everything in our power to see that you're trained in the best hospital. We've decided you're going to the Royal Infirmary, right here in Liverpool, so you can come and see us regularly. You'll make us so proud.'

Maxine's heart had plummeted. Her parents' dream wasn't *her* dream. But they'd been so good to her, sending her to grammar school when they could ill afford it. Yes, she'd won a scholarship but it hadn't paid for many of the books, nor the uniform and shoes, which had to be Clarke's. Mickey had turned out the biggest disappointment to them. He was nothing but a waster. And now they were pinning their hopes on me, she'd thought.

That first year as a trainee nurse had been a shock but the worst was over now – so the other nurses had told her when she'd been tempted to pack it all in. She was now in her third year and looking forward to continuing her studies and taking her finals, knowing she'd be needed, what with the war on – the same as Johnny with his medical skills. So why did he think he could wave her nurse's training on one side? He, of all people, knew what a commitment she'd made.

'Give up my training, do you mean?' she demanded. 'When I've worked so hard.'

'Well, I suppose it wouldn't hurt to finish it,' Johnny said, his eyes fixed on hers. 'But there's no need to continue when you've got your certificate.'

'Johnny, why does being married have anything to do with my nursing?'

'Because you're my wife, and I don't want you working.

What would the lads say? "Can't support your wife, Johnny-boy?" No, I'm not having that.'

'I'm not interested in "the lads" and what they think,' Maxine flashed. She tried to keep the bubble of irritation pressed down. 'We're talking about *me*. My parents nearly killed themselves to pay for my training. Think what a waste that would be. What am I supposed to do all day long? It'd be different if we'd been married longer and I had a child to look after.'

'We can easily remedy that right away.' Johnny gave an exaggerated wink, but if anything it made her even more cross. It wasn't a joking matter and she knew she needed to stand firm. 'You could help your mum . . . especially as your dad isn't well,' he continued. 'That's where your nursing will come in handy.'

'Mum wouldn't want that at all. She prides herself on looking after Dad. They've sacrificed everything for me, and if I left they'd be terribly upset.'

'We'll talk about it some other time.' Johnny drew in the last puffs of his cigarette as though it was the end of the conversation as far as he was concerned. He was sitting on the edge of the bed and reached over to stub his cigarette into the ashtray on the bedside table. 'Come over here, Mrs Taylor.' He spread his arms.

'No, Johnny, it's too important. We'll talk about this right now.'

'Let's not spoil our first night, Max.' Johnny looked across at her, his bright blue eyes afire with anticipation. 'We haven't got much time together.'

Maxine hesitated. She didn't know what to do. If she let this go she'd be paving the way for him never taking her seriously – that his needs and wants were more important than hers. That his decisions didn't invite even discussion.

After all, she had only a few hours ago promised to love, honour and obey him. She sighed, trying to dispel the little spurt of anger. No, she was sure her vows hadn't meant he could make all the decisions that concerned her.

Or was she being unreasonable now they were married?

'Johnny, I know women leave work when they get married but this is different. The war's started. We don't know how long it will last but I want to do everything I can to help. Everyone who can will be doing the same. Mum's even talking about organising knitting circles to make socks for the soldiers.'

'My mum never worked another minute when she married Dad. You'll be doing your bit by helping your mother to look after your father.'

"Doing your bit". He made it sound almost inconsequential. She remembered learning at school about the women in the last war – the one that was supposed to have ended all wars. It hadn't mattered what class the women had been, they'd all risen to the occasion. Most of the rich had never lifted a finger before, and those girls in service in grand country houses, desperately needing the money to help their families survive, would rarely have mixed with any other but their own kind. It was amazing what they'd achieved in so many different walks of life, and nursing was one of them.

Johnny had changed. Or was it her? But she knew without any doubt that even if war hadn't been declared she would have still carried on with her nursing. She gritted her teeth. Maybe now was not the time. Johnny was waiting only a few yards away . . . waiting expectantly for her.

She only hoped their first night together would not be as painful or embarrassing as Linda at the hospital had warned her.

406

Acknowledgements

This novel would never have been written if it were not for two smashing women. One evening I met author Kat Black for the first time at the Romantic Novelists' Association Conference. She liked the sound of my latest historical novel and next morning she introduced me to Helen Huthwaite, then the Senior Commissioning Editor of Avon HarperCollins. As a result of that meeting Helen asked if I would write a brand-new series set in a Dr Barnardo's orphanage during the Second World War. Less than a year later *An Orphan in the Snow* was born. Thank you both so much for giving me such a fantastic opportunity.

Heartfelt thanks to my dear agent, Heather Holden-Brown, of HHB Agency, aided by her charming assistant, Cara Armstrong. How lucky I was to meet you at that Historical Novel Society Conference, Heather. Your experience both in the publishing and agency world is second to none.

Then I must thank Phoebe Morgan, Editor at Avon HarperCollins who began the publishing process, and placed me with my delightful and talented senior editor, Rachel Faulkner-Willcocks, together with all the lovely friendly team at Avon HarperCollins. You make me feel like a celebrity.

Thank you to Megan Parker at Dr Barnardo's headquarters in London for gathering much of the information I needed to create an authentic setting for the orphanage. She provided fascinating details such as the wide variety of country houses that were transformed into Barnardo's homes, the different duties of the staff, together with some charming photographs of Barnardo's children during the Second World War. I've kept several of those faces in mind when they appear in the story.

Huge thanks to Ray Jones who appeared on the TV series 'Long Lost Family'. He'd been a young orphan in one of the Barnardo's homes in Scotland during the war. I managed to contact him and he kindly answered all my questions, providing me with facts and snippets I would never have found in books or Google. He generously invited me to contact him whenever I needed any more information.

Grateful thanks to my husband, Edward Stanton, who has an eagle eye for anything military, being an ex-RAF chap, not to mention spotting those blasted anachronisms. I'm in my writing cabin for hours most days and thankfully he rarely grumbles when I don't cook *every* meal from scratch.

I belong to a writing group extraordinaire; we're all published writers and call ourselves the Diamonds. The four of us, Joanne Walsh, Terri Fleming and Sue Mackender, with April Hardy as an honoury member who occasionally turns up from Dubai, meet every month and critique each other's work with much brainstorming and belly-aching laughs.

Alison Morton is both a friend and an amazing critique writing partner who reads practically everything I write with red pen firmly in hand. She calls it 'brutal love' and she's nearly always right, darn it!

Then there is the Romantic Novelists' Association – a unique organisation for making writerly friends who support one another through good and bad and are never more than a tweet away! Writing books can be isolating – and not everyone has the company of a fluffy white cat with amber eyes who regularly spreads himself over the mouse mat so I can barely move the cursor, as does my adored cat, Dougal!

And finally, I would like to acknowledge the wonderful work of the founder of the orphanages, Thomas John Barnardo (1845–1905), an Irish philanthropist. At first he took in all boys because he was unmarried, but upon his marriage to Sara Louise, who worked side by side with him, they were allowed to take in girls as well. A staggering 60,000 children have passed through Dr Barnardo's homes.